WILBUR SANDERS

Like the Big Wolves

Q

Quartet Books

London Melbourne New York

For George

THANKS

Thanks are due to many people for their help with this book – people who have been generous with their time and expertise, as well as in less palpable and more personal ways. George Roman taught me more about Hungary than I could have found in any book, and he's been, in person, a constant source of encouragement. Mike Gillespie played a similar role in relation to the craft of sculpture, not merely by telling me about sculptors, but also by being one. Clive Wilmer, whose English version first introduced me to the poet Radnóti, has not only allowed me to quote, but has tolerated some opportunistic tamperings with, his and George Gömöri's translations (*Forced March*, Carcanet Press, Manchester, 1979).

I should also like to thank Chris Hann, who arranged some invaluable contacts in Budapest; Ranjit Sondhi, who offered advice on matters Indian; and Mr John Alderson, who kindly acceded to a request from a perfect stranger to look over my final chapter with the eye of an experienced police officer. What I did with all this friendly advice is, of course, my responsibility not the friends', but I hope they won't feel it was entirely wasted on me.

Finally, I must thank Stanley Middleton for things too large and amorphous to be specified, though, if his modesty permits him, he will know what they are.

W.S.

First published by Quartet Books Limited 1985
A member of the Namara Group
27/29 Goodge Street, London W1P 1FD

Copyright © 1985 Wilbur Sanders

British Library Cataloguing in Publication Data

Sanders, Wilbur
  Like the big wolves.
  I. Title
  823'.914[F]   PR6069.A51/

  ISBN 0-7043-2488-1

Typeset by AKM Associates (UK) Ltd, Southall, Greater London
Printed and bound in Great Britain by Mackays of Chatham Ltd, Kent

ONE

Entrepreneur

Morning in Mayfair.

The huge black porter of the Connaught, in his top hat and tailcoat, was requisitioning the pavement for some distinguished patrons. One or two passers-by, finding their way blocked, flattened themselves to slither past, but most stood, forming an obedient gallery. After all, it might be someone famous about to tread six paces of common earth between the carpeted stair and the waiting limousine. The little crowd – expectant? impatient? bored? – stirred and shuffled, bumped against itself, recoiled, and apologized.

'Careful, darling.' Smiling vaguely into space, a woman disentangled her child from the gentleman's briefcase. 'We'll wait, darling, shall we?' she fluted, making sure the gentleman didn't mistake it for an apology.

'Why?' asked the child, with the serenity born of knowing that they would. A tasteful miniature of her mother's elegance, she tucked in her chin to admire the clasp on her neat plaid cape. Beside her, two office girls prattled, spinning slim ankles on stiletto heels, while a char, returning from the dawn shift, gazed up the stairs with tired, unbelieving eyes.

There was a stir in the depths of the lobby; the glass doors opened, and a knot of liveried attendants spilled out, almost hiding the celebrities everybody had stayed to see. At the back of the crowd some late arrivals craned for a better view.

Just as the cortége reached street level, some sort of striding Valkyrie came shouldering through the crush, gave a chop to the porter's raised arm and, without looking to left or right, swung across the prohibited space.

'Well! I ask you!' The char appealed to the outraged proprieties.

The distinguished patrons just perceptibly paused – their faces, already closed against publicity, taking on an additional blankness,

1

before the black giant stooped to ferry them across the dusty inches they shared with the rest of humanity. There was a flash of mink, a glimpse of tailoring complete as a suit of armour, and the limousine door clicked shut, enclosing the vision behind immaculate glass.

The watchers exhaled a collective sigh. Was that all? Nothing more? Had it or had it not been Celebrity they had just witnessed? Should they too, perhaps, have shoved rudely past, like the broad-hipped girl who could be seen now swinging round the corner into a cul-de-sac off Carlos Place? Was it awe they were feeling, or contempt?

The long black car glided off.

'I don't know, Miranda,' said the mother, brisk and business-like again. 'Somebody important, I daresay.'

No doubt it had been. Fleeting smiles were exchanged, as the lives of those who still had to elbow and jostle for their bit of pavement touched for an instant. Then the street resumed its ordinary life and motion.

The tall girl strode past house-fronts of decaying elegance, making for the foot of the court and a squat, ugly, thirties-ish building. In its ground-floor window, vermilion and sulphur-green, glowed a barbaric man-sized sphere in which the gangrenous mildew peculiar to citrus fruits had been caught with hideous exactitude. 'The Rotten Orange', announced Art Nouveau letters of the highest chic – adding as an afterthought: 'Unfashionable Frocks for the Girl of Independent Mind'. (So? Slaves of the mindlessly fashionable might blush and tremble . . . in their mindless fashion.) Let into the Orange, behind the glass, a display shelf disguised as a removed segment so effectively tromped the oeil that people had been known to walk the whole length of the court to check whether it was really there or not. By these allurements had an unpromising blind alley been turned into a fine commercial fly-trap.

Apparently unimpressed, the girl of independent mind picked her way over the delta of dust and slurry that choked the gutter, glanced in passing at a parked delivery van, and pushed open the shop door.

The bell pinged. The door clashed. ('Dollybirds and Gogogirls must be kept on a leash,' read another painted legend.) At the rear of the shop a young man and woman looked up, while a third person, grey-haired, in a reefer jacket and cravat, crossed to intercept . . . too late. The abundant scents of fresh corduroy and cotton-size, all the subtle fragrances of the fashion trade, filled the air – with perhaps a

2

whiff of conspiracy too, from the couple who now half-rose from their chairs, as if they had been caught out

The tall girl bore down and stood over them. 'We'll have that weary witticism off the door for a start,' she announced, veering off and rummaging in a drawer. 'Here,' she said, holding out a bladed scraper, 'it'll come off with this. It really dates us too drastically.'

The young man came towards her, his hands held out in appeal: 'But Anya, I spent a whole day doing that sign.'

'Weren't you paid?'

'I expect so. I can't remember.'

'Well, now I'll pay you to scrape it off . . . Oh, forget it! I'll do it myself.'

The young man watched as his rainbow-coloured letters came curling off in tight little ringlets which she caught deftly in her other hand.

'Sheet of paper, Stacy.'

The assistant obliged, adding in an undertone, as she spread out the paper, 'There's the rep from Sagittarius here. Been waiting an hour.'

The gentleman in the cravat inclined frostily from the waist. Anya peeled off a couple more strips before handing the scraper to Stacy and stalking to the wheeled rack of dresses. The rep followed. She riffled down the row, catching up occasional items roughly by the hem, rubbing the fabric between thumb and forefinger, dropping it. She reached the end and looked at him inquiringly. He was paid to sell, so let him begin.

He jolted into motion: 'This line here is much in favour this spring,' he said stiffly, indicating a gauzy print number with large tricoloured flowers all over it. 'Bobby's Boutique took six dozen,' he plaintively appended.

'Uh-huh? Don't like the colours.'

'Or it comes in these alternative shades.'

'Nor those. That print's not by your own designer, is it? What's his name again?'

'Henschel.'

'Yes. Got anything of his?'

'Regrettably . . . not today.'

'Bring those next time. The cut doesn't matter. He's good. Anything else?'

'I do have one last year's line . . . at a clearance price.'

'I'll bet!'

'It did quite well, last year.'

'That's why you're flogging it cheap this year, I know. Show. My God! Look here, Stacy. A puke-pink tea gown with appliqué tit-cups in apple-green. Go on,' she nudged her victim, 'you've got to laugh. Have you tried the W1 jumble-sale circuit?'

'I'm only asking five pounds.'

'Sorry, I'm out of the rejects-and-seconds market these days. We got started that way – persuading the middle-aged *ingénues* of Mayfair that all sorts of tat was high fashion. But I'm legit, now. Quality, you know.' (She said it in a way that implied he wouldn't.) 'That's what you should bring me. Quality. Like what's-his-name's florals.'

'Henschel . . . I see.'

She appeared to ponder for a moment. 'I'll take a dozen of those filmy, flowery things – some people seem to go for them, God knows why. What colours?'

'There are three shades.'

'Half a dozen of each then. Usual sizes.'

She turned away. The rep still hung arrested.

'That's it,' she said over her shoulder.

'I'll make out an invoice.'

'Do.'

The assistant was making signs of a clandestine, excitable kind, and mouthing exaggerated syllables.

'Don't mumble, Stacy. What? Customer in the cubicle? Doing *what*? . . . Oh. Can't decide? I'll take over. Are you with us for long, Magnus? Want something to do?'

'I was just talking to Stacy.' Moving to her side, he lowered his voice, '. . . about the Family Difficulties, you know. How that girl keeps up her good cheer is a marvel!'

'Living with me, you mean?'

'With these continual traumas. She's a lesson to us all. I've been actively suicidal myself, with far less provocation.'

Anya contemplated him musingly: 'I can just see you being "actively suicidal". Anyway,' she resumed, 'if you're staying, you might give your mind to a new window design.'

'You . . .' He caught his breath. 'You're not scraping off the Orange too, are you?' He had enjoyed many a useful *entrée* as the designer of the Rotten Orange, '. . . you know, dear, that clever, off-beat boutique behind Berkeley Square,' and reeled now at the threat to his professional standing.

'No, no. The *other* window. The Orange is old hat. Familiar local sight. Nobody notices it any more. We want something to go with it – catch the eye from the end of the court.'

'Ah, I see. Do you want something *on* the window, or *in* it?'

'I dunno. You're the expert. See if you can come up with something.'

She pulled back the curtain of the changing-cubicle with a clatter, greatly startling the woman in her mid-thirties who was perched unhappily on the wooden bench in her bra and pants, her long dark hair falling forward on to her knees. Marooned amid a sea of dresses, she raised a pair of haunted eyes.

'Don't get up,' said Anya breezily, picking her way in. 'Here comes help. Looks as if you need some.'

'Oh yes,' she sighed. 'I'm so confused. I don't seem to be a "girl of independent mind" at all.'

'Too many independent minds, more like it.'

'That's just it.'

'It's an old story. Not to worry. Let's start at the beginning: *why* are you buying a frock?'

The customer gazed at her mutely with her big eyes.

'Go on. Tell me why. It helps to know. To please yourself? Mother? Husband? Bloke next door? A lover . . .? What?'

'To please myself.' She smiled shyly. '*And* bring on the lover. But,' she caught her bottom lip under her top teeth, 'just look at these rolls of fat. I think I'm past it.' She took pinches between her fingers, rapt in the pathos of it.

'Nonsense!' Anya was definite. 'I could show you a thing or two worse than that.' The customer looked, and felt bound to concede the point. 'No,' Anya dismissed the problem, 'it's how you feel about yourself. It's what clothes are for. Now . . .' She stood her *protégée* on her feet, ran her fingers lightly down from her shoulder to thigh, and cocked her head, while the novice sucked in her tummy and waited. The transformation was beginning. She could abandon herself to hands that were lovingly professional. Her eye had brightened and her bearing was already more sprightly – even a little provocative.

Anya read the signs and went to work. An hour later, after armfuls of garments had been ferried in and out, after much coaxing and teasing and merriment, spiced with touches of indiscretion, the new woman sailed out the door loaded with Rotten Orange carrier-bags – out into the streets thronged with potential lovers . . . and went to have lunch with her husband. It is unlikely that he regarded the cheque, which Anya shut in her till with a brisk click, in the same complacent light as she did. But virtue is its own reward, and Anya felt she had performed a small service for her sex, sending one more girl out into the world with a spring in her step and a few less years on her back. The burden of undeserved antiquity, after all, was one of the great evils of life. She fought it wherever she found it.

'You're shameless,' said Stacy, stepping lightly across the carpet, her arms loaded with unbought dresses. 'I don't know how I managed to keep my face straight.' (She had been heavily involved in the operation – appealed to for confirmation, decision, judgement: 'Doesn't that suit her, Stacy? Isn't it stylish?' 'Perhaps an inch up on the hemline?' 'Sure, but isn't it "in character"?' etc.) 'Venal,' Stacy concluded. 'Venal – it's the only word for it.'

'Who's venal?' Anya brushed it aside in disdain. 'She didn't take a thing she didn't like. You saw that dowdy little body cowering in the changing-room. Shocking! So shocking that it had you yelling for help. And what walked out my door? A girl with strut, and style, and swagger. A little Cleopatra! It's a creative talent. A vocation. Some have it, some don't. That's nature. No point in your being envious.'

'Oh my!' mocked Stacy, 'what one fat cheque'll do for the ego!'

'As a matter of fact,' Anya threw out, 'she was *so* delighted that she kissed me before she left. A great fervent smackeroo right on the mouth.' She tapped her lips derisively. 'Not that I was surprised,' she continued airily. 'She'd been making up to me the whole time, waving her tits and showing off her little bum – Don't you like me really? Aren't I a pretty little peat? – you know how they go on. It's not me that's shameless. I positively have to fight them off.'

Magnus, roughing out some ideas for the window, had looked up sharply. Anya caught the movement: 'Oh yes,' she jeered, 'the secrets of the girls' changing-room. That turns you on, doesn't it? That sets the fevered little imagination pulsing, eh? If I was to tell you some of the torrid scenes acted out behind that thin curtain, you'd hardly contain yourself. I've got my eye on you, little man. You don't walk invisible when you wear trousers as tight as you do.'

'Don't be obscene,' said Magnus. 'It doesn't suit you.'

'I think it suits me very well. Don't you, Stacey? . . .' She broke off suddenly. 'What *is* that racket?'

'It's been going on all day,' said Magnus.

'Longer,' Stacy corrected.

'I know. Are they building? Or demolishing? Or what? Surely that old crook of an Afrikaner hasn't got his planning permission after all!'

They all sat still, listening to the irregular chinking sounds that came through the back wall. There was a pause. Then they resumed at a different pitch. Major structural work it had to be. And besides, there was all that white slurry running down the gutter of the side lane. Boesma, the landlord, had stolen a march on them. For all they knew a workman might be about to burst through the rear wall of the shop in a shower of bricks and mortar. Anya rubbed her hands and hoisted her skirt with a violent circular motion that preluded battle. 'Right!' she said, then, 'Oh fuck! Just look at that!'

They looked, seeing at first only a startled customer about to back out hastily through the door.

'Not you, dear,' boomed Anya. 'Come on in. Jesus, just look at those bloody footprints!' The dark-blue carpet had snow-white spirals leading hither and yon among the dress racks. 'Shit!'

'Don't shout,' said Stacy. 'They're yours.'

'Well, that does it. I'm going round to see what the hell's going on. Come in, dear, come in. Stacy will see to you. I'll be back.'

Down the side lane, she knew, was a . . . oh, something or other . . . part of the same building. Garage, warehouse, factory – she'd never bothered to check. And in the last month someone or something had moved in. That – come to think of it – was when the white slurry (on wet days) and white dust (on dry) had begun to plague them. And now this hammering. It was more than a little worrying. She had come to a reflective halt at the corner of the lane. A passing workman interrogated her with his eyes, then walked on.

She had no lease. Her rental was absurdly low because the landlord (a chance South African connection she had stumbled upon and exploited) was trying to get permission for commercial development of the whole site. Wanted to knock down the tiny two-storey irrelevance and put up a skyscraper or something. And he reckoned, no doubt, that a leaseless tenant on a peppercorn rental could be more easily evicted when his planning permission came through. The arrangement suited both parties. But Mr Boesma might have been interested to learn that most of the objections from local residents that flowed into the Westminster Planning Department originated from the proprietress of the Rotten Orange who, in her spare time, was working her way through the Electoral Register. Now, however, she feared she was to discover that it had been all in vain.

7

She had reached the large sliding doors. Closed. In front of them, a padlocked iron grille. Silent as the tomb. The chinking sounds had ceased. Dammit! That workman! Must have knocked off for the day. She'd have to come back.

Disgruntled, she scuffed her way back to the shop. 'Gone,' she announced to nobody in particular. 'Knocked off for a six-hour tea break more than likely. It's half past ten, after all. What can you expect? I'll catch the buggers tomorrow.'

Magnus was beckoning confidentially from his table: 'See what you think of this,' he said.

She crossed, picked the sketch up, stared, shook it, held it at arm's length, frowned.

'It's only an idea.'

'No need to be defensive.' She patted him on the neck as one pats a well-meaning but stupid dog. Magnus almost snarled; but he was not *that* stupid.

'Shall I rough it out in colour?' he suavely queried.

'Why not? It might serve.' She turned on her heel. '*If* you can't think of anything better.'

The young designer seemed to have thought of several better things . . . but the object of them had disappeared into the stockroom. He shot a crooked grin in the assistant's direction – inviting collusion – and began gathering his papers together.

'I'm off,' he said grimly.

'Have a good day,' came the reply, serenely mocking.

For Anya, a bed was a throne. She did not retire for the night; she removed the seat of government to the bedroom. Propped against a morain of tumbled, multicoloured cushions, her large figure framed by a reredos of Turkey rug pinned to the wall, she held council, scrawled notes, gave sentence, and issued edicts.

'Are you making coffee, Stacy? I'll have another. This one's disgusting.'

Stacy appeared briefly to collect the mug which was held out to her. Anya eyed her thoughtfully over steel-rimmed spectacles, before returning to her magazine.

The drapes on the tall windows were made out of a stuff so impenetrably thick, that there was no telling what lay beyond it. Traffic, humanity, a mild evening in early spring, all were indiscriminately excluded. The electric fire, its three bars glowing, pumped several kilowatts of heat into the already fuggy air, where smoke from Anya's eternal Cocktail Sobranies hung in layers right up to the high ceiling.

One of the cats, sniffing at the gold-tipped dog-ends, sneezed and blew ash about the quilt, was cuffed and tossed to the floor. Comfortable informality was one thing, squalor another. She brushed the ash away, made a heap of the scattered newspapers, letters, magazines, upended paperbacks, and crowned it with a ravenous-looking bulldog clip holding a wedge of invoices between its jaws. The other cat, a marmalade, had humped down beside a platter sticky with the juices of crumpets and honey. Apart from the rasping of his tongue, the only sounds were the faint buzz of the fire and occasional sighs of impatience from his mistress, who was in the process of being unimpressed with somebody-or-other's Spring Collection. She turned the pages with loud flaps, as if testing the strength of the paper on which it was printed.

One had to keep up with these things, she supposed . . . but really! It was all so boringly known. Each footling innovation totally deducible from the exhausted fad it was replacing. 'Revolutionary New Designs' they called them. Sad, pusillanimous little revolution that went round and round like an old goat at the end of its tether, hoping that the grass would have grown again by the time the circuit was completed. Is it time yet, darlings, to revive 'The New Look'? Or should we wait a wee while longer for the next season? Some revolution!

She removed her glasses, folded them, and ran her hands through the heavy mass of auburn hair, shaking her head as she did so, to relax the neck muscles. She was just stretching out to see what the Beeb had to offer, when the phone rang. Her hand hung in air.

'Hello?' Stacy's voice.

A word or two of greeting, then a long silence. Anya strained her ears. One of those hearty, pleasure-loving Cambridge boyfriends, was it? No. She'd be bubbling and twittering. Magnus? He usually elicited mocking tones when he came a-flattering and a-wooing, not this portentous silence. Please God, not the poisonous family again! Not the Carcinomas of Croydon. They'd had about enough of that squalid tragedy, she and Stacy. And since the father had had the abjectness to contract cancer too – so as not to be outdone by the mother – it had taken quite a grisly turn.

Nothing but Mmmm's and Ah's and Oh no's from Stacy. Sounded bad. It had to be the Surrey leper colony. Which meant it would go on half the night. You could forget coffee! She reached out for a tall glass of abandoned vermouth where slivers of cucumber and medallions of lemon leaned disconsolately together, took a tentative sip, and spat it back into the glass.

Well, she'd be in for a long heart-to-heart tonight, and no mistake! She frowned, and the straight chiselled lines of her face took on an added austerity, rehearsing a prohibition. There would be, the frown notified the world, no encouragement of confidences from *her* end, none! The trouble was that the large dark eyes, with their steady clarity of gaze, their careless directness, promised such candours that they undid the prohibition. People feared, yet confided in her. That was, after all, how she had first met 'Eustacia' (ridiculous name!). They'd found themselves working together, one summer, behind the bar of a Cornish pub. And on the very first night, as they mopped up after closing, Stacy had spilled it out all over the place, like puking. Love life, sex traumas, the curse, family nasties – the lot! Disgusting incontinence! Fascinating too, of course, these spy-holes into people's foul little secrets.

'But I can't come *now*!' Stacy's voice, astounded. 'I know, Gaby, I know.' (Ah, the younger sister.) 'It's awful for you, I know, but I can't come, really.'

Pause. The kettle was screaming on the gas.

'All right then, why don't you come here?'

Anya sat up so violently that the crumpet-plate slithered to the floor and the marmalade cat had to sidestep nimbly to avoid following it. Come here? Not bloody likely! What? And have that pompous bully of a father storming in again and staging his obscene domestic dramas all over her carpets?

She jacked herself up on her fists and her voice boomed through the flat: 'Stacy! No! D'you hear? NO!'

'What? OK,' came the girl's agitated voice. 'She can't come anyway. What's that Gaby? Just a minute . . .'

The kettle abruptly lowered its hysteric note and Anya, too, subsided.

Should she get the suppliers' bills done before the storm broke? She eyed the clipboard with distaste. Pah! let 'em hang on another day or two. They'd nothing to worry about, and they knew it. Kept them on their toes anyway, to wait a bit for payment.

Things had become very emotional at the telephone. Anya fanned herself with the fashion mag and wondered at the avidity of curiosity that was heating her cheeks and brightening her eyes. Nothing like somebody else's misery to raise the spirits and fire invention. As the dramatist of her world, Anya had been too often let down by stale material to reject a scenario as promising as this one. When was the woman going to get off the phone and give her the dirt? Come on, come on!

Ah! The handset pinged at last, and there came a rattling of cups from the kitchen. Bless the girl! Even in these extremities, she didn't forget the coffee. You had to give it to them: there was something in this suburban upbringing. Anya replaced her spectacles and composed her face so as not to smirk too openly.

Stacy came in, red-eyed. Silently passing the mug across, she sat down on the bottom corner of the bed and proceeded to twist, fold, and shred a fistful of tissues, into which she was trying not to drip. Like Anya, she was tall but (unlike her) leggy, tapering, with the curious elegance of a borzoi and something of that creature's air of scenting its world through fine nostrils rather than encountering it direct. Her movements – the way, for instance, she perched on the bed's foot, legs tucked under her – had a sinuous ease about them, flexile and free, all except the hands which were tending, now, to clench, knot and flutter as she pressed the wrists down furiously into her lap.

'Well?' challenged Anya, in some impatience, forgetting all her resolutions. The query simply released a flood of tears.

Stacy mopped and dabbed at her face in humiliation and rage. 'I never want to cry again,' she said angrily. 'Never. They're not worth it.'

'So what have they done now?'

'He's . . . d'you know what he's done? Brought that bloody woman home. Right under Mummy's nose!'

'What? The Slag from Sevenoaks?'

'Yes. What a bastard!' Angry tears started again into her eyes.

Anya, feeling the great gulps of laughter rising from her belly, made a desperate attempt to suppress them, realized it was hopeless, and gave vent to whoops of appalling merriment that rang round the room. Whoop! whoop! hoot! By the time the spasms had subsided, *her* eyes were full of tears too.

Stacy looked at her incredulously. 'You're a great comfort!' she said sarcastically.

'Would you rather I cried?'

'No.'

'Take what you can get, then. Go on! He brought her home . . .'

'Yes.'

'Was your mother there?'

'I don't think so. Gaby found them together in the bedroom.'

'Actually fucking?'

'No. Just groping, I think.'

'What did he say?'

'He said, "If *you* were dying you'd want your pound of flesh too, before you went." '

'He didn't! "Pound of flesh"? Those very words?'

'Those words exactly. It's a few *hundred* pounds of it on *that* one, I can tell you. She's disgusting. All flab and girdle and whiskers. How he can stand her is beyond me.'

Anya felt the demonic merriment rising. 'Not whiskers too? Not whiskers!' The whoops broke out again.

'Whiskers like an old sow.' Stacy was catching the infection. 'She shaves them . . . It's true, I swear. She shaves them, but they . . . they come up . . . come up again . . . All over her face.'

They both gave themselves up to idiot mirth. The scene in the bedroom had become a farce of heroic proportions. Stacy wiped her eyes for the twentieth time while the shivery little giggles subsided. Eventually she felt she might risk a smile: 'You're an old bastard too – laughing like that. Just like him.' Another involuntary gulp. 'Can I come into bed with you?'

Anya stared hard: 'What's this? what's this? I'm having no dike's picnics in *my* bed, my girl. Where did you get that idea? Just watch it!'

'Oh, come on. What're you afraid of? I won't rape you. I just need a bit of maternal comfort, that's all.'

'Maternal? you little slut! There's no more than five years between us. I'll give you "maternal"!'

'You know what I mean.' Stacy was unabashed.

Disgruntled, Anya heaved herself to one side, sending small ripples across the deeply sprung mattress, and Stacy, having removed the sheaf of papers, slipped under the covers and snuggled against her with a sigh.

'I know it's childish,' she said, but without apology. 'That's how I feel. Don't you ever feel childish? Needing a cuddle? This way I get it over and done with. Is there anything wrong with that?' She laid an arm across Anya's broad chest and gave her a peck on the cheek. 'I'm very fond of you,' she crooned, half in satire.

'Mind my coffee,' Anya growled.

12

'I am, truly.'

'I suppose you think that licenses anything?'

'Yes,' replied Stacy impertinently, and proceeded to demonstrate her conviction.

Anya gave a yelp: 'Keep your fingers to yourself.'

'Just testing.'

'Pfft! I must say you've cheered up mighty suddenly.'

'That's what the love of a good woman does for you.'

Anya gave an amused snort and they relapsed into silence.

'You've no idea how peaceful this makes me feel,' Stacy said at length. Her whimsically caressive voice was not the least of her charms. She sighed. 'I expect I never had enough petting as a child.'

'You're one of the most over-petted girls I ever set eyes on,' Anya commented, looking down at the top of her head from an angle that rather compromised her asperity.

'Not like this. Not calm. Always anxious. Over-stimulated.'

'You mean your incestuous "Daddy", I take it.'

'"Incestuous"?' Stacy shifted her head to inspect Anya's face.

'Why d'you think he blacks your eye every few months? On political grounds?' Anya inquired scornfully. '*Because he can't fuck you*, for Christ's sake! It's obvious.'

Stacy took it in broodingly. 'D'you know what he said, the last time I went home? "The only thing you lot will ever take from me, is money!" ' She sat up, rigid and aggrieved. 'It's such a lie. He forces it on us. Bullies us with it. I *hate* his money!' The tissues were in play again.

'So does he. But you're such a tight-arsed little bitch that you won't gratify his obscene lusts. So what *else* can he do but corrupt you with money? And Jesus? are you corrupted!'

'I am not!'

'What about the car you drive round in? What about the tickets to Glyndebourne? The account at Harrods? All the glittering years at Cambridge, eh? Regular little Lolita. I bet you were lying on the hearthrug and kicking up your chubby little legs before you were five.'

'Doesn't everyone?'

'That's how depraved you've got: you think everyone does it.'

'Didn't you?'

Anya paused. The image of her father passed briefly across her mental horizon. He too had demanded, with a soft, butting pertinacity, the consolation that his marriage was not providing.

Like some kind of woolly obstinate sheep, he had obstructed to the last her exit from the family pinfold. So fleecy and warm he seemed, and yet, when you pushed against him, how immovably planted on those little iron-shod feet. Now and then, still, a disconsolate bleat would arrive by Suid-Afrika Flugpost, to remind her of that soft tyranny. But she had never kicked her legs at him – *there* she could exonerate herself. Her steely determination to take nothing of her mother's had saved her from *that*.

'No, I did not,' she pronounced.

'Didn't what?' The reply had been so long coming that Stacy had forgotten the question.

'Kick my legs at my father.'

'Oh? Must have been a funny childhood.'

Yes, Anya had to admit, it had been that. And she would not have minded attempting a clinical dissection. But not with Stacy, whose fevered love/hate relation with the paternal carcinoma precluded all objectivity.

'Right!' she said abruptly, thumping the comfortable mound of Stacy's backside. 'Right! That's it! Get your bum out of my bed. Ten minutes' consolation is more than any human being has the right to expect.' Then, as the girl moaned and wriggled in protest, 'How many times do I have to tell you that life is one long string of disappointments? Out! Out!'

The girl slid out and, trapped between affection and resentment, stood at the bedside staring at the tangle of tissues in her hands as if wondering where it came from.

'Gaby needs me,' she said. 'I'm her only ally. Because Mummy won't admit what's going on. But I daren't go home. I get sucked into the vortex and it makes it all ten times worse.'

'Work it out for yourself. If you haven't already. And I'll tell you what else . . .'

'Yes?' asked Stacy expectantly.

'*You*'re opening the shop in the morning. You. Not me. I'm having a lie-in. All this emotion drains me.'

And reaching for the file of invoices with one hand and the coffee mug with the other, she held the girl with her eye, and ended the audience.

Stacy walked out on her long legs, head held high, her narrow, sloping shoulders unbowed – tossing the tissues into the corner waste-paper basket as she went.

'And thanks for the coffee,' Anya called after her, taking her first sip.

It was stone-cold.

Anya slept late the next morning. Stacy had gone; the cats were yowling for breakfast. She padded about, opening windows and curtains to let in a crisp spring morning. The flat became suddenly light and airy, smelling of coffee. She sat straddling a kitchen chair, elbows planted on the table, gazing abstractedly across the frothy new green of the park. Sunlight glistened on a curled genie of steam that rose from the bowl she held in her hands. Why not prolong the pleasure by walking? This was no morning to go underground.

Carelessly halting the traffic in Exhibition Road, she stepped off the kerb, crossed, passed through the iron gates and strode off towards the lake, the long dipped vista of the Row smoking hazily blue on her right. A horse was galloping up the rise towards her. A slight fair girl, thighs packed tightly into white breeches, rose and fell in the saddle, in loud conversation, it appeared, with her palomino. The rumbling and panting crescendoed as horse and rider leant into the turn, depositing a steaming offering almost at Anya's feet. They were receding now, passing the 'No Galloping. By Order' sign. Ah, the ruling classes! Make laws for others to observe, and drop shit at the feet of anyone who ventures to notice. Who in hell, anyway, could afford to stable a horse in this part of London? Who could afford such a horse? It probably took a full-time groom to keep its silvery tail so combed and pomaded. Not that she minded. Not in the least. She admired. When the sweet young thing got out of her jodhpurs, after all, she would probably come to Anya for a party frock. The thing about wealth was not to abolish it, but to spread it around. Like muck, it made things grow.

She strode on, making for the Serpentine where, in the distance, workmen were varnishing the bottoms of upturned boats, getting ready for the season. A small explosion of colour on the edge of the park caught her eye. Good Christ! Now they were playing toy soldiers! Red coats and shiny tin hats jouncing up and down in rhythm like an unimaginative *corps de ballet*. Solemn little manikins, a dozen of them, trotting po-faced, as if they hadn't noticed what century they were in, while the Exhibition Road juggernauts and double-deckers thundered around them. What a hilarious country this was! She never tired of its absurdities. Not that she was knocking the Household Cavalry, or whoever they were. That was good for trade too. I mean, how many fat industrialists, their wallets bulging with Deutschmarks, would cross the Channel in order to see the TUC executive in mustard-coloured cardigans and flat caps posing for a group photograph? It simply didn't have the same cachet.

A tattered gentleman stretched out on a bench, a tent of soiled newspaper triangled over his head, reared up at Anya's approach, caught her eye, and replaced his sunshield. Let him just try it – putting an armlock on *her* social conscience! Let him try! She hadn't built a flourishing business out of £300 savings and a talent for extorting credit, in order to have her conscience wrung by the whining lachrymose ruins that lay dozing about the parks of Britain. If there was any one thing wrong with this country it was the hangdog puling defeatism that tried to justify itself with historical theories of class. What class did she come from? She neither knew nor cared.

The dosser sat up and watched her go, his face eloquent with distaste: what a tartar! Scowl on her fit to sour milk. Clumping along with her great boots as if she was going to grind you underfoot. He was wrong to imagine Anya made a particular point of trampling over people: she made no more point of it than she did of avoiding them. But her stride was no chance mannerism. She had tried, briefly, a long time ago, sitting with her knees together and mincing when she walked. But at the turbulent stage of her adolescence when it had become plain that she was going to be 'a big girl', she had opted firmly for *being* it. Not for her the stooping and sidling which concealed stature, the effacing of oneself in doorways in apology for what nature had done. At age sixteen she tilted up her chin, thrust out her chest and, cleaving the wind with her straight strong nose, strode into her future. The future, with some notable exceptions, had parted and made way. But the slope up the far side of the park had her puffing within seconds. Some endangered sparrows skittered out of her path. Jesus! she wheezed, I *am* getting fat! The voluminous billowing skirts might conceal from the world the scandalous breadth of her beam, but they couldn't fool her. And remembering the svelte brown goddess of her Cape Town beach party days, she experienced a twinge of remorse.

Ah well! svelteness was overrated anyway. Just look, for instance, at the idiotic pair of health-farm idols cavorting in bronze at the centre of that fountain. She might be gross but she was not epicene: no one could mistake her for a boy. Sweet Jesus, what did these artists think they were doing. A pair of flying nudes, male and female, legs aseptically interlocked, defying gravity and sexuality both, leaned backwards, holding hands in a parody of ecstatic flight, or dance, or something. 'Aryan Youth Celebrating the Purity of the Bodily Impulses' perhaps? A circle of jetting water might just have made it tolerable, but at this time of year Paolo and Francesca had to perform their mating dance above a stone basin choked with Coke cans, crisp packets and dog shit. The sculptor must have been out of his mind.

She clattered down the steps of the underpass, her nose wrinkling at the stink of exhaust fumes from the Park Lane racing-circuit. The tiled walls were new, but the aerosol artists had been hard at it. Those who were completely illiterate sprayed up a Nazi swastika, a CND chicken foot, or a strictly non-partisan phallus (she drew no distinction betweeen these manifestations of mindless inarticulacy). 'Free Nelson Mandela', urged one bright-red can-wielder. The imprisoned Congress freedom-fighter (about whom her father used to write cautiously inflammatory articles) seemed oddly domiciled in a Park Lane subway. 'Nigs out'. Well, make up your minds: do you want them out or in? 'Pakis are shit'. 'Croydon skins pis on Jews'. (Wonder if Stacy knows this curious fact about her home town?) 'Jesus saves'. (Oh yes?) 'But Brooking scores on the rebound'. . . . Not greatly impressed by the intellectual life of the district, Anya ended her passage through the underworld and emerged into the daylight of Mayfair.

She quickened her pace. This part of the itinerary was full of delights. 'Lovely Legs of Mayfair (Hosiery) Ltd' with its rank of six yellowing waxen legs – never changed since she'd first set eyes on them – looming over the litter of upended flies that lapped against the window. 'Ashkenasy's Ancient Arts'. Now, what would the old fraud have to offer this week? She could see him eyeing her sideways from amidst his native jungle, judging her probably far too fleabitten to call for the exercise of *any* of his ancient arts. Above the bristling undergrowth of bureaux, bidets, escritoires, armoires – all hideously bulbous and grotesquely gilded – soared standing candelabra, gross and elephantine, reaching up to a tinkling sky thronged with chandeliers. There was hardly room to move in his wonderland of exquisite vulgarities.

At the side of each window, as ever, pairs of eight-foot steel urns mounted guard, with their bevy of gawky Grecian matrons clubfooting it round the circumference. Would he ever get rid of these monstrosities? Perhaps he liked them and refused to sell – who could tell, given the general level of his tastes? And yes, there was a new treasure – all scrolls, balls and bulges. How could you describe it? A gilt, glass-panelled howdah? A china cabinet disguised as a sedan chair (with quilted, red satin interior)? A Louis Quatorze telephone kiosk? It was wonderful, with its alabaster orb atop and its brass Cupidon sprawling amid the legs, positively crushed under his burden of bows, arrows, garlands, torches and God-knew-what-all. How much would he sell that little marvel for? she wondered. It would have to run to thousands. And to cap it all, there were buyers for this rubbish. Apart from the steely Grecians, nothing loud, large or ostentatious stayed long in the window. She stood in the road and laughed outright, while the dignified proprietor stared into the middle distance.

Refreshed by derision, Anya crossed to the gardens and threaded her way along the winding path lined with benches upon which nobody ever sat, ducked through the iron gate, and out into the creamy-pink rococo of Mount Street. In the poulterer's window a dozen pheasants reclined gracefully on a decorative fan of wheat-ears. Gorgeous smouldering colours in the plumage. A pity to eat.

A slight screech of rubber signalled that she'd crossed the road, to where her friend the porter was strutting and sunning himself at his usual post – decidedly the most impressive thing the Connaught had on display, she always thought. Seeing her, his face broke into a broad smile as he swept off his topper and bowed low, forward arm dangling in the manner of a trainee extra at an acting academy: 'Mo'nin', ma'am. De wedder am entirely to yo' taste, Ah trust?'

'Why sho', precious. It entirely am.'

'Mighty glad to hear dat, Missy. Mighty glad.'

She never knew what these satirical impersonations did for him, but it cost nothing to go along with them. There was a piquancy in seeing someone employed as a decorative nigger, doing an impersonation of a decorative nigger – much to the puzzlement of any patrons who happened to be within earshot. Let him salvage his dignity that way, if it pleased him . . .

But enough of idle hedonism. She turned into her dilapidated little court, and, having notified Stacy of her arrival, went straight round to the rear premises. This time she really must settle their hash. Inside they were chinking away steadily.

'Oy!' she bawled, and rattled the iron grille. 'Oy! you in there!'

There was a pause, the door slid back, and she found herself looking, through the grille, at a tall, stringy, dusty-looking individual in dungarees.

'Are you in charge here?'

' "Charge"?' Some sort of middle-European accent. Wasn't going to understand a word.

'Are you foreman?' she bellowed, as to the deaf.

'What foreman? I dwell here. Work.' He had a cold chisel or something in his hand.

'What are these alterations I hear going on? I'm your neighbour,' she added belatedly. 'Next door.'

'Yes, yes, I know. We have seen ourselves. Please to come in.'

He pushed back the grille and ushered her in with what she thought an unnecessarily florid gesture.

The room was high, light, and spacious – probably an old taxi depot or car-repair workshop, complete with skylights. In the far right corner, a kind of mezzanine office, glassed in and reached by ladder, stood on piles. Through the open door she made out the end of a bed. Chests and workbenches round the walls were covered with pots, pails, cans, rags, fasces of steel rods, of wire, of wood, bags of mysterious powders. A large crucible of something dark and glutinous congealed over an unlit paraffin stove. Some sort of frozen black quadruped snarled at her out of a darkened corner; and on a shelf, at odd, inconsequent angles, a whole army of plaster heads and busts lolled and wallowed, like some medieval headsman's personal collection. Blobs and trails of plaster were spattered across the concrete floor, and the white dust was everywhere.

It began to come clear. That seven-foot block of dark-grey stone standing on wooden baulks in the centre of the room was the source of the clinking. She caught sight of other items of sculpture scattered about – metallic mostly. Would it be bronze? She knew next to nothing about it. The scene had taken her so much by surprise that she had lost her momentum, and with it, her sense of grievance. Memories of late adolescence, too, were stirring – prompted by an elusive yet pervasive smell whose associations she couldn't quite pin down.

She pulled herself together: 'I've come to complain,' she said in her usual resonant tones.

The lean sculptor thrust his hands into the front pockets of his dungarees and watched her with, she suspected, a smile playing under his thick, untrimmed moustache. She became distracted by the muscular hairy forearms, whitened with dust. ' About the dust,' she concluded.

He made a movement with his shoulders. 'There is much,' he conceded.

'There certainly is. And not just here. It runs down the lane and piles up outside my shop. And then people tramp it in, all over the carpet. It's impossible to get rid of.' She had become quite heated, less about the problem of the dust, perhaps, than about the ridiculous sound her complaint was acquiring in her own ears.

'Oh, I well know,' said the sculptor.

'Why does it run down the lane? Why?'

'Every night I wash up – wash down. With hose. Also the plaster it runs out. So I suppose.'

'Will you stop doing it, please? It's a great nuisance.'

He gave a theatrical shrug: 'This is my dwelling here. I do not like with dust to sleep. With dust to eat. Is enough I work with dust. So I think.' He was perfectly good-humoured, as if confident of being understood.

'Well, I *don't* think.'

'Sure,' he said soothingly, as if he knew better. 'What is it you say? "Live and Let Live"? Is the name of local pub hereby. And a very nice pub too. Often I go. Some day I take you there perhaps? A drink of neighbours? What do you say?'

Anya detected herself finding this inconsequence faintly charming and struggled to recover a proper asperity: 'It can't go on, you know. My people spend half their time hoovering.'

He looked around him, nodding sagely. 'Perhaps I give up sculpture,' he said, pursing his lips. 'Twenty year is long enough, I think. You reckon I should give up? What do you advise?'

'I warn you, I'll complain to the council.'

'I do not think so,' he observed drily. The change of tone was startling. For the first time Anya felt she had heard a real voice.

'Why not?' she demanded

'Because . . . excuse me . . .' he shrugged dismissively, 'in this building, with Mr Boesma, and the little rent, and the little rates, and the developments of Mr Boesma, I think we do not need the council. Not you. Not me. We have both work to do.'

'You know about "the developments of Mr Boesma" then?'

'Sure. When I would move in, my friend . . . the painter what was here, you know? . . . he told me.'

'I didn't know there *was* a painter here.' She spoke as if she had been cheated of something.

'Yes. For three year. But he was all the time worrying about the lease – about the not-lease. All the time worry. Also, he feels the cold. In his bones, so he say. So at the last he has gone away. Me, I need a cheap studio, big like this. Cold I do not feel. So I take it. And try not to worry. Is very cheap.'

'You don't make much on the sculpture, then?'

He measured her with his eye, reluctant to waste explanation on the uncomprehending. 'Once, yes. When I come first of Hungary. For a while I make much. But my last exhibition was, I think you say, cat-as-trophy.'

'Catastrophe. Didn't sell?' ·

'Hardly nothing, God he knows why, not me. I do the same work what I have done in 1959. Or in 1962. I do it only better. Properly. This time I know what I do. I understand. In 1959 they have all gone crazy for me. This time they tell me it is "Old Hat". Thus,' he gestured around the studio, 'I get back a lot of Old Bronze Hats, and not very much money. You want to buy?' he asked with a certain reptilian swiftness.

'I might. Who knows?'

'I joke.'

'So do I. Now about this dust.'

'Ah so. It is plaster dust. I work in plaster.'

'So I gathered. But that's no reason why *I* should work in plaster.'

It seemed to amuse him. 'Well,' he said, laying a patronizing hand on her shoulder – which she promptly shook off, 'for this present, there is not plaster. So it happens. I have delivered this week a big block of stone. On this I work. It makes good dust, clean dust. You will like this dust.' He heaved against one corner of the monolith – so that it rumbled through a few degrees on its turntable – and became momentarily absorbed in the surface it presented to him.

'Provided,' Anya interposed, battling against his growing abstraction, 'provided I can put up with the racket.'

He looked up. 'Oh, is very musical. So I think. I have not carved stone for long years. Is a pleasing sound.'

'I see I may as well save my breath.'

'No, no,' he demurred courteously, wresting his attention away from the stone. 'Not so. I like you to talk. You *move* when you talk.'

'How do you mean "move"?' Anya asked suspiciously. The voice had been assured, factual, all the silly playfulness gone out of it. It was the voice of the professional, not to be controverted.

He made to explain: 'When you talk, you are . . . *mobile*.' (He pronounced it French-fashion.) 'Not your mouth only. Everything moves.'

'Everything except your mind. That doesn't seem to shift an inch.'

'Ah,' he said, spreading his palms, 'you understand how is it. You are a woman of determination. I am a man the same. That is how we make our works, is not? By determination. Is better that peoples know her own mind. Much better. So I think.'

Anya wondered whether "mind" in Hungarian was of the feminine gender, or whether she had just been the recipient of a somewhat barbed innuendo. His English seemed to come and go rather wilfully.

'Well,' she said truculently, 'now that we know that we are both determined people, what happens? Nothing, I suppose.'

He laughed and spread out his arms, cocking his head quizzically: 'We should be friends. So I hope.'

'Mister Whoever-you-are,' said Anya, putting her hands on her broad hips and planting the heel of one boot in front of her as if drawing a line of demarcation ('Kovacs,' he supplied, 'Laczi'). 'Mr Cove-arch-lartzy,' she went on without a pause, 'I distrust your charm.'

'You must not worry. Is very superficial.'

'I never doubted it. That's why I distrust it.'

'You see? We *shall* be friends!'

Anya spun on her heel, determined not to be flattered into submission: '*When* you stop fouling my pavement, perhaps. Not before.'

Having terminated the interview with this cadence, she had nothing to do but make her exit. But her speculative eye was still drawing up an inventory amid this clutter of objects, and when it fell on a notice board near the door she instinctively paused. Here was a wealth of matter for deductive ingenuity, and Anya was chronically inquisitive. The board must have been transferred bodily from his last lodgings, for the grit of decades lay upon its litter of business cards, bills, press clippings, invitations to private views and pinned-up sketches. But right in the middle, grimed and curling at the edges, was a big publicity photograph of the expensively glossy kind, showing three huge spidery-skeletal figures circling each other in a kind of grave dance. It might have been the three Graces. But it might equally have been a medieval dance of death, for the figures were opened out with large spaces where their chests and viscera might have been, and their heads bore only rudimentary features, like skulls. She went closer. Something about the grouping, about the implied movement, something, even more, about the lanky, spindly grace of these walking lattices of bone pleased her very much. Could it be Mr Ashkenasy's Greek matrons they reminded her of? Or Stacy's long-legged elegance, was it? . . . No, of course! It was that pair of whirling nudes on the edge of the park. *Here* was what that clumsy sculptor had been trying for, and could not achieve. His travesty of abortive flight, so kitsch and ludicrous, had been crying out for the harmonious relation and refinement of these forms. There was no loud insistence upon movement, yet the very stasis was instinct with it. They paced in grave pavane, and space went still about them. She peered at the print and made out, pencilled in the margin, the words 'Dance of Liberty'.

There was a sudden growl behind her. 'I should get rid! I forget.' And Kovacs's hand reached rudely past, to tear the offending object off the board. He stood with it gripped in his hefty paw, making noises of disgust in his throat.

Anya was roused. At last she had touched a chord. 'How big are they?' she inquired, insidiously naive.

'What? These? About two metre. Bigger than me.'

' "The Dance of Liberty" you call it?'

'Bah! *I* do not call. The gallery, *he* call. I was a child. I know nothing. They say to me "What it is about?" About, about! Sculpture is not "about". Sculpture *is*! But still they say, "What it is about?" So I say, "It is dance." I say, "Maybe it is about being free in the dance." "Oh?" They say, "The Dance of Liberty"? "Maybe," I say. To me it sounds the same. Those days I do not well understand English. So it becomes. Is foolishness. Foolishness!'

'The figures? Or the title?'

'Both, both. Liberty? Bah!'

'I like it,' she said flatly – because she did – though also in the hope of producing more sparks. .

'You must *not* like!' He was vehement. 'It is bad work.'

'But I do.' She was all serene lucidity. 'Just because *you've* ratted on your own work, that's no reason why *I* have to. The Dance of Liberty. It pleases me. Title and all.'

'You look at me,' he said, gripping her arm roughly and turning her to face him. 'I tell you how it is. I am coming from Budapest.' Suddenly he released her, striding away several yards before rounding on her: 'Where is no liberty. In 1956, liberty is bleeding in the streets. I come away because I cannot stand to see liberty bleeding in the streets. Good. I come to London. It is different. Nothing is bleeding in the streets. Peoples do not ask for my papers all day and all night. I do not in cellars hide from the police. My friends they do not fall their eyes and whisper in a corner when I speak what I think . . .'

(She wondered how he would manage to converse in a confined space, he strode about so furiously.)

'. . . And I can make things like I want. Not heroical peasants, and worthy factory workers, and a bust of the Comrade President only. It is different. I make them like I want. Like I want! There is a woman. I give her legs like a giraffe.' He hit the photograph a smart crack with a back of his hand. 'Liberty. So. I take a man and I put a hole where his chest should be, and another at his guts. Wonderful! This truly is liberty. Perhaps tomorrow I put a pumpkin where his prick should be. More liberty! Wonderful! And *why* I do all this? you ask me. Simple. Because there is no reason why not. And I tell you *why* there is no reason why not – because there is no reason *why*! Do you see? In this country where you can do anything what you like, is no reason for doing anything at all. I show you . . .'

He strode across to a shelf and hauled down a curious abstract compilation, planted it on the floor in front of her. 'This I make for exhibition in 1959.' He prodded it with his foot. 'You know how? I take a pile of old trash from my waste-box and I stick it altogether, very artistically, in one big pile. I cast it in bronze. "What it is?" they say, and their tongues are hanging. "It is a barricade," I say. Wonderful! What a clever fellow is the young freedom-fighter of Budapest what makes sculpture out of rubbish. How he enjoys our British liberty. Now we will buy his whole works with the funny titles and put them in our ballrooms in honour of British liberty. Ach, I am like a baby. All the time liberty is bleeding in the streets. I know nothing. Nothing. This is not liberty. Liberty for what? Liberty for to be bought and sold, like a cabbage. Liberty to do anything what has not been done before, because only it has not been done before. *Why* it has not been done before? Because it is foolishness, that is why.'

He was glaring at the photograph so murderously that Anya held out her hand: 'If you don't want it, give it to me.'

'You should not like.'

'Pfft! I like what I choose. Give it to me.'

He handed it over.

But submission only provoked her further: 'So,' she eyed him wickedly, 'although it was "bad work" and you despised the buyers, you made a tidy little profit on your "foolishness", did you? Or did you refuse to take the tainted money, on aesthetic grounds?'

'In 1959? You joke. I was young man. Broke. No home. No country. What should I understand? I needed the freedom. To work. To work *in order to understand*, you see?'

'Oh, I see. So you flogged the shoddy goods, pocketed the cash, and bought liberty with it? I thought only corrupt capitalists did that sort of thing.'

He met her mocking eyes, accepting the challenge: 'Very good,' he said, between his teeth, 'one day I explain to you liberty. Also why you *think* you have it only. You British, you are very ignorant. Some day you will lose thus even the liberty what you have. And that is not very much!'

'Quite enough apparently,' she retorted in high sarcasm, 'to keep you from returning to Hungary, home of the free. Here you are – two decades on – managing somehow to put up with our lack of liberty. I've met your kind before. They come round to my flat and scoff my best French cookery and guzzle my château-bottled claret, and as they settle down to the cognac in front of a good log fire, they tell me about the evils of capitalism, and how no conscientious person could really consent to make a living as I do, out of the pampered dowagers of Mayfair, and how I should give it up – I really ought – because it's not worthy of me. What a load of hypocritical shit! Why do they always wait until after the meal – these . . . "After Eight" revolutionaries – before discovering their consciences? Just like you – sell first, agonize afterwards. And from what I can make out there's not much to choose between my dowagers and your art-collectors. Same people probably. You're in the muck with the rest of us, boyo. Down in the rich, fertilizing, fulsome muck! So don't you come the high and mighty ideological purist with me!'

It is hard to say what Anya expected in reply to this tirade. Nothing, possibly – or perhaps a very great deal. But she was waiting, visibly, to see what would come. He had picked up one of his chisels and was throwing it speculatively from hand to hand. His demeanour disclosed neither a definite anger or a distinct in- difference. It was a kind of abstract energy as yet undischarged. He put down the chisel.

'Perhaps you would be surprised,' he said, speaking with deliberation, 'but this to me is not new. I have heard before. Just once or twice.' Irony glinted for a second, then disappeared. He lowered his eyes and thrust clenched fists down hard into his pockets. 'Is perfectly true: like other peoples, I fill my belly in order that I can afford my conscience. It is not nice but it is nothing new. I have seen the other: I have seen peoples what try to make justice with an empty belly, and it does not succeed. Not for long. The hunger is too loud. Perhaps . . .' He seemed struck by a thought, and looked at her inquiringly. 'Perhaps when I explain to you liberty, I explain also Hungary? You think so? I think it is necessary. But perhaps then you would not be listening.'

Contemptuous though she was of people who 'explained' things to her, Anya met the change in his tone with some conciliation: 'Oh I can listen well enough,' she said airily, 'when people tell me something *new*.'

'Ah so! It is a long time that you have not heard something new. Good! I give you something new.'

He gave, in fact, an impatient sigh, and his eyes crept back longingly to the pair of steps beside the vertical block of stone where he had so far done little more than square off, to secure a firm base, and try a few exploratory cuts.

'But not today,' he said. 'Today I work.'

He was only half attending, and Anya saw that if she prolonged her stay, he would presently forget her altogether.

'Me too,' she said briskly, wrapping the folds of her vast cardigan about her. She understood that painter, the previous tenant: it was decidedly frigid in here.

'Happy chipping!' she remarked in valedictory flippancy. The patronage slid straight off him.

'Yes,' he said, taking up the chisel and a little square-headed lump of a hammer. Before she was well out of the door the clinking sound had resumed. All day – coming in irregular bursts that were impossible to ignore, and punctuated by false lulls – her ears were wrung with it. 'Very musical', like hell!

It was still going when she shut up shop that night, and set off for Princes' Gate.

T W O

Sculptor

At six, a shaft of sunlight woke the sculptor, lighting up the wall as if a switch had been thrown. Though it had been stained coppery-brown by the studio skylight, and divided into lozenges by the panes of the former office, it served as well as any pristine rustic sunbeam would have done. His feet were already planted on the bare boards, feeling instinctively for splinters, before his eyes came open.

That was a good sign – waking like that. Being up before you knew it. That was the way productive days began. The cold air which he drew into his lungs seemed to expand his chest cavity as if he were growing on the spot. It roused him to his feet, all his muscles stirring. It had been weeks since he had had a really productive day. Months, more likely. Determined not to waste it, he grabbed a fistful of clothes, scrambled down the ladder and ran the cold tap into a bucket in the porcelain trough. And stood there, his eyes focused keenly on some point miles beyond the walls of the studio.

Water was brimming the bucket and running down the sides. Noticing, he turned off the tap. He had fallen into a restive reverie that now sought its own origins without success. It was chilly standing about naked. The big wolf – in plaster temporarily sloshed over with metallic paint – leered at him from the corner, tongue lolling. What was it after now, that misfit? Like all unfinished work, it hung about the edges of consciousness when he least needed it. He reached into his mind for something, as an unoccupied hand gropes in a pocket for a pebblestone.

> Be tough as the big wolves, who bleed
> From many wounds, yet live indeed.

That was all very satisfying, and Radnóti was a fine poet, but it did not answer to his abstraction. And what (he came awake with a jolt), what was he, Laczi Kovacs, doing making animal pieces anyway? Next thing it would be families of badgers, or hand-crafted garden gnomes. There was only one animal that demanded his attention – the one that was now standing about like a zombie and coming up in goose-pimples. Crossing to a clear space near the sliding doors, he slung the towel across a trestle, upended the bucket over his head, and began violently to rub himself down.

Red blotches appeared on the muscular sierra of chest, shoulder, bicep, spread to the valley of the breastbone and down into the knotty hollow below the rib-cage which had the pinched look of his own wolf. The selective muscular development that went with his trade had given him a slight round-shouldered stoop; and the absence of any flesh without a manifest function gave his nakedness a curious kind of hungry pathos – as if, with such strength, he might have won more of the roundedness of joy. Not that he indulged such thoughts. Pathos was a category he scarcely recognized – and certainly never as applying to himself.

With money tighter than ever (he was thinking), he couldn't seriously propose having the wolf cast – even if he was happier with it than he was. (He sawed at his shoulder-blades with the towel.) That could cost five or six hundred pounds. He might cast it himself for much less, of course – perhaps would be obliged to: whom else would he trust with all that complex undercutting around jaw and tongue? Couldn't do it here – far too big for his home foundry – but at the art school, yes. Bill Madison would help with the pouring: Bill's indiscriminate fascination with technology got him regularly involved, as assistant, in other people's craft-mysteries. Except . . . (he flapped the threadbare towel in an impractical attempt to render it less sodden) . . . except that he would have to write off a couple of weeks on his own work. That wasn't what he had bounced out of bed for this morning. No, it would have to be a professional job. (The sawing and pummelling resumed) . . .

But what was he thinking of? At the only foundry he could trust, he already owed nearly a thousand in bills. Old Fenwick had been extremely forbearing. He seemed to enjoy the sculptural work for its claims upon his finer skills, and subsidized it out of his industrial earnings. But he could hardly be expected to come up with another massive loan before the first even looked like being paid off. Being misled by Kovacs's early successes was one thing, but failing to see the light after four unpaid years was another. He did not easily see how he could hope to mount an exhibition of bronzes ever again –

unless some gallery would pay his casting bills in advance. The teaching covered only running expenses.

Money, money money! He got the last of the water out of his ears and began to rub his hair dry. And last week he had put himself further in hock with his latest fancy – two and a half tons of purbeck. The same old trouble as with Fenwick: he quite fatally inspired trust. It was all the fault of the Budapest Academy of Fine Arts: his technical training had been so thorough that he could meet the craftsmen, in stone or metal, on their own ground – even teach them a trick or two. And for a fellow-craftsman, you know how it is . . . they would stretch a point here and there, financially. They almost insisted on it – 'No, no my old son, don't you worry. You'll pay in the end, we know that. And the bugger's only lying about the yard getting underfoot. You take it. It's worth it to us to get the space . . .'

Just like that. There had been a kind of fatality about it. All he had to find was the transport cost. True, he never could pass a mason's yard without nipping in for a quick shifty, but how was he to have known that he would hit it off so well with the new proprietor . . . who would therefore take him round the back to look at the big grey block . . . ordered by a contractor . . . but now found to be surplus to requirements? Or that he would be suddenly overtaken by the old passion for stone which had not troubled him for years?

The block spoke to him. Within seconds he had been mentally locating the box of tools gathering dust under one of his benches, congratulating himself on having a studio large enough to house such a monster, and wondering whether the disused baulks stacked under his bedroom-on-stilts would serve to make a turntable. In the event he did not 'decide' to take the block. By the time it presented itself as a matter of decision it was too late. And he was glad of it anyway. Damn the money!

Standing on one leg to dry his foot, he found he was staring at a dark runnel where the water from his morning shower had streamed out under the door, leaving whitened banks on either side. Tttt! Another distraction! That Wagnerian giantess from next door. Should he do something about it? The splendid morning was already beginning to fray at the edges and his spirit chafed.

But if there was one thing that Kovacs did not like, it was leaving another person in possession of grounds of complaint against him. It flawed the perfection of his indifference. Especially if they could be removed. He pulled a heavy check shirt over his head, climbed into his dungarees, rolled up the cuffs and, hauling out the hose, attached it at the sink.

A quarter of an hour later, with the water from the hose splashing down a gleaming drain-grate which had not a trace of plaster near it, he leaned on his broom – an odd, gaunt, bare-footed figure in a deserted London street – and contemplated the facade of the Rotten Orange. Bizarre at any time, it was doubly so at the bottom of an empty court in the faint pinkish light of an early morning that was still studded with the mercury-blue flares of paling street lights. The overnight spots lit the windows from within, so that they gleamed like some emanation of phosphorescent decay in the dark of a cave.

All the sculptor saw, however, was a piece of meretricious flotsam cast up by the op/pop vogue of the sixties – and that had been meretricious enough in all conscience! How could they be so clever and so stupid at the same time? By mistaking Publicity for Expression, he gloomily supposed. London was nearly all Publicity. Call this a city? Canned music thumped and twangled at you from the interiors of shops, spilling out across the pavements like an unclean tide. Walls of banked electric lettering pumped their mindless iterations into the eye's mind. Shopkeepers looked like pimps, and pimps like shopkeepers. It took a persistence amounting almost to genius to discover a decent approximation to a European café. Nobody seemed able to do anything but sell! If this city had a soul, it hid it well behind the neon lights and the hoardings and the big brazen shops. There was, about it all, something not properly human. Not human as Budapest had been . . .

No, it was not just piety, or nostalgia. Even when he saw the mother-city last – scarred and cratered, a wilderness of tank carcases and uprooted trees, dangling cables and shattered glass – even then you did not fear for its soul. Perhaps least of all, then.

The sun came round the corner and peered into the court. At the far end, a door opened and a char in a headscarf banged the contents of her dustpan out on to the pavement for the municipal cleansing department to deal with . . . Throughout the uprising, no matter how devastating the night's bombardment, the housewives of Pest would be out in the morning lull, cleaning up the pavements. It was, you could almost say, *the* characteristic sound of those days: not guns, not tanks, not the chatter of small-arms' fire – but the sound of tinkling glass being swept into domestic dustpans. What they had hoped to achieve was a mystery. There would be the same shattered rubble to deal with next morning. But they would not admit it. The devastation was transitory. Russians might come and Russians

30

might go, governments might fall, revolutions and counter-revolutions succeed each other without sense or meaning, but what endured from age to age, suffering no diminution and requiring no justification, were the constitutional cornerstones of the state: a scrubbed doorstone, a swept pavement, and domestic self-respect. Still, he supposed it wasn't the char's house, so why should *she* care? The flats of the Budapest housewives, allocated by the State, were more truly possessed by their inhabitants than most owner-occupied houses in London. It was the possession, the being-at-home, that mattered – not the legal title: that merely reflected the vagaries of the prevailing political system. To give people homes . . . now *there* was an objective for the planners, the bureaucrats. Not that they would know where to begin, poor babies. They had no idea how to make things grow; they knew only how to impose, how to drill, and box and package.

Looking at the fantasticated window of Anya's boutique, however, he was inclined to let the British planners off. How could you ever create conditions of growth for a people who fell over themselves to be imposed on in this gross fashion? And no doubt it would be the same inside as out. He squinted into the darkened interior. As he thought . . . masses of froth, flounce and flummery – all the standard invitations and allurements to female vanity to trick itself out for consumption. Femininity as commodity. Dress as publicity. Sell, sell, sell! Yet she – the madam of this establishment, presumably – she was no mere commodity. Why did she lend herself to the corporate betrayal? She with the monumentally planted calves, the strong hips, the broad chest and deeply-cleft breast . . . with that clarity and defiance of gaze . . . there must be some wilfully embraced self-parody in her choice of occupation.

He would like to do her in bronze, he realized. Stone rather. Granite! She lent herself so prodigally to sculptural appreciation. But it was out of the question. Impossible! She would talk him to extinction. She would insist on his knowing her opinions – that scummy froth on the surface of all active brains – while he was in search of the mind which expressed itself in body and limb, mass and movement – that weight of mobility and repose which had struck him at a first meeting so forcibly as to make him comment on it out loud. A little impertinently, if the truth were known.

That had been very unguarded of him . . . he who was so wise (poor burnt child!) about women. Furthermore, he had hoped – also aloud! – that they would become 'friends'. Had even offered to explain to her Liberty, Hungary, and Frugality. Oh dear, oh dear! . . . Of course he had told himself, at the time, that he was 'managing' her as one manages a spirited horse – exploiting the old trick of accent, the emigré's quaint licensed courtliness, under which, it had been his experience, British women became unnaturally docile (how else had he acquired a British wife? how else lost her . . . when the charm began to wear thin?). But his self-deception, now, seemed flagrant. He had meant it. He had been galled, stung, and – let it be admitted – piqued. Did he still mean it? To be friends with such a woman would be no small undertaking. And he had reason to distrust himself in these matters.

His eye fell on the clothes-horse mannequins of the window display, with their waxwork sinuosities, their fatuous struttings, and his mind recoiled. So that (God help them!) was their conception of the human body! Could any good thing come out of this Babylon? Could any rational being make a life out of selling clothes? Out of the sub-civilized obsession with dressing up Nature? If he hoped to get back on his feet with another exhibition – and hope was strong in him this morning – he must steer a wide course around these banalities. For banality didn't merely lie alongside you, neighbour you; it mined, it eroded. It insisted that you talk to it about its trivial preoccupations. It filled up your ear and obstructed your eye. It shattered concentration.

He might, he supposed, ask her to sit to him; but his experience of amateur models had not been happy. They bestowed themselves upon you. They were convinced you were in search of their treasured, sacred egos, and insisted on helping you find them. Unable to sit still and be, they simpered and twittered. It was exhausting and unfruitful.

He shouldered his broom. He was forgetting what he was about: what in God's name had he been sweeping streets for, if not to purchase immunity from such invasions? So . . . now he had it, let him use it. Executing a crisp right-face, he marched up the lane – playing the military clown in sheer relief at his recovered freedom. The qualm had passed.

The wolf still leered at him as he coiled up the hose, but he ignored it. He'd settle its hash some other day. Larger matters were in hand. He patted his lovely stone, so darkly immanent, running his palm down the sharp vertical edge on one corner which already gave the mass a character all its own. That character he must carefully and lovingly elicit – allowing the stone to speak. When he withdrew the hand, it felt empty. He took up an apple and bit thoughtfully into his breakfast.

His exploratory chippings at the purbeck had revealed what he had to reckon with there: for a limestone, it was unexpectedly, gratifyingly tough. This meant that his first maquette was wrong – too waxily curved and recessed. (Was there even, perhaps, a perfidious kinship to the dress-shop mannequins?) It was not, in any case, what the stone asked . . . something craggier, grander . . .

He lit the stove under the modelling-wax, caught up his battered, spattered copy of the poems of Radnóti and, pulling a stool up to the bench, fell into an active musing where he read and drew, and pondered, without distinguishing between the activities. The book seemed to help.

Lajos Kovacs had been a boy of ten, hiding from the Russian bombardment in the cellars of Pest, when Radnóti – too weak to continue the forced march into Germany – had been shot by the roadside. That was in 1944. The poet had not lived to see the Rakósi terror, or the hopes and fears of the fifties. But you couldn't tell that from his poems. He might as well have been writing of the world he never saw, as of the one in which he died. At all events, they spoke direct, those poems, to the Hungarian exile in a strange city. They spoke in the mother tongue – the tongue of the mother he could not remember – and he did not so much read them, as allow them to work upon his blood.

> I lived on this earth in an age
> When poets were silent: waiting in hope
> For the great Prophet to rise and speak again –
> Since no one could find tongue for a fit curse
> But Isaiah himself, scholar of terrible words.

It made no odds that this was peaceful London, in the year of grace nineteen hundred and seventy-four. Anger was timeless.

He had no doubts of his right to it. Somewhere in Siberia his father rotted – whether above or below ground he would probably never know. And his crime? He was a subversive: he had enjoyed life. And he had done it impenitently in the wrong company. Undelighted by the new breed of joyless, hatchet-faced work-fanatics who became the servants and tyrants of the Republic, mistrusting their humourless single-mindedness, he had declined to change his way of life. The charge against him was absurd: he was no counter-revolutionary. As a lawyer he had been acutely aware of the iniquity of the feudal landowning system, and the prompt and efficient reforms of the Russians, when they came to power in 1945, had warmed his heart – as they had warmed most humane hearts in Hungary: they could hardly believe that, after a century of struggle, it had actually come about. Land for the People, and people on the land. Along with everyone else the elder Kovacs thanked God for the brotherly assistance of their socialist friends from the East.

But his sympathy with the agents was not as complete as his sympathy with the acts. And in November 1956 he was found to have the wrong friends. It had been very sudden. In October he had had the right friends – Imre Nagy among them. And in December, along with thousands of other unwitting fascist-revisionist-bourgeois-reactionary bandits and assassins, he was herded on to a train at Budapest station, and sent east under the guns of those same socialist brothers – a deportee and prisoner.

There had been nothing anybody could do about it then, and there was nothing now. Kovacs had spent days in the anterooms of the Embassy in Eaton Place where a former classmate was now an attaché. It did him no good. He might as well have been sitting on the kerb outside. The wall of silence was complete. Oh, there was still powerful need of that 'fit curse'! The anger did not go away . . .

The tip of his pencil moved on the page, seeking some form for the fitness. 'A great Prophet . . . scholar of terrible words.' It would have to be a figure. He had no patience any more with abstractions, however organic. Man, man – that was the only subject. He flipped pages. 'Wrath nurtures you,' he read. How to draw wrath? How do you write wrath in rock? Rock was certainly the place to write it – wrath being timeless. A prophet, a leader it had to be. The tall stone deserved nothing less. But how must it lie in the stone? He was not illustrating poems, he was carving a block. Just as he went to push the book away, something caught his eye:

> Come let us go:
> Gather the people together. Bring your wife. Cut staffs.
> For the wanderer, staffs are good companions

The pencil, responding, made a hand, gripping . . . gripping a vertical. A staff, that was it! – an axis, a pivot for the composition. He could feel the straight edge behind his back as if he were pressed against it. The pencil moved faster, flying wider. The clenched fist

34

was growing an arm, the arm a body, the body a head . . .

He sighed and wriggled his buttocks, settling them into the hollow of the stool for comfort and permanence.

The morning was beginning to justify its promise.

Kovacs would have been hard pressed to explain how he came, that evening, to be sitting in one of the scrubbed-board booths of the Live and Let Live, facing a pint of mild and Anya Jevons. The simplest way of putting it might have been to say that Anya had 'taken him up' – and in fact he had a little of the feeling a rabbit might have when 'taken up' by a hawk. Not that he was going to admit to fear, but a little dizziness perhaps . . .?

She had dropped round to enlist his active support in the campaign against Boesma's developments. An objection from 'a resident artist of international repute', she thought – one who was liable to be put out in the street by the scheme – would help stiffen the cause. She was not one to let small personal embarrassments obscure the larger public benefit. One thing had led to another . . . and here they were. On the table between them lay such catalogues of his past exhibitions as he'd been able to rustle up – 1959, 1966, 1970 (1962 seemed to have gone missing somewhere), together with a print or two of commissioned works. He did not like bringing them here to this public place, but Anya had insisted.

She was in the process of mounting a private photographic retrospective. Having decided overnight that he was a major sculptor, she was acquainting herself with his *oeuvre*. The decision – about his major status – had been greatly helped by the fact that she knew no other sculptors, though she had once looked long and hard at a Henry Moore she had come across somewhere on the Embankment (she hadn't known it was a Henry Moore, but that didn't stop her studying it with much satisfaction).

Kovacs had been 'taken up' many times before. You might say he was an old hand at it. And he knew of old, too, the little 'oh's' and 'ah's' and 'mm's' of mock appreciation, the accelerating flip of pages which signalled flagging interest, and finally, the offers of reluctant critical dissent with which his admirers eased their exits. From the door, they would fling him salutary advice about where his true talents lay and how best to develop them. Some even proposed a subject for his next piece, before departing, conscious of a service to the Arts worthily discharged. And over the years, craftily, he had

35

developed his defence: a mask of deceptive blandness which smiled and blinked and demurred, giving nothing away and letting nothing through.

But Madame de l'Orange did not fit these categories. She had none of the pseudo-technical cant, the aesthetic jargon to fall back on, so she kept coming at the sculptures in a kind of headlong rush. The collisions were instructive, revealing to him meanings he had certainly never intended, but which he was not ready to disown either. Not yet. It was like listening to an over-familiar symphony in the company of someone hearing it for the first time: what had seemed obvious showed itself for strong, and the hackneyed, one realized, had become so perhaps because it was memorable. It was really very gratifying – and all the more so because there could be no suspicion of flattery. As the pages turned – neither with that telltale acceleration, nor with mechanical regularity – he found himself incongruously hoping that the sculptures would manage somehow to live up to the strange, imperious demands she was making of them.

The landlady, clearing glasses and mopping tables, lifted the pile of papers to wipe under it, and paused. Her blooming middle-aged buxomness, highlighted by a big black beauty-spot, had often been turned on the Hungarian in the domineering provocativeness that publicans' wives specialize in.

'Is this you, Laczi?' she asked coquettishly, noticing the name on a catalogue.

He shrugged. She weighed the booklet in a pair of reflective hands, holding it at arm's length, possibly to get it in focus.

'I knew you were something in the arty line,' she said, 'but I didn't know you were such a celebrity. Well, well, well. D'you think we might rate one of those little blue plaques one day? "Laczi boozed here"? Bond Street galleries, if you please!'

'Is good address,' Laczi agreed,' but I do not myself dwell there. I only make for them their rotten profits, so *they* can dwell there.' He laughed. 'You must not be so very impressed.'

'Oh, you're very modest, you are,' she said with jesting patronage. 'A right little violet, until someone contradicts you. We all know you. You should hear him,' she appealed to Anya. 'when he gets warmed up. Shouts the place down something shocking, he does.'

'Once!' Laczi held up a solitary finger. 'Once in many years.'

She gave a sniffy solitary laugh and passed on.

Anya was watchful: 'You like playing the dark horse, eh? How long have you been coming here?'

'I don't know.' He pondered it. 'I think I have started to come when I must taught at the art school. The instructors they like to drink here. I suppose eight, ten year.'

'And in all that time, you never let on what you do for a living?'

'Why I should? Is nothing to do with them, and they do not care in any case. Like she say, "something in the arty line". Is quite enough to drink beer by.'

He drank some

'Secrets!'

'Pardon?'

'You. You're a hoarder of secrets.'

'Ach, so they say. Because I do not spill myself all over like a sloppy bucket. Is not so.' He looked away frostily into the middle distance. She followed his gaze with amusement.

'Someone you know over there?' She knew there wasn't.

'No . . . Yes, but it does not matter.'

'You're certainly no sloppy bucket, my Hungarian friend, but I'll have your secret all the same. What about these explanations you promised me?'

He raised polite eyebrows and cursed inwardly.

'Of Liberty, you remember? And Hungary. Let's start with Hungary. Why did you leave?'

'Ach, you have heard. There was a revolution in '56. Uprising, street-fighting, what you like. The Russians they come with tanks. There are many who leave. Also me. You know it all.'

'In '56 I was a little girl splashing about in the bright-blue sea. How would I know it? And there may have been "many who leave",' she parodied his accent, 'but why do *you*? You sound as if you're guilty about something.'

'What should I be guilty?'

'I don't know. You tell me.'

He had a brief tussle with an impulse to do just that. But it would have meant unbarring some long-closed doors in his castle, so instead, he grinned defiance at her: 'No, I don't tell you nothing.'

'Why not?'

His hands fluttered upwards in a gesture of impatience: 'Is too dangerous. Last time I tell a girl about Budapest and the troubles, she up and marries me.'

Anya went off in hoots of laughter. 'We'll treat that as a joke,' she said, subsiding. 'And I give you my solemn word not to marry you.'

'Thank you,' he said with a gravity that could have been satirical, 'but I should not promise ever to explain. Explaining is big mistake. Over and again I discover how I cannot do it. When I would try, peoples think I am a freedom-fighter and a hero. Or else they think I am trying to pretend to be , and this is just as bad. For the English it is all a romance – a novel, and they do not like that I should take away their novel.'

Anya dismissed this evasion with a wave of her hand: 'That's tremendous! You'll kindly let us know that we're ignorant fatheads, but you won't take the trouble to set us right. Did you fight or not?'

'I fighted.'

'Then . . .?'

'I am sorry,' he said with lordly indifference, 'I know how it would not work. I know it good and long, so I do not take the same mistake two times.'

'You *make* enough mistakes telling me so. Aren't you ashamed to have such bad English after all these years?'

He squirmed rather under this charge. He wasn't sure he had not been retreating into foreignness and letting his grammar wantonly deteriorate in the process.

'I don't hear your Hungarian very good,' he retorted. 'Aren't *you* ashamed?'

'Nothing to do with it! I learned Xhosa, when I could have got by perfectly well with English. It's a matter of self-respect.'

'Xhosa?'

'Native language. South Africa.'

'Ah, so you *are* South African! I have thought I am hearing some funny vowels . . .'

'Was!' she said shortly.

'Just so. I *was* Hungarian. Was! Is! What difference does it make? It does not stop because I wish.'

'When *I* wish, it stops!' she declared in ringing tones.

He shook his head sagely: 'I understand. We have both secrets, you and me. Perhaps is because we have betrayed both the motherland.'

' "Betrayed"! Pfah! You lot are always talking about "betrayal" . . . and "oppression" and "revolution". Sheer cant. I've heard it all before.'

'Is wrong word. Not betray. We have cut off something. Amputate. So it bleeds, aches.'

'You may be bleeding for your stinking country, man. Not me.

They can all go to hell. A continent of shits!'

'This is your way for to show your hurt. But still it is there.'

She slammed her hand down hard on the table: 'As a moralist, dickhead, you're a bloody good sculptor. Don't give me that patriotic shit! I know your little game: one whiff of South African blood and all the curs of enlightenment are in full cry. Every little yapping radical panting after my guilt-complexes. Show us your racist scars, the wounds of white consciousness. Bare your conscience! Tell us how hideous it was! Grovel before our liberal purity – we who never buy South African oranges, not even when the Israeli ones have run out. Big deal! You know nothing. Nothing!'

She pivoted in her seat, flinging an angry leg across her knee, and glared haughtily into space. The black waves of anger that came at him from the averted face surprised him by their intensity; but he was arrested rather than intimidated. Here, apparently, was another one with reserves of wrath. And the profile she presented, with its austere planes and clean angles showed that it was no muddy resentment, no petty pique that he was dealing with, but a big anger, big like the girl herself – though he could not at all make out its sources. But then why should it need a cause . . . with such a profile? And what a splendid balancing mass of red hair it was, that hung roping down her back. Trapped between the artist's impersonal allegiance to the truth of body and substance, and the abstract combativeness of relations merely social, Kovacs found himself addressing the body-person rather than the talking head, uttering his thought without any view of the possible consequences: 'I would like to model you ,' he said meditatively, 'when you are like this.'

'What?' she very nearly yelled, swinging round to face him, eyes blazing.

'When you are angry. Make a sculpture. It is a fine head.'

'Fine head!' she exploded. 'Don't you understand, little man? I am angry because you make me. Blundering around like an inarticulate baboon in the private affairs of someone you don't know. How dare you!' she shouted, and the hand banged the table again, forcing up the shoulder in a pose newly expressive of the energy he had been admiring.

He shrugged: 'It doesn't matter. Is a good anger, whoever caused it. A big anger. It would make a good sculpture.'

'You bloody aesthete! What would you know about anger?' she said, tossing her head scornfully and pushing the hair back from her temples. Her face was flushed and she looked capable of violence.

39

He hoped the landlady would not intervene – as she had a knack of doing when voices were raised: it would push her over the brink. But the brink of what? He was totally at sea. And what was the significance of the theatricality he sensed behind a fury which he nevertheless judged to be genuine?

For some reason it had become very important for him. . . not to make friends with her – for that he cared nothing . ∴. but to make her recognize an equal. What would he know about anger?!

He leaned forward, insisting that she meet his eye: 'I *know* this anger,' he said in a low sibilant voice, as if he were threatening her. 'I know it just as good as you. It is this what we have been talking about, is not? Is also what you have been looking at.' He slapped the pile of catalogues with an impatient hand. 'Anger! The wrath what nurtures. This is what my work is. Why would you think it is yours only?'

He leaned back in his seat, his challenge delivered, holding her eye steadily, defying her to laugh. The glance that followed lasted long enough to pass beyond the exchange of hostilities and the tabling of credentials. Quiet came over them both, uneasy yet restful.

The difficulty of finding something to say on this new basis, however, was dissolved by a hearty voice: 'There you are Laczi old son. What're you drinking? Evening!' (nodding at Anya – who detected in the accent a hint of the professional Yorkshireman). 'Hello!' (sighting the catalogues). 'What's this? Reliving past glories? Not like you, Laczi.'

'You show me some present ones, and I stop.'

'Aha!' The chubby face beamed. 'Wrong department. Genteel failure is more in my line. Where's Binkie? Ah, here she comes. Mind if we join you? Good. Bill Madison.' He thrust his hand at Anya at a queer horizontal angle, sat, leapt up again to admit Binkie (who was as bony as he was rotund), sat again for a second – beside Anya this time – then bounded out to get a round. Kovacs followed him.

A small waif seemed to be wandering lost among the tables. Binkie reached out an arm and hoisted the unprotesting boy like a sack of potatoes on to the seat beside her. He put his chin in his hand and regarded Anya with an unblinking limpid gaze.

She stared back. The mother apparently felt no need to talk to people just because they were there, and Anya found herself meeting the silent scrutiny of the son for longer than was amusing.

'Hasn't anyone told you it's rude to stare?'

40

'No,' said the child factually; then, as an afterthought, *'You're staring.'*

'What's your name?' She sounded as if she might report it to the authorities.

'Caspar. What's yours?'

'Anya.'

'Anya?' The child turned it over, getting accustomed to it. 'Anya bananya . . . bananya anya . . . Anyway,' he said, 'I'm a pastrycook.'

'You don't say.'

'I make gingerbread mans.'

And he continued to stare at her from between his fists. Her interest in his small intransigence flickered and died. She had thought she had detected a mind, but it was only the familiar infantile inconsequence after all.

Bill returned, slopping drinks.

'Didn't catch your name?' he queried, slopping Anya's for her.

'I didn't give it.' With a beer mat she dammed the trickle that was headed for her lap.

'She's called Anya,' said the child.

'Anya, eh? Russian?'

'No.'

'Just curious . . . no offence.' Bill Madison's broad smile, certainly, could give none. 'My vice,' he shrugged. 'Inquisitive.'

'Since he knows it,' remarked his wife, 'you'd think he might give it up, wouldn't you?'

Anya relented: 'My father was hooked on Chekhov. You know . . . the insipid little golden-haired idealist in *Three Sisters* who believes in Work and a Wonderful Future. That was the Anya I was supposed to become . . . you remember her?'

She had been addressing the woman, but it was the man who replied: 'Can't say I do. I'm no book man. I just make pots.'

Suddenly Kovacs was back again, bustling, intrusive: 'You too read Chekhov?' he questioned, as if it mattered.

'Do you?'

'But of course!' He seemed not to have noticed her indifference. 'In Hungary we must all learn Russian. In order to read Lenin, Gorky, Mayakovsky . . . the Party classics. Most of us try not to learn anything. Is unpatriotic, you see. But for myself I discover Chekhov and I forgive the Russians for him. A great man. A great humanist.'

'You think so?' In spite of herself Anya's voice rose in contradiction. 'He gives me a pain in the crotch. Doesn't have the courage of his own ill-nature so he smears it all over with jam and compassion. Humanist, you call it?' She gave a snort of derision. 'If you think humanity is composed of whining dwarves and congenital halfwits, the humane thing to do would be to put them down – not "pity" them. Pathos! He stinks of pathos.'

He was watching her, rather than attending to her words. 'So what does humanity compose of, then? Big wolves?'

An answering gleam showed for a moment in her face – as if a lamp had flashed somewhere in the darkness.

'If only it did,' she mocked. 'I suppose,' she went on, wearily dismissive, 'I suppose it is a "big wolf", what you in your studio make, eh? That leering black creature?'

'I stop him at present.' Kovacs was cheerfully unoffended. 'He is, unfortunately, only a puppy what has overgrown. He has many teeth but no bite.' Mocking in his turn, he now grinned at her: 'I am pleased. This time you dislike the right thing. You are making progress.'

'Gee thanks.'

'Our Laczi,' put in Bill, with the air of contributing an insight pleasing to all parties, 'is very strong on the right and the wrong things to like. Everything black and white. No grey zones for him. If only he didn't change his mind every other day,' he clapped the Hungarian warmly on the shoulder, 'we'd make him our oracle, eh Laczi?'

'Already I am your oracle, my friend. That is why you gather my mistakes in little bundles up, and never believe what is true I tell you. That is what peoples do to their oracles, is not?'

Bill laughed the delighted wheezy laugh of a child who has made a pet animal perform a promised trick. From the swift way Anya averted her nose – just like a cat offended by a tainted dish – Kovacs gathered that something did not please her. Was it Bill's amiable, foolish homage? or the way he failed to repel it . . . ?

But why did he take the trouble to inquire? Who was she to thrust her judgements on him? He scarcely knew her and was not at all sure he liked what he knew. Yet, in a disquieting way, he was in more instant communication with her fluctuations of mood than with anyone else in the room and it made him a sudden stranger both to himself and to the familiar pub setting.

So that, when Bill broached some trifling matter of art-school intrigue, he plunged into the discussion as if it were of ultimate and burning concern. Whereupon Anya's nose came further into play. The spectacle of two males playing at man-talk, like boys playing at gangsters, always excited her scorn, and the intention to exclude her was so transparent as to be laughable.

Keeping them under distant surveillance, she turned to the Wife-and-Mother who had hitherto maintained a studied detachment. She expected little of such sullenness, and offered less. But a desultory question or two revealed that 'Binkie' was the same Beatrice Madison whose glowing embroidered landscapes she had coveted at more than one craft-and-fabrics show, and that she, Beatrice, knew all about the Rotten Orange. Surprise, surprise! With stirrings of more active sisterliness, Anya began to pump and probe. 'Binkie' was emerging as a woman of sharp-edged self-sufficiency and – once you set her going (she plainly *needed* someone to set her going!) – a lively and caustic observer of her world. There was none of the husband's intellectual flatulence about Beatrice. She seemed to have ceded to him all the dubious territory of benevolence and senti-mentality, and to have set up on her own as the sharpshooter of unwarrantable pretensions – male and other. Kovacs's self-importance, in particular, sustained some shrewd nicks.

Anya was delighted. This was very good. Possibly because she felt that she herself had generated the vivacity, she passed in a very short space from bored indifference to the active partisanship of a promoter; and if there had been anybody at that moment to show her off to, Anya would at once have put Binkie through her paces, rather in the manner in which Bill had put Laczi through his.

But the men talked on, heavily oblivious (or so it seemed) to the girls' laughter which broke over them from time to time like a spatter of hard, cold rain. Once or twice Kovacs lifted a wary eye, sensing derision, but he had decided to sever that subterranean link with her fantastical moods and was being deliberately unreceptive. Let her laugh. It hurt no one.

Wedged in his corner of the settle, Caspar watched both camps impartially with bright, circumspect eyes. He had perfected the art of invisibility. No one pestered or so much as noticed him . . .

Near closing time, they were joined by a West Indian couple. The man, burly and taciturn under his black donkey-jacket, looked as if some prankster had folded the paper on which his torso was drawn and given him someone else's lower half, so incongruous with his style and sobriety (not to mention his workman's boots) were the bright checked trousers in which his legs were encased. Glancing at his wife's florid get-up of emerald-green fedora and billowing polka-dot neckscarf, Anya attributed the imposition to her. She knew the type – the sort of burgeoning black extrovert who had to have everyone around her in fancy dress to satisfy her sense of occasion. Puffing with pleasure, she sank into the space Bill had made for her. The collusive air these people had that they were all 'such characters' was beginning to get up Anya's nose.

The black woman was immediately all over the boy: 'And how the fourth wise man, this evening?' she inquired taking Caspar's chin in her broad hand and laughing at his solemnity. 'I do declare he getting wiser by the month. How old you is, boy?'

'Seventy-seven.' Caspar withdrew himself with dignity.

'Too old to have his chin chuckle, he thinking,' she sighed. 'But I don't believe you seventy-seven just yet. I think it not till next month, you hear.'

Her man, who had been watching proceedings with a wrinkled brow from which grey hair frizzed and receded, remarked suddenly: 'In Peru, there a tribe which live to a *hundred* and seventy year old, more. Is because of the water have zinc in it. Stop the rust. Helluva thing, man!'

Everybody but Anya seemed to know how to take this oracular pronouncement. Nobody laughed. His wife fluffed herself out like a settling hen: 'You an old fool, Sam, reading old-fool books you don't understand. I bet it those old *National Geographics*, eh?'

Sam appeared inured to contradiction and merely repeated, 'Zinc stop rust. Everybody know that.'

'It did never stop yours. The inside of that bald head of yours is fulling up with rust, it look like.'

'Zinc stop rust,' he repeated simply, and sat there, head cast back, with all the dignified self-possession of a plain mind and a powerful physique. He didn't care to convince anybody and he had no interest in argument. After a moment he began cracking and bending dead matches, building a little jointed pyramid, and casting furtive glances in the boy's direction to make sure he was watching. As it neared completion Caspar pursed his lips and blew. It collapsed. Sam laughed and began again.

Anya found herself watching the big, deft, calloused hands in unwilling fascination. It had carried her back suddenly to the maids' annexe in Constantia, to long, puzzling conversations with the garden-'boy', who was full of reported marvels, and who made things for her . . . to those years of seemingly endless leisure that she spent among the black servants. There had always been something going on down there – laughter, drama, anger, stories, tears. The big white house was an antiseptic vacuum by comparison. And here she was again in the grip of that warm enfolded sensation which, again, she must fight off.

The black woman wanted to be introduced. Anya, this was Annabel. Was it indeed? And this was Sam. What Anya most wanted to know was how in the name of thunder the Hungarian came to be mixed up with this pair of oddities. It smelt very suspect. But there was no way of asking, so she settled, like Sam, for taciturnity.

'I mean to tell you,' Annabel had turned back to Laczi, 'I got my shift arrange so I can come Thursdays. So you don't get nobody else for my job, you hear.'

'It's yours as long as you want it.'

'Well, I want. It cheer me up after a week of the hospital. It good for a laugh. All those kids with their crazy ideas and their crazy clothes. Hey! I did tell you what happen last week? Going out, 'night, I meet a monkey on the stairs – look first like a monkey self, but then I see it a monkey-suit with a boy inside. "Who you is, boy?" I ask him. "No monkeys does be allow in this building." "Who me?" he say, "I ain't no monkey. Can't you see? I an Urban Gorilla." And then he jump me like he mad and yell "Yerrraaargh!"' She wiped her eyes. 'Like I did say, it make a nice change from bedpans and sick-dishes. Urban gorilla, eh? "We all radical, these days," he tell me, "so I go be an Urban Gorilla." "You about as radical as a cartload of clowns," I tell him. But he just laugh.'

'Annabel models for me at the art school,' Laczi explained for Anya's benefit. She read the explanation as shamefaced.

The black woman beamed: 'That's right, I a model. Don't ask me why. Ask him. It his idea.' She plumped and prodded herself around the ample midriff: 'That look like a model belly to you? They model legs? No sir, they doesn't. But he say yes. He say I got a classic bum. All these year I walking round wagging my classic bum and nobody didn't tell me. Now I laying on it, two hour a week and getting pay! I come like a big-shot. You know he got a statue of me, in the West End self, you seen it?'

Anya shook her head.

'I have a good laugh every time I pass. See those insurance boys and bank tycoons haul their tails in and out their big glass doors, and all the time an old black queen sitting up there looking down on

45

them. She a model too?' she asked abruptly of the sculptor. If she was, Annabel clearly would have to take her seriously.

Laczi decided to gamble on a temporary immunity: 'So I hope,' he said.

'Settle the hourly rate before you start,' came Binkie's warning voice.

'Oh, if I do it, it'll be for the pure love of Art,' Anya remarked caustically.

'Then you *will* sit?' His genial pleasure seemed untouched by her tone.

She froze him with a look.

'Harlots,' muttered Sam into his beer, causing a sudden hiatus in the conversation. Anya was glaring at him. He raised his head in surprise. 'Harlots does be showing their bums.'

'You don't know nothing about it, Sam!'

'I seen harlots,' he replied stolidly. 'Helluva thing!'

Bill nodded in absent-minded sympathy. 'I'm afraid,' he said, embarking on another anecdote, 'Laczi is a bit tough on his models. I met one storming out of the studio one day, and you know what had happened? He'd been struck with a bright idea for another piece he was working on, and completely forgot she was there! Gone off into a corner, the absent-minded genius! Left her there in the buff, shivering and neglected.'

'I pay her to sit still,' grinned Laczi, judging that impenitence was expected of him, 'so she sit. Not a squeak from her. How am I to remember such people?'

'He do that to me once,' said Annabel brightly, 'but I have a fit of the coughs and he remember quick sharp.' Laughter bubbled out of her throat and spilled down her breasts. Bill, too, caught the infection.

Anya rose suddenly, swinging her bag over her shoulder: ''Night,' she said in a flat monotone so remote from their hilarity that it sounded like an accusation. She towered over them for a moment then strode out the door and into the street. It had happened too quickly for anyone to speak or move.

'What we say?' asked Annabel in surprise. 'She vex at us?'

Laczi raised a face that looked suddenly tired: 'No,' he said distantly, 'only at me. But it is not to worry. It doesn't matter.'

He did not explain *what* didn't matter – his blunder, or her going. Nor could he have said what his blunder had been. It could have been a dozen things. He had the comfort of knowing there was nothing he could do – this woman did not lumber others with the implementation of her own decisions. But this did not stop him straining his ears for the sound of her receding footsteps, outside in the empty street . . . By and large, he assured himself as they died away, he liked that guillotine decisiveness of hers more than he was perturbed by its causes and consequences. There was nothing wrong with it. It made for clarity.

Bill was pulling a glum face: 'You bought yourself a bundle of joy there, old son,' he commiserated, proffering discreetly the supporting hand of male solidarity.

But Kovacs either did not notice, or did not need it.

'It doesn't matter,' he repeated.

Sam was pointing with concern to Caspar's head, drooped at an impossible angle to his spine. 'He asleep? Or dead?'

'Of course it doesn't matter,' remarked Binkie briskly, as she hoisted the child and prepared to leave, herself. 'You just bored the girl to death, the pair of you, that's all. Why would that matter?'

Her husband and his friend stared at her with the startled defiance of boys who have been disturbed at some absorbing but illicit game which they cannot now resume.

THREE

The Sitting

Beatrice may have been right. Anya was many things by turns and nothing constantly, over the next few days. But boredom did not seem to be her problem.

When Stacy questioned her about the encounter, she got a voluble and ribald account which did not entirely cohere. Their Hungarian neighbour, she gathered, was quite colossally conceited and surrounded himself with a troupe of toadies who paid perpetual homage to his genius. He even kept a pair of parody Blacks in tow – so he could play at solidarity with the Oppressed Masses, she presumed, but without being obliged to take them seriously. Mercifully one member of the hallelujah chorus was a very sharp lass who had her head screwed on the right way and was taken in by none of it. God knew how she put up with her husband's abject idolatry.

'Sounds pretty insufferable,' prompted Stacy, hoping there would be more to come. It came.

The genius's pretensions, it appeared, went with a quite absurd humourlessness. Kept on dragging out catalogues of old exhibitions and breathing solemnly down her neck while she looked at them. Educating her taste for her – by issuing orders. Like this! Abhor that! Venerate the other! Right little Prussian! Yet he was quite amusing too in his heavy Central European way, and particularly funny when he tried to play the ladykiller. It was like being courted by a Centurion tank. Would Stacy believe it – the only way he could find to declare his passion was to suggest Anya should model for him – as if no greater honour could be proposed to womankind than to recline on his casting-couch.

'And will you?'

For reply there came a puff of scornful laughter.

Stacy chewed it over: 'Sounds like about Force Three, on the Jevons Scale,' she opined. (The girls ran a rating system on the males of their acquaintance.)

Anya concurred. An absolute maximum of three. This one was no earthquake. (Those who made the earth move were calibrated at ten.) And Stacy should *see* the way he lived! It was the complete piggery back there. You'd find more of the graces of civilization in a black shanty town. If the truth were known, he probably pissed in the same trough as he washed in.

'I think he's quite talented though,' she wound up in an offhand tone, indicating the matter was closed.

But Stacy was an old hand at these games: the purpose of the visit had *not* been an exercise in aesthetic appraisal.

'Will he write to the Planning Department, though?' she craftily queried.

'Oh yes . . . at least, I think so.' Anya pushed it aside. 'It seemed all right. I suppose he can write it in Hungarian and we'll get it translated. His English is beyond belief.'

Stacy permitted herself a small smile: 'You'll be visiting again then?'

'Like hell I will. Let him come to me.'

The sculptor showed no sign of doing so. In the piggery things were not going much more smoothly than in the Rotten Orange.

There was a V-shaped flaw in the purbeck. Of course he'd known about it – that was why they'd dropped the price (apart from their having already screwed the contractors for a penalty payment on the cancelled order). But it was beginning to look like one of those wicked faults that runs halfway through a block and keeps changing direction. The composition would have to be built around it, and the constraints were getting tighter at every turn. Twice now he had had to ditch a promising design and he was bracing himself for the third. Pursuing the fault into the meat of the stone had become a nerve-racking business, and besides, after his long lay-off, the carving was taking quite a toll: his hands were blistered and the muscles of his forearm ached under the weight of the lump-hammer. Even in the dead of night he would wake with sudden cramps, and nightmares to match.

It did not improve his temper to note how much of his remaining attention kept circling around the events in the pub – as he searched stray remarks for hidden meanings, grew enraged at his own responses, and invented the crushing replies he had failed to make at

49

the time. Was it Sam's 'harlots' . . . or that silly quip about models being paid to sit? . . . or the presumption that she would sit? or . . . ? Whole new dialogues began to unwind in his brain, but they all ended the same way – as the maddening female rose to her feet, shouldered her bag, and stalked out of the door. Bearing the secret of her contempt with her. He did not permit people to walk out on him!

When, on the fourth day, there was a clatter at the iron grille and the doors rumbled back, he was taken by surprise. It was the one issue he had not foreseen. Anya stood silhouetted against the street.

'How's it going?' she asked, hand on hip, cigarette on lip, like some buckskinned heroine of the wagon trains arriving with coffee for the boys.

'Bloody awful!' he growled.

She pulled a sympathetic face: 'What's the trouble?' She sounded as if she had undertaken to set it instantly right.

'I have sold to myself a pup.'

'Oh?'

'This stone. It is rotten. Flawed.'

'Send it back.'

'Two tons and one half? It costs to move stone, you know. Anyway, I was aware.'

'Work around it then. Like Michelangelo.'

(Was she jeering?)

'A few more inches like this,' he said, thrusting a hand into the fissure he had cut and scooping out the spoil, 'and I have not one block but two.'

'Isn't that a bargain? Two for the price of one?'

'You can joke.'

'Anyway, I've come to model for you. Give you a break.'

She stubbed out a cig on the side of her boot.

'Now?' He was flabbergasted.

'It's Saturday. Early closing,' she said, as if that explained everything. 'OK? You did want me?'

He clapped his hand to his brow and gave vent to a sigh of exasperation.

'What's wrong now?' Anya was enjoying herself. She lit up another little black-and-gold cheroot and puffed absorbedly.

It was probably the visibility of the enjoyment that made him turn on his heel and wheel out a low trolley on squeaking castors, grab a stool by one leg, a cushion with his other hand, and shove the whole assembly across the floor with his foot.

'Sit here,' he ordered.

She did so and watched amusedly as he bustled about, black-browed, setting up the modelling-stand, assembling materials for an armature, wiring it together, and beginning, finally, to flesh out the metal cage with fistfuls of clay.

'This I know will be *un abozzo* – an abortion. But since you are here, I try.'

'Don't despair,' she said gaily, 'you never know your luck.'

'My luck today,' he retorted, 'is a thing not to talk of.'

'Meaning me?'

'Meaning you at the end of everything.'

'Thank *you!*' she laughed. 'I see what you're doing, of course: you're trying to make me angry. Calling up a bit of "the wrath what nurtures". But you'll have to do better than that. I've had a good day.'

He grunted, beginning to lose himself in his own activity, and she was silent for some minutes, watching with interest.

He worked quickly in the early stages, peering at her from odd angles as if detecting weaknesses in her bone structure that could easily prove fatal, then splattering the head with quick dabs of clay. From time to time the trolley shot from under her and she had to clutch at the stool, as he gave it an unexpected shove with his foot. To get her in a different light, was it? He didn't explain. She felt oddly left out of account, but the relationship was changing under the sharp impersonality of his scrutiny. Changing, she felt, for the better. She was used to being looked at, but this was different. There was no invitation to self-consciousness, which had then to be resisted. No censure, no flattery, no emulation of any kind, just an intense contemplation which deepened the verticals of his frown and screwed up the corners of his eyes. It was better than flattery. Unconsciously she had tilted up her chin to receive it.

'Take off your jersey,' he said suddenly, imperatively.

'Only the jersey?' she laughed, as she complied.

'You,' he remarked drily, 'have been read too many scenes from the life bohemian. Is not so. I wonder only that it should be a bust, not a head.' He regarded her sideways, making no account whatsoever of her bare shoulders. 'Yes. Is so. But not today. Today the abortion only.'

'Tomorrow the striptease.'

'Like I say. You read bad fictions.'

'Oh, I don't just read it, my friend. When I was younger I lived it.'

'In South Africa, eh?' he asked pointedly.

'Cape Town, yes.' She was imperturbable today. 'I knocked round with the arty fringe as a teenager. I guess that's where I got my primitive ideas about artists. Some of that lot didn't seem able to get their brushes out of their paintpots till some girl dropped her knickers. And then they'd suddenly lose their passion for Art and come at you slavering. Ye-es,' she mused, round the side of a freshly lit cig, 'it *was* all a bit like bad fiction . . . consumptive painters, bilious poets, eternal students of nothing in particular, and grunting jazzmen who "didn' do nuthin' maan but jes' blow that ole horn". All fabulously radical, mind you. Just like your Earth-Mother friend was saying the other night – we're all radicals now. Was there ever a time, I wonder, when students weren't?'

'I wonder if you know what it means – "radical".'

'Oh,' she tossed it off carelessly, 'it was "radical" enough in the shebeens of District Six. And the brandy they stewed up in the outhouses was pretty radical too, as I remember it.' She sniffed. 'I don't like to boast (nasty habit!) but it wasn't just discreet mixed parties for our gang – hobnobbing with the multi-racial intelligentsia in middle-class suburbia. Oh no, maan! We got out and about, down amongst the cesspits and shitheaps. You needed to be pretty "radical", I can tell you (or pretty stupid) to go visiting the black locations. The police aren't too polite with whites who cross that frontier. You could end up with your nigger-loving skull kicked in.'

'This is true what you tell me?' She had delivered it all with such scornful laziness that he wasn't sure.

'Why shouldn't it be? I'm not the pampered bourgeoise you take me for.'

In spite of himself Kovacs was amused: 'Now that,' he said, laying his lump of clay on the stand and wiping his hands, 'that is *not* the mistake I take about you.'

'*Make*!' she corrected brusquely. 'What is, then?'

'When I know, I tell you.'

'I'll look forward to that.'

He eyed her with mistrust: 'You think already you know it?'

'P'raps.' She blew smoke in his direction.

'To yourself you are the great knower, eh?'

'I have a talent.' She carried it off lightly. 'In an enlightened country, they'd pay me to exercise it. Here, I have to indulge it in private life.'

'At present, on me.'

'Well, you're indulging your talent on me.' she retorted with some warmth. 'There's got to be a bit of reciprocity.'

He pursed his lips and took up the clay again. There had been a touch of the ultimatum about her last remark.

A longish silence ensued. The amber light filtering down through the stained skylights made of the room a warm brown pool in which sound and movement turned fluid, lapping away at the edges of consciousness.

They were both startled by the rattle at the door.

'What now?' growled Kovacs. 'I think I move studio to the Victoria Coach Station and have some peace.'

He crossed and dragged back the door.

'Oh, is you.'

'What a welcome!' came well-modulated feminine tones, 'after all the ado I had finding you! May I come in?'

'Yes, yes. Of course. Please.' To Anya's surprise, his manner had turned suddenly *gallant*. She swivelled round and (Snap!) was amused to see that their visitor was wearing one of the filmy flowery things she had ordered for the boutique, earlier in the week. Plus a large floppy hat like a floral pancake. People did seem to go for them, God knew why! And her ridiculous Hungarian was sidling crabwise in front of the royal progress, all his dignified mien melted into the stoop and crouch of subservience. Anya smelt money. A patroness, no doubt. And she, Anya, would be expected to become invisible out of sheer deference. She got down from the stool.

'Oh, I'm interrupting a sitting,' said the mellifluous personage in gracious surprise. 'You should have said. This is very ill-timed, I'm afraid.' She wielded the armoury of courteous commonplace with much charm; but there was power too, in the light voice and slight figure.

'My bum's numb anyway,' Anya declared. 'I could do with a stretch.' She waved them both away. 'Carry on, dooo!'

'That's kind of you,' said the woman. Her simple civility absorbed, without repelling, Anya's parody of it.

Anya was piqued. She should, of course, under the usual codes of social decency, have excused herself at once and slipped out. Whatever this woman's errand, it was no affair of hers. But having written the afternoon off, she didn't see why she shouldn't take advantage of any stray enlightenment that came her way. Her study of the sculptor had not yet included his encounter with somebody

53

capable of pulling rank on him, and she was curious to see if the present abjectness would persist.

'I shouldn't have troubled you, Laczi,' the stranger was saying, as he dusted down a seat for her, 'but I thought you'd want to know. There's an agent of Fenwick's looking for you.'

'Agent?' Laczi sounded startled.

'Sorry! That was inept of me. A messenger. A debt-collector, not to put too fine a point upon it. You know about it?'

Kovacs had clapped a hand to his brow and slumped in a chair.

'Of course! For what do you take me, to forget a bill of hundreds? But why now? Why of all days, today?'

'It was two days ago in point of fact,' she corrected. 'However . . . it seems that old Fenwick has retired and the new broom, his son, is bent on sweeping exceedingly clean. He's been going through his books. That much I elicited from the check suit and trilby that called on me. He didn't know where you were, you see. Found you'd moved, and came to me. The only other address in the book, I imagine,' she wound up, half in apology.

Only other address? Anya, who had been poking about among the jumble of casts against the back wall, pricked her ears. Could this be the wife? Her swift reflex of attention had caught Kovacs's eye.

'I will not be very long,' he called, as if to reduce the distance between them.

'You go right ahead,' she fluted back, 'I'm enjoying myself.' The glint of malice in her eye met something cognate in his, a fleeting grimace of complicity, and when he turned back to his visitor his tone had altered subtly: 'Amanda, I am sorry you are to be bothered thus,' he said.

'Not at all.' She slid off her hat, laid it in her lap, and smiled at him. 'I am sorry to bother you. Especially when you have taken the trouble to go into hiding.'

He gestured about him in protest: 'Who is hiding? This is not hiding.'

'You know what I mean. You've earned your privacy and I'm the last one to wish to violate it, you know that. But . . .' She didn't so much falter, as exhale an exquisite hesitation.

' "But" what?'

'I would like to put this tactfully, but I suppose it can't be done.'

'Go on,' he said implacably.

'If you're in debt, there are ways . . .'

'I do not take from you. That we have agreed.'

'But Laczi . . .' her voice went darkly contralto, 'the funds are available. *More* than available: languishing for employment. You fall within the exact terms of father's trust – "for the encouragement of the visual arts, payment of artists' material costs, labour, and so on". What could be more apposite than a sculptor's casting-bill? *Ça fait ta botte.*'

'It is the money of your family.'

'Is there something wrong with my family? Believe me, I respect your scruple, but you carry it to absurd lengths. After all this time!' she appended reproachfully. 'It is a simple business matter: you are eligible for a grant, and you don't become *ineligible* just because you are the divorced spouse of one of the trustees. Come now. Don't deny me the pleasure of helping you a little. Come now, what do you say?'

She sat there, sweet reason incarnate, leaning slightly forward with her small elegant hands folded in her lap, her short fair hair curling appealingly under her ears. Who could accuse her of bullying?

Laczi, however, did not seem inclined to proffer his thanks: 'I promise nothing,' he said stiffly. 'I give it some thought. OK? If it will be yes, I write to the trust myself. If it will be no, then I don't.'

She shook her head sadly: 'Still the same stubborn old Bruin.'

'When it is my independence what you take from me, I am stubborn. Not otherwise.'

She rose, as if weary of the discussion: 'Your independence, Laczi, is a thing I neither envy nor covet.' She turned away from him. 'And I cannot imagine the woman who could prise it from your grasp. Certainly it is not I.'

It may have been chance that brought Anya within the field of her vision while this sentence still hung in the air, but the consequences of that chance were distinct and determinate. Their eyes met. They exchanged defiance. But more importantly they exchanged intelligence. And it was as if, in the curious way two women may, they had disposed silently of the man between them in a compact perfectly understood by both. Nothing whatsoever had happened but, in the time that nothing took, Amanda Kovacs had abdicated, and Anya Jevons (though she would certainly have denied all ambition of succession) had been notified of the fact. It brought a small flutter of triumph to her heart. It brought also scorn – for the male package so ignominiously consigned, for the woman who hadn't known how to keep him, scorn above all for herself, caught in that ancient vortex of female vanity. Oh, the ignominy of such triumph! For a second, she felt herself fanned by the wings of a great fear, as yet invisible, but passing somewhere near. This she did not need and could not desire. It made such havoc in her emotions, stirring up all the sleeping lustful beasts she had been at pains to pacify. Let it not begin again, dear Christ!

She turned her back abruptly, examining the casts for distraction and relief. Had the black man been right? Was the harlot in her stirring again? Perish the thought!

'Oh, one thing I nearly forgot,' the woman was saying as she walked to the door attended by her ex-husband, 'Juhacz is looking for you. Says he has a proposition.'

'Juhacz has a proposition; also the sea is wet. What should I care?'

'Shall I give him your address, if he calls again?'

'Do what you want. So it is out of my hands.'

'Very well then. And the debt-collector I shall leave to make his own discoveries. It is after all what he's paid for. *Au revoir.*'

As the voice at her back faded musically away, Anya realized what it was she had been staring at. It was a portrait of the speaker, Amanda Kovacs herself – done perhaps a decade ago? – in yellowing plaster. Going on her knees and shoving a few other pieces aside, Anya tried to extract it. But it was heavier than she had expected and, halfway to the bench, began to slip inexorably from her fingers. With a wild wrench and a lurch she heaved it the last few inches, steadied it where it stood rocking, and sank panting into the nearest chair. My God, what a dead give-away! Panic and a kind of ghastly relief swept over her.

And then hilarity. She began to laugh, helplessly, hugely. But it had so nearly happened! (She could hear him closing the sliding doors.) If he should have seen her – dashing his wife to the floor to shatter in a thousand pieces – what possible explanation? Oh, oh, oh! whoo, hoo, hoo! She gave herself up to it, only rendered more helpless by the thought that the wife, passing down the lane, would certainly hear the maniacal whooping and conclude that *she* was its subject. But there was no helping it. The whole thing was grotesque, monstrous!

She wiped her eyes and looked up. Kovacs stood, hands in pockets, watching her quizzically. His grin of complicity had returned: 'So what is so very funny?'

She shook her head dumbly, making him wait, buying herself time. And the more sobriety returned to her, the more certain she was that she was not going to tell him – no more than she would have told a witch-doctor that the human hair in his ju-ju bag had come from her own head. It was too risky. Anya had a superstitious respect for what other people called accidents.

But he was still waiting for an explanation. She pulled herself together.

'Nothing,' she said shortly. 'Nothing is funny.'

'Such a laughter for nothing?'

'That's right.' Her jaw clamped shut like a vice.

'Well,' his left shoulder, lip and eyebrow went up in a half-shrug, 'so long as the laughter is not for me.'

'And what if it were? What would you do?'

'I don't know,' he mused lazily, 'perhaps I strangle you. Probably is not worth it. Hey now!' He had noticed the bust, and turned to her sharply. 'What is that doing there? That cast?'

'I put it there.'

'Why?' His tone was edgy.

'To look at, of course. Is it forbidden?'

He subsided. 'No. Nothing is forbidden.' He walked across to the bust and his fingers moved in quick touches across the hair and ran down the cheek. The gesture was abstracted but not absent-minded. Anya imagined he was caressing it, as sculptors are alleged to do with their own statues.

'You prefer her in plaster?' she inquired.

'Prefer?' He was mystified.

'You treat *that* more nicely than you treated *her*.'

'Oh!' He saw her mistake without feeling much impetus to correct it. 'I treat her like she treats me – we respect ourselves at a distance.' His hand had come to rest on the shoulder of the cast, affectionately proprietorial.

'It'd need to be at a distance!' she exclaimed. 'At close quarters it'd give you frostbite.'

He laughed: 'Is not all so bad as that. So . . . what do you think of the bust then? Tell me what you think.' He stood aside, displaying it.

'Is this Lesson Three?'

'Go on. Tell me.'

An appeal to her judgement was not a thing Anya was able to resist. She gathered her forces, confronting the unwinking gaze that came at her from the bench-top.

It wasn't bad. All the breeding was there: the fine, slightly flared nostrils that appeared to breathe lightly, the small soft ears, the

57

mouth strong without brutality, irregular eyes faintly narrowed under firm brows. And she liked the way he had resisted the blandishments which might have smoothed it all out into a neutral paste like a sucked sweet – amorphous charm without pock or wrinkle. This face had been lived in, exposed to the elements, crossed by passions, however discreet. But the neck, and even more those bared shoulders and the beginning of breasts . . . here she paused. There was something here she did not like. It was strong, but her dislike of it was stronger: 'I think it's cruel,' she said shortly, a little surprised to hear herself urging this as a defect.

'How, cruel?'

'Heartless. I wouldn't stand for having my boobs looked at like that.'

He folded his arms in sardonic defiance. 'You must explain.'

Indeed she must: 'Those shoulders.' She pointed an accusing finger. 'It's flesh, I suppose, but it's flesh that never wanted to be looked at. All hunched and shrinking. You shouldn't have done it!'

'I should lie perhaps?'

'It's only a man's truth. It's the way you look that causes it. You can call it truth, but it's just the age-old male lie.'

'You don't know her,' he remarked dismissively.

But she was having none of that: 'I didn't until I saw this. Now I do. And I know you, too. Why is there no tenderness?'

' "Tenderness"!' He waggled the back of a hand at her in derisive continental fashion. 'Do I put in "tenderness" like – like paprika in a stew? Never mind what else would be therein, always a little pinch of tenderness to improve the flavour.' He flung away a few paces, then turned on her, growling like a bear. 'This is nonsense what you talk. The tenderness must come, it must gr-r-ow out of the clay – out of the seeing. And moreover,' he said, leaning back against the bench, judicial, minatory, 'who are you to be telling me about "tenderness" – you who have been laughing yourself sick a few minutes ago about God knows what?'

Anya made a *moue*: 'Do you think she heard?'

'The rest of Mayfair heard. I suppose also she.'

He waited for further light, now that she had broached the matter. But it did not come. She was staring at the bust again, screwing up her eyes.

'I suppose you're right.' She made the concession as if it had been wrung from her reluctance. 'There's a special kind of asensual Englishness that you've caught there. A kind of truth, I suppose. I see it a lot in the shop – beauty with no bloom on it. Comes from having so little sun, I reckon. Nobody goes naked naturally, so when they do, they look as if they've been stripped and violated. It's not so much nakedness as exposure. And the skin shows it.'

She noticed he was attending very closely. Too closely.

'Do you want to go on?' she asked, jerking her head in the direction of the modelling-stand.

He gave a start, snapped his fingers in irritation, and strode rapidly to the clay, which had begun to harden. He sprayed it liberally with a handgun, feeling the surface with deft splayed fingers as he did so. No harm done. Now . . . did he want to continue or not? That was the question. He sighed heavily and frowned down at his scuffed and spattered shoes.

'If you do,' she was saying, 'I'm willing. Nothing else to do with the afternoon in any case.'

Still he hesitated.

'I don't put in no tenderness.'

'You can save your tenderness,' she retorted, 'for where it's needed. I'm sorry I ever mentioned the word.'

'OK.'

He snapped out of his brown study, drew up the trolley, pointed her to the seat, and the sitting resumed.

Before long he was in difficulties. The interruption had broken his flow and he found he was modelling a nose here or a chin there, but not a head anywhere. It would not cohere. He took a small hatchet and gave the jaw a smack with the butt-end to bring it further forward. Anya suppressed her reaction of alarm, but the violence of it had startled her. She fingered her jaw. Nothing amiss there . . .

On the modelling-stand, the sculptural chiropraxis had only made matters worse. Now the jaw was too *far* forward. He sliced an exasperated wedge off the chin. It was getting on the girl's nerves – this battery by proxy.

'I suppose,' she said, as if making light conversation, 'that you'll accept her offer in the end? Heroic independence notwithstanding?' (It was the next best thing to smacking *him* in the jaw, and it could be done without shifting a hair.)

His head jolted up: 'You make an interest most unwholesome in the affairs of other peoples.'

'Oh don't hand me that privacy shit!' she replied in high tones. 'You thrust me right into the middle of it, with no option of retreat, and now you expect me to be deaf, dumb and blind. What's so secret anyway? Any fool can see it.'

Laczi seemed not to relish her sense of his transparency.

'What is secret,' he hissed, 'is what is between a man and a woman. And any fool should know that!'

'Oho!' she gloated. 'What a great big secret that is – four inches long and made of meat.'

'You talk muck!' he said in disgust, giving himself with increased fury to the application of clay.

'The secret between a man and a woman,' said Anya, setting him an example of superior lucidity, 'is a fiction invented by people who have something to hide, and who want to believe they have succeeded. You don't believe me? Shall I tell you what your so very secret marriage was like?'

'If I were you,' he said softly, 'I would find some other way for to recommend yourself, not by spreading muck upon the other woman what you do not know.'

There was a murderous pause, during which Laczi added some quite unnecessary touches to the left cheekbone.

'Shall I tell you, little man,' said Anya in a low voice which held promise of a quite shattering crescendo, 'why I would not be found *dead* in your bed – not if the Home Secretary, the Archbishop of Canterbury and the Wizard of Oz came to me on their knees, begging me to do it? Shall I tell you?'

'Who can stop you?' He too was rigid with rage.

'Right. First.' She checked them off on her fingers, so as to forget nothing. 'You live in such fatuous self-opinionated insulation that you don't notice when people try to tell you the things you need to know. Second, you surround yourself with toadies and sycophants so as to hear nothing but the sound of your own praises. Backscratchers all, to a man! Third, you suffer a complete collapse of your sense of humour whenever your shaky self-esteem is threatened. Next and lastly, you have an extremely kinky attitude to women and, if that thing over there is anything to go by, you've got the erotic sensibility of a conger-eel. I doubt very much if you're capable of fucking anyone but yourself. Oh, *and* Art. I nearly forgot Art.'

At the far end of the room, a drop detached itself from the brass tap over the trough and fell into the bucket with a tiny crystalline explosion. Plink!

It had been a long time since anybody had addressed Laczi so directly (that part of her indictment held some truth). Furthermore, it had become his habit over the years of his exile, to try each case at his own introspective tribunal, before rushing into a sentence which had first to be cast in a foreign tongue (thus people sometimes believed they were being ignored). So he did not immediately reply . . .

He made, instead, some attempts to shore up his sense of humour – it wouldn't do to have that giving way now! And his kinky attitude to women was some help in this respect. It was *so* kinky that he found himself half liking this woman who had just flayed the hide off him. And that, if you thought about it, was quite funny. Yes, he could see the humour of that. What he could not at all see the humour of, was the invidious comparison with a conger-eel. Even though he was hazy about the fish, he was in no doubt about its offensiveness. *That* he would have to rebut. But how? Certainly not by trusting himself to the treacherous language of the English where she was so much the virtuoso. No, but in his own true language . . .?

'Come,' he said, holding out his hand as if to take hers. She stared at it in disbelief, but made no move. 'Come,' he repeated , indicating the direction with his head, 'I show you something.' Balked of her revenge, she followed at a distance. What did you have to *do* to strike some answering fire from this stone-chipper? Was he a totally torpid lump of phlegm?

He pulled the dust-sheet off a life-size bronze and stood back. She looked.

'Well?' she said after a few moments, turning to him.

He mimed mute.

'I see,' she said, taking over from him. 'This is the mystery witness for the defence. I'm to take this into consideration, along with the other crimes, and you rest your case. Is that it?'

He gave a kind of shrugging nod.

'Huh! Not much to do with anything, as far as I can see. Nobody said you couldn't carve metal . . . or whatever it is you do to it. It was your dealings with humans that were in doubt. Still . . .' she took her chin in a judicious hand, 'if you want an opinion . . .'

She gave it her attention.

'What's her name?'

'Ilona.' He cleared his throat. 'Ilona Veszi.'

One of Anya's eyebrows flickered. She had a shrewd notion why this piece was kept apart in a remote corner of the studio. She had been specially favoured and was now to prove worthy of it. His aspect of simultaneous pride and timidity told the whole tale. But it also provoked her by its naïve expectancy. Anya was not a person to whom you said, 'Don't disappoint me!' – and then stood by, waiting for a response. Whenever presented with a sensitivity test it was her habit to fail it so spectacularly that the tester would never again insult her with another.

So now: 'I'm afraid, my friend' (as if at the farther end of a long tunnel, she heard the familiar grating tones she so little admired in herself) '. . . I'm afraid that you are trying to pull an old-fashioned weepy on me. *Bad* mistake! You've picked altogether the wrong girl to impress with the eternal truths of human banality.'

('Here we go,' she thought, 'over the top.' But it was the fallacy of her chronic embattlement to feel the exhilaration of the charge so keenly, as never to be able to wheel her galloping forces until it was too late.)

'You see,' she went on, heading inexorably for the big smash, 'I am totally immune to sentimental blackmail.' In the stillness her voice had become unnaturally loud. She squinted malevolently at the bronze.

'Don't tell me!' she jeered. 'She Died in Battle, wrapped in the Flag of her Country, and with her Dying Words she cried, "God Save Hungary!" While the Band Played On! How kitsch can you get? And what've you got her kitted out in all this macho gear for? A nice girl like that! Pfft! Look at it! Battledress, and helmet, and boots five sizes too big. Where's her rifle then? . . . Oooh! there it is, for a wonder! My God!' she wound up, a little breathless actually with her own temerity, 'you're even kinkier than I thought. Did you fuck her in jackboots while you were at it?'

Perhaps she expected to be stopped before going so far – for, unable to generate her own prohibitions, Anya depended on others to set her limits. But not a sound came from him. The silence was unnerving. Why, why would he not speak, so that she might know what it was she had done? She could *feel* him there, behind her, not even breathing, rigid as a ramrod. Were there reserves of wrath of which she knew nothing?

Refusing to glance in his direction, she affected to re-examine the bronze – in the spirit of frank reappraisal. But panic was bleeding her impermeability. The figure in battledress had become an accuser, too. This keen bright flame of a fighting girl rained contempt on her indulged aggression. They were ganging up on her these two, destroying her in a savagery of silence.

There was a sudden expulsion of breath at her back, and her

elbow was gripped with a ferocity that sent stabbing pains right up to the shoulder.

'I think you better go,' said a voice like death. She was being steered to the door. 'Go! Now!' She experienced a tumultuous conviction that there were a thousand things more she must say, but she could think of none of them. They were nearly at the exit . . .

'Stop it,' she cried, shaking off his grip and rounding on him. 'Look! why can't you *tell* me, instead of going dumb?' She waved her arms in several directions at once. 'You show me all these things. How am I supposed to know what they mean? What is it I'm supposed to be seeing? You *know* I'm ignorant. Why can't you tell me?' She was almost weeping with exasperation.

'You would not begin to understand.'

'Why not?' she cried, aggrieved.

'After what you have just now said? Never.'

'Try me.'

There was an inner tussle and, again the great exasperated sigh: 'Pah! I waste my breath.' He veered off, fetched a furious circuit, then bore down.

She held her ground, but he stood so menacingly close that the breath he was wasting was hot on her face: 'I tell you then. What you find to be so very funny, is truth: she died in battle. So! You are pleased, eh? Crying "God save Hungary!" Yes! Her blood . . .' The voice came harsh and strident. 'Her blood make a pretty puddle in the cobblestones for you to laugh at. So laugh then, laugh! Because you . . . you do not know nothing. Such things to you are "kitsch". Good. So you better go. I have no place, me, for peoples what call kitsch to the dead and the brave.' His eyes glared into hers as if he hoped to sear her brain.

'How was I to know that?' she cried, faltering under that glare. But of course she had known it. And now he knew too. It was a knowledge that only fuelled his rage further: 'Her boots . . . what you do not like . . . shall I tell you? She wears her boots too big because that is all the boots there are and in shoes she get her feet crush with rubble and shrapnel. This to you is "macho"! Good! She has a rifle why? Because without it she will be sooner dead than she is. This to you is "kinky"! Wonderful! You who never fought for nothing in your life, who never drop your blood since you fall off your tricycle and cry for your mamma! And is it *you* – this overfed little girl in a frilly dress – is it you to tell me about "jackboots", ha? Because you read it somewhere in your storybook? Fairy tales, ha! I tell you, this storybook where you are living your silly little life, it is a story about a real country. But this you will never know. So how can I talk to you? What is there to say? You much better go.'

His voice trailed disgustedly away. The futility and dejection of it all overcame him. He let the gesticulating hands fall to his side and lowered his head.

Shaken and pained, Anya rubbed her elbow. If the nerve wasn't damaged it would be a wonder. He had the grip of a demon. But she'd asked for it – that, and a good deal more. She had known what she was doing. But now that she had done it, she no longer knew what it was – and she was in a state of anguished anxiety to find out. She could not ask him. And she could not go away.

So there they stood, stranded in the backwash of their own spent violences, neither of them able to find motive for speech or movement. They stood, and did not look at each other.

Prolonged beyond a certain point the silence of mutual antagonism changes its character. The antagonists have not gone away when they might. And in their minds a question begins to form soundlessly like a bubble: Why is he still here? Why am *I* still here? Is there something still unfinished . . .?

And if either should happen to catch the passage of that question over the face of the other, or if (as in this case) one of them should be so inconsequent as to let a big fat tear roll down her cheek and splash on to the dusty floor, then there is a chance that they may, given time, find out what it is they have been quarrelling about.

The loudly defiant sniff with which Anya attempted to arrest the passage of a second tear proved her undoing. Or it proved Laczi's. At all events, they could stand there no longer like dummies. The secret was out.

Half an hour later, the sitting – which had been resumed yet again – was finally abandoned. The whole thing had acquired a frivolously festive air and Laczi's concentration was shot to ribbons. After he had caught himself completely destroying the plane of the cheekbone with an ill-judged addition, he took a step backwards and landed a playful punch just to the left of the nose. With a smack of wet clay, the whole face squashed and buckled.

Anya swerved up in agitated protest: 'What did you do that for?'

'Ach!' He seemed to find her reaction funny. 'It is the abortion what I told you. A waste of clay. You cannot work like this in fits and snatches, like the intervals of an opera.'

'But it looks awful!' Anya was staring at her own crumpled features with comical fixity.

'Is the latest fashion in sculpture,' he explained, doing his best gallery-guide impersonation. 'Who wants a head what looks like somebody any more? All the old frauds do that – Michelangelo and Rodin and Epstein. This is now out of mode. Now we do something new – a face what has been in a smash. A face of the mashed potato.' He grinned at her.

Chilled suddenly, she wrapped her cardigan about herself.

'You shouldn't do that. It gives me the jim-jams.'

Laczi stared. 'You are superstitious!' he exclaimed in amazement.

'You've been gawping at me for three hours,' she said scornfully, 'and you've only just discovered that? Of course I'm superstitious! I don't know how you make out as an artist if you're *that* slow on the uptake.'

'But it means nothing,' he said, beginning to pluck clay out of the armature in fistfuls and fling them back in the bin. 'If you take everything in a symbol, there is then nothing what has a meaning. Is an old fallacy. There are not symbols. There are only acts.'

'What would you think of the act I performed today, I wonder,' she said, 'when I all but dropped that bust on the floor and smashed it.'

'What bust? That of Amanda? You did?' He was greatly taken with it.

'You see? You're laughing as if it meant something.'

'Well, did it?'

'Of course! What d'you think I'm saying, numskull?'

'You intended to smash it?'

'No. It slipped.'

'So? It is not an act, because it has not an intention. And because it did not happen, it is not a symbol neither. It is a nothing simply.'

She looked at him, darkly pitying: 'God preserve you in that cheerful frame of mind.'

'But you look here to me,' he said cheerfully, clanging down the metal lid on the clay-bin, 'why you go in for omens such a big way today? Today is not the day?'

'Oh, isn't it. Why did you punch me in the face then – today?'

'Correction. I did *not* punch you in the face. Perhaps I should. But I didn't. Now is too late, no?' He put his hand through her arm, pulling her playfully towards him.

She shook him off. She found his proximity too disturbing, and cast about for some mitigation.

'Look,' she said finally, in a businesslike voice, 'I know that true artists don't eat, and that if they aren't chilled to the bone it corrupts their genius, but . . .' She wrestled with a qualm, then plunged ahead: 'Why don't you come round to my place and eat a decent meal for once. I'm not going to be seen walking round with a cadaver.'

He glanced down at his own wiry frame with comical surprise. What was she talking about?

'I have all the fat what I need,' he said, 'but for you . . .' he was all magnanimity, 'why not? Just this once.'

'Don't worry,' she said haughtily, 'it will only be "this once" . . . And you can wipe that silly grin off your face! You look like a demented rabbit, baring your teeth like that.'

But still he grinned.

FOUR

Hungarian

In the year or more that Stacy had been living with Anya, they had
evolved an elaborate double act which was kept on the road by a
series of comic fictions. The fiction, for instance, that Anya's
behaviour was shiningly consistent from end to end, and that it was
only her friend's stupidity that made her occasionally think
otherwise. Or the fiction that, whereas Stacy was hopelessly
nymphomaniac, Anya enjoyed total invulnerability to the opposite
sex – whose besieging hordes she was eternally fighting off. And
there was the unifying fiction of their relative roles: Stacy's as pupil,
totally docile to reproof and incapable of criticism; and Anya's as
benign guide and conductor through the tortuous passages of life,
happily blessed with the gift of infallibility. On this basis they had
developed many a happy, po-faced routine.

So when Anya brought home her conger-eel, the impossibly
conceited Hungarian sculptor – the besotted admirer she could not
be bothered to give the time of day to – Stacy saw at once the rich
potential of the material and went gleefully to work.

Wasn't it strange, she marvelled aloud, that she'd just been
wondering whether to prepare supper for three! (Never mind that,
she was told, the cooking was to be put in competent hands tonight.)
Relieved of that responsibility, Stacy began wondering whether
tonight mightn't be the night she went on the town and actually laid
hands on the man of her girlish dreams. Didn't Anya think it was an
auspicious night for that sort of an enterprise? (No, Anya didn't. She
thought Stacy was looking unwholesomely hectic, and that she
ought to go and sit down next door and cool off a bit.)

Seeing at once the wisdom of this advice Stacy sat down with the
sculptor in the drawing-room – squatting disciple-like on the carpet
with her long legs crossed and one of the cats twined about her arm –
and began to be quite unnecessarily charming – plying him with

questions, wine, nuts and compliments. Since Anya, by definition, had only a scientific interest in the man, it could do no harm if she expended her nymphomaniac passions on this, the nearest available male object. Anya banging pans and chopping vegetables in the kitchen, heard the husky seductive tones and smiled to herself. Stacy was really far too good at that sort of thing to be wholly in control of her own act. Lucky for her that she had someone experienced to keep her on the rails!

The voices had changed, becoming more animated. She kicked the kitchen door wide open: 'No whispering!' she commanded. 'You're being overheard.'

They were talking sculpture, with Stacy proving unexpectedly knowledgeable on the subject. Unlike her friend she was familiar with the monumental bronze of Annabel – passed it regularly on the way to her hairdresser's, actually, and had often admired (or so she said). Lying probably. Not that *he* noticed. He was responding flagrantly to the girl's provocations and kept striking a skittishly saturnine note which didn't suit him one little bit. With a half-peeled potato in her hand, Anya went to stand for an admonitory minute in the doorway – letting Stacy know she was being watched. Up leapt the girl, all compunction at the thoughtless way she had been monopolizing their guest, but then it had been so long since she'd had anyone to talk art with. Not since Cambridge days. But she really must scoot, if she was going to corner that hapless male and force him to buy her a meal. So nice to have met Mr Kovacs. After hearing so much. From a ducked head she shot her friend a wicked glance and went to her room. What the Hungarian made of all this extravagant by-play was anybody's guess.

Anya returned to the kitchen and merely grunted when Stacy, pulling on a black sealskin coat, paused at the door to flutter her eyelashes and hope that she was 'doing the right thing' going out like this, and would Anya be all right?

'You know,' she concluded in a voice that pretended to be confidential, but was in fact, slightly raised, 'I think we may have to revise that Force Three estimate. Ni-eeght.' And went, leaving a small stir of flirtatious flippancy in the air behind her. Anya smiled appreciatively. She didn't think much of the chances of the hapless male who tried to resist Stacy when she was in *this* mood of triumphant insolence. Actually, in all its subtlety of nuance and innuendo it was a bit wasted on the obtuser sex, which would only goggle and drool, instead of savouring its finer flavours.

The flat door banged. The sound had a startling conclusiveness –
irreversible.

Don't leave me!

For a second Anya panicked. Was not sure she hadn't actually
spoken the words. Was powerfully tempted to run to the head of the
stairs and call Stacy back. She dithered on the kitchen threshold.
The silent room where he sat (doing what?) held all sorts of
unforeseeable terrors which the girl's chatter would immediately
disperse. But it was too late now. Too late!

What an imbecile she was, rushing into things like a cow at a gate.
What had she brought him here for? The situation, now that they
had been so pointedly left alone together, held quite horrendous
possibilities of embarrassment. It would be two or three hours
before she could send him home. 'Two or three hours!' she mentally
wailed. Perhaps he was capable of walking out on his own initiative
if it proved too ghastly? But she feared that continental gallantry
would prevail. For three grisly hours! Her mind raced: should she
send him packing? Now? Give no reason, just get rid of him? Really,
it might be the only clean solution. She'd suffer for it, but the
suffering would at least have an end. The other way . . .

He was in the doorway, bearing bottle and glass, questioning with
eyebrows and shoulders: pour you one? She swerved aside into the
kitchen, knocking a colander to the floor with a clatter. He must
have seen.

'Yes,' she said loudly as she stooped to retrieve it, 'I could use a
drink. Yes. Pour me one, yes.' She was acutely conscious of the
broad backside she was presenting him, and spun around as if she
had been attacked.

'It won't be long,' she said '– the meal.'

'No worry.'

Either he'd not noticed or he was being odiously tactful.

'You wait next door,' she said imperiously. 'It'll be quicker.'

'Sure,' he said, in soothing tones, handing her the glass. To her
annoyance, her fingers touched his as she took it. He would think
she had done it on purpose – she knew what men were like. She took
a too large and too noisy gulp, then realized that he had spoken:
'Sure, I go.'

Her eyes darted to examine his: the words had had a peculiar
earnest finality. In the half-second during which she thought he
meant he was leaving – thought that he had understood everything
and, out of kindness, was leaving her to a preferred solitude – she

realized two things: how much she *needed* him to be percipient on this scale, if their relations were to be endurable; and how much she didn't want him to walk out on her, now.

She lowered her eyes. The realization had restored her calm. She even recovered some attention for the braised-meat dish she was running up by her usual method *viz* opening the food cupboard, facing the spice rack and awaiting inspiration. He had withdrawn as bidden. The panic had passed.

So had quite a lot of things . . . some of them for good. This was probably the last time that she thought of embarrassment in connection with Laczi Kovacs.

A few minutes later she carried in the dishes, and amid the ensuing cheerful clatter she saw that he had accepted the whole situation with uncomplicated directness. Nothing was pre-empted and there was nothing to justify or explain. Here they were. The evening stretched ahead invitingly.

They tucked in with gusto and, once the meal was demolished, the gusto transferred itself to their talk. On both fronts, food and conversation, Laczi surprised himself with his own voracity. He hadn't known he was so hungry.

It was not until she woke the following morning that Anya remembered her moment of terror, and then it was only with a kind of fond incredulity. What an idiot she could be at times! She sat up. He was not in bed. She could hear his loud spluttering ablutions from the bathroom, then the quick hard step which the carpet could not muffle (he must have very bony heels!), the thunder of water into the stainless-steel sink, the snapping of impatient fingers while the kettle came to the boil. New sounds. Queer the way every man had a different set of characteristic noises. Queerer still that these, though new, did not strike her as alien.

She was half inclined to resent the fact he was paying her no attention. Given the not very extraordinary success of the night's doings – no worse, perhaps, but certainly no better than your average first night . . . given that, most men she knew would have been all over her like a rash, making passionate amends, promising her the erotic moon and stars 'next time', and generally reflating the punctured male ego with the usual blasts of hot air. . . . In other words, being very very boring. Much better that he went and gargled and washed his face. Who wanted men that scaled you like a mountain in order to plant some incomprehensible flag on your summit? It was pleasant to bed one that didn't have a thesis to prove on you.

'Can you find the coffee?' she called.

'Yes. I find.'

'I have it black.'

'Me too.'

She lay back and listened. He was making it all so ordinary. Again there came the reflex towards resentment and again the instantaneous check: in ordinariness lay the pleasure. She was lapped by an extraordinary luxury which was not languorous but full of sharp expectation. It was as if, instead of its happening every day of her life, no one had ever brought her coffee in bed before. Absurd!

He came, cleared a space, laid the tray carefully on the bedside table. Mugs in hand, they sipped without noticing, their eyes held in a long exchange of unconscious intimacy – a peaceful blankness which took in nothing distinctly. Then, kneeling on the bed, he reached forward and took the back of her head in one large cupped hand and looked at her. Looked . . . and yet it was not looking, so much as holding her, whole and entire, between eye and hand – as she was to see him later cradling a wax model, weighing, inspecting, assaying. The eyes, calm, abstracted, severe even, but unseeing, took all of her in – relieved her of herself. He had not bothered to dress and she realized, from the way this did not matter, that nakedness for him was not an issue but a condition.

She could not remember being looked at like this before, and the light touch on the back of her neck stirred her as many a more explicit intimacy had never done. It was a caress of which nearly all the content was implicit. Nothing promised, yet everything contained. Something peculiar was happening to the Necessity of Disappointment – that iron rule which had grown, over the years, into one of her guiding dogmas. How strange to be without it! It left *her* naked of all her ironies. She reached out and touched the little branching tree of hair that grew vertically up the knotted muscles of his belly.

'Right then, Mr Chips,' she said brightly, brassily, 'off you go. Nobody's keeping you. '

He sat back on his heels, cocking his head at her, quizzically unoffended. You couldn't say he was handsome.

'I can see,' she continued in a lofty tone, 'that you're fidgeting to get back to your precious block of stone. Don't let me detain you.'

He laughed quietly, but still held her with his eyes, denying nothing. She waited for him, for *something* from him, but nothing came.

'I'll call round this evening, shall I?' she said at last. 'It won't hold you up?'

He smiled faintly: 'No,' he said. 'If it would, I would tell you. Come about seven. There is then no more light to work.'

'About seven.'

He brushed her cheek with his stubbled lips, climbed into his clothes, and left Anya to ponder.

Was she sorry he had gone so soon? Probably not. She had seen far too many slipshod dilettantes lying abed and proclaiming a voluptuous salvation-by-passion. She was glad his nature was hard, determined, purposive, just as she was glad the muscles in his belly were taut like a drum. They were both things that felt good when you touched them. And besides, his departure left space and quiet to review the change that was beginning.

It was Sunday. Stacy had not returned. It wouldn't be at all a bad thing to have him out of her hair for twelve hours. She hunted the cats out on to the little balcony roof-garden, turned the key on them, and gave herself up, in a great cloud of cigarette smoke, to meditation.

The door of the studio being open, Anya walked in on what appeared to be a spirited dispute in Hungarian. Kovacs's *visitor* at least was being spirited, waving his chubby hands about with vigour and occasionally restoring himself to calm by smoothing down the sleek black hair that sat snugly on his round skull. He seemed a strange mixture of urbanity and excitability, the agitation of voice and gesture emerging oddly from the beautifully tailored suit of expensive buff-coloured cloth. The olive skin of his face had been barbered to the smoothness of wax. Anya noticed it, because he turned repeatedly, with courtly deference, in her direction – requesting the civility of an introduction.

But Laczi was remorseless. The introduction was refused along with all other requests, and civility had no place in the process. Eventually, the visitor appeared to capitulate. He turned up the flats of his soft palms and gave a small sigh. Well, well, the sigh said, still the same old Kovacs I see! Anya contemplated the little tableau. 'Stubborn old Bruin', Laczi's wife had called him at the end of a very similar scene, making much the same gesture accompanied by the same sigh. Affection and exasperation in almost equal quantities. Did he deliberately elicit this? Was this where all his admirers were doomed to end up?

The two men exchanged the farewells of fraternal unmeaning that pass between compatriots in exile, and with a half-bow to where Anya stood aside at the exit – 'Excuse the intrusion, I beg you' came wafted to her in impeccable English – the visitor angled his forward shoulder and passed deftly out of the narrow opening without soiling his clothes. Anya watched his retreat down the alley to where a white Mercedes waited, gleaming.

'Who's that one then?' she inquired.

Laczi took the corners of his moustache into his mouth and muttered unintelligibly. Another habit he would have to be broken of.

'Could it be "he who has propositions as the sea has water"?'

Her retentiveness startled him: 'You are the great listener, eh?'

'That's right. And you have been cautioned. What's his proposition this time?'

'Some foolishness.'

'About what?' She was not to be fobbed off. If she was taking over, she was taking over.

'Ach, he wants me to make him nudes in bronze. Smooth little nudes, just so. Not too big. Not too many. Tubby little odalisques for the mantelshelves of his fat friends in the Chamber of Commerce.'

'I bet there's money in it. He looks grotesquely affluent. That suit was pure mohair, you know. You wouldn't notice, but I do. From the best Savile Row tailor too – it must have set him back three or four hundred.'

'So I think. Like you say, he is grotesque.' Laczi dragged the door shut.

She blocked his way: 'Well, are you going to do it? You're short of the ready, aren't you?'

'You joke. I have sent him to pack.'

'Was that wise? Can't you run him up a few?' Laczi pulled a face. 'It wouldn't take you long,' she persisted.

'It takes long, and I do not have the time.'

'That's the whole idea: with the proceeds, you can *buy* time.'

'Besides I am not Aristide Maillol, so why I should pretend? I do not make women with buttocks of water-melon and thighs of wax. Not with faces of the sublime cow neither. Such women I do not see, or if I see I do not look.'

'Oh, I don't know,' Anya tossed out, strolling ahead of him, away from the door, ' I think there's something to be said for water-melon buttocks.'

He followed undiverted: 'Let it be said then by somebody else. Me, I have better things. My stone has today come good. The fault has finish. Not too deep neither. Now I can begin. Make a maquette – a model. That's good, no?' He stood with his hand on the dark stone.

'Yes. Very glad for you. But shouldn't you treat your retail outlets with more respect? I think you need a marketing manager.'

'Retail! Markets! Pfah! You talk like the Juhacz.'

She eyed him closely. 'I suspect that you've done quite well out of "the Juhacz" and it galls you to admit it.'

'Phoo! A commission here and there. I admit. I am corruptible like the next fellow. But only when I choose. I do not corrupt to order. I have only to do with such a man when I cannot choose. He is Hungarian of the wrong sort.'

'Oh really?' Anya affected nonchalance but was immediately alert. 'What is "the wrong sort"?' Again she walked ahead, leaving him to follow.

'A *puszta* landlord,' he said '– a bloodsucker of the big estates he was, what saw his chance and got out with his loot before the communists could catch him. Now he is tycoon – a builder of cubical glasshouses and renter of luxury flats – a "property developer" I think you say.'

'Oho!' Anya turned round and laughed in his face. 'A property developer, and your patron! My, my!'

He was not put out: 'Patron nothing! He is a tick in a sheep.'

'With you as the humble sheep, eh?'

'When it suits me, I pick him off. Meantime, I don't care.'

'You just "itch" a little,' Anya needled.

'Perhaps a little,' he conceded with a shrug, dismissing it. 'How was your day? Also good?'

They had come to a standstill by the workbench and, absent-mindedly, Anya began pulling out drawers, turning over the contents.

'You mean, did I find that my fault had an end, too?'

'What fault?' he protested, 'I don't see no fault.'

'Maybe it's still to be discovered.'

'You don't mean that.' He seemed very sure of it.

'Not today perhaps. Today I am an optimist of weak wit and impaired judgement, so I don't mean it today. But I will later.' She had found something in the drawer. She held up an old-fashioned photograph frame. 'What's this?'

He took it from her eagerly. Under the glass, instead of a snapshot, there was a yellowing sheet of newspaper, badly frayed at the edges, print blurred where it had been folded, saying something or other in the incomprehensible language of his country.

He embraced and kissed her on both cheeks: '*Wunderbar!* I thought I had lost. Hey! this makes for me my day.'

'What is it?'

'This,' he said proudly, holding it up in his two hands like a favourite grandchild who has just done something very clever, 'this is Hungarian of the right sort. This you must know. In '56, when we fighted, it is to be able to say a thing like this. I like it very much that it would be you what finds it. That is good.'

She peered over his shoulder: 'You'd better translate it then, flower. I'm a little bit left out in all this euphoria.'

He pulled a dismal face and ran his hand up the back of his head so that his hair stood comically on end: 'Translate?'

'Just give me the guts of it, I'll handle the felicities.'

He looked dubious, then brightened: 'Why not?' he said, gathering animation as he went. 'I want you should know it, so why not?'

'Good. Just let me find my specs.'

So began the process of Anya's initiation into things Hungarian. It was also the occasion when a fleeting ambition to learn the language took a heavy fall from which it never recovered. Xhosa had been nursery-school stuff compared with this copiously intractable lingo which yielded not a morsel of common vocabulary to the English-speaker. Why, she complained, couldn't Laczi speak like a Christian and an Indo-European? No, she was having none of it.

That evening, nevertheless, they did manage to hammer out a version of Gyula Háy's article (from the *Budapest Literary Gazette* for June 1956). For Laczi the process was clearly fascinating. Anya, though she tried to deceive herself, had finally to acknowledge indifference. As manifestos went – and she had very little time for the genre – it was engaging and sprightly enough. But its touching importance and urgency for him was, as she had feared, something she saw without understanding. She fumbled for palliatives: had something been lost in translation? she asked. No, the translation was very good – she had caught the spirit very well. She read it over again, looking for the thread to the labyrinth without really believing it existed:

It is the writer's prerogative to tell the truth; to criticize anybody and anything; to be sad; to be in love; to think of death; not to worry whether light and shadow are in balance in his work; to believe in the omnipotence of God; to deny the existence of God; to doubt the correctness of certain figures in the Five Year Plan; to think in a non-Marxist manner; to think in a Marxist manner – even if the thought thus born is not yet among the truths proclaimed to be of binding force; to find the standard of life low, even of those people whose wages do not yet figure among those to be raised; to believe something unjust that is still officially maintained to be just; to depict troubles without immediately detecting the means of remedying them; to consider ugly the New York Coffee House, declared a historic building, regardless of the fact that millions have already been spent on its restoration; to notice that Budapest is falling to ruins since there is no money to repair the buildings; to criticize the way of life, the way of speaking, and the way of working of certain leaders; to wonder whether it is deducible from the fact that things *are* done thus, that they ought always, and forever to be done thus; to ask questions and expect an answer . . . All this we must do; all this we dare scarcely attempt; all this, undone and unattempted, creates a prison worse than any they can put us in for doing it.

'Nice, that last sentence,' Anya remarked, keeping prudently to the inessential. 'There's no denying it, I've got the makings of a great stylist. Especially given the platitude it adorns . . .' She let the thought trail off.

But he had heard: 'It doesn't speak to you, then?' he asked in a voice so dejected that she almost felt compunction. 'It passes you by?' he persisted.

'About half a mile above my left shoulder and travelling at speed. I'm sorry, but it's just an anthology of obviosities. When I've said, "Yes, of course!" what happens next?'

It was fortunate that they had passed this way the day before – in the case of Ilona, the girl freedom-fighter. Otherwise Laczi might

76

have said some irrevocable things. Besides, this time, he could detect no deliberate provocation. It was just flat incomprehension. The onus of explanation seemed to fall upon him: 'Shall I tell you a story?' he proposed.

She was willing. What else had she come for, but to be told stories? For the next hour he made the most concerted effort he had ever attempted to put a foreigner on the streets of Budapest and let her breathe the sharp morning air of national liberation. He gave her the atmosphere of breathless rumour, of incredulity, of hope and cynicism. He tried to put her among the little excited knots at street corners, stirred to new agitation by a running messenger who had just heard something on the radio: the demonstration was banned; everyone was ordered back to work. But the polytechnic students were already marching! The polytechnic students had been arrested. (No they hadn't.) News, news! The ban on demonstrations had been lifted. Everybody was going to Bem Square. No, everybody was going to Margit Island. No they weren't, they were dismantling the statue of Stalin in the Municipal Gardens. (When they'd finished that, someone commented, they would be 'dismantled' themselves – probably for a stretch of twenty years.) But the ban *had* been lifted. And had they heard, shouted a passer-by who was going somewhere in a great hurry, the whole Petöfi Military Academy had joined the marchers? Come off it! The crack troops, the ideological storm-troopers from the Military Academy, joining a demonstration? Believe that and you'd believe anything. 'Don't you know where you are?' demanded a wit. 'This is Hungary, Comrade. Remember the old joke: one man went out on the streets with a placard, and what happened . . . ? A whole squad of mounted police had to turn out and disperse him.' There was knowing laughter. But still the reports poured in. Could it all, just possibly, be true? People were saying things aloud that they never expected to say to their pillows. And nothing happened. Nobody came. No secret police of the AVH with their dreaded blue insignia. No police whatsoever. The streets just kept steadily filling, and the little red, green and white cockades kept appearing from nowhere, until you began to feel conspicuous without one.

And then, as if it had been prearranged, this great concourse of people began to move one way. It had *not* been prearranged. Nobody knew where the current was taking them, nor what they would find when they got there. But it was as unthinkable to stay behind, as it would have been unthinkable, twenty-four hours ago, to go. Somebody up front knew where they were going. It would be all right. Look at the numbers.

But was there anybody up front? Or was it just the Spirit of Hungary invisible but potent astride a horse of smoke?

Coming out of a side street, they found themselves suddenly milling about on the outskirts of a vast crowd. Tens of thousands of people (not that you could count them – you just sensed it). It was Bem Square after all. You could see the barracks to the right, and the statue of the hero of the 1848 War of Liberation decked with flags and wreaths, youths clambering all over him, and one leonine old man up there, a megaphone in his hand, declaiming something from a sheet of paper. Neither Laczi nor the greater proportion of those in the crowd could hear a word he said. Who was he? Some writer or other. Does it matter? Never mind, Comrades, why split hairs? They cheered when he got up and cheered when he finished. No doubt he had said a lot of true things. This was a day when true things got said.

And then, in the stir of vacillation that followed the end of the speechifying, there was a tidal movement to the right. The crowd was facing about. Everybody was looking one way – towards the barracks. They had noticed the rows of soldiers standing silent behind closed windows, watching. Were they armed? Most likely. An uneasy silence fell on the murmuring sea of faces . . . So that the voice that yelled was unnaturally distinct: 'Long live the Hungarian Honved Army! Hungarian uniforms for the soldiers of Hungary!' The crowd took up the chant: 'Long live the Hungarian Army!' from thousands of throats. The windows opened. There was a moment of frozen silence. Was it about to begin again? You read about such things, but in actuality . . . ? Something small fell among the crowd below the barrack windows. Word spread with miraculous speed: a soldier had torn the Soviet star from his cap and thrown it to the crowd. It was beginning, right enough, but it was something completely new. The star insignia were raining down as other soldiers followed suit and, released into the euphoria of the impossible, the crowd went wild. It was at this point, Laczi thought, that someone started singing the National Anthem.

'I don't know how many we were. It might be fifty thousand, it might be a hundred thousand. But if we would not have too big a lump in our throats, we all sang. Have you heard singing like that ever? Nobody ordered, nobody planned, nobody gave the note. But everybody sang. We were all together. For what? We did not know, and we did not care, because we were together. And we had not been together like this for maybe twenty year. Do you understand?' He gripped her hands where she sat. 'Do you understand how is it that everybody wept? Old grannies and shopkeepers, students and little kids, prostitutes and soldiers, the cynics and the sentimentalists all the same? We wept for nothing. We wept for hope, do you see? Because we had never expected that we would be able to hope. We had forgotten how to do it. We had forgotten we had forgotten. And now we were hoping again, and it pained us. That is what politics is about – to give a great people hope together. To use the hope what they have, to put it to work and build something what will last. And that is why it does not make anything, that you British have already all the liberties what Gyula Háy hopes for – that they are "obvious", like you tell me. Maybe so they are. But they are no good to you unless you have them *with hope* – like he does there in that writing. It is not enough just to have this liberty. You must use it also to make something, or else it is nothing worth.'

He realized he had been standing gesticulating and sat himself down on a stool, his hands dangling between his knees. He looked up at her, half-ashamed, half-imperious, from under his brows: 'I make a fine speech, eh? Maybe I find myself a megaphone and a statue?'

But he need not have been defensive. She had been listening.

'And what came of his hope?'

'Háy? They put him in prison.'

'So . . .?' There was no intention of triumph, but she did not succeed in keeping its sound out of her voice.

'So, maybe he is still there. I don't know. People disappear. But it doesn't matter.'

'You may say so. *He* might think differently. *If* he's still there.'

'No, you are wrong. He knew the cost and still he chose.'

'And you knew the cost and chose not to.'

He smiled wryly: 'I thought it would be here that we wind up. Never mind. I told you before, I chose amputation. I don't know if it is much better. And I don't think I really chose either. At a time like that, there is not a lot of choice. Do not think I am keeping secrets like the dark horse. I want you to understand; but I cannot tell to you the things what I do not myself understand.'

Anya looked at the ragged page from the journal. It was still not real to her.

'Did you know this Háy?' she asked.

'Not really. He was friend of my father's.' He began picking at a callus on his hand – a habit she had already mentally listed for reform.

'Where's your father now?'

He picked more furiously.

'Siberia.'

She couldn't stop now: 'Alive? Or dead?'

'They won't tell me,' he said in a low voice. She had cured him of the picking – the hand fell limp between his knees. 'Or they can't.'

Anya drew breath. It was enough to get on with. And she was weary with concentrating. She put both hands on his shoulders and shook him as if he was a sleepwalker she had to awaken.

'Interrogation is over,' she said cheerily. 'For the present.'

'You are very wrong,' he said unsmilingly. 'It is never over.'

A week or two later, as she was busy reducing the piggery to a degree of habitable order – since she occasionally slept there it had to be made tolerable – she came across a copy of the *New Hungarian Journal* and started dipping at random . . .

'The winning of the support of the toiling masses,' she read, 'has demanded a radical break with all erroneous conceptions and prejudices and a return to the correct Leninist style of work.' Oh really? she mocked. And why not *embrace* the erroneous conceptions pray? And return to an *in*correct style of work? Tut, what pusillanimity! 'But we laid no less stress on the task of separating from the real enemies, and leading back to the right path, those who had been misled – whose number was not small!' Ah, the dear old 'right path'! Always there when you needed it! What a blessing it must be – especially if you had been 'misled' – to have such leaders! How could a nation not puerile *acquire* such leaders? . . . 'This policy rested on Marxist/Leninist principles, was sincere, communist, and hence humanist.' And *hence* humanist! Who was this blockhead? She turned back a few pages. Janos Kádár! 'Our scientists and artists, whether they are or are not members of the Party . . . participate actively in the development of the arts and sciences and in the elaboration of solutions for the problems of our society. The country provides all possible requisites for the creative work of Hungarian scientists and artists . . .' I'll bet it does. Right down to the possible requisite of a prison to sit and rot in. Like Háy, with his lofty idea of the writer's destiny.

'Laczi,' she trumpeted from the office/bedroom, 'who's Kádár?

Isn't he the Russian stooge who took over in '56?' She had been doing her homework: she hated being dependent on other people for her facts.

'Something like that.'

'You're not going to defend him, for Christ's sake?'

'I might.'

'But I thought he was the one that jailed all your heroes and crushed your precious liberty. *And* deported your father.'

'That is so. "Heroes", you say? I tell you something about heroes. There is one of our poets writes . . .' She came to the head of the stairs, as he fumbled for the vocabulary, ' "A People protected by its martyrs must be cowardly people. For were they courageous, how would they permit their heroes to perish?" Something like that.'

'Oh *very* high-minded! But your Kádár did these things all the same, didn't he?'

'He had no choice.'

'Oh, don't start that dialectical crap again!'

'OK, I don't. You ask the question. I answer.'

She thundered down the ladder, bearing the obnoxious journal. She slammed the thing on to the bench and directed him with an accusatory finger. See this . . . look at that . . . how about this?

'Yes?' he said, looking up interrogatively.

'Jesus, you're not that stupid. This is the most arrant nonsense that ever dripped off the end of a pen.'

'Probably.'

She put a theatrical hand to her brow: 'Go on. Enlighten me.' She slumped in a chair. 'But do it gently. I don't think I can stand much more. And for Christ's sake,' she appended, as he prepared to do so, 'stop chewing your bloody whiskers!'

'Kádár,' he began with a grin, but measuring his speech with care, 'was an ignoramus, and a bully, and he has murdered like the others. You are a Hungarian politician – you have blood on your hands. Háy also has murdered. He – and the others like him – they might have shut their traps and then there would have been no Russian tanks, and thousands of people who now are dead would be alive. Who is to say who is right? Both ways there is a cost to pay. And besides, Kádár and Háy agreed both of them about the goal, the objective. Oh yes . . .' he fended off her protest. 'Give it here. I show you.'

He thumbed through the pages searching for something.

'Ah, here. See, this is Kádár. It is his sixtieth birthday and he is

81

reflecting. Perhaps it is his first time ever, I don't know. But he says this: "Marxism/Leninism taught me that if I wanted to be human, happy and free, a man free in mind, I could not be it alone. I could be it only together with the working people; and only if I tried to understand this ideology still better and if I lived accordingly as well as I could, only then could I bring these things about . . ." Háy would not disagree. He did not want liberty on the back of the working people. He wanted it *for* them. The question was, how? For Kádár, the way of Háy would *destroy* the liberty of the working people. So he crushed Háy. And the others. For the sake of the working people. Do you see?'

'Will you *stop* saying "Do you see?"!'

'Sorry. You see, I do not think he was a happy man when he was doing this. He was not a contented villain. Somewhere here . . . "It is a pain for the soul," ' he read, ' "when men ask, as with me, whether one is an honest man . . ." No, not that. That is just whining . . . Ah, here: "In the old world I also dreamt of liberation, socialism, communism, and even though it was doubtful whether I would live to see the day of Liberation, there was no doubt in my mind that, when the day came, all that was needed were a few sensible ordinances and socialism would become a reality." '

Anya yawned. He held up a finger: 'Now hear this: "That was over a quarter of a century ago, and it has since become clear that things do not get done in quite that way." ' He looked up, only to encounter a gorgon stare. But he was not to be deterred: 'You see it is no good to have the big ideals, unless you know the reality about how to get them. "Things do not get done in quite that way." That is the problem. Who loves best his fellow-men, you tell me: that one what leads them at once into the wilderness, without maps, without food, without a plan? or the one what holds them back, by force even, until he has a plan and equipment? It is not so easy as you think. It is easy to hate Kádár.'

'Don't you?'

'Of course I hate. I hate the thing he is. I hate what he does. But maybe I shouldn't. Since then he has done much for Hungary.'

'But for shit's sake, Laczi! All this Marxist/Leninist claptrap? This mindless, witless slogan-shouting? If you had any brains to start with, they'd be burnt out after two pages!'

'It is a language. You can say in it things what you can't say in another. Maybe they would be important things. Who knows?'

She appeared to be pondering, but she was really only recoiling before springing: 'You know, my friend, I think you're a coward. All this fair-mindedness of yours is just pusillanimity. Pus-ill-an-im-ity,' she repeated, when he looked blank at the word. ' "Who knows?" ' Savagely she mimicked his shrugging, purse-lipped delivery: ' "It's not so easy" – "Who can tell?" – "Perhaps this . . . perhaps that" . . . What is all that but cowardice, you tell me?'

He paused, licked his lips, pursed them . . . then, with a reflex of amused recollection, altered his expression: 'I tell you one thing,' he said. 'I don't think beside you I am going to sleep very quiet.'

'I didn't come here,' she retorted, 'to induce sleep.'

'So I think,' he replied, in his habitual phrase.

South African

Talk was something Kovacs enjoyed. But in moderation. He saw he would have to make some provision for silence. To some extent the trading hours of the Rotten Orange protected him. But not entirely – it was inconveniently close. Besides, the enemy was within: he was pleased to see her. Instead of finishing the section he was working on while she talked, he found he was laying down his tools before she was well through the door. This had to stop. He had broken out in a rash of new ideas which he had hardly had time to get down on paper, let alone in wax. And he must make the most of the clear light of high summer – which meant working long hours.

The solution was plain – that stony taciturnity, developed over the years to fend off the babbling, twittering world, had now to be applied to a painful case. He braced himself for the ordeal. He did not go so far as to envisage losing her altogether. She was no fool: she'd see what he was about. In the comfortable way we all have, he assumed exactly the degree of clairvoyance in her which he needed if he was to pursue his own course with a tranquil conscience. What he had not foreseen was that the strain of renunciation would give a sourness to his demeanour which was open to more than one interpretation. The sacrifice whose difficulty was a tribute to her, might look, to somebody unapprised of his motive, like a difficulty in enduring her company.

At first, however, it seemed to answer. She dropped in less often, took a dutiful interest in the purbeck's state of health when she did, and generally left it to him to decide when they were to spend time together. And he, pleased to find his faith in her percipience justified, was usually in high feather when he rewarded himself with a spell in her company.

But this ration-book version of a love affair would hardly have satisfied an accommodating female for more than a month, let alone an Anya. While Laczi happily slaved away at his Prophet, heaping up small hills of spoil as he roughed out the figure – or while he took a few days off to run up waxes of the new ideas that were coming at him from the pages of his Radnóti – all this time Anya was growing restive. She could see *he* was absorbed and content, but what was that supposed to do for *her*?

'That's all very well. But can he be trusted?'
Anya had finally worked round to the question she had to ask, though it made her very uneasy to be asking it.

Bill Madison's small eyes, always mobile, began positively to dance when she brought this out, and his face creased in a dozen quizzical lines: 'Why's it me you ask, heh?'

'Well, you know him better than I do, don't you?'

'Do I?' he parried in his wheezy fat man's voice which always suggested a joke not far away. 'I didn't think my judgement counted for much with you.'

'Certainly,' she retorted, 'I'd be more interested in it, if I thought you were capable of resenting him.'

He met it with a shrug: 'Resentment? No. Not my style.'

He made it sound like a boast.

'I'm collecting data,' she pursued, defying him to take umbrage. 'I can't afford to be too choosy about the source. Who else can I ask?'

'Quite a few. D'you want a list?'

'Can he be trusted? I'm asking *you*.'

'Right,' he agreed amicably. 'So you are. And *I* don't know where the question came from.'

'We're already shacked up, for Christ's sake, and before things get any heavier I want to know what I'm buying into. Is that strange?'

It might be, his shrug said.

'I saw him with his wife once,' she continued. 'I didn't like the omens one bit. Depressing little spectacle that pair made! What I mean is . . .' She sighed with exasperation at being driven to such bald-headed explicitness: 'Has he ever cared for anything but himself and his sculpture?'

Still he preserved a canny and observant silence.

'I see,' she said with some impatience. 'He *can't* be trusted, but you're too loyal to say so.'

Bill pulled an owlish face and shook his head knowingly from side to side. He was enjoying this.

'Shall I tell you,' he said at length, 'why it's me you've come to? "before things get too heavy" – as you say? It's because you *know* what I'm going to say, and it happens to be the answer you want to hear.'

'Oh, very cute!' She brushed it aside for the ingenious fatuity it was.

'That's right,' he went on, nodding happily at her. 'If you wanted to hear about his *un*trustworthiness, his selfishness, and so on, you knew where to go: you've met her. There aren't too many Kovacses in the directory. But you came to me. Why?'

A moment ago his high good humour had been incurring her scorn, but now she was not so sure. She was not narrow-minded: she was prepared to award points to those who were sharp enough to distrust her. She conceded him an equivocal, wary smile.

'Lass,' he said, his broad frame expanding in his chair and the regional burr going broader with it, 'if it's my blessing you want – God alone knows why!' He paused and beamed at her: '. . . you have it!' And he laid a friendly palm for a second on the hand she held unconsciously clenched on the table between them. It was the kind of presumption she normally detested. Men had had their eyes blacked for less. Instead, she felt herself flush with a warmth of unexpected recognition. He had misread her motive absurdly – absurdly – yet she felt absurdly pleased. It was like winning first prize in a competition you didn't know you'd entered. So after all, his friends approved! So she *didn't* have to fight the whole current of his past. The relief that swept over her gave her the first inkling what a weariness of spirit the fight would have been. It also apprised her unexpectedly of the value she set on this little fat man's goodwill. She was bound, in honour, to make some amends.

She began to take him in more attentively. Bill stood the scrutiny with something between bashfulness and bravado.

'You make an odd pair,' she said after a pause.

'Me and Laczi. Why? Most pairs are odd. What's so queer about us?'

'Well, him all spikes and principles . . .'

'And me so bland and mediocre, eh?' he laughed.

Her shoulders convulsed in a shrug which was not exactly a denial.

'Say it! No,' he continued with sudden sobriety, 'I have one virtue for Laczi: I know my trade, see? I'm "the good workman", worthy of his hire.' He shrugged. "S true, actually. You can't teach me a damn thing about clay technology. It all began when I showed him a trick or two about his modelling-clay, and we just went on from there . . . Anyway, you're wrong about the spikes. He's tolerant as hell. Too damn tolerant, if you ask me. Puts up with all sorts of fools out of pure good nature. But perhaps I shouldn't grumble,' he wound up in a half-aside.

Anya brought her fist down hard, with sudden conviction: 'That's right! That's *it*!' Something had struck her forcibly and it was not the aside, which had passed her by. 'It's his tolerance I distrust most.' She leaned forward heavily grinding one elbow into the table as if preparing for a bout of arm-wrestling. 'And I'm sure as shit not going to be "tolerated" myself.'

Bill cocked his head like a sparrow and put up a pair of approving thumbs: 'Good for you!' he barracked. 'That's the way to play it. He could use an equal. And there aren't a lot around. I reckon you'll do.'

At this blatant flattery Anya gave a grimace of disgust, but failed to conceal her pleasure. *She* reckoned she would, too. That, she realized, was precisely the role she had chosen for herself.

She was distracted from her mission, however, by news from Cape Town. Peg – the indomitable, the inimitable, the invaluable Peg Houghton – was coming to England. As recollection flooded over her, she began to wonder how she had managed to live without Peg for ten long years. Stacy was all very well in her way – good at the all-girls-together routines – flighty enough to make entertaining watching; and reliably vixenish when the dog-foxes threatened to invade the inner sanctum. But she didn't have Peg's monumental stability. She couldn't, like Peg, shed intractable circumstance as a seaboard rock shed waves: she tended, instead, to wring her hands and shred her hankies. And much as Anya believed in the sisterhood of her sex, she *did* require a touch of the heroic from them.

Long before Peg's foot touched British shores, Laczi had been regaled with their exploits together, at school and university, beach and *braaivleis*, to the point where he began to nurse a discreet scepticism. The stories had one curious feature in common: Peg was always the initiator, the leader, the sheet-anchor, while the Anya who figured in them remained shadowy and, to Laczi's view, hard to recognize.

When, as kids, they went round the suburbs ringing doorbells, it was Peg who rang and Anya who hid. And on the famous occasion when a *hausfrau* set her boxer on them, and the boxer bit a perfectly innocent passing black, and the black very naturally kicked the dog, and the *hausfrau* called the police – it was Peg who stood up to the stupid bitch of a woman and made her climb down, though she was only thirteen at the time. Get that! A thirteen-year-old kid, caught out in a silly prank, and she bawled out an adult till the woman was actually apologizing! It was true that Peg appeared to be a couple of years the elder, and that all this had happened a decade or more ago . . . but something definitely didn't add up. He kept his reservations to himself. The event would show.

The great day dawned. The little cupboard of a boxroom had been cleared and the obliging Stacy had moved into it. She was becoming accustomed to invasions and incursions and consoled herself with the thought that, as with Laczi, the new arrival would probably add a new active ingredient to the social brew that her friend liked to keep bubbling away in the flat. The conditions of life with Anya might have been inconvenient at times, but she had never had to complain of boredom. Also she was curious to meet a person of whom Anya spoke with almost unrelieved admiration – though she expected, in the face of such a portent, to feel rather dwarfed.

That was the first surprise for her, and for Laczi. For Peg was short and dumpy, with a hard little moon-face and a sharp nose on which round gold spectacles perched nervously. They had been expecting a matriarch of hieratic splendour, some sort of Amazonian queen. And then she talked ceaselessly about the petty politics of the Cape Town English Department where she was a lecturer, with Anya, stoogelike, feeding her questions about personalities, scandals and liaisons.

As that material wore thin, they turned to the girls they'd known at Herschel (one of them making quite a go of it on the BBC as an interviewer, Peg had heard? – Yes, that was right). And whatever happened to Marylla, that tall girl whose family used to take the cottage next door on those dreadfully boring holidays at Knysna? Also in England, Anya had heard. Did she remember those wild toga-parties in District Six? And the night Toby held a flagon of red to his mouth and glugged it down till he passed out? Toby was a colonel in the army now, would you believe it! And so on . . . all the usual harmless stuff of which reunions are woven . . . you tried to make allowances, but it was hard to know how to hold your face, Stacy found. She had been willing to be impressed, but who could be impressed by this interminable rattling train of trivia? Given Anya's preternatural nose for personal limitation and lumpishness, the case of Peg was turning into a major enigma.

Laczi, of course, with the aid of his famous tolerance, was being the perfect Central European gentleman. He sympathized with Peg over the complications of getting a trunk from Southampton to London ('I know this is a backward country, but three weeks to travel a hundred miles?!'); was suitably intrigued to learn how a reader of too many nineteenth-century novels could be misled by the contemporary English vernacular (when the purser suggested she might 'take a coach' to London, she'd thought he was taking the piss, she really had!); and was prompt to deplore, once given the cue, the fatuity of the British drinking laws, the mulishness of the British public servant, or the squalor of the British public toilet. And yes, he had to agree, there were an amazing number of blacks about London. Not that she objected, mind you. Quite the reverse. But there were more than she'd expected.

It was probably the conspicuous exercise of the Kovacsian tolerance that alerted Anya. At first, loyal to her friend, she tore a strip off him for being insulting and patronizing. His suave manner didn't fool *her*, and he could just cut it out, thank you very much! But then she began to worry. She had expected Peg to talk South Africa out of her system, get over her strangeness in a new place, and begin to take an interest in what was going on around her – notably Anya, Anya's shop, Anya's man. But the days passed and no such transformation took place.

No effort had been spared. Peg had been taken to the Rotten Orange, where she gazed about her vaguely, found the prices unexpectedly high, and mentioned the name of a similar establishment opened recently in — Street. The National Gallery fared little better: wasn't the collection rather light on good Pre-Raphaelites? A Brecht play reminded her of Athol Fugard's latest masterpiece. It hadn't come to London yet? But it must have been four years ago it was premiered in Jo'burg! Though Peg seemed quite oblivious to it, the atmosphere was becoming dangerously charged, and Laczi found himself, every night, saddled with the task of defusing it sufficiently to see them all through another twenty-four hours. And every night the task was becoming more difficult.

It is well known that when people are about to have a blazing row they invariably book a table at an expensive restaurant of the plush, hushed kind. Laczi, unacquainted with this law, thought they had turned the corner. When Anya proposed they go as a foursome to her favourite Italian eatery, he encouraged her in the scheme. Sentimental old European that he was, he probably retained some naïve notion, inherited from his father, that good wine and good food (rarely though he encountered them) were the bond and cement of friendship.

They might have proved so, perhaps, if Peg had been properly impressed by them. But instead, before they were well into the *tournedos rossini*, she threw off some slighting comment about the relative quality of British and South African beef, followed it with a doubt that Château Léoville-Barton was really much better than a good Constantia . . . and the battle was on.

Anya sounded her bugle: 'Is anybody asking you to pay for them?' (When she entertained she never inspected the bill, merely dropped her Diner's Card on the plate and looked away. And it added fuel to her fury now, that she had been made to recall the inflated prices in this place.)

Peg blinked from behind baffled rims. She had intended no slight. She had thought Anya would have been *pleased* to be reminded of the good things of home.

'If you want to live on mealies and Cape plonk, why did you come, eh? Nobody's forcing you to eat it.'

In one predatory swoop, she snatched the plate from under Peg's nose and stood up, staring about for the waiter. A few heads turned.

Laczi and Stacy made motions of restraint, but since they had both seen it coming and had sat there paralysed their protest had the ineffectuality of the doomed. The waiter, alert but anxious, sailed up to their table, inquiring with clasped hands – *Prego?*'

'Is there anything wrong with this steak?' Anya demanded, prodding it rudely with a forefinger.

'Wrong?' he queried, offended. 'What there shoulda be wrong?'

'This lady thinks there's something wrong with it.'

He wrestled with his pride, took a swift look at Anya's face, and opted for diplomacy.

'Very sorry, madam. I take 'eem away.'

'No,' cried Peg in a high alarmed voice, trying to repossess her dinner. 'It's fine. I like it. It's perfectly all right. Please!' Anya tightened her grip on the platter.

The waiter stood baffled.

'Take it away,' commanded Anya, wrenching it from Peg's unnerved grasp. This time the whole restaurant heard. Heads bobbed up all over the place, then, as if in danger of bombardment, ducked back low over their plates, leaning in towards the candles, whispering. 'And bring another.' He hesitated. Anya glared at him. 'I'll pay,' she boomed.

The waiter bowed hurriedly and departed. *Ch'altro fare?* It was an old and valued customer. What was he to do? A volley of Italian went off like cannonshot in the kitchen, before the spring door swung to and muffled it. The chef might be having to take the brunt, but he was not taking it lying down.

A deadly silence fell at the table, broken only by the sounds of Anya eating with violence and breathing heavily.

'Look, Anya,' said Peg hesitantly, 'you know I didn't mean . . .'

'I "know",' retorted Anya through an obstructive jawful of meat. She spat it out disgustedly on to the plate. It tasted like sawdust. 'I "know" that you've done nothing but gripe since you came here. Gripe and bitch and whine. Turn up your nose as if there was a turd under it. Look at you! Look at you turning up your nose! Where's the turd? What is it that offends your precious nose?' With a contemptuous forefinger she flipped Peg's nostrils upwards, driving her head back in fright.

'What've I done, for Christ's sake? I only said . . .'

'Why come six thousand miles, where's the point? If you're going to sit there like a deaf mute and notice nothing? Twittering on about Cape wine, and Cape beef and Cape boutiques, and your fucking department and its fucking infantile politics! Who wants it? Who gives a shit?'

'You did!' exclaimed the astonished Peg, getting some re-inforcement from a justified indignation. 'Who pumped me with questions? You! Isn't that true? Didn't she?' she appealed to the others. 'Who started the Herschel reminiscences? You! You!'

'You're so besotted with yourself and your little world that you can't tell simple politeness from boredom. And then – God save us! – all that fake white-liberal rubbish that you parrot out of the *Argus*, and all the time you're quivering with embarrassment because there are blacks on the trains, and blacks on the stairs, and if you don't watch out there'll be a black in your bed.'

'Oh no you don't!' Peg's voice rose high and clear. 'Not *me*. That's *your* speciality. I leave that to *you*. Don't you come the righteous prig with me, Anya Jevons, when I know, and you know, what a squalid little *kaffir-boetie* you were in your heyday.'

'Out!' roared Anya, rising and pointing to the door. 'Out!' And when Peg sat frozen, she began pelting her with anything that came to hand – potatoes, bread, napkins. A wine-glass overturned with a splintering sound as several waiters converged on the table. In one swift movement, Laczi took Peg's coat from the back of her chair, captured her arm, and marched her grimly through the devastated zone and out the door.

Stacy sat mesmerized and tingling.

'I ama sorry madam,' (he did not sound at all sorry – menacing rather) 'but thees musta be stop. Atta once!' He signalled his troops to close in.

As if by sorcery, the winged Victory turned into a rag doll. With a puff of expelled air, Anya flopped into her chair and sat there immobile. The rest of the room was crackling, but she had gone limp with the laxity of the dead. She was fumbling in her purse with inept fingers.

'Add up the damage,' she said tonelessly, head down over the bag, 'and give me the bill. Here.' She thrust the Diner's Card at him. He took it by its extremest tip, as if avoiding contamination, signed his assistants away, and retreated on patent-leather toes, reassuring with a glance here and a word there, as he passed other tables. The storm had blown over. It had alarmed him less than most. He was not Italian for nothing.

Stacy, though her heart still pounded, felt her self-possession ebbing back along the startled veins. What a performance! She had better stay. Anya had the look of an incompetent general who has been deserted by his troops and knows he has deserved it. Another desertion and her cup would run over.

Several minutes passed. The candle flames in their chimneys of ruby glass grew tall and steady. The murmur of voices and chink of cutlery again lapped quietly against the damascene wallpaper. Soon no trace would remain of the raucous vulgarity that had shamed them all. Anya prodded and shovelled amongst the congealing sauce, before letting her fork fall with a small silver clang. They were taking their time with the bill. Trying to think of extra charges. Well, let them: she was not going to so much as look at it.

It was Stacy's curiosity that was the first thing to surface in the general torpor. It seemed to her simplest to satisfy it, so she asked, 'What's a *kaffir-boetie*?'

Anya raised her head, to measure the spirit of the query. She seemed satisfied.

'Nigger-lover,' she muttered, then, waving the matter away, 'I'll tell you some other time. Thanks.' She took her credit card from the proffered plate. 'Shall we go?'

Stacy downed the last of her wine with regret. It was really rather splendid stuff. What could 'a good Constantia' taste like, if it competed with this?

'I'm ready,' she said, taking her wrap from the waiter with a conciliatory smile . . .

Outside it was raining steadily.

'That's *another* place I can't go back to,' said Anya, as they picked their gloomy way through the puddles. 'Isn't that te-*rrif*ic!'

'It's overpriced anyway,' Stacy remarked sniffily. 'Don't know what you ever saw in it.'

'Thanks for staying.' Anya's smile was undeceived.

'Oh, I didn't "stay". I was just paralysed with embarrassment.' It was half true, but she was also glad she had stayed. She would do it again. But how often? she wondered. There was a nemesis about Anya's affections and rages, from which prudence tended to stand well back. Who could be sure that one would not oneself be the next target?

Laczi, when next seen, was standing well back.

He returned to Princes' Gate after midnight, sodden and ominously silent. When Anya berated him for walking out on her, she was met, not with contrition, but with a tirade that lasted ten minutes and covered a lot of ground. She retired, shaken. Of course he was in a bad mood after having had to comb central London in the dead of a wet night, finding Peg a hotel. All on foot probably – he would never call a cab. The irritation was understandable. But in the end he must see that she had been justified. You couldn't tolerate provinciality and insensitivity on that scale. It was simply an insult to your intelligence. It wasn't as if he'd ever had much time for Peg himself. It was just chivalric humbug. He'd come round.

But he was so far from coming round that he walked back to the studio that night – at 1 a.m., in the rain – and, three days later, had still not reappeared. She could hear him from the shop, working, but he did not emerge. The weather stayed damp and gloomy. It was her move apparently . . .

'I thought you must have shacked up with Peg,' she said breezily, when he pulled back the door, 'to teach me a lesson. Is she here?' She walked in, resuming possession. Bravado seemed the best tactic; and besides, she had no intention of holding a conversation under the cataract formed by Laczi's defective guttering. 'Can I make some coffee?' She pulled off a wet headscarf.

'Sure.' He would not wrangle over a cup of coffee. The silence inside was alive with disseminated drippings where the skylights were less than watertight.

She made for the end of the bench where the gas ring squatted among rafts of dead matches and beads of solder, and began filling the tin kettle. Really, he needed a decent coffee-making machine.

'But when you have made,' he said, 'I think you got a history to tell to me.'

'A history of what?'

'A Cape Town history. A "Kaffir" history, no?'

'Oh that? I don't mind.'

And in truth she didn't. It would be a relief to get it off her chest. It was the one important bit of her youth she had so far suppressed. Well . . . omitted anyway. How, in the course of her excited teenage slumming in the locations she had got mixed up with this black youth (she embarked on the tale) . . . a bit of a rebel, a bit of a spiv, and, as she belatedly discovered, a bit of a crim. Her gang (Peg among them, Laczi deduced) were all peculiarly fascinated by blacks and talked overheatedly about free sex among the races, even going so far as dancing with them at location parties, revelling in what they thought of as the licence of 'dancing with the body instead of the feet' (she gave that phrase in her best mincing Afrikaner English, handing him his coffee). It was partly because it was all *talk*, that Anya despised it so heartily. Besides, she danced better – well enough to bring a glint into the eye of this Thandi, which the others certainly couldn't do . . . Well, things trundled along. He was flatterable and she was provoking. It took its course. In time, she grew reckless, vainglorious, flaunting herself and her rashness. And every imprudence she committed was endlessly dissected and applauded by the gang. Go on, go on, they kept saying. It's good, it's noble, it's moral, it's *liberal*. Keep on doing it for us; it saves us the risk and the bother. Soon she was pregnant. And she was getting some novel views on the ways a good-looking black youth went about maintaining himself in style . . .

And so the little saga unfolded itself. Warming her hands on the coffee-mug, though without denying herself the pleasure of stray embellishments, she tried to give the essential facts. She was doing for him, in the matter of South Africa, what he had done for her, in the matter of Hungary. She found, to her surprise, that she was recovering forgotten detail, and that the new version sounded truer.

'What you've got to grasp,' she said, 'is that when a black clubs a white and hijacks his wallet, he's Being Moral. He's being an Afro Robin Hood. You can even extend the principle to robbing your brother-black. That's moral too: if a black's got anything worth taking it's probably because he's a "sellout", or an informer on retainer from State Security, or just a plain boot-licking Uncle Tom. Money? Possessions? Property? That's all a part of the great white swindle! You'll never get what you're entitled to, so anything you can grab is a blow for justice (not that you believe in justice!).

'It seems light years away. What was I . . .?' Anya did the sums. 'Nineteen, must have been. Perhaps twenty. I couldn't see anything wrong with it. Seemed more honest than what the white conscience-wankers were up to. The ones I knew, anyway, were having themselves cheap thrills at my expense – watching me "build bridges across the great racial divide". Some bridge! Nobody, you know? . . . not one of them had the decency to take me aside and say, "Now look here, chickadee, are you sure you know what you're doing?" Not one! No, they didn't want to interrupt the show – scared they might miss the next thrilling episode, the shits!

'Whereas Thandi . . . Thandi had guts. And he was a realist. He was going to milk the system and live proud. I think I was part of the system for him, though he showed me a good time – in and out of bed – I'm not complaining. But the one thing he wasn't going to feel was responsibility. A black man who feels responsibility for a white woman – her, with all the hounds of hate and retribution slavering at her heels . . . well, he'd have to be going soft in the head. Thandi laughed himself silly when I told him I was pregnant. Went round bragging about it. Showing off my belly, before there was anything to show. It was all quite stupidly dangerous – you know about the "morality" laws? – but I wasn't noticing anything. This was just exactly the kind of excitement I was after. The risk only gave it an edge. So . . .'

She paused, as if some picture was becoming distinct in her mind.

'I think that was why he wanted me on the last job – to see how far he could push me, before I reverted to type. Oh, I'd been hanging about on the perimeter – bits of petty theft and housebreaking – trying to look tough and probably getting in the way. The gangster's moll, signed on so as to make it look more like the movies. But the last one was for real. And I think he rather relished the ring of it: "pregnant white teenager, daughter of prominent journalist, arrested in location gang-battle". When I got in the car – did I say I was driver for the night? – and saw they had guns, I realized, but it was too late then. They were stewed as prunes and steaming with aggravation and they would have used them on me, if I'd given them any reason . . . Well, it was pretty sickening. They beat the other lot to a pulp with pick-handles – including their women – didn't use the guns except to threaten, but I'm not sure it made much difference . . . And then I had to clear out the pockets of these bits of human blubber. Some of them still whimpering and groaning. That about finished it. We nearly got caught on the way home. Thandi went to ground. Didn't see him for weeks. I drove out into the hills and chucked the rings and watches and money and stuff over a cliff, and decided to be a good girl from then on. Keep away from bad Kaffirs.'

'And the child? What happened to the child? You say you were pregnant?'

She stared at him, flabbergasted by the question. Was he mad?

'Think man! One more piece of coloured shit, to be kicked round by the other pieces of coloured shit? *I got rid of it.* Or rather, my very frightened and high-principled Daddy did. I think he must have looked in the Yellow Pages under "I for Infanticide" and then used a pin. I doubt I can ever give birth, thanks to that brandy-sodden butcher. But that's "life" isn't it?' She laughed as if it was – and hurt.

Laczi wrestled with this novel idea: 'You have tried?'

'To give birth? Not really. I generally get a fit of the cold flushes, before it's too late.'

'The cold flushes?' He thought it was something gynaecological he hadn't heard of.

'I go off the idea.'

'Ah!' It was only a monosyllable, but it sounded relieved. 'And Peg – where was she?'

'Precisely. Where *was* she? In the bloody gallery, of course, with the rest of them.'

'This you knew before,' he reminded her.

'This I have been forgetting,' she retorted. 'And I'll tell you what else I've been forgetting. When I was sick as a dog after the insanitary curette-job and my father was scuttling about Pretoria trying to get me out of the country before the Greys caught up with me, the faithful Peg kept at a very safe distance, Ver-y, ver-y safe! In fact she didn't come near me. Not that that made her anything special. They all knew a state-certified leper when they saw one. Pfah!' She made a noise of disgust. 'I suppose you can't blame them.

I wasn't a pretty sight. The leprosy might have been catching for all they knew. I don't blame them.'

Laczi appeared to be pondering the evidence.

'I would blame them,' he pronounced at length, judicially.

That surprised her. She pressed him for his reason.

'I blame anybody,' he said, 'who would commit a political act when he would not be ready to follow home the personal consequence.'

She looked let down: 'But that's not the point. Stuff the politics! It's a personal betrayal, regardless of the politics.'

'Ha!' He pounced on the remark like a retriever on the game he has been searching for. '*That* is your so very big mistake. Over and over I see you do it. You make the personal to bear too much. You load it up with things what it cannot carry. And then when it cracks, you cry out betrayal. How could the miserable Peg be all at once the five hundred impossible things you make her? The moment you start telling me about her, I know that. She will crack. She cannot carry it. And so it happens.'

'So it's my fault now?'

'He looked as if he were about to tear his hair – or hers: 'I do not *care* about "fault"!' he bellowed, rattling the air with clawlike fingers. 'Make it *my* fault if you want. The reason you English are so stupid about these "personal relations" of yours, is because you make so big thing out of them. What *are* these "personal relations" I am every day hearing about? They are a branch of the *social* relations that I never hear about. Everywhere I see it. I think it should be call the English Epidemic. For look! It is like this also with the kids at the art school – they must make at once "personal expression", so they have no time to get a skill, no patience to understand what is structure. I tell them: look! your beautiful souls, what you want so much to express must be express in matter. But they do not want to understand matter. Matter is for peasants, matter is for bricklayers and they are Artists. Personality! I am sick of it. You must understand first the structure!' He moulded the structure in space with his large flexile hands.

'Your Thandi, now . . . with him it was a personal relation, eh? Not a bit! You tell me over in a dozen different ways how it was political first, personal after. And when the political cracks up, all the rest tumbles down. You! you have a big heart and a large mind, you do not go in fear, but you burn it all up on trivia. Personal relations! You are angry with the injustice of life, so what do you do? You fuck a black man! You throw potatoes at Peg! What kind of solution is that? You don't know even who is your enemy. If you find him first, then perhaps you do not waste so many potatoes.'

Anya sniggered: 'I knew the waste of potatoes would offend you, my frugal friend. That's probably what drove me to it.'

'But you do not throw them at *me*! You see what I mean? You do not know who is your enemy.'

'Oh, so it's you?' she jeered.

'No,' he grinned. 'Wrong! I am your friend. I tell to you the truths what the others do not. But,' he fended off the imputation with a raised hand, 'I don't expect no gratitude. I don't do it for no personal reasons. I make contribution only to the general social good.' The gratification this brought him gave a twinkle to his leer of fatuous complacency. Such virtue, he implied, was its own sweet reward.

'My next lot of potatoes,' she remarked sardonically, 'I'll save for you. And that's a promise.'

He positively chuckled with delight. It was as if he could have hoped for nothing better.

It seemed they were reconciled to each other. It seemed they hadn't quarrelled. It seemed they always quarrelled. It seemed that it didn't matter.

As the months passed, Laczi found ways of reconciling his highly developed taste for privacy with his relish for her company, while she found ways of preventing that reconciliation ever becoming secure. It could have been exhausting, infuriating, dispiriting; instead they both thrived on it, enjoying a kind of excess capacity which they were then able to harness for their respective fields of productivity.

After months of neglect, born of boredom, Anya began to lick her business into shape. She brought the books up to date as never before – not, it is true, going so far as to admit seriously the existence of tax inspectors, but far enough to be able to survey her ground of commercial vantage and to identify the places where the screws might be applied. She studied her opposition and discovered where she could undercut them most savagely at least cost to herself. She conned a lighting salesman into replacing all the spotlights in the place free of charge, by graciously permitting him to use publicity stills of the Rotten Orange to advertise his gear (she also managed to secure half a dozen of the big colour blow-ups for her own use).

Intuitively identifying the travelling reps who could least afford to leave without an order, she ground them down to within an inch of their commission. She drew up a table showing the maximum period that her various suppliers would tolerate non-payment and by exploiting this tolerance to the hilt was able to carry greatly increased stocks at no cost whatsoever to herself. One or two weak-kneed wholesalers had got into the horrid double-bind of fearing to supply an order that might never be paid for, but fearing even more to risk (by refusing supply) the much larger sums she already owed them: these wholesalers were favoured with particularly large orders, and delayed payment in excruciating instalments. There was no malice in these transactions: she took the world as she found it.

And she kept up the highest standards of business ethics: she refused to stock a product in which she did not believe, or of which she was not proud. This probity was made practicable by the surprising extent to which a large profit margin *assisted* her belief and her pride in a product: after all, if it were not good in itself, how could it survive such a large mark-up and still sell? And when she found that, mysteriously, she no longer believed in a particular line, in accordance with the same high ethic she made a sacrifice of it to the grateful customers who had come bargain-hunting. Thus what had been an error of taste and judgement when it was not selling, became an act of generosity towards the tasteless but well-meaning public which now bought it. Either way, one was keeping up the standards that one owed to oneself and one's establishment. She had nothing to reproach herself with.

It was not surprising: a system in which value is determined by saleability has the perfection and reciprocity of the circle: nothing can enter it and nothing can violate it. And anyway, it's no more than what the rest of the unscrupulous world is doing. In a world of Boesmas, Juhaczes and Magnuses, fine scruple would be fatuous.

Anya's depredations were not motivated by greed. Except where food was concerned, she was not greedy – and even there, it came over her only in bouts. It was rather her passion for independence, her steely determination to be nobody's pawn or clog, that made her an entrepreneur; and conversely, it was her contempt for those too feeble to achieve such independence which enabled her cheerfully to exploit them. According to the evolutionary morality of economic survival, if they couldn't get their stupid little affairs in order, the failure demonstrated their feebleness. Like many self-made persons (and they are by far the most interesting kind) Anya could never be persuaded that there were elements in individual success which were not necessarily of the individual's making. To say so was simply to confess to feebleness.

In this simple, lurid world, Anya bustled and thrived.

But she had one problem. Long before the shop had begun to echo to the sounds of the mason's hammer, Anya had been grooming Stacy to take over as manager. Almost from the beginning of the enterprise, she had foreseen the day when she would be unable, literally, to endure another hour in the place. It was exciting, it was hectic, it was fascinating . . . and on certain, damp, grey evenings, it bored her to extinction. So she had been laying contingency plans. With some reliable person in charge, she calculated, she could syphon off enough to live on, without the tedium of actually working. And then she could do all the enjoyable creative things that had gone into abeyance since her teens – read more books, take up the 'cello again perhaps? or singing-lessons? Stacy, of course, might not *want* the job – might have other, more independent plans. But that was all right: it simply meant that the grooming for the job would have to include *making* her want it.

Anya kept this idea to herself, so she thought, but Stacy was perfectly aware of it, and sensed that they were headed on a collision course. Her tutelage had been all very well in the stagnant lull that followed graduation – indeed it had been very welcome! She had had nothing more definite to propose and she had needed to get clear of her father. And her two-and-a-bit years as a frock-shop flunkey had been fun, no denying it. But she too had had her previsions of tedium – particularly of late since Laczi had monopolized much of Anya's free time, so that there was less of it to spare for her young friend. Though the girl's contingency plans were nowhere near as fully drawn as Anya's, Stacy was not proposing to become the adjunct of her friend's convenience. That would be gratitude run mad.

She began to cultivate Magnus's company – rather to Anya's disgust: Magnus might be used (he had contacts in the club-and-party world), but befriended? Surely not! And the notion that the girl might actually be sleeping with the little toad was repugnant to her. That would be a lapse of taste that was almost criminal. Had they not agreed that Magnus's rating was an irretrievable Two? Only two notches above faggot-zero and one above impotent flat calm? Bed with that? She would not believe it of Stacy!

She determined, however, that *she* would not be the first to speak.

No one was going to accuse *her* of an unwholesome fascination with personal relations. It was not her style to go nosing about in someone else's love life. If Stacy wanted to spend her nights helping Magnus to get his pecker up, that was her affair. Meanwhile the sight of Magnus's smug buttocks winking about her shop, or disappearing up the road beside Stacy's long legs – 'Just slipping out for a quick sarnie. Back soon!' – was turning her stomach. For all his compact, hard-chested, narrow-waisted, over-groomed presentableness, there was something about the Magnus walk that could only disgust. He claimed to be a regular weight-trainer, but he was a jellyfish for all that. It was as if he had some vile grey spongey substance where other men had joints. He slithered into rooms. He flobbered and flumped all over chairs, and he talked endlessly in that rapid, insinuating, confidential marshmallow voice of his – so swift to compassion! So slow to wrath! So full of soul! So saturated in cunning! And now the viperous creature was wrapping himself about Stacy! If it had been her concern, she might have permitted herself to hate him.

But she had other concerns. She must look to the future – a future very probably without Stacy. She plunged afresh into the commercial jungles.

In all this Kovacs appeared to take no interest – perhaps out of cunning, or incomprehension, or feebleness. He was careful, anyway, not to imply that the lack of interest came from a mind intent on higher things. He offered neither comment nor suggestion. She would not, in any case, have endured his intervention – let alone his morality. The Rotten Orange was her passport to personal freedom – freedom even from him – and was therefore sacrosanct.

But probably he was just too preoccupied.

The Prophet was almost fully roughed out. He had worked painstakingly, making each cut with as much care as if it was to be the last . . . as it very well could be: without warning, a plane, a surface might declare itself complete. The stone would tell him when that moment came. The original maquette had already been left far behind in these progressive yieldings to the suggestions of the material. That, actually, was where it had all begun – with a yielding: if there had been no flaw in the stone, the figure would not now be standing with its head thrust forward at an angle that was anatomically impossible, but expressively potent. The need to support that head-mass had suggested in turn the columnar treatment of the draperies. As the Prophet gripped his staff in a knotty claw, the great concave sweep of his cloak emerged from the rounded hump of the boulder that was his back – and this was so because every time the sculptor had taken a tool to it, he had sensed that the boulder he had first loved was the matrix of his forms, and had best not be disturbed. A boulder therefore it remained, at that point.

There was a period when he fretted about the Prophet's rear end, fearing some failure of spatial imagination, but now as he dinged away at buttock and loin and thigh he became convinced of the wholeness of his conception. The hump-backed seer had a nobility of muscle in his hinder parts which was worthy of the god he served. And the dark purbeck, even under its bloom of powdery dust, promised just the right degree of grainy substantiality.

Meanwhile a swarm of competing conceptions buzzed about his ears. Re-creating for Anya the Hungary of Háy and Kádár had, like a day of sharp sun, given wings to many crawling, sluggish thoughts. As an artisan, he distrusted literary inspiration; but that tattered volume of Radnóti kept blossoming in his brain in intensely visual, bodily shapes.

Most of these shapes were floundering about in the roadside mud – the road the poet tramped on the long forced march from Serbia to Gyor. Grey indomitable figures they were, calling to each other out of smoke or fog:

> A fool he is who – poleaxed – rises to walk again,
> Ankles and knees alone moving, itinerant in pain . . .
> 'Don't leave me, friend, yell at me: I'll get up
>   off the ground.'

This one was humped and crawling, pushing at the slurry of mud (criss-crossed by tyre- and tank-tracks) with incapable ramrod knees. But he would get up. The will is indestructible, if futile.

Another, on the farther side of fatigue and despair, trudged through the same slurry. His wrists were chained to companions who were not there. 'Keep walking, you, the Death-condemned!' And he does. The automatism of exhaustion.

Another is being executed:

> His body – which was taut
> As a cord at snapping-point – spun as it fell,
> Shot in the neck.

A kind of helmeted beast leaps the prisoner from the front, smothering him with its belly, arching over his skull to place a pistol at its base. The pair reel and topple before the inevitable groundward crash – jaguar and prey. The Execution.

> I muttered to myself beneath my breath: 'This
> Is how you will end. Lie still. Lie still.
> Now patience is flowering into death.'
> '*Der springt noch auf,*' said someone over me.
> ('This one's still kicking.')
> Blood on my ears was drying, caked with earth.

This one was still moving – but only just – a minimal muddy survival, the legs thrusting (or maybe merely twitching), the body broken beyond repair.

There were other inhabitants of this world – a peasant woman huddled into the angle of two walls, fists thrust in mouth; a baby, a grotesque *putto*, cast forth naked on the slime of the world he would never have chosen. And there was the horror itself of realizing such things:

> I started up in terror and sat there – in my sleep
> Mumbling, then declaiming, screaming unintelligibly,
> And I flung my arms out wide, as a bird ruffled with fear
> Will beat its wings when, without warning, a shadow
> sweeps the garden . . .

Before Laczi had time to reflect, he was compiling an exhibition. It cohered. It bred. Clay – no, rather plaster hacked into bronze it had to be. These folk were of hewn bronze, and so was the tank-scarred mud he visualized so vividly – seen last on the streets of Budapest, probably, where cobbles had been prised up for missiles and barricades.

He made a couple of waxes. It was viable.

Though he disapproved of such behaviour, he began to use the models at the Thursday life class for the project. Leaving the students to tag along, skimping their instruction, greedily, surreptitiously he filled his sketchbook. Already in his mind they were halfway to bronze: four, five, six figures – some of them large. Perhaps he would have to swallow his pride and apply to Amanda for subsidy. Time would show. Meanwhile, he went home to the

Prophet, to the maquettes, and to Anya. He was living in a peculiar ferment which was satisfactory to neither of them, but which could not be relinquished.

Occasionally he woke in the night, like the man in the poem, streaming with sweat, choking in the grip of nightmare. Shouting in Hungarian (that language of ill-omen), he seemed to be giving orders – orders which *she* could not understand and *he* could not remember afterwards. There was much that lay unknown between them, perhaps unknowable. The wings of a great fear.

The young man presented his card:

---

detritus

advance-guard of the avant-garde

exhibitions

permanent collection

giles borthwick: director

. . . and a Cork Street address.

Kovacs inspected it, handed it back.

The bearer was well enough dressed in his hacking-style suit, his purple-striped shirt with gleaming white collar and cuffs, to be the director in person. Some whizz-kid of the art world. Squandering the family fortunes, probably, to buy himself a reputation as an aesthete.

Kovacs thought it best to put him out of his misery: 'I think you come to the wrong address,' he said. 'This here is the *old* guard . . . you know? what comes from behind to kick the avant-garde in the pants?'

'Very salutary for us all,' said the young man affably. 'That's partly why I'm here. We're planning an 'Artists of the Fifties' show – one of those "whatever-happened-to-so-and-so?" events. And you are high on the list.'

'As one of the so-and-sos what has gone missing?'

'Precisely.' He had such a grave air of bestowing favours that the sarcasm fell harmlessly to the ground. The sculptor's quickness to understand clearly pleased him.

'And who,' inquired stolid Laczi, 'will pay the foundry?' It seemed the simplest way of terminating the discussion.

'Foundry?'

'Casting-bills, you know. I work in bronze.'

'That's negotiable.'

'You mean *I* pay, you negotiate?'

'Not necessarily. We can make an advance against sales.'

Laczi shook his head with aged sagacity: 'When I want for to make myself a millstone,' he said, 'I do it with my own two hands. For what am I a sculptor?'

Giles Borthwick indicated with his hands and eyebrows how well he understood the difficulty. 'Can we at least talk? See what might be arranged? I should very much like to see your current work, if you don't mind.'

'Why I should mind?' Laczi inquired, more of himself than his visitor.

'It's not entirely an idle request,' the young man pursued. 'We do buy direct into the permanent collection from time to time.'

Laczi let his surprise show: 'So! You must be well loaded! And also so new?'

'We opened last year. Yes, we do ... ah ... have funds.' He gave a smile of modest discretion. 'Would you mind if I asked ... er ...' Anxiety peeped for a moment through the serene exterior. 'You're not under contract to any dealer?'

'Since 1970, is nobody.'

'No shows planned?'

'Here, yes,' Laczi tapped his forehead. 'But here only.'

'May I see what you have?'

'Please.'

There was quite a lot to be seen – particularly from the disastrous 1970 exhibition, 'Warriors', which had scarcely sold at all. Old Fenwick's bronzes these were, if each had his own. Perhaps he should send him one as a retirement present.

Borthwick paced discreetly from sculpture to sculpture, cocking his head and canting his torso at the best angle to take them in; made notes with a pencil chained to a small marbled book; took his chin in his hands; lowered two fingers into a waistcoat pocket; most conspicuously did *not* jingle small change in his pocket. He knew what was due to art. 'Previous exhibition?' he inquired, and jotted down the reply. 'Early work? . . . 1962? Interesting. You began in abstraction and moved to the figurative? . . . I do so agree: the terms are approximate at best . . . Now I do sincerely admire that wolf: '*farouche*', as the French say – both fierce and shy . . . And this?' He had returned to the Prophet, around which they had been circling for the past half-hour. He now gave it his full attention.

'Now that,' he announced, 'given the right space and the right presentation, would make an excellent centrepiece, don't you think?'

Without some notion of the circumference, Kovacs found himself unable to say. He had not got round, indeed, to envisaging it being looked at by other eyes at all.

'I must say I'm delighted,' said the delighted Borthwick, completing another turn, 'to see that someone has looked at his Epstein without being overwhelmed by panic. There are so many who . . .' He completed the sentence with a deprecating hand. Kovacs gathered that he did not much like Epstein.

'It is not of course *à la mode*,' he conceded to some invisible caviller, 'but . . .' he held up a staying hand, '. . . fashions, after all are not mandatory.'

Though clearly expected to congratulate Borthwick on this discovery, Laczi maintained his silence.

'I am wondering,' said Detritus's enterprising young director, running thoughtful fingers through his hair, as people do when wondering, 'I am wondering, you know, whether you haven't enough unexhibited work for a one-man? Or could have.' He glanced up at the Prophet with a shade of nervousness. 'This has too much substance – too much "mass" – for a mixed exhibition: the other work would suffer. Whereas with your own work it would blend. Are there other things, as it were, "in the pipeline"?'

Laczi, though not greatly interested in the blending qualities of his work, or indeed in pipelines, explained some of the Radnóti projects, declined to produce sketches, mentioned again the high cost of casting, but did not absolutely rule out the possibility of reaching an arrangement for a one-man show in, say, a year's time? His benefactor seemed pleased by this outcome and showed it by putting a second pair of fingers into his other waistcoat pocket and drumming gently on his ribs. He had not, of course, expected any definite commitment at such short notice, but he was sure some sort of informal contract could be drawn up on this basis. Buttoning up his notebook with its neat snap-fastener, he bowed and departed.

Laczi, left to reflect in peace, concluded that the 'Forgotten Artists of the Fifties' exhibition had been a front – a ploy to abash him with his own unimportance – and that Giles Borthwick, director, having indulged his egotism as patron and entrepreneur, would promptly forget the whole affair. What business had the outrider of the avant-garde hobnobbing with Old Testament prophets and executed Hungarian prisoners. It was hard to imagine a setting more inhospitable to his kind of sculpture than the sort of gallery 'Detritus' appeared to be.

Instead, three days later, a draft contract was delivered by hand, offering a guarantee to cover half the casting-charges. The exhibition was scheduled for the next August. Mixed up in Laczi's shock and incredulity there was an inexcusable elation. But he took it philosophically: 'Well, since already I am half corrupted,' he thought, 'I suppose I had better apply to my wife to finish the job. Who knows? They might all sell.'

SIX

Devils

'What're you doing here, Magnus?' Anya, struggling to extract the latchkey which had again jammed in the lock, made no attempt to veil her distaste for the figure she saw distributing itself over the sofa in her drawing-room.

'Talking to Stacy,' he replied, as if it should have been obvious, and implying that he certainly wouldn't come here to talk to *her*. At the same time he cautiously lowered the leg that had been stretched out horizontally along the sofa, then interlaced his palms behind his neck, to illustrate his nonchalance. She contemplated this intrusive bug, wondering whether it mightn't stink if crushed.

'Hi!' Stacy's head bobbed round the corner of the door, then disappeared. 'Magnus has brought some wine. Want some?'

'Take them to your own room, please. I need the desk.'

The desk, though it bulged with papers, was never used.

'OK,' chirped Stacy. 'Come on up, Magnus. We can have our party in the dorm.'

They sidled past Anya as she stood partially blocking the exit, bottle and glasses clinking. There came a muffled explosion of laughter from the first landing. Giggling idiots! She sniffed suspiciously. They'd been smoking pot. That was the excuse, she supposed, for the imbecile grins. Why was it always the feeble-witted that insisted on making their wits feebler by artificial means? And Stacy knew perfectly well the stuff was banned in this house. Lawless in most respects, Anya drew the line at drugs. If she was going to get raided for something it would be for something she enjoyed – and the ritual of the sacred Joint had always left her cold, sober, and censorious.

She tipped the prohibited ash into a bin. Really that girl would have to go. After all that had been done for her, she was turning into a comprehensive bore. Unfortunately there was no replacement for her at the shop. What a bloody mess!

She flung a few magazines into the pile in the corner, picked up a half-drained glass, drained it, and pulled a face. Was that the best the fastidious Magnus could manage? This piss of an anaemic gnat? Still grimacing, she replaced the glass on the marble-topped table. They were all turning their backs on her. The whole damn lot. Kovacs with his eternal stone-chipping. Stacy with her girly randiness. No fidelity in any of them. She was going to have to look elsewhere for a life.

Go back to Cape Town perhaps? Pick up the threads. It always tempted her as the gloomy English winter set in. At least the sun shone there, and it was home. Why not go home? . . . Home to Daddy? Home to Mummy – who would whine about how she didn't know why *she* had to make do with *two* servants when everyone else had *ten*! Wasn't it giving them *employment*? And wasn't that what they were supposed to want? she would demand. And how *hard* it was, dear, having to live by Daddy's queer conscience, when you couldn't for the life of you (could Anya?) understand – you really couldn't – what he wanted the government to do! After all, you couldn't give everything *back* to the blacks, could you? . . .

Home to that? And home to Peg?

Morosely she rummaged in the drinks cabinet, poured herself a vermouth and flumped in a chair, chin on chest, spreadeagled legs rested on their heels. (Nice girls don't sit in a chair like that, dear!) Shit and shit again! Turning out her pockets for the packet of Sobranies she found the leaflet, shook out its folds and refreshed her memory. 'Anti-Apartheid League. Hampstead branch. "The struggle in Namibia". Meeting to be addressed by prominent SWAPO guerilla leader. Members only.' Maybe Laczi was right. Maybe this – or something like it – would provide the larger impersonal theatre she needed. She was so sick of little people and the messes they made.

She smoked in silence for a while.

But that was as bad as going back to South Africa. All the old types – like the fierily fanatical girl who had contacted her about the league: there she'd stood, brave and bristling with the statistics of outrage, while her face, in its pinched and desperate lines, recorded the ravages of a failed expiation. Nothing smelt ranker than a sick white conscience when it started to go off. And what were they mixing in for, the fools? It wasn't their business any more. It was the blacks' battle. And the *baases* who had lived off the fat of the land for generations would just have to go down with the ship in the end.

Nobody would have time to sift *their* precious consciences for redeeming scruples, when 'the day of bloody reckoning' came. They might as well spare themselves the effort.

Unless, of course (her nose wrinkled with plausible suspicion), it was in order to *hasten* that ecstatic consummation that they worked. It was one balm for a corrosive self-hatred, she supposed, to throw yourself bodily into the purifying flames of the final holocaust, and be consumed scruple and all. Anya's view of political motive tended to discount avowed aims in order to fasten on the unavowable, which explained all.

Her hand closed on a six-inch bronze warrior, dark-dapple-green like moss-agate, with his sturdy little rectangular shield and his squat indomitable helmet. It was something she had admired – like royalty, and like royalty, she had been given it. She looked at it where it lay in her palm. Always battles. Battles and embattlement and weariness of spirit. (There was no face under the helmet, just a jutting jaw and a prow of skull cutting through space to no destination.) That was all Laczi seemed to know about. There was no salvation to be had from him. She turned it over, put it down.

The day, the evening, life . . . everything was at its lowest ebb. There was nothing you could think of doing that wasn't stunningly futile.

She dragged her leaden body to bed with the deliberation of one who never intended to rise from it again.

She stayed there, in fact, for three days, morose, monosyllabic, sleeping away vast torpid tracts of time for which she had no use. She was not ill. Illness brings with it the complementary notion of cure. This was something worse than illness.

So for three days Stacy ran the boutique single-handed, quite enjoying, in fact, the self-determination and the freedom from interference. In the evening she skittered in, fetched something for Anya from the take-away, going about her affairs with a chirpiness that might have been aggravating, had Anya been noticing. But she was quite sunk in her own depression. Of Laczi there was no sign.

On the fourth morning, Stacy found her in the kitchen, studying the washing up.

'Has Magnus been staying here?'

'I pay rent . . .'

'Has he?' Anya's voice rose menacingly.

'Yes. What of it?'

'We agreed . . .'

'Who "agreed"'? *You* decreed, more like it.'

'If you don't like the terms . . .'

'You're right. I don't.'

'. . . you can get out, d'you hear?'

'I hear. You needn't shout.'

'And when he's gone, you can sterilize the sheets.'

Stacy's jaw dropped so far that she seemed unlikely to retrieve it. The enormity of this woman could still amaze her. She gasped for speech: 'You're incredible! I don't believe it! Anything else you'd like me to do? Lick your boots? Lie prostrate and be walked on? You're worse than my father – and I thought *he* was the last word in insane jealousy.' The girl's eyes were blazing. 'I sleep with whom I damn well like, you stupid old cow!'

'You can sleep with the hunchback of Notre Dame, as far as I'm concerned, but you can do your copulating between somebody else's sheets. You're out. As of now. *And* you're fired.'

'You just beat me to it. By seconds.' Stacy stamped her foot in fury. 'Get . . . get knotted!'

She stormed out and up the stairs to her room. Anya could hear the clash of drawers, and doors banging, also something suspiciously like the sound of sobbing – but she blocked her ears to that. She wasn't wading into the snivelling quagmire of Sympathy. Even less, Remorse. They passed each other grim-faced on the main stairs a couple of times, but when Anya returned from the shop that evening, the only trace of her lodger was a forlorn stack of cartons outside the flat door, awaiting collection.

She went upstairs. The bedroom was bare and echoed unnaturally when she opened the door to inspect. Only a faint whiff of the musky perfume the girl used hung on the air. Anya turned the key in the lock.

She resisted the temptation to go straight round to the studio. With the exhibition date fixed for the following summer, Laczi had gone into a frenzy of activity. Tonight he and Bill were to pour one of the smaller bronzes. She wouldn't get three words out of him. Besides, the momentum of her own repudiations was beginning to frighten her: it could easily carry her so far beyond any possible destination that there would be no return. Kovacs too she would send to hell – if she had to – but not yet – only when there was no other course left. She went to bed . . .

She woke in the blackness created by the heavy drapes. Her heart was thumping dully. It was impossible to guess the time, indeed the notion of time seemed absurd in the preternatural stillness. But now she was sure of it: 'he' was standing in the corner of the room, beside the mirror – the black man. She couldn't see him of course, because he was black. But he was there. It was no use calling out. There was nobody left to hear. She had sent them all away. And she knew him of old: now that he had come he would stay all night – there was no sending *him* away.

Her breathing had become harsh and difficult. The more air she gulped down into her lungs, the less breath she seemed to have. She heard her own drowning gasps above the cavernous knocking of the overtaxed heart, which seemed to be accelerating insanely. Numbing cold was seeping up her arms and legs, a chill quicksilver sweat which only gave a keener edge to consciousness. Inch by inch, he was edging her into the vortex – forcing her down, fully conscious, into the fear of fear from which more fear was born, dropping helplessly in an endless void. The blood clamoured in her ears, deafening all reason. Unconsciousness, the death of the mind, had become the ultimate blessing and the ultimate terror. But the nearer she approached it, the further it lay from her.

If only he would move! If only he would cross the pallid blotch of the mirror and let her see him, perhaps then she could take a grip. But he was too cunning for that. He was cunning beyond all cunning. That was why he did nothing. That was why he stood in the empty space beside the mirror for the rest of the night, the black devil who terrified her because he was not there.

The spiral of hyperventilation is a common medical phenomenon. The excess of oxygen produces a chill, which produces fear, which produces an excess of adrenalin which, in the absence of any object for the fear, generates more fear and thus more adrenalin. The escalation can be very rapid. It can feel like the onset of death. It is the normal metabolic process, but reversed – so that, instead of the stimulus producing an endocrinal response, the endocrinal response, self-generated out of nothing, creates the stimulus which is not there. It is all very simple. It is a fear of nothing, from which devils are born. In well-lit rooms our healers may set it in a book.

The light was very slow to penetrate the dark room where Anya lay, gasping – as she truly believed – for her life. It would have come no quicker if she had been instructed in the aetiology of phobic anxiety. For what was it that first set her gasping for breath? Where was the first fear born? Was it a fear truly groundless? Or was there in her nature a ground so ample as to be unthinkable?

A stiff, pained little note arrived from Stacy, giving a forwarding address and requesting a week's outstanding wages. The money was despatched, together with a note not at all stiff and rather more painful (for the recipient, at least), in which Anya allowed herself to square some other accounts before her purpose cooled. She did not particularly intend to wound. She just wanted a termination which could not be mistaken for anything else.

Next she advertised for a replacement at the Rotten Orange, and was swamped with applicants. It made her wonder why she had hovered for so long. Stacy had not been indispensable at all.

Kim, the new assistant, was dark and extremely pretty, with wide brown eyes and a wide soft mouth. In repose, her features fell naturally into a smile that was half cheesecake, but half unaffected charm as well. Because Kim believed, as Stacy and Anya had never done, in the power of a dress to chasten and subdue all but the most recalcitrant circumstances, she was an excellent saleswoman. She gave to the purchase of a new skirt the dignity of high art and the solemnity of religion, and Anya watched her at work with a wonderment which was *not* going to develop into satire. Certainly not! Such dedication was too valuable to be mocked. (Laczi, who had shown some inclination that way, was notified of the fact.) The only problem was that Anya found it impossible to have a rational conversation with Kim. The daily drama of the changing-cubicle, the daily comedy of life in Mayfair had vanished like smoke and she was left to console herself with the steady rise in the daily takings. Since she was still thinking in terms of eventual escape, this consolation was not to be despised. Kim was a treasure, a real treasure!

One evening, as she was clearing the till and bagging the money, a face that seemed unpleasantly familiar appeared first at one window, then at the other, and finally peered through the door into the darkened shop. He must have made her out back there in the gloom, for there came a rap on the glass, and a rattling of the handle. Before he knew it, the fool would be setting off the alarm. She went to the door.

'Oh,' she said, taking a step backwards. It was Stacy's lunk of a father.

'Can I see you for a sec?' He was already halfway through the door, staring about him in a heavy stunned fashion.

'She's not here.'

He looked puzzled, disoriented.

'No, of course not,' he said, coming to. 'It's you I want to talk to. I know . . .' he went on, putting up concessive palms, 'I didn't make a very good impression last time. I wouldn't blame you if you wanted to chuck me out again. Temperatures run a bit high in our family . . . but that's no reason,' he reminded himself, 'why other people should have to put up with it.'

'No,' said Anya implacably, 'it isn't.'

'No,' he nodded, as if pleased by her assent, 'but the way things are now . . .' As he moved forward he appeared to stumble, then sank without invitation on to one of the bentwood chairs, lowering his head between his hands. Anya presumed this was another of his acts – a heart-rending alternative to the maniacal raging he had turned on for them last time. Or perhaps he was drunk. The big clumsy body with its over-large hands and feet moved her no more than did the haunted eyes that sought hers from the swarthy pock-marked face.

'She's going to be all right,' he said, as if this was the sentence Anya must have been waiting for.

'I dare say,' Anya remarked, with bitter flippancy. 'When wasn't she?'

'When I say "all right" . . .' He ran aground for a moment. 'What *is* "all right" anyway? God knows . . . What I mean is, they got the stomach-pump to her in time.'

Anya leapt aside as if she had been stung.

'What?' she yelled. 'The silly little bitch! She didn't try to . . .' She had lost the use of her jaw.

He saw his mistake.

'I thought you knew, I thought it was you that took her in . . .'

'The stupid cunt! What did she want to do that for?' She talked as if the girl had made an attempt on her, Anya's life.

'I don't know. I thought you'd be able to tell me. That's why I'm here. Please, what's it about? Is it us? Is it me? I've not been too brilliant a parent lately. Tell me what you think.'

'You'd better ask her,' muttered Anya.

'I can't,' he groaned, and it sounded like a permanent, not a temporary impossibility. 'And anyway she's too shaky to be put through it now. But you – you've been a . . . if you don't mind me saying so, a kind of mother to her since . . . since we "drove her out"

114

(I suppose that's what it amounts to). Does she talk about us? Eh? What does she say? You can tell me. Don't beat about the bush. I'm past shame. People are what they have to be, and I'm no exception. There are no secrets any more, so why pretend? Not after this.' Anya stood locked in stupefaction.

'Please!' his hands appealed to her. 'There's no one I can turn to. Her mother and I . . . we don't talk. Even less after this, you can count on it. She'll make it all my fault, of course, but she won't say a word. She's "loyal", you see.' He laughed with extravagant bitterness, a big lacerated laugh that jangled Anya's nerves. 'Ha! My loyal wife! Let me talk to you please. I think you might understand. Nobody else will.'

'Don't be too sure.'

'You're her friend, I know. It's only natural. But you don't sit in judgement, not in eternal frozen judgement. I can see that. I'm not stupid. Have you got anything I can drink? I'm all done in.'

He looked so annihilated, she thought she might allow him this concession.

'Brandy do?'

'Just the ticket.'

She went to the closet and the first-aid cabinet, and filled him a tumbler. He poured half the fiery stuff straight down and gasped his thanks.

'It's how I keep going,' he explained, and immediately plunged off again: 'The silly bitches won't see how I love them, that's the trouble. I have my own peculiar way of doing it, granted, but they won't see it. They call it bullying.'

'They'd "see" better if you didn't black their eyes.'

Again he laughed that naked, frightening laugh.

'It's my only way through, girl. Got to get through the wall of silence somehow. What else have they left me? Do you know how silent a house can be, with three women who won't admit you exist? Have you felt that? No, of course you haven't. You don't do it to each other, do you? Only to your men. And then when they break out and smash a bit of furniture, you get your heads together in a corner and twitter away about brutality – haven't I seen it! . . . I'm sorry.' He gave a sigh that must have emptied his lungs of all air. 'This is stupid. It's not you I'm talking to. Just a piece out of the never-ending monologue. I'm friendless, that's the trouble. Can only punch and kick and curse and blame somebody else. And talk to myself, like now.'

He got to his feet. His whole movement was shambling and unco-ordinated. How he must have been provoked over the years by Stacy's gazelle-like elegance! Anya found herself wrung by an unprecedented and quite unforeseen compassion. It wasn't that he was dying. That didn't touch her – it was unreal. It was that, given every sufficient reason, he was still refusing to die.

'Thanks for the drink,' he said, grasping her hand in both his before she had offered it. 'You've been a brick. But there's nothing you can do. Even less than I can. Never mind. That's the way it is. Sorry to have bothered you.'

He released her; but she still felt constrained to something.

'If I were you,' she said, meeting his haggard gaze properly for the first time, 'I wouldn't take all the blame on myself. There are a few other shits around who've had a hand in it.'

'Ah no,' he waved it away. 'No. I appreciate the gesture, but you know better. You know better. Goodbye.'

She let him out and a moment later heard a car start up outside with a roar and a squeal of tyres. The way he drove out of the court and round into Mount Street, he must have felt his life-expectancy had sunk to zero.

She was shaking all over, like someone in shock. What did she have to go making admissions of responsibility for? Why had she joined him in his obscene games of guilt and self-flagellation? Nobody was responsible for anyone else. Nobody!

And she'd forgotten to find out which hospital!

She snatched up her coat, banged the till shut, noticed the money-bags on the counter, rammed them into the first-aid cabinet and left the shop. Halfway up the court she remembered she'd also forgotten the burglar alarm. Dammit! They could have the lot and welcome! She strode ahead, ignoring traffic as she crossed roads, and driving unwary pedestrians against walls and into gutters. Turning a corner into Berkeley Square she ran head-on into someone. It was Magnus. He took a step backwards and glared at her.

'Oh it's you,' he said, in a voice rich with hatred. 'I was just coming to find you.'

He waved a piece of paper at her which she guessed, rather than saw, to be her letter. 'I hope you're pleased with your work.' He bared his teeth at her. 'I hope it pleases you, what you've done this time, eh? As if the kid hasn't enough to cope with, without you – you callous bitch!'

Anya's wild ferment of feeling congealed instantly. Without

warning she was ice-cold and ice-hard. She looked him over from head to foot, her lip curling.

'Just tell her from me,' she said in withering tones, 'to try and do it *properly* next time, there's a good boy.'

She spun on her heel, putting distance between herself and Magnus's distorted, lurid face. She no more knew where she was going now than she had known a moment before, but this time she ran, as if from the scene of a crime. And as she ran a diabolic laughter bubbled in her throat.

When Laczi went to answer the batterings at his door, he found her on the verge of hysterics.

For the next few days she stayed in the studio and consented to be nursed back into some kind of calm. She told him it all – voluminously, obsessively pouring it out. He was repelled by what she had done, could find no way of condoning it, but he was also fascinated. The scale of the havoc she wrought, the area of blasted devastation . . . it was impossible not to be a little impressed. The size of her affection for Stacy too – an affection now perverted and laid waste – was plain enough to him. The rough tough manner need fool no one: she had loved her like a daughter, attending her progress with all the anxious proprietorial fussiness of maternity. But she was not ready yet to own it. She reported the father's suggestion to that effect as some kind of impertinent outrage. Clearly she did not know what to do with her passion for moulding other lives, especially young lives, and preferred to pretend it did not exist.

When Laczi allowed himself to look into their future – and he did it as little as possible – he felt desperation, mostly. He would not desert her now, he knew that – but the prognosis for such loyalty was gloomy. His heart sank when he learned about the black man in the darkened bedroom. She told it unemotionally and with great precision. It was not that she was unhinged. She was clarity itself. But that only made it worse. There was a devil in her very sanity, and he had never intended to set up house with the devil. Superstitition and nightmare were anathema to him – the phantasmagoria of romantic indiscipline and excess, he judged them. Yet here it was, being brought right home to his hearth.

The worst thing was that, in all his unrelenting fidelity, there was very little warmth. He found her, in her troubles, as ugly as she clearly found herself. It wasn't just the matted hair, the dirty

117

dressing-gown, the smudged and blackened eyes with which she punished herself and the world; the sluttishness revealed a hobbled, haggard soul in which hope appeared to have died.

And then, one day, for no discernible reason, her spirits revived. Torpor, gloom, resentment took wing with the early-morning birds. She was up before he was, clattering about downstairs, stoking the studio stove, and singing. Porridge, she informed him loudly as he dressed, porridge was what they all needed. Low spirits were a consequence of malnutrition. You needed a solid base for the day's activities. A canny race, those Scots. She didn't know why she hadn't realized it before: she was suffering from a porridge-deficiency.

By the time he arrived, the pot-bellied cast-iron stove was beginning to glow a dull red, she had so fanned and befuelled it. He sat down in the comfortable circle of heat, while she, dutifully pecking him on the brow, set the steaming stuff before him.

'Great, isn't it?' she purred, tucking in with gusto.

'Amazing,' he replied noncommitally. 'You can feel how it is doing you good.'

'All the way down!' she concurred with enthusiasm. He could not read her tone. Here was another Anya.

Having washed up and set the pot to soak, she sailed round the corner to the shop, still mildly effervescent.

Well, whatever it portended, there was an immense weight off his mind. He worked furiously all day and in the evening, gratified with his progress, took her to the Live and Let Live, to have a bar snack and possibly meet some of the art-school crowd. Anya, dressed with the kind of regal nonchalance that attracts eyes without exciting envy, was unrecognizable as the same person who had sought refuge with him a few days back. Picking their way to the bar to order, he felt pleased, proud, vindicated, having her there with him.

Someone dark and bearded seemed to be signalling further down the bar. With her elbow and chin she directed his attention. He glanced up, stared, then exploded with wonder, his arms flung wide in the gesture of expansive welcome which revealed, occasionally, how much he must have scaled himself down to fit safely into British drawing-rooms: 'Karoly!'

'Lajos!'

In the surprised space cleared by their shouts, they embraced, laughing and clapping each other on the back, falling at once into a rapid exchange of questions in Hungarian: Karoly! You, in London? Since when? Why? And what are you doing? Me? I live near here.

What? A recital? When? Tickets? But of course – first thing in the morning! Was it not amazing? And how had Karoly come to be let out of school? Must have been a very good boy.

'No,' said Karoly, smiling broadly, 'just a very good 'cellist.'

'Ah,' Laczi agreed with warmth, 'but that is nothing new.'

He must meet Anya. Come . . .

The evening so warmly begun showed no sign of cooling as the party filled out. Bill and Bea, Annabel, a young instructor and a couple of students from the art school turned up. Conversation, conducted in a crazy mare's nest of cross-talk, was possible only in raised voices. You answered questions intended for other people, relayed the answers, shouted your own comments, bumping and butting against your companions in the tangle of invincible cross-purposes. The friend, the very good 'cellist, swallowed without trace in the *mêlée*, surfaced from time to time, smiling at anybody and everybody. This was far better than he had expected of the chilly British.

Anya collected and devoured her chicken and chips without noticing she had done so. Her wine-glass seemed to be perennially empty and perennially refilled. The rounds she insisted on paying for would have damped the spirits of a more prudent drinker, but she just dug deeper into the bottomless purse containing the day's takings. She had, actually, a fleeting impulse to scatter the remainder on the table and set fire to it, as a small burnt offering to the convivial gods. But something or other distracted her. It was very hot and airless inside. She fanned herself with a menu-card.

They were attracting the attention of a knot of youths standing by the door that led to the toilets. One crop-haired acned lout was making remarks probably abusive and pointing their way. But the landlord had an eye on him, and anyway the insults could not be heard above the hubbub.

Annabel struggled to her feet and tried to squeeze past Anya.

'I think I go make the big piss before I bust,' she said with a wink.

'I'll come with you,' said Anya, rising too, and finding that her sense of the vertical was not entirely secure. She shoved her way out.

There seemed to be a blockage. Anya bumped into Annabel's broad back. What was this? The acned lout was barring the way.

'Where you goin' Miss Sambo?' he jeered. 'Gwina give de big black hole a wash?' His mates laughed the hoarse uncontrolled laugh of retarded adolescence.

Annabel by-passed the obstruction with exactly the required

grimness and determination. Anya watched her receding back, but did not follow. Her glittering eye was fixed on the offending scum, though for the life of her she could think of no plan of action. 'I heard that,' she told herself. 'I heard what he said, the little shit. With my own two ears I heard it. What? Am I going to let that sort of thing happen in my presence? Eh? The insulting of respectable coloured ladies by little pimpled turds? Am I hell?'

Inspiration came to her. Gathering herself for the charge, she lunged with her shoulder, landing on the chest of the little pimpled turd with a great thump that sent him reeling back over the legs of his cronies, who scrambled aside. From the corner of her eye she saw that the landlord had a foot on the bar, about to vault over. Yippee! She hoisted her skirts and, taking the advantage of surprise she drove again at the enemy with her shoulder and, before he could regain his balance, forced him in a headlong rush out the open door and into the street, where she pinned him against the wall. His face had gone green with booze and fright. In a minute he would come at her with his fists. She took a step backward and, gathering everything she had in her throat, let him have it full in the face. He emitted a thin scream of fear and rage, covering himself too late with his hands.

Anya stood with her fists on her hips, feeling very pleased with herself. Her lungs took in great gulps of the wintry air which did not seem, however, to bring sobriety any closer. Words had completely deserted her, but why waste words on this cowering lump that leaned cursing against the wall, trying unco-ordinatedly to wipe the mucous off his face and then flapping a contaminated hand to get rid of the stuff? She'd really given him quite a gobful, she noted with satisfaction, as she turned unsteadily to go inside.

He might have followed, but the landlord had already ejected his cronies and was dusting his hands in the doorway with the air of a satisfied workman looking about for the next job.

The youth veered aside and swaggered off after his pals, pausing to bawl an obscenity when he had reached a safe distance.

'Bloody squaddies!' remarked the landlord in disgust, letting Anya slip past.

She was so exhilarated by the recollection, next morning, of this little piece of racial reconciliation, felt so tenderly protective towards all the Annabels of this big, bad multi-coloured world, that she decided she *would* go, after all, to the Anti-Apartheid meeting. They turned her away at the door. She was not an ANC member. She had no affiliations with the movement. Nobody could vouch for her. And, as if that wasn't enough, she was white. She mentioned her father and they laughed in her face. She'd have to do better than that. Didn't she understand that the league was being persistently infiltrated by BOSS agents, and that just a single agent on the inside could undo years of patient work? Lives were at stake. A name carelessly mentioned in the wrong company in London today, might be tomorrow's 'suicide' in a Jo'burg jail. They couldn't afford to take risks with people who came in off the street. They hoped she'd understand, but frankly, they didn't care if she didn't. That was the way things were. (Anya was getting rather sick of 'the way things were' and the people who kept instructing her about it.)

Another repudiated revolutionary, who had remained hopefully hanging about the doors, offered his commiseration . . . and his company, if she was going somewhere. She informed him she could do without both. He laughed in hangdog desperate fashion.

'They think I'm a BOSS agent! Me!' he said in heavy Afrikaner English. 'What a laugh!' He laughed.

She looked him over. A poor specimen.

'I reckon you probably are,' she said contemptuously, and left him to his foolish mirth.

Several months later, hounded by British Immigration and in difficulties with an expired South African passport, she realized that she should have heeded her own jest. The league might not let her across its threshold, but the agent of her homeland had seen her knocking at the door of subversion, and had included her in his November listings.

That, too, was the way things were. Who would change them?

The Exhibition

Laczi Kovacs thought of himself as a humanist of Marxist leanings – militant, but a man of peace. As the time of the exhibition approached and the studio slowly filled with the Radnóti pieces, the scarred and cratered flesh of these bits of humanoid shrapnel had him wondering if his credentials were sound. Why should a pacific humanism gravitate so exclusively towards war, death and battle?

The Prophet reassured him a bit. He was glad it was large enough to dominate the show. And he consoled himself, now and again, by giving a finer polish to some of its serener passages – scrubbing away with file and abrasive till it felt rounded and stabilized to the touch. Usually he distrusted high-gloss sculpture, associating it with the mechanical patina of the temples of commerce or, further back, the brutalized colossism of the Pharaonic power-cult. The Prophet, anyway, remained definitely *hewn* as far as his head, hands, feet and limbs were concerned. But Laczi found himself working over the concave amphitheatre of his cloak for days on end, in search of some abstract purity and simplicity that would contain and resolve the tension of the pose – the energies of denunciation and striving which propelled the scrawny, thrusting neck and the clawlike grip of the hand.

It was not that he wanted to make the Prophet caressable. Perish the thought! Sculpture that asked to be fondled inevitably turned saccharine as a Victorian nymph under the touch it solicited. Stone! . . . he wanted to put the viewer in touch with the solidity and stability of stone. And only a resolved, harmonious form could do that.

But scattered around him, in hollow bronze, lay these bits of human debris. It was like a morain of destruction. Blood and mire. Mire and blood. He could justify it, of course – with the argument he regularly turned on his students. Ever since the Greeks (it ran),

122

bronze had formed a language for flesh, and it had served so long and nobly that it had almost *become* flesh – a second nature for the sculptor. The skin of bronze could be as fine, as subtle, as delicate as the skin of a woman. But lately bronze had also become the language of the machine and the projectile, the metal which subjugated and maimed that same flesh. Conclusion: modern metallic sculpture must express and exploit this material paradox. He believed this. He practised it. And yet the contradiction remained . . . along with his insidious preference for stone.

Looking back, he seemed always to have lived with it. As a student he had taken a job in the machine-shop of the Red Star Tractor Factory – hoping that he might pick up there a practical grasp of metal technology which the art academies could never teach him. The place itself had been a travesty of human productivity – as factories usually are. Driven to exhaustion by unreal quotas, plagued by clapped-out machines, and goaded on by piece-work scales which never brought them within sight of the theoretical minimum wage, the hands had abandoned themselves to sullenness. They knew life was made for something better, but there was nothing they could do about it except keep their heads down over the lathes and milling-machines. If the treacherous and ill-maintained monster did not actually claim a limb or a finger, it nevertheless turned you into something mindless as itself.

Yet even here the surreptitious 'homer' – keyholder, ashtray, pencilboxes, pendants, door-bolts, daggers, salt-cellars – lovingly made from waste material in time that could not be spared, flourished like an illicit passion. The metal that tyrannized and laid waste was also the object of loving skill.

Laczi's first response to the paradox had been a 'homer' of his own – a mechanical man clownishly welded together from a hotch-potch of waste from the reject-bin. Pistons, rods, rockers, washers made up this machine-person hermaphrodite with a limp dangling spring for a schlong and two valve-heads snapped off at the shaft for boobs. It caused much mirth and derision in the shop. But, like the idiot novice he was, he made it too large to be successfully smuggled out of the factory gates. His pay-packet was docked, his employment book endorsed, and the little excursion into creativity flung back into the waste-bin . . . Tough!

Another image remained with him from the Red Star days – glimpsed one frigid December day through the door of the welding-shop – a figure in mask and apron satirically turning the oxyacetylene blowpipe on its own guts in a vain attempt to counteract the icy cold. That one he had worked into a bronze for his first English exhibition in 1959. In the sculpture, the welder had scorched a hole right through his hollow belly.

It was strange how often, since then, he had reverted to images of humanity turning upon itself, self-consuming, self-devouring. Surveying the results of his latest bout of work it was a question whether, fifteen years later, he had cleared himself any more space. He seemed locked still in antagonism and battle, self-annulled and self-annulling. What was it all a struggle *for*? Mere survival?

Well, he rinsed and scoured, burnished and polished away at the bronzes; but whenever he straightened his back and lifted his eyes to the Prophet he sensed that they belonged to a past he either *had* left, or soon *must* leave behind. There were ways of remaining a prisoner of conscience which were not, in the end, conscientious. He had, after all, left Hungary nearly twenty years ago. Though he could have, he had not been back. Wasn't it time to acknowledge that his life had changed beyond recall? Had he any right to go on lecturing others from a position of righteousness he had effectively abandoned? More to the point, how much longer would the others let him?

In the flurry of final preparation he let the matter drop. There would be leisure for it soon. He had enough on his hands keeping track of the ingenious Mr Borthwick.

Left alone for a few minutes in the director's office, he had found on the desk a 'preface' for the exhibition catalogue which amounted to a sustained and abject apology. An apology for showing anything so anachronistic as Kovacs sculpture in a gallery renowned for its progressive outlook! Borthwick had succeeded in excusing himself for this lapse, on some ground of flabby eclecticism, and he had done his best to excuse Kovacs. But the whole thing was in obnoxious bad faith, and likely, moreover, to give the art pundits the kind of hint for pack-hunting that they rarely needed. This last argument, bearing as it did on Sales, carried some weight with Borthwick, though he couldn't for the life of him see why Kovacs made such a fuss about being labelled a reactionary dinosaur since he was so plainly bent on being one! But he graciously gave way, stipulating only that some alternative material should be provided for the catalogue.

Anya was prompt with the answer: forget the essay in critical aesthetics. Hadn't he seen how regularly artists sabotaged themselves with these ill-judged excursions into rhapsodic prose? Why not print, instead, the poems that had given rise to the work? . . . There was no translation? Well, they would have to make one, wouldn't they?

Anya was not herself greatly impressed with the hapless Radnóti – too much of the gloomy Middle European soothsayer about him. Getting frog-marched across Europe, pregnant with presage, and shot at the roadside, though it made a stirring tale, hardly turned you into a poet. Still, she had great faith in the power of her own style to lend him the distinction he would otherwise lack. And Laczi's accompanying sculpture could be left to do the rest.

He didn't argue. They set to work. She was glad, in all truth, of the distraction. Troubles had been mounting up . . .

Troubles that arrived by mail she always dealt with by redirecting them to fictitious addresses. Particularly unwelcome items tended to wind up in Central Chad or Outer Mongolia. Knowing that she had overstayed her time in Britain (and preferring not to be reminded of the fact), she had made no exception for the fat manila envelopes that arrived every so often from 'The Home Office, Lunar House' (wonderful address!). But now, given new teeth by recent legislation, Immigration was snapping at her heels. Inland Revenue, there was every reason to fear, would come yapping after. Officials at South Africa House, without actually committing themselves to a refusal, were being stony-faced and unco-operative about the renewal of her passport. And it peculiarly irritated her that she couldn't dismiss from her mind the elegant solution that lay ready to hand: she could marry Kovacs, who was a naturalized British citizen. *Not* that he'd asked. *Nor* that she'd accept. Quite out of the question. But there it lay – the solution – niggling and nagging. It was as if there was a conspiracy to filch away her independence, one way or another. If she escaped the marital dungeon, they would pack her off, houseless and stateless to the prison-camp of her birth. Recent letters from home reported alarming mental deterioration in her mother: the little woman had never had much capacity for anything, but now, apparently, she was well-nigh incapable. Senile at sixty! It was bloody typical!

Faced with this agglomeration of aggravating circumstance, Anya could devise no strategy. The legal resources, too long neglected, were all ranged against her. There was no telling Kovacs, for he, with his devious mind, might spy the solution *her* devious mind was bent on suppressing. The only constructive thing she could do was . . . eat. Huge brown mounds of black forest gateau began to appear in the flat; chocolate eclairs (so much cheaper if bought in two-dozen packs from the cash-and-carry), cherry pies, cream-stuffed brandy-snaps, vanilla slices deliquescent and fondant, those really mouth-watering French flans filled with gorgeous glazed fruit . . . the crumbs and smears of her gluttony were all over the sheets of the translation. And the sight of the mess only set her salivating anew. By the time she had gorged her way through *this* crisis she would be secure against marriage – for what man in his senses could propose chaining himself to the meaty-thighed mammoth she was becoming?

And *this* was the moment she chose to set up shop as a translator of Hungarian poetry! Well, what difference did it make – one absurdity more or less? Cake-slice in one hand, ballpoint in the other, she grappled with her world. The possibility that there might be some infringement of copyright involved was an inconvenience like the elephantiasis of her weekly food bill. She resolutely ignored both.

Two days before the private view, she looked up from the table in the boutique where she was restitching some careless seams on a jacket, to see Laczi standing in the door. It was the middle of the afternoon, but he was not in his working clothes. In any case he never visited the shop. She waved him to come in. He didn't move. She put down the garment and came forward.

'Something wrong?'

He seemed to have lost his voice.

'What is it?'

'Not here. I go round back. When you can . . . come.'

She had a word with Kim, and left hurriedly. Found him slumped in the old wooden grandfather chair, whisky-bottle in one hand, glass in the other. At four in the afternoon! All the moulds of his well-regulated life were being shattered today. He pushed the bottle along the bench to her. She shook her head, pulled up a chair opposite, and took his hand – a gesture which had never before seemed either natural or possible. She was helped to it, perhaps, by the need to stop him picking at the calluses on his hand.

He cleared his throat: 'Do I ever mention Bogati? Diplomat-fellow. Went to school.'

He hadn't. He shook his head in confusion.

'Not my cousin Juli? Juli Horvath? You remember?'

That rang a bell. The grim little tale had opened her eyes unaccustomedly wide on the realities of life in the Russified East. In the ferment of the '56 uprising, much scum had risen to the surface – scum of the right as well as of the left. One small neo-fascist group in the town where Juli lived, imagining itself licensed by the recent events, had issued a manifesto – a mish-mash of sedition and anti-Semitism, fanaticism and folly. Nobody in his senses could have taken it seriously. It was signed Janos Horvath. Or in English, 'John Smith'. There was no Janos Horvath, as the agents of Janos Kádár perfectly well knew. But reprisals and repression were the order of the day, so all persons of that name in Tatabanya were rounded up, interrogated, and then, with a few exceptions, they disappeared. Juli Horvath's Janos among them.

He left her with two young children.

Years passed in futile attempts to trace him, and eventually an official notice arrived informing Juli that her husband had 'contracted a pulmonary infection' in Siberia and was, in short, dead. The certainty, though ghastly, came also as a release, and two years later Cousin Juli married again. Her young railwayman seemed to have proved a good husband, and a kind father to the two children he inherited. There was a third child of his own marriage . . . The story so far. Anya checked that she had it right. She had. Well . . .

That morning, Laczi had received a message, on Embassy notepaper, from one Tibor Bogati, a former schoolfellow, who was now an attaché of indeterminate function at Eaton Place. Kovacs's attendance was requested – informally rather than officially. Information had been received from Budapest which might be of interest to him personally. Presuming it concerned his father, Laczi had dropped everything and run.

His expectancy was left to cool in an anteroom for ninety minutes, thus giving him time to regulate his pulse-rate and reacquaint himself with reality. It was a room he knew well: the high gilt mirrors, the empty grate, the black inexorable clock on the mantel, the inlaid marble floor, heavy maroon drapes at the windows with a filter of voile between them to baffle the inquisitive. The upholstery was browned with age and there was the pervasive pungent smell of floor-polish – half wax, half carbolic, which, to the experienced nose, *was* Hungarian officialdom. They must have imported it especially.

Plunged again into this familiar amalgam of opulence and austerity, he became estranged from everything else. The muted traffic outside in the Belgravia streets was an echo in memory. This already phantasmal London of chauffeured limousines, of wolf-hounds exercised by commissionaires and nannies exercised by prams, needed only the intervention of the Embassy voile to vapourize completely. He was back home and hating it.

Eventually the double doors were opened by a deferential bald-head, and Bogati stood there, profuse in apology: he begged Kovacs's indulgence; he had not been informed; it was 'inexcusable'. The apology lost some of its plausibility by being launched across an echoing marble floor to someone about ten yards distant; and the 'inexcusable' bald-head at his elbow – the same who had ushered Kovacs into this room an hour and a half ago – looked remarkably unabashed. In fact he positively sneered at the sculptor as he passed out, trotting in Bogati's wake.

Installed in the private office, Laczi became convinced that the attaché had been making a special study of the Western spy-thriller, he made such efforts to conform to its canons. He proffered a cigar from a huge box of inlaid walnut, 'remembered' that Kovacs did not smoke (since he had never known it he could hardly forget), inquired after 'mutual friends' by their first name (though Laczi knew of no intimacy to justify the presumption), mentioned others about whose fate and whereabouts Kovacs was apprehensive, as if they lived just around the corner and were daily visitors at his table; and wished to be brought up to date on the growing community of Hungarian artists and writers in London who were bringing honour to the homeland. The 'cellist Kiss, of course, he would have met up with? . . . No? (Laczi rapidly computed the danger to the 'cellist of a detectable lie, weighed it against the danger of undoctored truth, and arrived at his compromise.) Met only in passing? By chance? But London was like that – chance encounters of the most extraordinary kind were a daily occurrence.

And he, Kovacs, was about to mount an exhibition again, one had heard? What would that be? His fourth one-man show in 'the decadent West'? (The urbane smile revealed how consciously he fell into the received jargon, without quite establishing the spirit of the lapse.) Fifth? Indeed! He was making quite a habit of it. Of course he, Bogati, perfectly understood the commercial pressures upon artists these days. One must go where the markets were and London was, *par excellence, the* market. Take Kiss, for instance: if he did not get a chance to display his wares in Wigmore Hall, they actually declined in value. Art was, after all, a commodity, was it not? A form of production? He knew Kovacs to be a man who prided himself on being a workman. That was why it saddened him that he had not seen his way clear to returning to Hungary where his expertise and his breadth of experience could be invaluable to the rising generation of sculptors.

Oh, things had changed . . . In a happier and more prosperous land the arts of creative leisure had come back into their own. Even Comrade Kádár (he frowned inscrutably at his desk-top, flicking away a speck of dust) had been known to purchase a painting. Not a large painting, he admitted, now openly jocular, but a painting nevertheless. (Laczi recalled one of Comrade Kádár's more famous dicta concerning the arts: 'these fellows remind me of a botfly that settles on the reins for a second, and then imagines he is driving the cart.' He smiled as required.)

Was this all he had been summoned for? This parade of insolent power? But he knew better than to interrupt the leisurely evolution of ideas. He even made a contribution: 'I have considered returning,' he said, as carelessly as he could.

'I am glad to hear it.'

'I have never ruled it out.'

'That's good. You will let me know, I'm sure. I can – ah – expedite some processes for you. However . . . that is not why I asked to see you.' He arranged some papers on his desk with great gravity. Again Laczi sensed the ghostly presence of the hero of espionage.

'You have a cousin Juli, I believe. Juli Horvath, as she was.' He saw Kovacs galvanize at the past tense, and burst into genial laughter. ' "Was" before her marriage I mean. You are unnecessarily suspicious.'

Laczi was untouched by the comedy of it.

'I,' he said through his teeth, 'have a cousin – or so you assure me. But *you* have her husband. Or rather, you have his corpse. I would prefer not to be reminded of it. It makes me unnecessarily suspicious.'

'Now there,' exclaimed Bogati leaning back in his chair and spreading his arms wide, 'you see *how* needlessly suspicious you are! Janos Horvarth is alive and well and living in Hungary!'

Laczi took a few seconds to get his breath back.

'Released!' he muttered.

'With a pardon.'

Laczi inclined his head with satiric reverence.

'And the one who "caught a cold" in Siberia . . .?'

'Was another. Our Russian friends, knowing little Hungarian and less of the "Janos Horvarth Problem", made an administrative error.'

The casual enormity of it was greatly enhanced by the geniality of Bogati's manner.

'Some others,' said Laczi loudly, 'who did not have that excuse, made an "administrative error", as you call it, in 1957. Perhaps you would like to justify them?'

Bogati underwent a sudden change of role: 'I can*not* justify it,' declared this man of stern rectitude, saddened by a bad world, 'and if I could, I *would* not.' He leaned forward confidentially. Now he was the senior diplomat who permits himself a little unofficial latitude. 'I can say this here, *entre nous*, though if you were to quote me, I should of course deny it. But you should believe me. As you know, I was myself so little in sympathy with such doings that, in 1957, I had left our country. Do me the justice to remember that. No,' he shook his head, 'these excesses of zeal are painful to contemplate, and they have done much harm. You yourself show how much.'

'As far as I can see,' Laczi remarked bitterly, 'the "harm" is just beginning. What is my cousin Juli to do with two husbands and the children of two husbands? Will the Party show its regret by legalizing bigamy?'

'That is indeed a problem.' He looked appropriately pensive.

'So I think.'

'A painful problem. But not one that falls to the Party to solve, I'm afraid. But I thought you would want to be informed, in any case.'

'My gratitude, comrade,' Laczi declared thickly, rising to his feet, 'is not easily expressed.' He was determined to put an end to this farce.

Bogati contemplated the fingers he had interlaced in a small grave steeple. It gratified him really, to see how, even in this extremity, the troublesome fellow conformed to the unwritten code: never speak words, in an official context, which, if quoted, are not susceptible of an innocent interpretation: 'My gratitude, Comrade, is not easily expressed' – a beautiful example! In the West, they called it irony. In the East it had a richer significance. Besides, he could afford to relish it, because he had another card to play.

'Oh don't go,' he said, as if distressed at the possibility. 'I have a letter for you.' He held up a large envelope bearing the Embassy crest – it was the second of the kind Laczi had received that day. 'From your father.' He leaned forward, as if making a move in a

130

complex and subtle game, and placed it delicately on the outermost edge of the desk. Kovacs was to pick it up.

He did no such thing. He stood transfixed: with fury – seeing how he had been played with – and with panic – fearing what the thing on the desk-edge might contain. But it was asking too much of his self-possession to expect him to hold back the question which burst out in a strangled shout: 'Then he's alive?'

Bogati smiled. 'Would he be writing letters, if he weren't?'

'Much can happen,' Kovacs commented icily, 'in the time it takes a letter to get from Siberia to London, via Moscow and Budapest.'

Bogati's manner took on the exaggerated patience of a head-master: 'I see you think the letter has been tampered with.' (But one sweetly free of all resentment): 'Open it. See for yourself.'

'... much can happen,' Kovacs was becoming infected by Bogati's pedantic manner and ironic smile, 'not to the letter, but to the *sender*. I am curious, you see, to know *when* it was written.'

'I'm sure you'll find it's dated.'

Laczi laughed, hollowly. 'Many times over, I'm sure. With the date stamp, properly adjusted, of every censor's office between here and Vladivostock. But I would like, nevertheless, to have your personal assurance that my father is still alive.'

'My dear Kovacs, nothing would give me greater pleasure. But there is nothing certain in mortality. Why, I could not give it, if this letter had been posted yesterday in Brighton! You must see how it is: if you had asked for that assurance a week ago, concerning Horvath, I would have informed you, with appropriate regret, that he was dead. But I would have been wrong. And I was a good deal more reliably informed about Horvarth than I am about your father. This letter has arrived on my desk through the appropriate channels, but I can no more be certain how long it has been traversing them, than you can. It did not come accompanied by a *curriculum vitae*. In fact it came accompanied by nothing but an instruction to locate you and deliver it. This I have done. You must not blame me for the fact that communications,' he tapped the envelope, 'with the remoter provinces of the Soviet Union are erratic and unreliable.'

'Then I suggest,' snarled Laczi, snatching up his letter as if Bogati had been about to take it from him, 'that you send fewer of our compatriots to take extended holidays there!'

'We do not, Comrade,' Bogati was on his feet too, and his voice had gone velvety, 'send *any*! I hope you'll bear that in mind. We are dealing now with the consequences of a period when many errors were committed – and not *all* of them by the authorities. I suggest you take your letter and read it.'

'I intend to. But first you must tell me where I should address my reply.'

Bogati looked displeased. He moved a brass paperweight on the desk.

'I will have it sent on,' he said, without looking up.

'Through "erratic and unreliable" channels? I would much rather have an address, if you don't mind.'

This time Bogati turned his back.

'Even if I had it,' he remarked to the wall-calendar, 'such information is classified. Our Russian allies do not publish the location of their penal establishments. You can send it through the Embassy free of charge – or not at all. Will that be all?'

The immobile spine seemed to imply that it would. Kovacs had a sudden vision of a sulky and excluded schoolboy turning his back on a game he could not join, kicking at pebbles. Even at school, he had disliked Bogati. But at school he had been able to despise, and so forgive him. Now he suffered a powerful impulsion to gather the gall of impotence that was coagulating in his throat and spit it at that scornful back: 'With comrades like you, "Comrade",' he jeered, 'one does not need enemies.'

It was a random foolish shaft, but by some chance it went home. The sulky schoolboy must have been still in there somewhere. Bogati spun about in fury ... in time to see Kovacs stepping out briskly for the door and freedom.

'I'll thank you,' he quacked after the escaping quarry, 'not to use the vocabulary of the Revolution for purposes of puerile irony. Irony is the grunt of the decadent bourgeois pig and I do not permit ...'

But Kovacs had gone.

Anya's feet scraped on the gritty floor as she eased her backside. One leg had gone to sleep.

'Have you read it?'

'No.'

Now that he had told his tale, the deadly torpor had resumed possession. Also the pallor – he was a very queer colour.

'Where is it?'

He patted his breast pocket.

'Shouldn't you get it over?'

She was amazed at herself, at this vein of timorous solicitide which sought only the opportunity to console. She searched it for the falsity it must surely contain, for the self-regarding vanity of the compassionate. But she could find none. She was afraid for him, moved for him – moved also for the unknown Cousin Juli perhaps – that was all. She was, of course, intensely curious to see the letter, but that did not impair the solicitude. She watched his immobility for a further wary moment, then got to her feet.

'What a self-centred pig!' she exclaimed. 'There you sit, clutching the most dramatic document of my long and boring life, and you won't even open it. Read the damn thing before I piss myself with anticipation.'

He recoiled a little, but it brought him back to the present.

'Sure,' he said equably, 'I will read. But there is no point, you know. Either they will have censored it away to rags. Or it will say sweet nothing. Maybe they dictate it to him, I wouldn't be surprise. When I hold it in my hand, so, or look at the envelope, it tells me probably as much as I would know when I have read it.'

'Bah! All this sentimental titillation! It's like something out of a bad play.' She flounced away. 'Wipe your bum with it, see if I care.'

Fine smile wrinkles creased the corners of his eyes. Whatever heartache the letter might bring, the sight of her tantrums brought a compensating cheer. He began to revive.

'Anyuka,' he called. 'Come back here. You know what your name means, in Hungarian? Anya? Anyuka? I never tell you because it will make you mad.'

She tossed her head: 'Make me mad.'

'It means "mother". And now, see! You are playing for me the little mother. You are being my Anyuka, I think it very nice for you.'

She stamped her foot: 'Open the fucking letter, will you!'

He grinned. 'All right, all right! Keep your pants on.'

Inside the Embassy envelope was another, soiled and dog-eared. If it had ever possessed gum it had long since been steamed or slit or sliced away. He shook it. Three sheets of coarse greying paper fell out in his lap. One was smaller than the others, cropped at the head to remove address and date. Still deferring the plunge, he turned them over. The handwriting was firm and elegant – no sign of deterioration there – but it took detours in unexpected places. He squinted at the loops and bumps, then began to laugh: the paper was blemished with flecks of resinous pulp, vestigial splinters,

133

probably ink-resistant, and every time the writer had come to one of these obstacles he had steered around it in a little whimsical hillock of script. Like a handclasp in the dark, it charmed away the ignorant fears. It was all right; the old man was alive – still capable of being amused by the coarse obstructiveness of matter and of men, still making his wry, indomitable, uncensorable comment. It was more than Laczi had dared to hope. There had been little in his father's first fifty years of comfortable existence to prepare him for the twenty that were to follow. He had not, like some, been raised on prison gruel and trained to sleep sound on frozen boards. But he was surviving, against all the odds.

How much of a genuine message, then, had he been able to slip past the vigilance of the guards and censors? He read:

My dear Lajos,

I am sorry to have kept you so long in ignorance of my whereabouts, but I have been very busy. Besides it was only yesterday that I learned, from our most friendly and helpful Hungarian consul here ■ that our assiduous government has been able to locate you. No letter, obviously, was possible until this had been achieved and I must frankly remonstrate with you for being such a wretched correspondent. Surely, once in these many years, you could have found a minute to tell me where you are? I am touched, however, that those entrusted with the destiny of nations have found time to undertake the homely task which filial duty would not. And I regard it as perfectly natural that they should decline to venture such an important secret as *your address* on the discretion of an old man of unsound judgement. I have been assured however, that *this* letter will reach you.

It will come as no surprise to you to hear of my 'unsound judgement'. If it had been sound, would I be here? Besides, you have often reproached me with my unsoundness. There were fears at one time, I can tell you now, that it would prove incurable. I myself shared them. But I had not reckoned with the efficacy of the treatment that is available to Russian science, of which I have been a fortunate beneficiary. I think I can honestly declare that my judgement is sounder for it – though a complete cure is probably not to be anticipated this side of the grave.

I trust you are enjoying better weather than we are ■ though one mustn't grumble at what is sent from above. Every climate has its own peculiar virtues. This is a truth both meteorological and moral. It is, for instance, no doubt due to the salutary refrigeration of *baccilli* that one is as healthy as one is. One's only complaint is that some of the *baccilli* are unfortunately immune and flourish quite disgustingly against the odds. But I mustn't give the impression of ignorant repining. You would be surprised, my son, to see how, with age, I approach a resignation almost religious in its comprehensiveness. It can't be helped: I am 'going in the knees'.

I say 'almost religious', for to be fully religious at this juncture of history is of course impossible. Any truly empirical study of *homo sapiens*, even on the crude level I have been able to conduct it, disposes effectively of the hypothesis of God. I realize of course that my sample has been restricted and possibly misleading. But one labours, in the spirit of true science, to compensate for this by minuteness of observation.

As I say, I have been quite occupied. I have had my hands full. The other reason for my surprisingly good health, I dare say, is the *amount* of manual labour I have found it convenient to undertake. My soft lawyer's palms are not now, thank God, the subject of proletarian scandal that they once were, and I have eschewed the decadent arts of the manicurist for many years (I remember how you used to deplore that oligarchic aberration of mine). In fact I think I may say I have eschewed *all* decadent arts, and I hope, my son, that I may assume that you have done the same. It would be sad if you, who were raised in the nursery of revolution and nurtured on the broth of socialist transformation, were to fall helpless prey to the bloody claws of counter-revolution, to the fascist-reactionary-bourgeois-clerical-nationalist-revisionist-capitalist-imperialist demagogues, bandits, and assassins who lie perennially in wait for a young man's ideological purity. That was not what you learned at your father's knee.

But I think too well of you, and of myself, to believe that you will be anybody's helpless prey. And as that Star of the Russian dawn, that noble harbinger of the People's Revolution, Maxim Gorki, once wrote: 'The world will always be bad enough for the desire in man to make it better never to be extinguished.'

I may be going in the knees, but I can say Amen to that. I am sure the desire is not yet extinguished, my son, in you.

Salutations from afar,
    Kovacs Z.

Once he was relieved of it, Laczi realised what his dread had been
– that the old man had been broken and that the sound of his
whimperings would come distinctly through the prison-walls of
distance, time, and officialdom. But he was not broken: he was in
amazing heart. Laczi could see him humped over his pencil in an
ill-lit hut, like some wicked old child with an unseemly taste for
practical jokes, chuckling and gloating over his *double entendres*.
There were whole sentences which had no other function than to
drive the camp censor to distraction. Even Gorki's revisionist
sentiments had been protected by an emplacement of heavy-duty
panegyric of exactly the correct bore. In the end the censor had been
able to black out nothing but the two doomed attempts to name the
camp. It was a triumph of creative evasion.

Bogati, if course, would hardly have been fooled. And Bogati had
certainly read it. That was probably why he had been so tetchy on
the subject of 'irony'. Very likely. Laczi would have to think
seriously before sending anything back to his father through *that*
channel: officials riled by those they cannot touch tend to take out
their irritation on those they can. But meantime he was experiencing
a luxury of relief. True, nothing had changed: as before, so now –
there was nothing he could *do*. After two decades of Siberian rigour,
the old man could not have many more years of life in him. 'Going in
the knees' was his way of saying as much. Yet, though it was every
bit as impossible, it seemed now so much less urgent to 'do'
anything. For all their efforts, they had not been able to reform
Kovacs Zoltan. He was still gratifyingly 'unsound'. The *doing*,
therefore, could safely be left to him.

He folded the precious testament with care and replaced it in his
pocket.

But poor Juliska . . . he must write to her. She still claimed the
affection of the young man he had been when he last saw her.
Horvath would have returned a nervous and physical wreck – they
usually did. Even if she wanted to, Juli could never turn him away.
The guilt, the guilt! The young railwayman would feel it too. To be
free was to be guilty, never mind the usurped bed and board. He had
hugged a wife under warm blankets, and eaten enough to stay his
hunger, while the other, the scapegoat . . . out there . . . There was no
expiating it. What an unthinkable, stinking mess! Blood and mire
and the trapped creature struggling in it – what happy dialectic of
history was going to get him out? Poor Juli, with her broad, calm
peasant's face and braided hair, what was she to do? . . . And all the

while Bogati sat simpering with 'appropriate regret' at his polished desk.

Give me, *give* me a fit curse! Where are you, Isaiah, scholar of terrible words?

The evening of the private view arrived.

Bill Madison came to Princes' Gate in his old Bedford van to pick them up and found Anya in a petticoat and a rage because her favourite, state-occasions-only party-dress – a richly smouldering, dark-red affair, smock-patterned with filaments of gold – had split when she had insulted it with her overfed person. Laczi was in a mood of sublime whimsy and could not be got to admit that anything was actually happening, let alone to do anything about it. Beatrice was summoned from the street and proceeded to stitch Anya back together.

Meanwhile, Bill was explaining about some rapturous rural ruin in the Mendips that he'd purchased for a song, and insisting that they must all join him there for what was left of the summer. No one was attending sufficiently to be sure whether he was serious, though Bea, through a mouthful of grim pins, assured Anya that a tent in the Sahara would be more sensible, if she was thinking of a relaxing holiday.

When they eventually crowded into the van, they had collected a parking-ticket. This struck Laczi as peculiarly comic and he worked hard – the van becoming snarled in the Hyde Park Corner traffic – to persuade Bill to see it in this light. As a consequence of his persuasions Bill got distracted from his driving and had a slight disagreement with a cab – followed by a more substantial disagreement with its driver. Laczi, by now quite hilarious, promised to pay all fines, personally garotte the cabbie, buy Bill a new wing, a new van . . . anything . . . all this with the proceeds of the exhibition which, he confidently predicted, would be sold out by the time they got there – if they ever did.

They did. Made a late and brilliant entry, which was given additional splendour by Anya's high colour and flashing eyes, and Laczi's devilish euphoria. They had both been dreading it as an ordeal, but now that it was upon them they felt nothing. It was as unreal as the wine they gulped without tasting, unreal as the flushed and flitting Giles Borthwick in his brown velvet suit, unreal as the little gouts of red paper that seemed to be blossoming on the most unexpected plinths. Anya sailed up to report that there was a cluster of *four* on 'The Execution' – four drops of scarlet blood attesting the sculptor's successful crime! How could there be four? Laczi recalled with difficulty that he had marked some of the pieces as available in an edition of five, never imagining that he would be taken up.

The world had gone mad. One had only to go mad with it. He caught Bill's elbow, yanking him unceremoniously out of a conversation – now, about that new van . . . just say the word. Bill fell on his neck with noisy emotion. At last it had come – the long-merited recognition. And about time, too! He dragged him back to be introduced – to two potters, a painter, and a journalist whose name Laczi missed and whose enthusiastic comments he received without understanding, though he gathered they *were* enthusiastic. In the way a private view sometimes does, the whole occasion had become stamped with the impress of irresistible success, and the sourest critic in the milling herd was going to have to fight hard for his private severities.

He had caught sight of Kiss, but could see no way of reaching him. He waved. The 'cellist stood on a chair and cupped his hands: 'This is splendid!' he shouted in Hungarian, 'but where are the sculptures? Ah!' He shaded his eyes melodramatically, 'I think I've spotted one.' He climbed down from his perch . . .

'What the hell for I come here?' asked a disgruntled voice belonging to the hand which then clutched at his elbow. 'I don't see a damn thing and the people keep tromping on my corns.' Annabel swung on his arm, struggling to get back into the impossibly high-heeled shoes she had half-shed. Laczi, who had forgotten he had invited her, smiled now to see her. 'Is big success, man?' she asked, releasing him as she succeeded. 'Is sure one big crush. Where your Anya? I think Sam run out on me.' Just look for the thickest tobacco smog, he advised, or follow the trail of Sobranie butts. She'd be there . . .

Could that be Bogati helping himself to sherry? Surely not. He wouldn't have the nerve! . . . Would he? . . .

It had all begun (Borthwick now took possession of his ear in a confidential shout) when the Grand Old Man himself had bought 'The Execution' for his private collection – an unlikely enough choice, given his current practice and predilections, but there you were. It was done. The Old Man liked making these grandly simple gestures of approval and it had worked like a charm. A stampede had started – a veritable stampede.

Laczi had never seen Borthwick so animated. It had turned him into the boy he was usually so careful not to appear. And a rather likeable boy, too, Laczi thought. He patted the boy's arm and assured him that it was all his own good work, munificently adding that the lighting and presentation of 'Forced March' (over which they had squabbled) was completely vindicated and he must now confess his error. But one question: had he invited people from the Hungarian Embassy? 'Naturally.' Borthwick's eyebrows went up in surprise. 'Was that an error?' With even more surprise (at himself), Kovacs confessed that it probably wasn't. It had touched him in passing but left no mark . . .

He was hauled off to meet the Old Man who was at the centre of the only pocket of calm in the gallery's three rooms. About their conversation, next morning, he could remember nothing. They made words at each other, but the more important salutation had already passed: I like it so well, I choose to live with it. Laczi was tempted to ask why he had not chosen 'The Prophet' – more his style, he would have thought. But the price-tag was probably sufficient answer.

Anyway, a grave personage joined the select circle at this point, and the nervous hush that attends celebrity deepened around them: 'Very impressive, Mr Kovacs, very impressive. A literary imagination sculpturally verified – it's most rare to see it. I congratulate you.'

Kovacs winced. They were after him for his 'literary imagination' again. He had been forcibly acquainted with it before. Like a small boy dragged to the bathroom mirror to be shown the dirt on his face, he had had to acknowledge the stain without understanding why it should offend. What they mostly seemed to mean when they accused him of a 'literary imagination' was that he had a fondness for the human figure, and generally preferred it to be *doing* something. This time, however, although the stain had been 'verified', he was to be forgiven – forgiven the grubby face and the dirt behind his figurative ears. Well, so be it. Puzzled but relieved, he bowed his thanks and excused himself, nearly colliding with the ubiquitous Borthwick, who muttered something in an excited voice, hastening to attach himself to the grave personage. (It was not until he read the papers with which Bill came burdened next morning, that Laczi realised that the man must have been the Director of the Tate, who later, on the advice of the Grand Old Man, bought 'The Prophet' for himself and the nation.)

Hovering distractedly about a plate of *vol-au-vent*, he was buttonholed next by a gracious lady of high breeding, swathed in the kind of brocade usually reserved for royalty. Other faces had left him blank, but this one he remembered well. She had bought one of his early bronzes, beating his impecunity down to a mere £150 (less than the materials had cost him); and then, some years later, when he had needed the piece for a travelling exhibition, had insisted on *his* insuring it for £2,000. Oh (she had fluted), Mr Kovacs needn't imagine she was one of the ignorant who didn't know the value of his work – she knew it very well. No, £2,000 was the absolute minimum. That bust was quite irreplaceable – the centrepiece of her collection. (It *was* the only copy, was it not?) At the time of this conversation, it *had* been, but by the time it returned from its travels to its Knightsbridge home, it no longer was. Laczi, savouring his secret revenge, managed to bow his head under the rain of her complimentary condescension, with a very good grace. One of the red spots on 'The Execution', it transpired, was hers: this was one of the stampeding sheep who had jumped the hedge in pursuit of the Grand Old Man – though Laczi surmised, through the polite fog, that she had yet to discover what it was about the piece that she was supposed to admire. He did not much care if she never found out. This time at least she had paid the market price . . .

It was well into the evening before the company thinned and the sculptures became visible again in the strewn sea of ash, butts, crumbs, nuts and glasses. Laczi, feeling a bit queer in the pit of his stomach, sat and stared at these beached sea-beasts of his imagination. He had feared that, called together to assembly, they would convict him of excess, of an over-loud rhetoric. But they were simple statements of solid fact. Touch them. Pick them up. Fall over them, if you preferred. There they were. They repelled insinuation and defied exegesis. It was good.

He felt no particular emotion – it was as if they had all escaped him and he were now bidding them farewell. But like a wise parent, he relinquished possession in the name of a larger satisfaction: out there in the big world, there were ambassadors of the self – freely existent, self-determining entities which subtly altered the sum of objectivities. The world would never again be quite the same.

He lay back on his couch of quite sybaritic sponginess, allowing the room to swim hazily before his half-closed eyes. A great balloon of laughter was lodged somewhere in his throat and he was uncertain whether to release it or not. What he would most have liked to do, actually, would have been to sketch, in affectionate satire, this heaped and memorable battlefield in which a few survivors and scavengers still picked their way, bemused and nibbling: the durable dark masses of his sculpture properly contextualized by the wisps and flotsam of the social tide. Entitled, 'Detritus, 25/8/75'. He smiled to himself.

'A penny for 'em.' Anya sank beside him, laying a flushed and boozy cheek on his shoulder.

'A penny?' he exclaimed indignantly. 'For what do you take me? From today, are new tariffs.' He gestured about him in lordly fashion. '*Voilà*! The pennyworth is no more.'

'Feelthy capitalist schwein!'

She snuggled against him, stifling a yawn. It added to her comfort that he had permitted himself a little commercial gloat. It brought them together. Given time, he might even reconcile himself to the real world. Good! It wasn't that she grudged him the success. She was delighted for him. But it did prove conclusively that 'selling' and 'selling out' were two distinct things . . . so let him know it and have done!

She slid her neck along the couch to examine the familiar profile of her man of stone. Still there! The beaked nose, the ragged moustache, the sculpted jaw – impressive, as always, in their imperviousness. Was this a man to go in fear of a corrupt and venal world? It was all foolishness. They could never touch him.

Anya was not to know that the lines of austere bleakness, into which his face had now set, were recording a new thought – or rather, the return of an old. How could he – filthy capitalist swine – have dared to forget? Nothing had changed. To be free was to be guilty. Laczi had remembered Siberia.

EIGHT

The Cottage under the Crabtree

Two ruts wound uphill between profuse walls of hawthorn and bramble, throwing up from time to time a flinty central crown which menaced sump and differential. But the Madisons' battered shooting-brake was an old horse at these fences and slewed sideways to plant its tyres on the ridges – thereby abandoning its paintwork to spines and thorns, which raked it from end to end with the sound of fingernails on a blackboard. Occasionally a switch of hazel dipped and delivered a stinging blow right in the middle of the windscreen, making the occupants flinch and duck. The brambles, as they passed, twinkled with berries at all stages of ripeness, from acid-green to glossy black.

Bill, crouched over the wheel, was brimming with undisguised glee. He had sprung the biggest surprise of his shamelessly overt life. All he had to do now was to lean back and watch the world cope with it. It had been long a-planning, and the anticipation was correspondingly great.

He crashed down into first and revved for the final ascent – a steep curving pitch which had the rear wheels churning, before they swung hard right on to a platt of chalky gravel and halted, dust swirling around them. Bill tumbled out, skipped round to the other door (which opened only from the outside) and handed his wife down.

'There it is,' he directed, with impish pride, 'Madison's Madness.'

She lifted the boy out, buying herself a little time. She was still in mild shock, and his insistence was overweening. Deprived finally of further resource, she lifted her head and looked.

Under the tall diagonal of a crabapple (richly invested, she was pleased to note, with fruit that was just turning colour) couched a sprawl and a tumble of honey-coloured stone, with a low-pitched gable and an arm of dissident sheds reaching out towards her. It was one of those cottages that had begun life as a modest cube, but had acquired amplitude over the years as outbuildings spawned and rooms were tacked on, until it had become a farmyard complex of impenitent uncomformity, mellowed by time and weather. An ancient elderbush, groaning with fruit, half blocked the back door – which was one of those two-part horse-box affairs that opened independently above and below. It was also desperately in need of a coat of paint, her quick practicality noted.

Behind the house came a fuzz of trees, and then the hill took a sudden swoop upwards before flattening itself back into the sky – a bald limestone skull, thinly grassed, with criss-cross striations of sheep- and rabbit-tracks.

'Mmff!' she said, and releasing Caspar's hand walked forward to the door, thrusting aside the drooping scions of elderberry.

'It's not locked,' called Bill, standing to watch.

She tussled with the latch, then ducked suddenly as a bat skimmed out of the gap between greying lintel and decaying stonework and lurched drunkenly off into the tangle of lichen-bearded orchard trees at the rear.

'A bat, a bat, a bat!' shrieked Caspar, setting off in barefoot pursuit. He disappeared round the corner past a pile of faggots half buried in nettles.

Beatrice got the rotting door open, with a wrench and a squeal of rusty hinges, and peered into the gloom. More a barn than a house, with its naked hand-hewn posts and small cobwebby windows. The home of generations of mice – and worse – to judge by the litter on the floor. She was loath to enter.

'The roof's sound as a bell,' said Bill, now at her elbow, 'and that's what matters.'

His wife slid a hand thoughtfully into the broad slit between two blocks of stone, and held up a finger stained with brown dust.

'Needs pointing,' he conceded. 'Built before the days of mortar. But sound!' He thumped the stone with a fist. It moved under the impact, emitting a tentative genie of dust which hovered in the afternoon sunlight. Beatrice's mouth remained firmly closed.

On small feet and delicate ankles she picked her way round the corner of the building, her husband following, hushed. Double french doors, a late addition, opened here on to a grassy plot looking south. Rolling arable and pasture, hedged in a comfortable mosaic, fell away to flatlands of sedge-moor and drained marsh, rising again to the farther horizon in swelling blue hills. The prospect could not be faulted and she felt herself being insidiously beguiled of her resentment. A huge briar bush threw out arched sprays of yellow roses which blossomed winsomely against that blue remoteness. This would never do. She turned about to face the house.

'And what does one do for water?' she inquired, noticing there were no tanks and assured there were no mains.

'Ah!' he exclaimed in gratified tones.

Taking her arm he led her through the thick grass under the apple trees and up the slopes to where the skull of the down rose bald and sheer out of the undergrowth. Caspar joined the procession along the way, having lost his bat.

'I met a friendly robin,' he announced. 'He just said hello to me.'

There was a faint tinkling sound on the air and the grass was unnaturally rank.

Bill parted a bush to let her through into a tiny spinney of alder. She sank immediately to the ankle. He hauled her out.

'I said "where's the water?" ' she protested, 'not "where's the bog?" '

They skirted round the edge and reached a mossy cliff. Here, at waist height, two flat tongues of water protruded from a cleavage in the stone, small translucent spatulae that fell into a gravelly basin at the foot.

'All it needs is a channel and we're made,' he exulted. 'Beautiful water!' He offered her a cupped handful, at which she turned up her nose; but Casper lapped it greedily and then waded into the soft mud to get more for himself.

She turned and looked west through the trees, over the pantiled roof of the cottage, and across the blue-brown Bristol Channel, to the hazy spit of land that was Wales – placid rural miles that lay smiling in the westering sun. The quiet of it, broken only by the tinkle of water and the skirr of an alarmed blackbird, was seducing her again. Above their heads, on the hill's forehead, grasshoppers seethed and snapped in the brown grass. It was almost a relief when she was able to make out the faint subversive roar of the motorway which underlay the silence. At least there was *something* here that was not straight out of *A Country Diary*!

'Well, it's done now, I suppose,' she said through lips as vinegar-thin as she could make them. 'If you choose to blow your life savings on a bat-infested pile of rubble and mouse-droppings, who can stop you? As long as you don't expect me to live in it.'

'Live, *and* work. Those outhouses are a gift of a pottery.'

She raised eyes of supplication to the longsuffering heavens.

144

'You do like it, don't you?' he persisted, solicitous and complacent at the same time.

'If I do,' she replied, deploring his literal-mindedness, 'I'm most certainly not telling *you*. God alone knows what ghastly scheme will possess you next, if you're given any encouragement.'

They trailed back down through the 'orchard' – a handful of gnarled bewiskered trees, untended for decades. Bill shouldered a trunk violently, and a peppering of small green nuggets fell among the grass. He picked up one for inspection.

'It'll need a bit of a prune,' he opined, tossing it away for some destitute wasp to get drunk on.

'With a chain-saw?' Beatrice queried acidly, 'at ground level?'

Caspar, retrieving the thing, had taken a mouthful, but quickly spat it out.

'Is that a crabby apple?' he asked, cleaning his tongue on his sleeve. 'It *tastes* crabby.' His mother laughed.

'Well, William,' she said womanfully, 'let's see the worst. Show me the living-quarters.'

But the worst was already over. The autumnal charm of the place and of the season had begun its mollifying work. The three of them went indoors, stamped on floors, poked in cupboards, stuck poles up chimneys, prodded at plasterwork, tugged at casements, took brooms to cobwebs, flung rubbish out of windows, trampolined on wire mattresses and tobogganed down staircases, and at every turn of a corridor and every opening of a door they saw what the estate agents call 'potential'. It was amazing what potential the house offered: it was a function, possibly, of its lack of the actual. Nevertheless, within hours, the place had undergone the transformation in their minds which it was never to undergo in fact. It had become a project – only the more absorbing for its apparent endlessness. To the endless expense of it all they gave not a single thought.

By the time Laczi and Anya turned up, ten days later, the cottage under the crabtree was a hive, in or out of which some busy worker was forever buzzing. The queen bee, who had been cropping the tributary hedgerows, was surrounded by the opulent fruits of a very good berry season, and the great black cast-iron monster of a kitchen range (with the bird's nest removed from its flue and the flaked rust from its firebox) was filling the kitchen with smells of jam and pie-crust. Caspar, freed of his clothes in the warm sun, was commencing work on the leat that was to conduct the spring-water to the house; that is to say, he was having the most gorgeously extended game of mud pies that heart of boy could desire – interrupted only by occasional errands with the bucket. Since he always found something interesting and experimental to do with the water on his way back to the house, these errands were likely to cease before long.

And his father, thoroughly in his element, dragged his toolchest from room to room, quite without plan, hammering and humming, sawing and singing, tackling any job that caught his eye and forgetting any that didn't. The old Bedford bounced up and down the cart-track several times a day with loads of timber and cement and putty and sand and paint and plaster. The local builders' merchant, quickly recognizing the symptoms of acute pernicious DIY, had insisted on his opening an account. Why spoil the ship for a ha'porth of tar? Why indeed? Bill was in total accord. What if the sills under the casements had crumbled away to touchwood? Tear 'em out and replace them: the sawmill would cut 'em to size. And suppose the ancient plaster did drink paint like a thirsty desert – just slap on an extra coat. And if paint and plaster and all came off the laths in alarming great sheets – well, sweep it up and cart it out, and mix up a bucket of new stuff. None of this was insuperable; it wasn't even discouraging; for look how well it was beginning to look. What potential!

The newcomers were swept up, without pause or protest, into the wave of activity. Anya tied her hair up in a scarf and grasped a paintbrush. Where should she begin? What, here? But the plaster wasn't even dry. So what? Nor was the paint. Just slosh it on, girl. No time for frills. The van came groaning up the track, with a six-foot overhang of hardwood whipping dangerously up and down between the clanging rear doors. A job-lot from the sawmill. Going for a song. Now they could build the leat. Laczi was drafted and set out for Caspar's Bog with spade, hammer, saw and nails. It was done in a day – so successfully that the brick floor of the kitchen was under an inch of muddy water when they got up next morning. Bea, barefooted, stood in the lake and cooked breakfast, while the drainage problem was solved. A sunken bath in the room below the kitchen, to which they had not yet assigned a function . . . that was the answer. Bill clattered off in the van and returned with a fibreglass fishpond which they proceeded to set into an excavated hole in the dirt floor. All it needed now was a quarry-tile surround, and Bob's your uncle. Tiles? Nothing easier. The van departed again. Meanwhile the fishpond filled and overflowed. Ah! A plughole perhaps? With a soakhole under? That was the way of it. Never mind the mud. Purely temporary! The porous ground, full of cracks and crevices, would absorb anything . . . After a week of this, enthusiasm began to flag. But the worst was over. The place was livable. Karoly was due to be picked up from Bristol on the Sunday, all his immediate engagements over. Time to ease off and enjoy oneself a bit. Laczi went to meet the train in Anya's new car – a small, lemon-coloured consolation she had offered herself for the joint persecution of accountants and officialdom. If she couldn't meet the instalments they would repossess of course, but she'd be no worse off, and meanwhile she enjoyed enhanced mobility. The relief she felt in handing the shop-keys over to Kim and seeing London grow tiny in the rear-vision mirror, proved how right she had been. All that hassle and fume seemed a thousand miles away – which was about the correct distance. One had the right to an occasional immunity from the mad world one lived in.

Karoly arrived, wedged under his big black 'cello case in the back seat of the Deux-Chevaux. Now they had music as well. Nothing was lacking. Except, Beatrice intervened sharply, *except* hot water. How long were they to go round splashing themselves with spring-water and stinking like a compost heap? Could the men perhaps put their accumulated genius to work on that problem? Nothing simpler. What had clever William found in an outhouse, but half a dozen old flat-irons? Heat 'em on the range, dunk 'em in the water and hey presto! hot baths. They'll go straight through the fibreglass, Laczi reminded him. Uh-huh! Not if you sit 'em on bricks.

Karoly's arrival was celebrated by a communal bath, Roman-style. The betowelled and betoga'ed patricians of Crabtree Cottage lounged about the room, supping their wine (Karoly had come armed with a caseful) and exchanging ribaldries with the bathers. Anya found herself unaccountably stiff about such licentiousness, fearing perhaps to look like a hippo amongst gazelles, but she swallowed her pride and took the plunge. As she had feared, the water promptly overflowed. Why hadn't that happened with the others, godammit? But it was so warm and soothing – though a trifle opaque – that she accepted her wine-glass with a good grace and toasted the builders, even agreeing to move over and share the bath

147

with a wriggling Caspar. The colour of the water suggested that Beatrice had been right in thinking an emergency to have been close.

The largest revolution, however, was going on unobserved – unobserved, at least, by anyone but the boy. For the estate had hundreds of sitting tenants – now threatened with homelessness. Caspar met one of them in the larder, beady-eyed and waffle-nosed, helping himself to breakfast cereal. The bat community, too, was in an uproar, being forever banged and poked and hammered, in daytime, out of their cosy crevices. And the huge woodpile was a disaster area for the woodlice and ants and snails and beetles whose metropolis was being devastated with casual indifference, in order to stoke up the kitchen range. Predatory birds flocked to the feast. An evicted hedgehog was seen scuttling away from the outbuildings, and the rabbits in the nearest hedge-bottom held emergency council. Only the resident robin seemed unperturbed, following Caspar about as he did his rounds, perching on twigs near his face, and cocking an interrogative head before emitting his shrill comment. The more things were overturned the better he fed, so why should he care?

But Caspar was worried about the rabbits. *They* couldn't load their houses on their backs and decamp, like the snails. He consulted Anya, and took her out stealthily, one dewy dusk, to survey the problem. It surprised her that he had singled her out, but she went. She found him an amusing child, in his inconsequential oddities. A bit of an original – as most children so boringly weren't. A full-bodied but wraith-like moon was rising in a sky of duck-egg blue.

Abruptly Caspar snatched her hand and froze. Just beyond the orchard a pair was feeding, heads down, backs humped, all movement concentrated into one furious inch of incisive jaw and wobbling lip. With infinite slowness he led her forward. The childish hand was cool and firm in hers, unconscious of the contact.

Suddenly, and for no apparent reason, the smaller rabbit made a wild dash of a dozen yards, and humped down again. Caspar's hand gripped hard. No, they had not been observed, for the rabbits were demurely nibbling still. Something else was afoot . . . Yes. For now the larger of the two, a buck probably, was edging sideways as he fed, in tiny creeping spurts, closer to his mate until . . . an explosion of motion: the buck springs. But the doe is ready, has been watching out of the corner of her eye all the time, and is off like the wind in swift loping circles. Then squats like a stone. Nibbles.

The stalking resumes – unthinkably patient, tirelessly cunning.

The watchers begin to think the show is over, it goes on so long. But again comes the rushing charge . . . and this time the doe leaps clean over her wooer-pursuer, a foot in the air. Turns. Faces him. A long, wary pause. Or are they exchanging silent rabbit-laughs? It could be, for they both leap simultaneously in the air, forepaws raised and soft belly-fur exposed, execute a couple of furious circuits, squat, feed.

The human pair watched till the chill from the ground began to climb their legs. The end of Anya's nose felt sharp, and a moist droplet was forming. She sniffed – circumspectly, she thought. The rabbits raised two heads as one, paused half a second, and were gone.

They walked back to the house, the boy playing like a puppy across her path, watching her stealthily. With the cessation of daytime noises the mutinous roar of the motorway down in the valley became noticeable, as did its winking current of coloured lights.

'They look pretty happy to me,' Anya remarked. 'I wouldn't worry.'

'Can rabbits laugh?' Caspar asked, as if that would settle the matter.

'I think that pair were telling each other jokes, anyway.'

'Good jokes?'

'They thought so.'

Caspar stopped worrying about the rabbits.

But Anya began worrying about something else. It had been strange to stand half an hour in frozen stillness under a frail moon, watching rabbits. And a child's hand, unresponsive yet living, was an even stranger thing. She could still feel the imprint of the strangeness, cool on her palm. It was as if freedoms she had never been conscious of possessing had come suddenly under siege. She was not sure she liked the sensation.

Indoors everything was luminous with the flare of the hissing Tilley and the softer glow of hurricane lamps. The hearth was ablaze too; for the tangled junkheap of the outhouses had yielded another treasure – a four-legged basket-grate large enough to handle the longer logs and branches. Bill had been raiding the copse down the lane for fallen timber, though he was rather hazy whether it formed part of his land or not. They were consuming fuel, nonetheless, with a prodigality that envisaged no shortage – envisaged, for that matter, no winter. Well, sufficient unto the day was the firewood thereof – especially when it blazed like this.

Karoly and Laczi had their heads together, conferring with the 'cello about some Hungarian folksongs whose words were eluding them. Though *not* the tunes – which the 'cellist was playing in hilariously elephantine imitation of a gypsy fiddler. From time to time, Laczi bawled out the bits he could remember, and very rowdy and randy affairs they seemed to be, these songs. Bill, with Caspar's box of plasticine, was modelling a satirical portrait of them – two emaciated, paper-thin Hungarians, their throats open down to the tonsils, with a stout and solemn 'cello between them, looking disapproving. Anya admired it in passing. There was more to Bill than she'd allowed: she had thought all he made was boring old pots.

'There's stew on the hob,' Beatrice called, looking up from her embroidery. 'Help yourselves.'

Anya plunged the ladle into the steaming unlit cavern, dredged about for a minute and slopped her findings into two bowls. Caspar took his into a corner, like a squirrel with a nut.

The singers had fixed on a refrain that twirled and spun in wild accelerando, until Karoly snatched it away into a free cadenza. Not so much a cadenza, as an unending reel. It went on and on, with Laczi stamping and clapping and threatening to break out in actual dance, and the musician laughing at the antics he was provoking. The 'cello, like the singers before, was emitting those strange glottal cries, coiling upon itself in maniacal little curls of ornament (sounds she associated with flamenco dancers or *muezzin*-calls) and then whipping free in long rippling lines. For a moment it would all dissolve into a single inhuman note, without vibrato – white sound that could end only in madness – then off again, in hectic pulsation.

Anya bolted the last of her stew, mopped up with a crust and went to join them. She was being assailed by some unbearable poignancy emanating from them, though nothing about their behaviour was in the least poignant. It was as if the music came through the open door of a room she was forbidden to enter. The two men looked up. Again that sense of powerful exclusion! She snatched a stool and sat, leaning her head back against one of the bearer-posts. The great oaken shaft was vibrating to the 'cello's bass notes which came up to her, also, from the floor. She had heard Kiss's playing before – at the recital – but not with this kind of directness. It was of a quite magnificent and savage sadness. Why should she feel shut out? Sad that she had given up her music, all those years ago – was that it? To venture her dilapidated technique on the instrument or the ears of a virtuoso was out of the question, but the tone of the instrument filled her with envy. If she had had a 'cello like that to play, what could she not have done? Like all true musicians, Karoly Kiss made his hearers feel, not how far beyond them such music lay, but how nearly it fell within their powers. She watched with intent gleaming eyes – a child, fascinated – until he acknowledged her gaze.

'Are you improvising?' she asked.

His head see-sawed on his shoulders: yes and no.

'Peasant songs – fiddle music – Bartok,' he explained between phrases, '*und so weiter.*'

'A musical stew?' she proposed. He laughed, with a sudden flash of white teeth amongst his black whiskers, and nodded vigorously.

'*Ja, goulasch*, he said. 'As she is made in Hungary – a little bit of everything, with much . . . how you say . . .?'

'Pepper?' No, not pepper. 'Curry . . .? Paprika?'

'Paprika, yes!' His eyes lit up. Anya felt as if she had just won a prize for unusual brilliance.

'So what do we have after *goulasch*?' she pressed him. 'For sweets? Afters?'

Karoly looked at Laczi: 'Afters'? Laczi translated.

'Ah!' his eyes glistened. The *goulasch* ceased. His face became grave. The bow hung suspended in the air, then descended with tender potency.

A mellow tripartite chord that seemed to turn every board in the house into a resonator. The melodic line detached itself and set out, searching, undulating, soaring, sinking down, till it came momentarily to rest where Bach sank a bass marker-post in his musical territory, while the post at her head vibrated anew. Then off again, unwinding the glowing filament of melody. It was as if the sound took on the colour and warmth and depth of the waxen wood, reddened by the firelight, from which it was born. But it was also as if the bow, drawn with such delicate and inexorable firmness, was being drawn across the very root of her being till the whole instrumental body of her sang. She watched the sinewy arm, bared to the elbow, on which the black hairs glistened, mesmerized by the enchantments it wrought. Was it Tolstoy who thought music too dangerously seductive to be let loose on immoral humanity? How right he had been . . . The Allemande had come to a delicious arpeggiated close.

'More, more,' she breathed.

He played the Courante. 'More.' The Sarabande. That was nearly too much for her self-possession, the dark riches of the sustained chords searching her out in the thickets of unconsciousness where she wanted to lose herself. But the Menuetto reprieved, and the Gigue released her back into gaiety. Kiss threw off the final descending chord with contemptuous bravado, as if he knew his power to pierce and stir, and disdained to exercise it. God help her, but she was in love with the man for extracting music from a lump of wood! She sat up and shook herself. This treacherous capacity for abandonment she really must watch: it positively offered her up for violation. She glanced at Laczi, who had become as strange to her as she was to herself. His head was down and he was shaking it from side to side, as if in pain. He reached across and laid a hand on the 'cellist's shoulder, grunting something in Hungarian. His friend flashed him a smile that came and went like lightning across the handsome bearded face. Again Anya felt her bowels melting. She rose.

'Thanks,' she said in her most offhand tone, as if people were everyday thrusting unaccompanied 'cello suites upon her. She fetched wine and glasses and managed, after a few minutes, to reinstate a safe normality . . .

Or so she thought, till she and Laczi climbed into bed that night. Then it all overflowed – to his intense surprise, and intenser gratification . . .

It was just like Bill, she remarked, as they curled up together to consider sleeping, to have put them in a brass bedstead with a built-in alarm system. Listen to the damned thing! It jingled like a tinker's cart if you so much as blew your nose. Did Bill think they were eunuchs, or what?

'If he does, my treasure,' murmured Laczi, folding his arms comfortably about her lap, 'he has by now learned otherwise.'

He took a mouthful of the thick auburn hair, and fell to considering the cumulative richness of things, wondering how he had failed, in the past, to take it properly into account.

The renovations had staggered to a halt. Bill, after building a tiny sluice-gate to regulate the domestic water-supply, gave up. They began to go farther afield in the daytime – while Karoly stayed at home, fulfilling his daily quota. He was to play the six Bach suites in a double recital in October. The practising was no hardship. The hardship would have been to neglect it. They could see him from the brow of the Warren – set up on the south-facing terrace, complete with music stand, a tiny figure on a spindly chair sawing away to the birds and the distance. The sound carried to them in faint gusts.

On the spine of the hill was some kind of ancient fort – 'Celtic,' Bill said somebody had said. An affair of trenches and earthworks laid out with a perceptible symmetry under the sky and the high-sailing clouds. Like the fossil of some gigantic ammonite, Laczi suggested. They kicked about in the flinty gravel, half expecting to uncover spearheads and stone axes.

But the distances beckoned. Once the height had been gained, it was easy walking. Beatrice surprised Anya by falling into a loping stride which had the rest of them stepping out breathlessly to keep up.

They came upon a little dewpond. Water-supply for the ancient Celts? There was inconclusive speculation. Caspar, who had a compulsion to wade into anything that was wet, went in up to the ankles, cupped his hands and squatted staring at the frenzy of pond creatures that were evading his grasp. Larval wrigglers, water boatmen, fat tadpoles and long-legged flies hopped and rowed and juddered in all directions, or burrowed deep in the peaty mud.

'It's life,' he said, using the curious vocabulary of primary-school nature studies. 'There's life everywhere. Look at the life!'

''Tis new to thee,' quoted Anya confidentially to Laczi. But the Party Classics he'd studied had not included Shakespeare.

'What is new please?' he inquired. 'Life?'

'Forget it.'

'No. Life is to me not new. I feel today very lifelike.'

'Lively,' she corrected.

He was forced to sigh for her literal-mindedness: 'I joke.'

'Well don't, muttonhead. It's too hard telling the difference.'

Condemned to solemnity, it seemed best to indulge it thoroughly: 'This,' he gloomily declared, 'is anyway not life. Is death. We stand in the midst of death.'

She eyed him with contempt. He scrambled up a grassy pimple to demonstrate: 'This here is a graveyard.' They stood, in fact, at the hub of a wheel of radiating tumps and tumuli, 'About us always are the dead. We stand upon the grave's lip.'

Anya laughed – in sympathy, probably, with the grave that had its lip stood upon. He took the expected umbrage: 'Is no joking matter, this mortality.'

Bill came up: 'What's this? Mortality? On a day like this?'

'What the day has to do with it? Is transient like the clouds.'

'The Prophet, you know,' Anya explained, touching her head.

'Stonedust and solitude. Silicosis of the cerebellum. Silts up the brain.'

Bill nodded, not much interested.

'Isn't this splendid, though,' he persisted. 'The weather and all?'

'To hear you talk,' Anya retorted, 'anybody'd think you'd personally had the Mendips shifted so as to be under this bit of it. You don't own it, you know.'

Bill grinned, happily immune to satire: 'The way I feel, I might as well. It's the best thing I ever did, buying this place.'

'What I detest about Nature,' Anya remarked to nobody in particular, 'is the way it erodes one's ironies.'

'Apparently not everybody's,' murmured Laczi, descending from his tump and taking her arm. 'Come on, let's walk. It's what we came for, no?'

Having no map, they wandered at random. Ventured down the opening of a pothole, slithering on greasy rock until prudence dictated retreat. Wandered into a pine plantation where Laczi, to Anya's disgust, tried to recover his boyhood by climbing trees and Caspar proved the better boy. Detoured down a scrubby groove in the hill's edge, which turned into a dark dingle, and finally into a deep wooded coomb, walled in on both sides by high cliffs. A stream materialized. They followed it. It brought them out, as luck would have it, at a crossroads and a pub. Exactly at lunchtime, what was more.

Sitting in the pretty beer garden behind high brick walls which trapped all the sun there was to be had, they succumbed hungrily to the fortuitous and admired the roses. Caspar, after exhaustive inquiries among the flowers, estimated the bee population at 'eleventy thousand'. They bought another round. Though Anya chafed for her escaping ironies, a timeless kind of benignity, indolent and inane, increasingly prevailed. It took closing time to get them on their feet.

After following the wrong branch of the stream back up the coomb and taking several other false turnings, it was late afternoon by the time they got back to the hill-fort. Cloud shadows moved on the yellow-brown water of the Channel which looked solid as custard now in the westering light. While the Madisons zigzagged down the giant brow, to the tangle of trees and the terracotta roofs of home, Laczi and Anya opted to stay up there ('for the sunset', they said). They'd had about enough euphoria for one day and needed to reconstitute their asperities.

But Nature was making it difficult: on the seaward prow of their land-promontory, She (or those increasingly hypothetical Celts) had scooped out a small bowl and grassed it voluptuously. It sloped up at exactly the right angle to pillow the heads and shoulders of the lazy or the zonked. They flung themselves down . . .

Clouds, but not time, passed.

Anya gave a yawn and kicked at the grass with an indolent heel: 'What a fatuous way of spending a day,' she drawled. 'M'legs're finished. And what for? Scenery!'

She didn't move.

'I feel like a fag,' she sighed. 'No use telling you.'

He turned his head to look at her. There were tones in her voice these days that seemed settled, reposeful, as he had never heard them before. It was the same strong profile, the same penetrating gaze, but with a something . . . a bloom, a glisten on it. Perhaps it was the healthful effect of wind on complexion, nothing more. He realized what she had just said.

'You have been not-smoking,' he said in surprise, fastening on at least one new element in the compound.

'Only just noticed?' she taunted amicably.

'This is a revolution I am to witness?'

She stuck out her bottom lip and shrugged: 'Never had a spare minute. Forgot about it.'

She met his contesting gaze.

'All right,' she conceded, 'a revolution. Small one.'

The minutes passed.

'Speaking of revolutions,' she said, cocking an ankle up on her knee, 'there's been another. *You*'ve not talked politics for a fortnight.'

'Do I not?'

'Nup. Not a sausage.'

'This comes to you as a relief?'

'S'pose so . . . Dunno . . . Actually I think I miss it. Takes all the needle out of our dissensions. Not the same.'

'There is also a reason,' he went on.

'Oh-oh?'

'For Karoly, politics is not an easy matter as for me. He must return soon to politics – or else he must make the big political choice.'

'Defect?'

'Stupid word. But so.'

'I didn't know.'

'I only guess. He does not tell. It is very hard for him, whatever way.'

'Hard?' She caught at the word. 'You admit to some ease, then?'

He turned his head again, lazily, to read the question.

'What is this, you think? Labour?'

'But you like it?' From her interrogative sharpness it seemed that something hung on his reply. He gave it dispassionate consideration: 'Is very nice. For a bit. For a change. For too long it would be destruction. Already I am half-destroyed.'

'Mmm,' she nodded, watching him with appraising eyes, 'right! A certain sogginess *does* prevail. Today maybe it's only Reclining on the Bosom of Nature; but next thing you'll be Loving Humanity.'

He rolled his eyes in her direction: 'You think so? So desperate as this?'

'All too likely.' She mustn't spare him the painful truth. 'These things creep up on you. And given *your* native sloppiness, there won't be much resistance either.'

'Me? Sloppy?' His incredulity was positively beatific.

'And I *don't* believe in your "destruction" either. I think you play at it. It doesn't hold any real terrors.'

'And you?' he queried, lax and motionless, 'you do not play?'

'Ah no, my precious,' she said, rolling on her side and taking a pinch of his cheek between her fingers, 'I do not play. With me it's for real.' Her grip on his face was certainly real enough, and not entirely affectionate. 'Be warned in time,' she crooned, 'destruction is my native element.' Then she laughed and released him . . . letting the word float away – a whisper on the mild air . . . 'destruction' . . . as if contemplating its evaporation, though in no doubt of its return.

'Of course,' she added matter-of-factly, 'if you can't take a hint . . . on your own head be it!'

Perhaps it was because she now had his attention very thoroughly, that she affected to make light of it: 'Argh!' she went on, with mocking bravado, 'it's probably just as well. I couldn't endure growing old. Falling hair and sagging tits. *And* a mouthful of clattering dentures . . . Jesus! you can spare me that! That's why I can't raise a flicker of interest in the nuclear disarmers and the Armageddon-merchants. When it ends, it ends. And good luck to it! Why spin it out?' She was meeting his questioning gaze with complete steadiness.

'Goodnight humanity?' he suggested.

'You feel it too?' she queried quickly, almost hopefully.

'No,' he said flatly. 'Not me. I don't believe in ends.'

'You'd better believe in them, buttercup,' she said sharply, taking another pinch of cheek, 'you've got one coming.'

'Just for that reason exactly, I *don't*. When it will come, it will not be requiring *my* belief. Until then I do not believe, I work. I work as if it will not be. Is the only way. (Would you leave please my face alone?)'

Once more she gave him a tweak and released him.

'It's not *my* way,' she declared, leaning back on one elbow, still watching him.

Her mind was gathering itself for something. She took breath, paused, then let it come: 'You know? I think we need each other . . . "for Life", as it were.'

He nodded in complaisance. It was true enough.

'Sort of . . . complementary souls, wouldn't you say?'

He nodded again.

'Aren't we?' Her brows were contracting in inexplicable wrath. What had he done now?

'Jesus Christ!' She detonated under his astonished gaze, kneeling up to grab him by the jacket and shaking him violently: 'Shitty death! I just *proposed* to you, dumb-bell! Can't you do anything but nod at me like a clockwork poodle?'

Light dawned on his startled face. But he looked so comical as it did so, that the silence of the ancient Celts was shattered by the sound of Anya's hooting laughter. 'Look at you!' she pointed, between whoops of unenvenomed merriment, 'just look at the sight you make!' She leaned on her knuckles, head thrown back and heavy auburn hair swinging, giving herself up to it.

A small chuckle took possession of his throat. It was impossible to resent her derision, or her laughter, which was bouncing back at them now from the liberties of the surrounding hills. They heard it down in Crabtree Cottage and exchanged amused glances. What a character she was!

But Laczi who, more than most, knew what a character she was, heard only one thing in all the reverberating mirth – the authentic note of a spirit free like his own. Here was a woman with the courage to mock destruction out of countenance – or to die laughing.

He curtailed his nod of idiot compliance and pursed his lips in his favourite clownish expression: 'OK,' he said, humping his shoulders and spreading fatuous concessive palms. 'OK, marry me. I don't mind.'

NINE

Cornish

Anya re-entered London, to examine her old life, with eyes that were both wider than before, and narrowed with new scepticism. She was not at all sure that the old life would prove viable. Pasted on the facade of the Rotten Orange she found a municipal Demolition Order. Boesma had struck. She struck back as best she could by lodging an appeal at the Borough Planning Department, but it was only buying time, she knew. She wasn't sure that she cared any more. Let it end if it would.

Two days later, chance came to her aid. *Nova* was running a nostalgia feature-series on 'Boutiques of the Sixties' and a cadet reporter of great impressionability materialized on the doorstep, with a brand-new fountain-pen that refused to write and a clipboard full of foolish questions. Anya lent her a ballpoint, plied her inexperience with liquor, and set to work on her impressionability. The questions she ignored. The cadet reporter, nervously feminist on occupational grounds, was greatly impressed by this colossus of Liberation. With only a little bullying, she was induced to collaborate in Anya's fabrication of her personal legend – from the days of the Grand-Opening-and-Closing-Down-Sale of 1969 to the threatened eviction of 1975. By the time it had been properly elaborated, the proprietress of the Rotten Orange was emerging as a commercial tragedy queen of lofty principle going down grandly to ruin and liquidation. It read well.

The article came out, and at once the shop seethed with bargain-hunting necrophiliacs. Anya took her cue, and bought on a grand scale. The selling on a grand scale had already begun. It became clear that the real problem was not how to sustain, but how to terminate the bonanza (she was by now determined that it *must* end, no matter what followed; enough was enough). But the crowds continued to flock and to insist on buying anything she cared to hang on a dress rack. A well-liquored wake tends to make the mourners careless about their wallets, and these customers, amicably convinced that she was going bust, had no attention to spare for her pricing policy.

A month passed, and still the turnover was escalating . . . So that it came as a relief when Pal Juhacz, the infamous Hungarian property tycoon, presented himself as mourner-in-chief. He had engineered an introduction through Kovacs, and came bearing a proposition. An unnamed 'friend' of his, who was thinking of going into the retail rag-trade, was looking for a commercial base, and he had commissioned Juhacz to inquire whether she would be willing to part with name, stock and goodwill for a sum he was here to negotiate.

She looked dismally doubtful – how was a girl to make a living, if her living was taken away from her? But yes (a sigh), she might indeed be forced to consider the possibility. Why didn't he come round to her flat tomorrow evening and they could discuss it *tête-à-tête* over a dinner she would prepare with her own fair hands? She saw his eyes light up – whether with cupidity or concupiscence it was hard to tell – and decided that if the dinner wasn't nourishing she could always eat him for breakfast. It meant, of course, that she had to cook both the meal and the books in very short order, but she managed it, and over the mints and coffee they concluded a deal which would probably give Juhacz a hangover the next morning, but which was toasted that night in impeccable Veuve Cliquot. At the door she embraced him continental fashion, bestowed a chaste kiss on his receding hairline, and vowed her eternal gratitude – with which he had to make do.

Maybe he had known what he was doing all along. He seemed too wily and too travelled a bird to be blown very far off course. But Anya was astonished, none the less, at the size of the cheque she found herself paying into her account a week later. And on the heels of the astonishment, came mistrust. The bank-biro slipped from nerveless fingers and swung on the end of its chain.

What had she been about to give away?! She knew she was bartering her *independence* for cash – but if she were also signing away a goldmine . . .? Perhaps the Juhacz knew something she didn't. He might be sitting at his desk this very minute, chuckling over his contract. Never! She screwed up the pay-in slip and sallied forth. Never! Never too late to correct a mistake.

The mistrust grew monstrously as she sat in an outer office and listened to clandestine negotiations on the intercom which wouldn't have fooled a baby: unfortunely Mr Juhacz was not in at present . . .

It was not known when Mr Juhacz would be back . . . Yes, Miss Jevons's name had been mentioned . . . No, there was no point in waiting. He mightn't be in again for several days . . .

Anya contemplated the oak-panelled door, drawing up dispositions for a charge. It would be easy enough to bring off. But she quailed at the conversation that would then ensue. As surely as her signature was on the contract, she was in his emollient little hands. And wouldn't he let her know it! She'd made him sweat a bit along the way, and he wasn't the kind to deny himself a bit of sweet reprisal. Better not give him the chance. The most she could achieve would be to screw him for an extra hundred or two; and meanwhile he would sit and smirk, knowing it was chickenfeed beside the anticipated profits of his fictive 'friend'. Well, damn them both! What was done, was done.

She fixed the secretary's evasive eye: she might tell Mr Juhacz, *when* he appeared again, that Miss Jevons would be back. When? . . . Oh . . . whenever. No telling really. She might not be free again for several days. (Let him at least spend one nervous night wondering what her game was: it was the best that could be managed.) Gathering her bag and coat, she swanned out. Episode closed.

She took a cab back to the bank, paid in the cheque, then walked to the Orange. Kim, who was moving with the stock to the new location, had it all packed up and loaded, and came to make her farewells. Her big brown eyes were swimming with tears. It was so sad. She was very grateful. It had been the chance of a lifetime. And so it was 'reallysweet' of Anya to recommend her to Mr Juhacz. Kim was her own recommendation, Anya replied – which was true enough, even without Juhacz's weakness for a pretty face. Kim climbed into the passenger seat beside the pantechnicon driver (whom she'd already put into such a flutter that he couldn't find first gear), and waved her hanky out the window. The vehicle lumbered off.

Stranded on the pavement, in the watery sunlight of a November afternoon, Anya half expected to see the bulldozers move in at once, though they were not due for another month. It had all been sudden as a dream, and her brain reeled slightly. She could have used someone like Stacy, who understood the susceptibilities of entrepreneurs, to steady herself against. A pity, really, that Stacy hadn't been here to see the farcical/shady/triumphant debacle in which it had all ended. It was a pity Stacy hadn't . . . many things . . . but this was no time for regrets.

Anya's betrothed was occupied in making up editions of the bronzes which had sold at the exhibition. When that was finished . . . tie a quiet knot in a Register Office and see what was to be done with all this unprecedented loot and liberty which, to tell the truth, was beginning to scare her a little, there was so much of it. All very well for him with his damned vocation, but she'd just packed hers – such as it was – into a blue-and-white striped van and seen it trundle off over the horizon.

The spotlights snapped on in the despoiled windows of the Rotten Orange. Bloody time-switch! It'd run her up a tidy bill if she didn't quash it. She moved towards the door, but paused. The idea of that man-sized diseased fruit squatting there phosphorescing as the demolition squad advanced on it rather appealed to her. And they'd never find her to present the bill anyway. Boesma, vile old stinker, would get stuck with it. Not that he hadn't done them a service – in spite of himself.

It was time they both moved. Truly it was. London was an old rind and they'd eaten the fruit.

So . . . a holiday-honeymoon in Cornwall – the old haunts (she could get that mouldering skeleton out of the cupboard) . . . next, find him a studio in the country (any old barn would do – Cornwall was full of old barns – and look what Bill and Bea had done with their pile of rubble!) . . . And then . . . begin again. *She* had capital, *he* had work, they both had hope and health. Why shouldn't it work?

She pictured herself briefly as Rural Muse, in headscarf, oilskins and wellingtons, stomping picturesquly about the moors, pausing briefly to be sketched in windblown silhouette atop a strategic logan-stone. A shade implausible? Well, it'd make a change anyway.

She strolled round to the studio, to see what he thought of it.

With their portables safely stowed in the village's sole pub and their persons well scarved and swathed, they stepped out for a stroll before the light went completely. The village street presented the expected vista of out-of-season desolation. A seaborne gale was funnelling through the harbour entrance and gusting up the steep vee of the valley, and when they came out of the canyon between the forestreet shops, Laczi was knocked sideways by it. Citizen of a land-locked state, he had never accustomed himself to these maritime astringencies, and protested keenly. What the devil was wrong with observing this uproar of the elements from the comfort of their bedroom? It overlooked the harbour. But Anya wouldn't hear of it. In keeping with her new life, the metropolitan sybarite had turned outdoor spartan and her new husband was going to feel the difference.

Two kids playing tag about the huge rusty anchor which dominated the Platt, caught sight of Anya and high-tailed it off up a deserted side street, shouting. The couple stood leaning into the wind, staring out to sea over the stone arm of the breakwater, which was not preventing quite substantial inshore waves from rattling the moored fishing boats and churning up the shingle. Low cloud loomed in banks on the horizon and rushed streaming overhead. The kids had returned with two others and lurked in the shadow of the lifeboat house. Laczi had the sensation of being under furtive observation, but put it down to rustic inquisitiveness. His eyes streamed and there was an incipient ache in his ears where the icy wind drummed. He turned up his coat collar.

'I would prefer to walk,' he said.

They turned off the Platt, jumping down on to the roadway. A late shopper with fur hat and string bag was battling along the street towards them.

'Hullo Alice,' Anya challenged sharply.

The woman lifted round eyes, which went rounder. Her lips parted for a second, then she lowered her head and went butting past them.

'And good evening to you, too!' At the sound of Anya's ringing tones, a knot of men at the entrance to the fish store looked up. Recognition glimmered in their eyes for a second, but quickly gave place to the dull stare reserved for anonymous emmets. The circle which had opened for a moment, coiled in on itself again, resuming its chat in the clanging vowels and swooping intonation of the local speech. Anya, her head in the air, crossed the road to pass unnecessarily close to them. Laczi caught a glimpse of tarred piles of lobster-pots, a whiff of rank fish, and a snatch of conversation in which there seemed an unnatural density of 'hers' and 'shes', though most of it was as unintelligible to him as a foreign tongue. They turned up the Chapel Hill, gradually losing the sound as the wind took possession of the air.

Laczi regarded his new wife curiously. She had been rumbling with incipient revelations for days, but it looked as if she was going to have to have them winched out of her.

'Should there be a welcome party?' he asked.

'Cattle!' she hissed. 'Cretins!'

'But where are the *friendly* natives?' he laughed. 'You seem notorious enough, but I would not say, welcome.'

She tossed her head in disdain: 'Fool to expect anything else!'

'But what was here your sin? Can it be told?'

'Criminal idiocy!' she snapped. 'I was criminally idiotic. I tried to marry one of the cretins.'

He waited for developments, but none came.

'You tried to marry...' he prompted, '... and then there has come the cold flushes, eh?'

She shrugged. He emitted a small tuneless whistle, and nodded to himself: 'So. This is why we are here, you and me? You with your fresh cretin? To show to them all, what is what?'

'Very astute.'

She strode on ahead up the steep lane. On their right, where the hill slid precipitously into the harbour, you could almost reach out and touch the slate roofs of huddled houses. A gull, sheltering in the lee of a chimney, croaked tonelessly at them, shuffling its weight from one clumsy yellow foot to another. They emerged on to a level. The track plunged off to the right, through high thorns. Lights were coming on in the town.

Laczi decided not to press. They needed all their breath for the climb, and the day was failing fast. The dorsal profile of the inland horizon was so black against the rose-coloured sky that the retina invented an incandescent thread, whiter than light itself, at the point of junction. Below it, the limbs of the sleeping land existed more as a feeling of mass and power than as visible shapes. They toiled up the spine of the hill, only to be slammed by the wind as they reached the summit. Anya's nylon anorak slatted and banged like the sail of an ill-rigged dinghy, while Laczi had to steady himself with his hand on the stone wall. Air was being forced into his mouth and his cheeks were stung by the flying spray flung up and driven onshore from the Point two hundred feet below.

'Aiiee-hi!' he yelled in protest at the capture of his breath.

She turned to him with gleaming eyes. She had thought it was a shout of exultation.

'Goddam the natives!' she screamed. 'Let 'em all rot with their stinking fish!' She executed a small war-dance on the spot, ending by stamping on the faces of her yokel-foes. Another racing battalion of clouds passed low overhead. Against the drained sky, now turning slate-grey with intimidating swiftness, they seemed to emit light, luminescent.

'Hey!' he said sternly, capturing her arm. 'How about now you tell me, eh?'

She shook her head proudly.

Whereupon he shook her: 'Hey!' Again. 'Was it one of those fishers down below?'

'I didn't look. It's none of your business. It could have been.'

'Why you are so crazy? coming back like this? Tell me that.'

Again she shook her head.

'All right,' he said, quite out of patience now, 'is too obvious to tell. You come to slay the ghost. You wonder maybe don't you like the big knucklehead after all – just a little – you don't think so, but you want to look. But you bring me along too. As insurance. Just in case. Is so. I know. And now I will tell you why you *like* the big knucklehead at the first place.'

She watched him with steady eyes, though the wind was whipping her hair in ragged streamers all over her face.

'You like him because you say to yourself, "Here there is at last a man! Here is one what is not afraid of me. This is what I have been wanting all along." But *why* he is not afraid, eh? You tell me that. Because he is too stupid. He is too stupid to know fear. Because he sees a handsome face and a pair of strong legs, all he can think is how to stick his prick between. *Wunderbar!* But once he has stuck it, *then* he is afraid. He is afraid with the fear of a stupid man. This is the brute what you think you are wanting – but only until you get him, and then you see better. Then you show to him the door. Then you treat him like the shit he is. Am I right? Or am I right?'

She put both hands on his shoulders and looked him fiercely between the eyes: 'And you? you're *not* afraid?' It was a question, not a taunt, but she looked capable of throttling an answer out of him.

'I am not stupid,' he muttered.

'Nor am I,' she replied sharply.

Still the clouds came scudding, driven fast and low, swerving up over the lip of the cliff and pouring down behind the rim of the upland horizon. Twisting his head back to watch their flight, Laczi lost the horizontal completely. Massed, looming, glowing queerly in the blue afterlight, they usurped the earth's substance, unreal as a dream army marching across his upturned face.

As he lowered his head to face her, a patch of light fell on the pair of them. A tiny crescent moon of jewelled clarity was sailing up a gap in the sky, forming a pool of ultramarine around itself.

They stood and watched the magical apparition, while the last pigments drained away out of the earth.

'Let's go round to the next bay,' she said. 'We can make it.'

'You reckon?'

They set out briskly. Laczi watched the muddy turquoise of the working waves turning to black, an unwholesome florescence which the night was suppressing. He kept losing his footing on the huge corrugations left by herds of passing cows. It was almost totally dark when they reached the tiny stream that ran into the bay. He stood in the shingle and picked at a boulder. It came away in his hand in great flakes.

'Look at this,' he said in disgust. 'You call this stone? Some sort of rotten cheese, more likely. And that sea!'

'What's wrong with the sea?' she asked in high amusement.

'Is putrid. Not natural. Is no place for humanity. Makes me sick to look at it. I tell you, when the ancient man put his foot on dry land it was not in order for to go straight back to the swamps again. You can keep your rotten sea.'

'What are you so mad about?' she asked, amazed at him.

He rounded on her angrily: 'Because I do not want to share you with some mucking knucklehead from the deep sea. With some blue-eyed fisher-boy. Not with him, nor with nobody, you hear? So you keep him right out of my way, or else . . . or else . . . I don't know, I think I kill him.'

Anya laughed and kissed him on the nose.

'I didn't know you cared,' she simpered.

He shoved her off.

'I *don't* "care",' he said roughly. 'What should I care about how you . . . how you "put it about"? This is nothing to me. In emotion, it is nothing. But we have made agreement together. As rational people we have made agreement. And that is what matters, no? To keep our agreement.'

Another woman might have been repelled by so transactional a view of the case, but not Anya. She much preferred her romanticism dried and salted, and besides, it filled her with wonder, this rage of his.

'You have hidden depths, my precious,' she crooned.

She was profoundly gratified and did not bother to conceal it. The commitment had been made and it was solid. More solid than she had dared to hope.

They walked back in silence, hand in hand like children.

As they came over the brow of the Point, in view of the twinkling, glimmering town where it lay crouched in little pools of blue and pink and yellow light, he spoke again: 'I also,' he said, 'have a ghost. She has come to me when we were at the Mendips, and she does not go away.' He seemed to be in trouble with his lower jaw which swivelled about pointlessly. 'You see, it was at such a house party exactly – after my first one-man show – that Amanda made her proposition.' He released her hand and gazed doubtfully at his feet, though it was too dark to see them.

'Then, too, I didn't say no.'

She gave a little sniff of amusement; 'Do you always get your women to propose to you?'

He looked up swiftly, searching her dim face for its expression. 'Is worrying, no?'

'Who's superstitious now?' she taunted.

'Then it does not bother you?' He could not make out her face.

She made a mouth of derision: 'I am superior to these petty fates,' she swanked.

'So I think,' he said. 'Perhaps.'

Having submitted herself to the ordeal of re-entry, Anya was prepared, possibly anxious, to let the past drop. Nothing would come of it – it was dead and gone. She was even ready to give up the sea, if it displeased him so much. They decided to drive inland, find a cottage they could take for a few weeks, and then start in earnest on the search for a convertible barn.

Next morning Anya pointed the nose of the little chugging Deux-Chevaux inland in the general direction of the Moor, and followed it wherever it took her. Having admitted a possible pleasure in mere scenery, she was not going to enjoy it by halves.

They plunged down long winding tunnels of twigs and greenery, the filament of tarmac with its ribbon of grass at the centre unwinding ahead and the banks closing in until they feared they would turn a corner and wedge fast between them. Then the lane would give itself a shake and they would be humping over an arched stone bridge with a glimpse of millhouse and gurgling brook, or splashing through a shallow ford, and on up an impossible gradient, surrounded by forests of spruce, larch and fir, until they burst into the open flatlands where draggle-tailed sheep with hearthrugs thrown over their backs huddled in eroded hollows at the edge of the road, raising startled heads in mid-chew to stare at the noisy yellow buggy. The tyres clanged over a cattle-grid.

A church tower and a stand of bare beeches beckoned and in a minute they were in a cluster of rag-roofed, slate-hung cottages, scattered higgledy-piggledy about a green where dogs sniffed and rooted. A solitary child swung from a rope's end, rapt in its own slow, swooping motion. Even the fields seemed deserted, apart from the occasional clatter of a tractor, or a distant thud from a shotgun. If everybody was going about their business, it must have been very silent and secret business. Strange folk, the Cornish – occasionally roused to hostility, but usually intent on their own affairs with a quiet stubbornness that repelled intrusion.

They bumped across rails and blundered into a china-clay depot – astonishing in this context, with its rows of silent freight-cars and closed steel warehouse doors. Nobody stirring here either. The country seemed foundered in its deep midwinter sleep. Except that the wind still blew powerfully.

Hunger and the quest of a pub eventually propelled them up an unpromising lane which debouched on to a triangular green of grand proportions. It was fringed with noble old elms and beeches which gave shelter, but whose tops thrashed about in the upper air. No rag-slate here, but solid granite houses in huge cyclopian blocks framing gracefully proportioned windows. On the village's downhill boundary the square tower of the church reared up, silhouetted against the rusty grey of the wooded slopes beyond.

They looked at each other. This . . . or something like it?

One of the manorial houses was a pub, crimson-carpeted and snugly curtained. They were the only customers and had the log fire to themselves. They inquired. Yes, there would probably be several houses to let at this time of the year. And yes, they could certainly have lunch. How about a slice of pheasant pie? The landlady had some freshly baked. Yes? Lovely job!

A couple of men, big-boned and florid-complexioned, stumped in and banged the sides of their wellingtons against the grate, shedding mud and exchanging pleasantries with the visitors. The peaceful hush, only temporarily disturbed, flowed back over the room. Laczi and Anya found themselves talking in undertones.

It took only half an hour, after lunch, to find the owner of a cottage to let, and a few minutes to reach an arrangement for a fortnight. That left a couple of hours of daylight.

Again Anya drove at random.

'I must get a licence,' she said.

'You don't have one?' It was the first he'd heard.
'Only a South African one. Expired ten years ago.'
'I have put my life in your hands.'
'You have, haven't you?' she concurred, swerving needlessly around a pothole to see if he was scareable.
'One thing,' she said, screwing up her eyes as if she detected an approaching hazard on the empty road ahead. 'I let it pass yesterday. But don't you start telling me what I do and don't do. I don't allow it.'
'You don't want to know?'
'I don't need your interpretations.'
'Of what?' He was all innocence.
'Of my dealings with the knuckleheads.'
'Ah! So I was wrong?'
'Maybe. Maybe not. I just don't need them.'
'Knuckleheads?'
'Interpretations.'
'So.' He gave it some thought. 'But still,' he stipulated, 'when I think you need to know, still I will tell you. OK?'
'Mutiny,' she growled.
'Not so,' he replied imperturbably, 'this is not your ship only. Also mine.'
Ahead the road swooped up towards a jagged skyline, a saddle ridge and a jumble of granite blocks – as if some gigantic child had upended its toybox on the rounded eminence.
Anya pointed. 'Shall we climb it?'
'What for?'
'Because it's there?'
The road petered out in a stony car-park. They laced themselves into the boots Anya had insisted on their buying that morning. Yesterday's gales had swept the sky clear of cloud, but it was far from blowing itself out yet.
The track started as a boggy cutting, oozing with water, which quickly faded where other walkers had fanned out across the turf, each choosing his own route to the summit. Ancient hut-circles, dating from happier climatic days, were dotted across the slopes, and moorland ponies grazed among them, rumps uniformly turned to the wind and tails streaming between their hind legs.
The higher they got, the more the blast bit into their clothing, shoving them from behind like a great hand so that they stumped along stiff-legged and clumsy in resistance. The force of it was

amazing. No wonder that, when they turned to check how far they had come, they saw the Atlantic, ten miles away to the west, spatterdashed with whitecaps huge enough to be visible even at this range. Nothing but the odd icefloe stood between them and America – and it felt like it.

Needling granules of snow driving into their faces at storm-force persuaded them to face about and continue the climb. They had reached the skirts of the tor, and began scrambling up blocks that were sometimes six feet high and twenty feet in length. A midget climbing the Great Pyramid would have experienced similar sensations of endlessness and exhaustion. But they made it finally to the summit of piled megalithic scones with its huge poised egg of a logan-stone. Well, they *almost* made it – for, as the wind shrieked free of the last obstruction it unleased such a demonic blast that Anya pitched forward on her face and lay there laughing, or shouting, or weeping – it was impossible to tell which, because of the deafening passage of air across one's ears. Laczi winched her into a sitting position and they crawled a few yards out of the pandemonium and into a slit between two vertical pillars of granite which offered some protection.

'Aieee– yaiee – yaiee!' he yelled. And this time he did sound exultant. 'My God, what a place!'

Anya, wrestling with her laces, sniffed.

'Smells like a stone-age urinal,' she commented, regarding the packed, puddled earth with suspicion. 'Oh, fuck it!' Her fingers were refusing to obey her.

He was running his hands over the walls of their rock-chamber and pecking at it with his nails.

'Now this,' he said admiringly, 'is what I call a real structure. Built to outlast dynasties.'

'Without central heating,' Anya retorted, rubbing her icy hands and beginning to detect some resurgence of the metropolitan sybarite, 'it's more likely to freeze them to death. Jeesus!' She held up a frozen claw like a dead blackbird's, and mimed paralysis. He took it between his and blew on it hard, rubbing away between puffs.

'Will be all right. You know,' he went on excitably, 'I saw today granite – all over the place – but I did not see the scale – the spaces what it comes from. Is magnificent. I think tomorrow I bring my toolbag up and commence a sculpture-park. It will be my Capella Medici, eh? Right out here under the sky.'

Anya groaned.

'You wait here,' he said, ducking his head outdoors again, 'I go find somewhere warm. Wait.'

Some minutes passed and she began to recover her functions. She heard a distant shout, stuck her head out, but could not locate its source. It seemed to be coming out of the sky. It was. The logan-egg had hatched and up there, shag-haired and bristle-whiskered, stood the Phoenix of Budapest brandishing his arms and shrieking unintelligibly. She laughed in spite of herself as a gust caught him and sat him down, plump on his bony rump. Below the waist he seemed to have disappeared. On the crown of the stone there was a lipped concave basin, hollowed out by millennial ice and rain. He scrambled to his feet cursing. His fall had cracked the pane of ice and saturated his pants. He presented the tragic sight for commiseration but she only laughed more, made signs: Can I get up?

He reached her a hand, hauled away, and they both crouched in the basin surveying the country around – an unobstructed 360-degree view of an amplitude that would have been breathtaking, if all their breath hadn't already been taken by the wind. Even so, it was magnificent.

'You've convinced me,' he shouted in her ear. 'This is the place. We look no farther. And I will carve here granite. Granite!' he smacked a fist into his palm. 'The stone for a man! No more stones of cheese and soap. No more chalk and flour and dust and gypsum. Granite!' He clenched a defiant pharaonic fist: 'It is decreed.'

Like many a sensible man before him, Laczi had succumbed to the seductions of a good day. His concept of the good day was not like that of most – balmy airs, warm sun, and pacific social relations – but he was just as prone to make long-term projections on the basis of present good feelings. And why not? On what other basis does any large venture get under way? All you need is a bit of stamina to see it through. Taking life in the lump, Lajos Kovacs, sculptor, felt confident that he had that stamina.

Untouched by his vehemence, Anya smiled sourly. Her feet were killing her.

So that was how it came about that the couple set up house in a large barn (also granite) on the skirts of Bodmin Moor, converting the attached byre into living quarters, and converting their lifestyle into something so different from London life that, when they lifted their heads from their paintpots and cement buckets, or paused in their tilling or reslating, they were astonished at themselves. Or rather, Anya was: for it was, in a way, Laczi's old life of frugal self-sufficiency before he had met her which had been confirmed and ratified in this, the first joint venture of their marriage. It was only the rusticity that was new.

The summer that was shaping up was one so extraordinary that, before it was over, cabinet ministers were to hear themselves publicly abused for being unable to make rain; and in the village nearest the Kovacses, some ancient druidic rites (which seemed to involve a good deal of dancing naked about fires) were revived, in the hope that these might succeed where cabinet ministers had failed. From the rural vantage-point it seemed as if the entire British nation – while crying crisis and anticipating death by parching – had taken to the beaches and the hills, where it lay idly about, acquiring a suntan and an irresponsible attitude to life. Anglo-Saxondom was in danger of that headlong slide into hedonism which was supposed to be the prerogative of the Latin races.

But sunshine takes different people different ways. In an asphaltic overheated London, hedonism was more difficult; and the inhabitants of Southall and Notting Hill might have been forgiven for resisting the idyllic view of the Long Hot Summer through which the metropolitan press was 'phewing' its frivolous way.

So might another family of aesthetic refugees who had struck unexpected trouble in their Mendip retreat. Beatrice enclosed a cutting from their local rag, when she wrote in August:

'ETERNAL' SPRING RUNS DRY

Local potter, Mr William Madison of Crabtree Cottage, Watlington Coomb, has lost his water-supply. The ancient spring which wells out of the limestone on the west face of Cottesloe Warren has dried up for the first time in living memory. Our reporter consulted Mrs Maud Climpton, who was born in the cottage during the reign of Queen Victoria and who now resides in an Axbridge home. She told him that the spring used to be known in her family as 'Helicon', because (her grandfather used to say) it 'had been given by the gods' and it never ran dry.

What about it Mr Howell? Is a twice-weekly visit from the RDC water-cart the best that our new gods can do?

(Mr Madison is the inventor of those ingenious ceramic puzzle-towers which have become cult-objects on the fashionable London craft scene. Our readers may be familiar with the specimen of his work which graces the foyer of the Clevedon Assembly Rooms.)

Down on the edge of Bodmin Moor, Anya Kovacs scarcely allowed these things to impinge at all. Water restrictions forced some contemptuous evasions on her, but the other dramas of national life passed her by entirely. She had cancelled the papers and declined absolutely to join the village-store gossip about Immigrants and Riots. Anything which did not act directly on her senses had no existence. There were no Immigrants and no Riots in the West Country.

For months now they had lived out-of-doors, only going indoors to sleep, and sometimes not even for that. The land went tawny-brown, whitening under the drenching sun; and Anya, slimmed down and permanently in a bikini, went tawny-brown likewise – all except her hair, which had bleached to a coppery-gold, and her eyes which, clarified by a great good health, shone piercingly blue. Visitors – even those who were accustomed to being intimidated – felt like violating intruders before this supple-haunched, brown-limbed Diana. There was a glisten about her very movements which had hapless males drawing in startled breath.

Anya made nothing particularly of her striking good looks. She had never been less disposed for conquest. She only knew from the great fund of energy in herself, that she was stunningly well. Her youth, squandered and misspent, had been given back to her. It hardly mattered what she did with it. Nothing was out of reach: everything was possible. For the time, she immersed herself in cheerful domesticity. The hens she had let loose on the property had started laying real eggs in the nests provided, and the lettuces (stealthily watered at night when no spying neighbour could see her) had crisp little hearts. And as for the tomatoes . . . there had been no such tomatoes in the annals of horticulture.

Her first encounter with the actualities of granite-carving, however, came as a bit of a shock. She strolled out on to the slate-paved terrace one morning, to find Laczi laying into the newly-delivered block with a whip-handled axe. Blood was streaming down his forearms and dripping off his elbows. She nearly gave vent to the scream beloved of witless and inexcusable females, but she contained herself and made calm inquiry. It appeared that the cusps of granite were so sharp and came off at such a velocity that there was no avoiding spilling a bit of honest blood. Well, she'd see about that!

She was not going to bed nightly with an extended scab. She made him a leather apron and arm-guards, and *insisted* that he wear a face-mask – though, under the blazing sun, he was likely to suffer the fate of the medieval knight scalded inside his armour. The airless confinement, Laczi complained, was damned near boiling his brains in his skull. About the brains, she retorted, she didn't give a toss, but she *was* growing rather attached to the body. He'd just have to put up with it . . .

The balmy airs of a great content were beginning to enfold her daily consciousness. What was all this foolish talk about water shortages? On every side springs flowed and trees flowered.

TEN

Dozing over the Papers

'ROCKIN' THE RACIST BOAT'

Rock, reggae and soul are *our* music, and these streets belong to *us*. The Nazi slugs have no Music, no Joy, no Love and no Hope. All they have is Sir Robert Mark's Company Police to protect them. They may sport the Union Jacks, but this multi-racial country belongs to *us*. Punks of Albion *unite*!

Get out and *fuck* the Fascists!

Despite what Jimmy Shann/Mark Perry/Howard Devoto, or whoever's the current 'We-Hate-Fascists-And-We-Hate-Commies-Too' Pisspot Bard tells/sells you, those who insist on being 'individuals' above *all* else *don't* get glamourously 'Shot By Both Sides' – they wank their way down the middle of the road into obscurity.

Beginning in that long hot summer, as the *New Musical Express* was colourfully noting, there came a rush of racist beatings and killings, a burgeoning of neo-fascist movements, one or two worrying deaths in police custody, and outbreaks of street violence on a scale that made the mayhem and murder on the streets of Soweto appear less than comfortably remote. Apartheid South Africa and liberal Britain were of course light-years apart, but could anybody be sure they were not beginning to converge? Common to both was a coloured community which regarded the police as agents and accomplices of the forces they found ranged against them. Something ominously like battle-lines seemed to be being drawn up.

In Britain, of course, the press had not yet been bound and gagged into silence. The bully-boys, the racists, the fascists, were duly named and berated. These things did not pass unchallenged. But the practice of investigative journalism is surprisingly close to the rituals of primitive magic: there is an assumption in both that by 'naming'

175

you have somehow gained power over the forces of nameless opposition. Nothing could be further from the truth. 'You must understand first the structure.'

That was not so easy – even for those who had *not* cancelled their papers. Many a conscientious citizen was convinced that the scattered manifestations of 'public disorder' were connected. Like Laczi a few years earlier, they were seeing the much-proclaimed liberty of the British subject as a thing precariously held, and under siege. But could they agree who was the enemy, or how to resist him?

Hardly. The prescriptions were as various as the disease was baffling.

'CALLS FOR EXORCISM GROW'

Increasing numbers of people who believe themselves to be possessed by an evil spirit are being given exorcism by Church of England clergymen, sometimes by telephone. The latest phone-in facility has been set up by Canon Thorpe of the Southwark diocese. 'We get up to twenty calls a day,' he reports. 'I must confess that I am shaken by the evidence. The Devil is no medieval myth. He is here in our midst.'

That might not suit all tastes. But if you couldn't exorcise the Devil, you could always put a knife in him:

'My friend and me had been taking a drink in the Victory pub,' Rashpal Bhatti, twenty-five, of Ferndale Avenue, Hucklington, told our reporter. 'We left just before closing time to walk down the road to go to the Century cinema to see a film. We were on the opposite side of the road to the pub. Soon I am hearing shouts. I do not take much notice, as it is most rough around there anyway. All of a sudden I felt a pain in my back and these boys ran past me shouting. Then I fell to the road. I did not know I had been stabbed until my friend was picking me up. "You have been stabbed in the back," he says. I heard one of the white boys shout "Nice one" as they ran past me. I cannot describe the boys. They were about sixteen or seventeen – just kids. It was all so quick. There was no fighting. Why should I fight kids?'

. . . Like the man said . . . 'most rough'! On the same night, in the same London suburb, Gurdip Singh Chagger died of *his* stab-wounds, and a National Party spokesman commented, 'One down, one million to go.'

It was rough, too, in the Brick Lane area of East London (scene of the blackshirt riots of the thirties), where a Bangladeshi resident told a reporter how he had been held pinioned by two assailants while a third stabbed him with a broken bottle. Another had been half-strangled with a piano-wire, and yet another had had his ear sawn off. Most had at one time or another been most roughly besieged in their houses.

And it was decidedly rough in Leamington on the night when Moham Devi Gautam, widow, seventy-six, was dragged from her house by two white youths, and burned alive. Were such things done on Albion's shore? It seemed so.

Not everyone, of course, tackled social evils with criminal violence. Some took up their pens. Like the good citizen of Leamington, who was outraged to read in his local paper how an invalided Pakistani worker, married with three children, was receiving enough to live on:

So you bloated black pig you feel that the state is not doing you any favours by paying you £109 a week to sit on your stinking great fat arse. You think it's only doing its duty. Well you odious venereal-ridden black scum if I had my way I would do the state and the other hard-working Englishmen a favour by putting a rope around your fat slimy neck and stringing you up to the nearest lamp post . . . You may be laughing now, but mark my words the days are numbered for you and the rest of the filthy black scum in this country. The time is coming when you will all be herded into cattle boats and shipped back to the disease-ridding [*sic*] place from whence you came. Bloody good riddance you stinking fat bastard.

R. Relf 卐

P.S. COME BACK HITLER, ALL IS FORGIVEN.

Mr Relf's next reported literary enterprise was to pen a notice which appeared in the window of the house he was offering for sale. '*Viewing*: to avoid animosity all round positively no coloureds.' And the hand-made billboard outside read:

FOR SALE. TO AN ENGLISH FAMILY ONLY.

Proud perhaps of his happy turn of phrase, Mr Relf declined, when invited, to take the notices down. He did not, however, avoid animosity *all* round. He was jailed for the refusal. Being a man of principle, he promptly went on hunger-strike, and was later released on health grounds. The notices stayed up.

On Fleet Street, more accomplished penmen were at work:

SCANDAL OF THE £600-A-WEEK IMMIGRANTS
FAMILIES LIVE AT FOUR-STAR HOTEL

(The Government of Malawi [black], having taken a dislike to its Asian population, had suggested to them that they might go and flourish somewhere else – leaving their property and businesses behind, to pay for all the trouble they had caused. Some bearers of British passports, finding themselves thus stateless and destitute, headed north.)

Two homeless Asian families are living in style at a four-star hotel – at a cost of £500 from rates and taxes . . . When they arrived from Malawi, the African country where they lived, they had less than £80 between them – and nowhere to go . . . The families have taken over six double bedrooms – each with TV and bath. Breakfast is included in the bill. Each family is drawing Social Security benefits of £20 or more a week. And they have told officials that this is not enough. The bill sent to the West Sussex County Council for the first three weeks was £1,863.01.

The front-page headline next day read '4,000 ASIANS ON THE WAY'. (Under questioning, one of the refugees had guessed that there might be . . . perhaps another 4,000? who had suffered a similar fate to his own.) And the story was taken up on an inner page:

Yesterday the two families were evacuated from the hotel for almost an hour, after a telephoned bomb threat . . . The families have applied for an increase of their £46-a-week Social Security payments. They want £115 between them for meals . . . The Sulemans have only one complaint of life at the Airport Hotel – there is no mosque nearby.

Next day, the immigration figures had been updated:

ANOTHER 20,000 ASIANS DUE IN BRITAIN!

It seemed that the 'lesser breeds without the law' (to borrow Kipling's phrase of deathless ambiguity) were proving a pain in the neck all over the globe. In South Africa they were getting themselves gratuitously shot. In Uganda they were doing the shooting – thus proving how incapable they were of justifying the democratic trust that had been reposed in them. And were they now to take over the Airport Hotel without a murmur of protest? The Fleet Street sleuths who had uncovered the scandal, manfully shouldered their responsibilities in an editorial:

SYMPATHY

For the ratepayers of West Sussex (*and of every other area where a local authority acts on the principle that money grows on trees*) the *S-n* has sympathy.

* THE ASIAN FAMILIES neither wanted nor expected such treatment.

* THE HARD-PRESSED public certainly do not want to fork out for four-star luxury such as they cannot afford for themselves.

* IN OUR VIEW, the council's explanation that no other accommodation was available was simply not believable . . . Indeed, it appears that alternative accommodation has already been found! Does *ANYONE* believe that the council would have moved so swiftly without the *S-n*'s intervention?

PROTEST

It is all too easy to make the plight of sad families like these a focus for racial envy and hatred.

By all means, let us protest.

But let us send the protest to the right address.

To the Town Hall bureaucrats who so recklessly squander other people's hard-earned money.

As the running ticker-tape caption at the head of this page proudly proclaimed,

IF THE NEWS IS BIG IT'S BIGGER IN THE *S-N*.

Some news items, however, required no augmentation:

SOWETO RIOTS. 176 DEAD. 1,200 INJURED

But the interpretation of these figures remained problematical:

179

According to Minister of Police Kruger, most of the victims were shot by .22 bullets, a calibre of rifle which the police do not carry. The inference must be that *these casualties were caused by black gunmen*.

No police were reported killed . . .

Puzzling indeed! But then . . . that was in another country, and besides, the 176 were dead.

British Post Office workers nevertheless leapt to their own hasty conclusions and proclaimed a week-long boycott on communications to South Africa. They didn't seem so sure that it *was* another country. Invited to intervene in the dispute, the Attorney-General declined, and, as a consequence, a private prosecution was brought against the union.

In the High Court the Lord Justices had no difficulty in disentangling the issues:

Lord Justice D: What is to be done about it? Are the courts to stand idly by? Is the Attorney-General to be final arbiter as to whether the law should be enforced or not?

Lord Justice L: For seven days very great harm indeed will be done to the business world of this country who have business dealings in South Africa. Is the law so powerless that all it can do is prosecute little men, postmen, telegraph boys and the like for infringing the law, when one would have thought that the union, if it had bothered to look up the law, could have seen whether it was breaking it. When the whole country is affected by a deliberate flouting of the criminal law, somebody has the right to intervene.

Union Counsel: Absolutely – and the right and proper person is the Attorney-General.

Lord Justice L: But he will not do it!

The courts did not stand idly by. The bench granted an injunction against the Post Office employees, forbidding the boycott. *The rule of law must be enforced!*

. . . So, presumably, thought the retired military man who was rumoured to be raising a private army somewhere in the savage wolds of Surrey. So, certainly, thought the secondary-school headmaster who wrote to *The Times* advocating the return of the birch to our schools:

Vicious young thugs must be punished severely to protect the good children. Nothing less will bring violent young people to their senses. And the parents of persistent truants should he heavily fined. Indiscipline, disruption and vandalism starts in the home.

So too, apparently, thought the Metropolitan Chief of Police who gave priority to the training of officers for the Special Patrol Unit, a new group of crack troops specializing in riot-control whose green Transit-vans were to achieve an ambiguous notoriety over the next few years. One policeman, at least, was doing his bit to stem the tide of lawlessness.

But populace and politicians were not making the policeman's lot an any happier one ... as Laczi discovered, one late afternoon in June, when he rewarded himself for a week of lugging heavy slates about, by sitting down on his newly-paved terrace for an hour's indolence with the Sunday papers. It was months since he had last indulged himself like this, and he approached the virgin sheets with a kind of guilty lust for information. How much of the world's corruptibility would have passed him by beyond recall?

PHEW! How to handle ye olde Englishe heatwave. *Including*: fashions, food, entertaining, cosmetics. (on PAGE FIFTEEN)

The problem was pressing enough, but the solutions didn't really appeal. Eschewing page fifteen, he browsed, not quite at random, since the news itself was not random.

POLICE CHIEF TO RETIRE
Sir Robert Mark, Metropolitan Police Chief, is retiring next month. Senior colleagues say he would have gone anyway rather than work under the Police Complaints Bill, which introduces a new form of independent review of complaints against policemen.
   'I am appalled that the Complaints Board will contain political nominees,' he is quoted as saying, 'allowing them to exercise control over police discipline, a sadly retrograde step.'

The Chief Constable of Derbyshire seemed to agree with Sir Robert:

The people running this Board cannot understand the full
difficulties of police work . . .

(Laczi nodded sagely. He was not disposed to underestimate the
difficulties of police work: he had seen many policemen having
difficulties with their work.) The trouble with the Complaints
Board, complained the Chief Constable, was that

. . . they will be looking at things in black and white, while the
police always look at things in the round and deal with them in a
more flexible way.

'What're you doing?' called Anya, who was waist-deep among the
broad beans. 'Plotting revolution?'
'No. Just reading about it.'
He turned a page.

AMIN BID: '10 KILLED'
At least ten people were killed during the grenade attack on
President Amin on Thursday night, and the Ugandan leader
himself was slightly injured . . . Informed sources in Kampala say
that most of the casualties occurred when security men fired into a
crowd.
Last week the President issued orders that all Britons who meet
him must kneel and maintain silence until he addresses them . . .

Laczi chuckled. Well, well! Britain's white-haired blackboy had
discovered *one* way, at least, of 'looking at things in black and
white'. And you had to give it to him: it had a certain ironic felicity.
He wet a finger and folded the page under.
More foreign news:

CAIRO RIOTS
Cairo's poor were out in force yesterday, in the largest anti-
government demonstration of recent months. One banner summed
up their grievances: 'Sadat, oh Sadat, you dress in the latest
fashion while we sleep twelve to a room.'

Pretty unanswerable, Laczi thought. The immemorial cry of the
oppressed, eternally justified by the flagrant facts. '*Something must
be done!*' fulminated a thousand liberal editors in a thousand liberal

editorials. And nothing ever was. Why he'd bothered to spend good money on this catalogue of intractable miseries, he couldn't imagine . . .

1,000 VOLUNTEER TO RETURN TO IRON AGE

Who could blame them? He blinked at the page. What the devil was it about, though? Some exercise in creative archaeology by a bored BBC producer, it seemed. Fatuous ape!

RHODESIAN TALKS IN THE BALANCE

Ian Smith starring again – at Geneva, this time – in the long-running saga of white supremacy. Laczi let a jaundiced eye roam over it. It was only Idi Amin in reverse – the pot calling the kettle a Black:

'If any African wants to talk to me,' Mr Smith stated yesterday, 'here I am. Let him come. I shall stay here as long as there is any reasonable chance of making progress. But my time is limited. We have got important talks back home, not like these Africans who have nothing better to do than sit around here talking indefinitely.'

What did they *all* do but sit around talking 'indefinitely'? The much more definite Zanu official further down the column definitely had a point: 'If we want to talk to Smith, we pull the trigger.'
Laczi grinned to himself, momentarily less bored . . .

HATE MAIL FOR RACE CHIEF
Mr David Lane, the newly appointed Chairman of the Commission of Racial Equality, has been opening his postbag this week. He offered us two samples:
1. 'Dirty nigger-lover! Signed NF ⌐╫
2. 'Dear Mr Lane,
      A west-end whore is a far more desirable member of the community than you shortly intend to become because
         (a) she provides a service that some people appreciate – and you won't
         (b) she doesn't pretend to be a moral do-gooder in her desire to get easy money – you do.'

Sighing, Laczi let the bulky sheets fall in his lap and leaned back in the deck-chair. The sun poured down on his face. Behind the closed lids a brilliant yellow light was lanced with shooting tongues of scarlet – blood vessels presumably. How odd that he should feel a sneaking sympathy with that detestor of 'moral do-gooders'! How odd that he didn't care whether he did or not . . . How odd that it was odd . . . *if* it was . . .Policemen, Assassins, Negotiators, Fellahin . . . Commissioners of miscellaneous Righteousnesses danced amorphously before his inner vision, amalgamating slowly into the craggy figure of an Iron Age chieftain half-naked in a bearskin cloak, who was shaking him and telling him to wake up. He screwed his eyes shut more tightly. He'd earned his quiet kip and he was damned well going to have it. Let them all get on with it . . . whatever it was they were getting on with . . .

Anya abandoned him and went indoors.

The quiet kip was to last a long time. He scarcely noticed the mayhem at the Notting Hill West Indian Carnival; and the pitched battle with the National Front at Lewisham passed him by completely. 'ENOCH'S SHOCKER: SECRET DOSSIER ON MIGRANT RACKET' found him still dozing and unshocked. During the Grunwick disturbances he raised his head a little, and was particularly tickled by the picket who, when asked why there were so many people outside the factory gates, replied with artless candour: 'Why, man, it's the Ascot of the Left. You've got to be *seen* here at least – or better still, arrested.' He quite fancied Grunwick's boss, too: 'I don't mind being a scab, because a scab prevents infection entering the wound. I am fighting for the freedom of a small person not to be bludgeoned and misrepresented by the powerful machinery of vested interests.' This, from a small person paying his staff £25 a week when the national average wage stood at £76, had a touch of comic genius about it. It was almost as good as the Notting Hill Carnival Co-ordinator charged with failing to liaise properly with the police – 'That's all wrong, man. We had some very beautiful meetings with the police.'

The more farcical they all were, the better Laczi was pleased. It left him free. Hadn't he spent enough of his life carrying the troubles of humanity about on his shoulders? And what good had that ever done anyone? He was ripe now to give way to the most powerful impulse of his nature. He would be a sculptor first, and nothing but a sculptor. It was the only version of 'humanity' left him.

And so, for the first of many afternoons, Laczy dozed over the papers. . . The sun had abdicated its western throne long before any coolness reached the scorched earth. Heat beat up in quivering waves from the slate terrace. Some evening midges that had escaped the patrolling martins became entangled in his hair. They bit joyously, but Laczi slept on.

He awoke in the stillness of a velvety dark to the sound of water puddling into the parched dust of the vegetable patch. Owl-blind and disoriented, he fumbled for his shirt. What was she up to? Every light in the house had been doused. He squinted into the dark.

'If you are so ashamed,' he said censoriously, not quite sure where to direct the censure, 'don't do it.'

In the windless hush, he could be heard all the way to the church.

'Shut up!' hissed a voice further to the left than he'd expected.

He adjusted his aim: 'If it is public opinion what you would defy, defy it. Don't skulk.'

There was a sudden cascade of water, quite loud enough to alert the vigilant, and a galvanized bucket came flying out of the dark and crashed against his deckchair. Too late he put up a fending arm. Silly bitch! She could have brained him! Somewhere beyond the boundary wall a bush rustled violently.

'Skulk, eh?' She was looming over him, visible only by the black hole she cut in the diffused mantle of stars. 'Skulk!' Whipping off her leather gardening-gloves she dealt him a resounding clout to the side of the head. 'Who is it that's brought me to skulking?'

His initial fright was converting to anger: 'Is enough!'

He rose. But she held her ground – leaving *him* so little that they stood daring each other absurdly nose to nose.

'Who,' she demanded, 'has reduced me to the cultivation of compost and chickenshit? Was it me? Did I do that? Was *that* our little agreement?'

'I think we have this conversation indoors.' He'd never been able quite to match her relish for the grand public occasion.

'Pfah! *Now* who's skulking?' A derisive finger prodded him in the chest so hard that he fell backwards into the chair with a splintering sound of ripping canvas.

'Conversation?' she raged, kicking at it as he struggled to extricate himself, 'when did we last have one of those? Is there anyone within a hundred miles capable of conversing?'

Her grievance, repeated by every stone surface in the village, awoke echoes right up on the Moor. But even this monstrous reduplication which was filling the night was inadequate to the outrage. 'A hundred miles!' she yelled. 'Eavesdropping, yes . . . spying, snooping! Plenty of experts at *that*!'

It was a point of protocol with Laczi to deny her, as far as possible, the gratifications of violence. So once he was clear of the shattered chair, he came at her fast and low. Whipping her legs from under her, while she lashed out at his back with the gloves, he carried her roaring into the darkened house, slammed the door to with his foot and, with scant concern for possible injury, pitched her on to the divan. The backwash of his own violence had left him out of breath and out of temper.

'OK,' he announced, folding his arms truculently, 'we have one now.' Nothing but the sound of furious breathing came from the dim heap on the bed. 'A conversation,' he snapped.

Silence.

'You say you have wanted one. Right! We have one.'

'Nobody,' Anya's low voice came from between set teeth, '*nobody* does that to me.'

The somebody who just had, permitted himself a chuckle.

'Laugh again, and I'll *kill* you!'

He gave a snort: 'Better have the conversation first. Afterwards there will be problems.'

'God!' she exclaimed disgustedly, 'not the sweetness-and-light routine. You despicable hypocrite! Have the cleanliness to be angry!'

'I see. So it is an *un*reasonable conversation you would have.'

'I shit on your "reason".'

'And who is to wipe up afterwards, I wonder?'

'Oh you're a great little wiper-up, aren't you? You with your godlike, pusillanimous little intelligence. Intelligence! You'd *prefer* to do it by brute force, of course. But when that fails there's always rationality.'

Her home truths moved him only to mock apology: 'I cannot help it,' he sighed, feeling in the gloom for the edge of the bed, where he provocatively perched. 'Simply it shines out of me.'

A vicious kick caught him in the butt and deposited him hard on the flagged floor. Though the impact had been painful, he was chuckling again.

'You think I do this for your amusement?'

'It contributes,' he admitted ruefully.

'Well nothing – NOTHING – contributes to mine.'

There was a pause.

'I am sorry.'

'Your sorrow doesn't either, so you can stuff it up your Y-fronts.'

'I see.' Indeed, he was beginning to. He attempted some realignment: 'These months, lately, I have been too much contented, is that it? This is perhaps my sin? To be happy?'

'What's your happiness to me?'

He weighed it mentally: 'What is it to me? It is a condition – happiness. You have it or you do not. I thought you were "happy" growing the tomatoes.'

Her incredulity was monstrous: 'Is your *mind* going? Tomatoes? Me? Happy?'

'It seems I took a big mistake.'

She was too dispirited even to correct his grammar: 'It seems we both did.'

The silence had become profound, and he did not know how to break it. But he needed to see. He rose, flicked on the switch. The room congealed in sudden unnatural light, hard edges without depth. But her face was blank and closed.

Now, fearing it was too late, he really wanted to know: 'So tell me what I do wrong?'

'Wrong?' she echoed scornfully. 'What is "wrong", is that you have to ask.'

'Sure.' He felt its justice. 'But still I am asking.'

'Time, my friend, goes forwards, not backwards. You should have asked months ago. Where's the point now?'

'You are too fatalist.'

'And so would you be, if you understood anything at all. Christ.' She was staring at him, as if at so perfect a stranger that he felt himself becoming one, even to himself. 'Who the hell *are* you anyway? Sitting about cluttering up my life? You're more interested in your bloody newspapers than you are in me – I can tell from the way you fall asleep over them. Well?' she challenged, seeing his eyes going round, 'I suppose you'll tell me you've been "happy" in bed too? Eh? Is that the pitch of your expectations, you limp little worm? That's it, is it? Just enough to break your sleep and flatter your complacencies, before you pass out again? Well, doze on, my fine Hungarian friend! I won't be disturbing you for long. I want out. Out!' she repeated, defying his injured gravity.

Out? His questioning gesture seemed to stretch beyond the distant rim of the Moor to embrace the vast black dome above it, pricked by tiny alien lights. He was stupefied. Was this not large enough? For himself, he had felt liberated by the great cleared spaces of moor and sky – liberated from ambition, responsibility, greed, vulgarity . . . liberated even from passion. And he had imagined her as sharing the sensation. Surely she had? Hadn't they travelled together to this westward edge of human habitation precisely in order to breathe free air?

Only the air was *not* free. It was foetid – he could smell it now. One must get out. Out! Yet there was nowhere for her – for them – to 'go'. Not back. Not on. Nowhere. It was the edge.

Light was dawning bleakly for him: they had sought solitude and achieved unrelation. They had defected from an inane social reality, only to be clapped into the infinite jail of unbounded Nature, where Anya, raging and uncomprehending, was going slowly mad – shouting at the rocks and the sky in a vain attempt to elicit a response. At him, too . . . Nothing but echoes came back. Was this the nemesis of 'personal relations' predicted by the wise man of Budapest? He stood, self-estranged, strangling the ineffectual pity that welled up in him for the thing they had become.

If one understood anything at all (she had said it!), was one not *bound* to be fatalist? Nemesis, Laczi knew, was an old-fashioned word, propounding causalities where nothing but chance could be shown to exist. That things happened as they did, was certain: the rain did, or did not, fall. That they *must* so happen, or could be *made* to happen, was superstition – hence the dancers on the Moor. And Laczi emphatically did not plan on joining them: he was implacable in his hostility to superstition. But was it not superstition that was now paralysing the very thought of remedial action? A superstition of character that dared not envisage change on the front where it found itself most threatened? Assailed by her taunts he drew back upon a shrunken self, stupid with his own hurt. No more than she, was he capable of apology or reparation which, to his mind, only confirmed that the irreparable had already occurred.

Weary of his scrutiny, Anya flung the gardening-gloves into the empty log-basket. What use were weapons? The campaign was over. She rose to drag her mortal weight off to an unwanted bed. She had come to the end of her retrenchments and faced the blank wall with what courage she could. Stranded for a second at the door, she let her chagrin ring out, harsh beyond any personal bitterness: 'It was bound to end this way! Bound to! Disappointment,' she cried, ground down to her last brave irony '– it's the name of the game, isn't it? Disappointment!'

It chimed too horribly with his own thought to meet any resistance there. A man less experienced might have found standing-room for some frailty of hope (for it is experience that breeds mistrust). But he saw only Nemesis – a futility infinitely predictable and, once it had occurred, only futilely to be resisted. Deprived of all grist, the mills of his thought ground aridly upon each other.

So this was how it was to be. Another woman, another failure. There was something, apparently, that these women knew and needed, of which he was doomed to be eternally oblivious. Something he could hardly supply since he didn't even know he lacked it. And lacking it, he could never hold them.

She would go. He feared she could live only too grievously well without him. But could he, without her? To this fatalistic faithlessness, either alternative was equally fearsome: the possibility that he couldn't . . . or that he could.

It so happened, later that autumn, when the rain had started falling on the ruins of Anya's garden, that the following news item appeared in the *Guildford Examiner*. It had, probably, very few readers, and Lajos and Anya Kovacs, still fraily united under one roof, were certainly not among them:

SALE OF NAZI MEMORABILIA

Messrs Winny & Butt are to conduct an unusual auction next Tuesday. A collection of German military uniforms, weapons and other equipment, belonging to the estate of the late Mr Joseph Sladebrook, retired civil servant, are to come under the hammer in their Godalming salerooms.

Perhaps the most intriguing items listed in the catalogue are the complete set of propaganda postcards, circulated by the Nazis in occupied Holland, Belgium and France during the Second World War. These nauseous little bits of pasteboard, mainly anti-Semitic in character, reveal how far Adolf and his fascist henchmen were prepared to go in promoting the aims of their 'Final Solution'. They are indeed so revolting that this paper would risk prosecution under either the Obscenity Laws or the Race Relations Act, or both, if it reported their substance. Questioned about the propriety of displaying such material at a public sale, Mr Winny, the senior partner, commented: 'It is true that these documents may give offence in certain quarters, but they are by now a part of history. However distasteful we may find it, these things happened, and I don't see why those who take an interest in such matters, should be deprived of essential documents.'

Mr Winny expects there to be a large turn-out to Tuesday's sale. 'There is an expanding market in Nazi artefacts,' he said. 'We have had inquiries from as far afield as the Argentine and South Africa.' Asked to put a value on the collection, Mr Winny ventured to predict that it would probably bring in about £40,000.

One of those present at the sale was Constable Gordon Sagger. (Tuesday was his day off.) He did not inform his superiors – why should he, since he hadn't even mentioned it to his family? His 'collection', housed in a locked trunk in the toolshed at the bottom of his garden, was not something to be advertised. He doubted that even his understanding wife would enter into the motives of harmless curiosity which governed the hobby. He had mentioned it once, jokingly, to another PC at the station, but that was different – coppers knew the world and were not the victims of stupid prejudice. Even so, the bastard had thought it rather more of a joke than Sagger had liked, and he still subjected him, when nobody was looking, to the occasional sniggering *Sieg heil*!

PC Sagger's purchases at Godalming included: one German infantry bayonet with the rare dimple-edged blade favoured by a few Wehrmacht commanders, the dress-jacket of an SS Sturmbahnführer, and four of the French-issue propaganda postcards which did not form part of a set, and which were therefore auctioned separately (the set went for prices far beyond PC Sagger's means).

One of these cards convinced him that he would have to move his collection out of the toolshed. It was not the sort of thing to fall into the hands of a blooming teenage daughter whose purity was a matter of constant solicitude to him (there were so many perverts about these days). It showed a hook-nosed, emaciated woman, wearing the triangular Juden-badge, lying on her back in a shallow trench. A trouserless Fritz private, stripped for action, straddled the trench above the grimly closed mouth. To one side stood a jack-booted SS officer, apparently issuing an order. The legend read: 'Open up! The Führer has granted your last request – a square meal! (*un repas copieux*).' The previous owner had pencilled the English translation on the white border.

This, then, was the England Laczi and Anya had turned their backs on, to cultivate private pleasures. Though the pleasures had proved precarious, their rural idyll was to drag on for another year. Neither going nor staying made much sense any longer, so they did neither. They were waiting for a decisive event in which they did not believe.

It was Anya, probably, who suffered most from the benumbing stasis. And when, unexpectedly, it ended, it was Anya who broke camp and moved.

ELEVEN

Changes

One miserable night in November, Stacy pulled back the heavy front door of the Stoke Newington house. On the doorstep stood Anya. To say the girl was flabbergasted would be putting it mildly. Three years back she had believed her harried life hardly worth prolonging when this woman repudiated her. Since then, she had given their blasted friendship a great deal of thought (not so much lately – her life had begun to put forth leaves in new directions). But in all her ruminations there had been one fixed point: it would never be Anya who would make the first move. And here she was – looking rather pinched and ill, actually – making the first move. It had to be an appeal.

Such suppliance Stacy could easily have repelled. She was stronger these days and not afraid to make enemies. But there was something about those hollow cheeks and haggard eyes, something about the way she almost crouched on the step (or was she just hunched against the rain?) . . . something, anyway, that slipped under the palisades of justified resentment, and found her 'at home'. It was as if she had opened the door upon some Edwardian melodrama of betrayal and destitution and could only speak the lines that came thoughtlessly to her lips: 'Good God! what's wrong with you?'

Anya gave a thin, cynical smile: 'Look that bad, do I? Better let me in out of the rain, then.'

Stacy saw she had a suitcase, hesitated, then stood aside while Anya humped it over the threshold. But she could not let it pass totally unchallenged: 'Come to stay?'

The large eyes met her again, enigmatically: 'Not unless invited.'

Stacy tested her capacity to refuse and decided it would hold.

'Come upstairs,' she said. 'You can leave that there.'

The figure in a turtle-neck pullover turned on the swivel-chair at their entry. A fine-boned West Indian face with curling black beard and penetrating eyes.

'Wavell, this is Anya. Anya Jevons, remember? The Rotten Orange?'

The man nodded curtly, a sheet of writing-paper suspended in his hand.

'Every barrel has one,' he remarked cryptically, inspecting her without comment. 'You want me to go?'

This was for Stacy, who gave no sign.

He swept up the papers and tucked a book under his arm.

'I'll finish this in the kitchen.'

Anya sat down in her usual ample fashion, occupying as much floor again as the chair. It was unconscious, but already she had made herself at home. The familiarity of it took the edge off the tension Stacy was feeling. The time that had separated them began to go fluid, dissolving things she had thought solid, though she was not at all sure she liked the sensation.

'Are you still in Cornwall?' she inquired, then added explanatorily, 'My father mentioned he'd seen you there.'

Anya appeared to find the question difficult.

'I don't think I am.' The face was masked.

'You mean to say you don't *know*?' In spite of herself Stacy was amused by this woman who managed to spend most of her life 'in the melting pot'.

Anya pulled down the corners of her mouth: 'Say I'm "in transit" . . .'

'. . . but don't ask where to,' Stacy supplied, not without satirical intent.

Anya nodded. It was a relief to be so quickly understood. She had been right to risk it. She looked around the room, taking her bearings. One of the publicity stills of the old Orange faced her on the opposite wall. She thought she might risk something more. She indicated the closed kitchen door with a thumb: 'Who's he?'

'Wavell?' Stacy tried to resent the offhand impertinence of it, but failed. 'He used to be an attendant at the National – that's where I met him – when I was doing my Curator's course, but that was after you . . .' She waved it aside. 'He's doing the course himself now, as a matter of fact.'

Anya heard the note of quiet pride and abandoned that line of questioning. But she didn't quickly light on another.

'I've a job at Sotheby's,' Stacy volunteered.

'Like it?'

'Has its menial side – clerking rubbish – but it won't stay that way. Yes, I like it. How about you? Working?'

'I wish I was.' Anya was extremely restless, kept tugging at her hair and fiddling with her bag. 'Two years of sitting on my backside had driven me half crazy. That's why I'm here. I couldn't face another Cornish winter of crows and yokels.'

'Oh yes,' said Stacy, brightening, 'I *heard* about you and the yokels. Had a run-in with the garage-man, wasn't it? Tried to sue him?'

'How in shit did you hear that?'

'Oh,' Stacy pulled a puckish face, ' a little cutting from the *Delabole Post* was put my way, by a mutual friend.'

Anya made a noise of disgust: 'Don't tell me – Magnus.'

'Well,' said Stacy, large with mock conciliation, 'you know how it is: he likes to stoke up the fires of other people's resentment. It saves him from dealing with his own. He's obsessed with you still, you know.' She stretched her legs and waggled her toes. 'It got to be very boring.'

'But how did he come to be reading the *Delabole Post*, for Christ's sake?'

'Probably hired a PI, shouldn't wonder. So . . . the Cornish winter was too much for you? Oh, I can imagine!' She laughed a little at the recollection of her own days in that part of the world.

Anya was interested: 'You went down in the winter?'

'Sometimes. Over Christmas. My father said it kept the cottage dry. Mostly it just made *us* damp and dismal, but that's families for you. You knew Mummy died?'

'Yes. "Daddy" told me.' The acid tone did not seem to be directed at the girl. Anya paused. 'Sorry.'

'No, it was best.' She drifted away for a moment, then returned. 'What did he visit you for? Do you mind if I ask?'

'Pfah! Why do *you* think?' She roused herself to deliver the goods: 'It was grotesque! He made a great puddle of bereaved grief on the patio, stuffed himself silly in the kitchen, drank half my brandy, and then got down to business. Had me ticketed as a randy slut, apparently. Every unattached female is panting to be laid, of course. By definition! Either he didn't know I was married or he thought I was the kind that only played at it. Fuck knows why I ever took him seriously. I did once, you know?' She eyed the girl speculatively, recalling the occasion. 'No, you probably wouldn't. But I did. Gave

him the full female ear-of sympathy treatment – the dirty old lecher!'
She thrashed about in the chair for a moment, like a beached whale.
'I thought he was supposed to be dying anyway?'

'I don't think he can,' said Stacy. 'He tries hard enough, but he
can't seem to bring it off.'

Anya raised impish eyebrows: 'Family failing?'

It was her first clear hint of humour.

Stacy's shock lasted only for a second before she burst out
laughing. It was a clear, merry laugh with no retrospective bitterness
in it: 'Oh *you* haven't changed, have you?'

'Probably not.' Anya could not disentangle the reproach from the
appreciation. 'But you certainly have.'

'Well,' said Stacy cheerfully, 'you can't make a career out of
overdoses.' She sighed with exaggerated dolour: 'I saw there was no
future in it. Had to look for something else.' She dismissed it, rising
springily to her feet. 'How are the cats?'

'The cats?' Anya was finding the transitions a little breathless, '. . .
are completely wild. Gone feral. They disappear up on to the Moor
for weeks on end, and then come back and terrorize the village – as if
we didn't have enough enemies there already.'

'Poor dears!' sighed the girl. Did she mean the cats? or the
Kovacses?

There was a pause. Only one subject remained.

Stacy stood looking down at the sprawled Anya who, despite
some return of animation, still looked blanched and enervated. She
gave the extended boot a playful kick: 'Well?' she challenged, 'are
you going to tell me? or do I have to ask?' Her lips silently formed the
word 'Laczi'.

Anya stalled for a bit, but without conviction. It was becoming
inescapable that she had not brought her harp to the party in order
to hang it by the wall. She strummed and tinkered for a few more
moments, and then plunged off: No, it hadn't worked out. But no,
they hadn't split up either. It was all very well for him, besotted with
his blocks of bloody granite, but she was losing her functions and her
faculties. The conversation of chickens was limited – about as
limited as the conversation of Cornishmen, unless you gave yourself
up to clucking your days away. Oh, she'd made the effort. It wasn't
that she hadn't tried. Tried being the sculptor's muse, the hippie
housewife, the rural conservationist, even ran for the Parish Council
(three votes – hers, Laczi's and the village idiot's). Tramped the
Moor, bickered with tradesmen, got banned from the pub, and,

when denied all other amusements, fought Laczi. It had been madness to go in the first place, but an even greater madness to stay. So . . . here she was. She'd come to London to take the waters, find a job, do something – there must be *something*, sweet Jesus! . . . No, there wasn't much money left – all locked up in the granite jailhouse they'd built themselves. Sure, Laczi was all right. One of Britain's established fucking sculptors, wasn't he? A Tate Gallery bloody classic! He'd got what he was after. Never mind him. What about me?

'I'll ask Wavell about a room.' Stacy rose.

'Hang on. Don't rush your fences. Whose house is it?'

'Mine. I'll ask him.' She was halfway to the door.

'No.' Anya was imperative. 'It doesn't work. I don't make the same mistake twice.'

Stacy's laughter bubbled up irrepressibly again: '*Don't* you?'

'Take your damned percipience where it's wanted,' grumbled Anya. 'No,' she resumed gloomily, 'I'm not cut out for sharing – anything. It just doesn't work.'

'You don't seem to be cut out for solitude either.'

'Very astute!'

' "Very astute!" ' Stacy echoed mockingly. 'Don't you just bring it all back? Whatever people say to you, you've always thought of it already. But what good does it do you? Why don't you let yourself be surprised for once?'

'It doesn't depend on me,' retorted Anya hotly. 'Let the damned boring world do something about it.' She gathered herself, her limbs and her handbag together. 'Look, I'd better be going if I'm going to find a bed for the night.'

'Stay here why don't you? One night!'

'No thanks.' She rose. 'You can call me a cab, if you like.'

Stacy shrugged, went to the phone.

'Come to Sotheby's tomorrow,' she suggested as she dialled. 'We'll go to lunch. One o'clock at the main entrance. It's in Bond Street. Hello. Can you send a cab . . .? Five minutes? Good.'

She put the phone down.

'I can't,' said Anya flatly.

Stacy looked hard at her: 'You're not walking out on me for *another* three years, are you?'

'I've got to visit a quack.'

'There *is* something wrong. I knew it.'

'If you'd been attended exclusively by senile naval MOs forcibly retired for incompetence, there'd be something wrong with you, too.'

'Attended for *what*?' Stacy insisted, while her mind raced over some nasty possibilities.

Nothing came. It seemed that the cab would have arrived before Anya got round to answering. She stood, stymied, in the middle of the floor, kicking at the carpet like a delinquent. It had been her firm resolve *not* to broach this matter with anybody, and yet by some perfidy of her nature she was already halfway there. Whether she would have made it unaided over the second half is open to doubt, but her old flatmate, remembering her as garrulous to the point of obscenity on most medical matters, was able to guess what ailment might bring on this unnatural reticence. In tones so awed as to be almost comical she breathed, 'You're pregnant!'

Anya laughed harshly. It was not so simple. 'Ha! me? Not likely,' she said. 'This girl's gonads are fucked up for good and all. Don't you fret yourself, I shan't be being anybody's little *anyuka*.'

Stacy's steady gaze absorbed the harshness, transmuting it into a kind of luminosity: 'But you tried . . .'

'Ach, it's not too bad,' Anya tossed her head bitterly, thrusting back the unruly hair. 'I just need my guts totally rebuilt and I'll be right as rain.'

Several times this evening, Stacy had felt the tidal pull of something more powerful than sympathy. But it had been resistible – associated with a sweet ineffectual nostalgia, the ghost of a self she had not been sorry to put behind her. This time she was in the torrential present, and her feet nearly went from under her. Perhaps that was why she put her hands up to the ravaged face of her old employer and drew it firmly down on to her shoulder – to steady herself. But also, perhaps, in the complicated ledgers of a stormy friendship there were still some unpaid debts. She gazed across the room unseeingly, conscious only of a cold cheek that lay strangely against her own, and of a vague hope that Wavell would not choose this moment to come into the room. Her fingers ran absently through the hair – smoothing, soothing – and down on to the broad back, where they came lightly to rest. And this too was totally new, and alarming in its newness. Anya had gone limp and still – with relief, despair, humiliation . . . it was impossible to tell.

Downstairs someone clattered the letter-flap, then banged on the door. The whole house echoed with it.

Stacy murmured into the hair: 'It's the cab.'

There was a muffled groan. Anya drew herself upright and looked into the girl's eyes with uninterpretable sternness. What was she saying? Perhaps she wanted to issue a warning. Perhaps she saw it was unnecessary.

Stacy wet her lips: 'You'll get in touch?' It was both a question and an order.

Anya nodded.

'Good luck with the doc.'

Anya went.

For an enterprise so hopelessly unplanned, Anya's return to the metropolis went surprisingly smoothly. The medical consequences of the miscarriage turned out to be not too dreadful – amenable to pills not calling for surgery. Before the week was out, a tiny flat fell vacant not far from Stacy's place, and she moved in at once. Stacy fussed and ferried, bestowing gifts of furniture and curtains, and enjoying the reversal of roles. Anya was relieved to find that the girl still took money from her father, and chalked it up for future use. She might suffer from fits of political fanaticism. Looking at Wavell, she rather feared she did. It was always useful to know where to throw a switch, in the event of an ideological overload.

But Wavell caused her other anxieties. He wore his steel-plated self-sufficiency and implacable handsomeness like the caste-mark of a born ruler. It was impossible not to be impressed. He only had to walk into a room. And if Anya happened to be in it there was no mistaking then his conviction that a white South African and an abuser of Stacy's good nature was someone who, if not actually an untouchable, certainly belonged to the lower orders. Anya's acquaintance with blacks had been mainly in the servants' quarters or on the Cape Town locations. Wavell came of a different breed. He breathed the hard, purposive air of the radical black movements, wrote for *West Indian World*, was active in community politics, and showed no sign of the cultural cringe which had disfigured the independence even of a Thandi. In place of Thandi's gangland defiance, there was an icy calm – towards her, that is. Not towards Stacy: those two were very intriguing to watch together. He seemed to have brought out the aristocrat in her, and dispossessed for ever the spoiled child of the middle classes. In their relations, there was a courtly considerateness which ran to few words, but which showed, nevertheless, how much they felt they owed to themselves in the way of dignified civility. Just occasionally, in their company, Anya had a startling vision of herself as underbred and loud. That, no doubt, was what the Magnuses of this world had always thought her to be. But the critique, this time, came from a source she couldn't so easily discount – not least because it was a critique that nobody bothered to make, unless it was herself. Had she been in more buoyant health and spirits, she would probably have got around to resenting and resisting it. As it was, she found herself lying low and waiting, with an observant watchfulness that brought many new matters to her attention.

It was Wavell who, soon afterwards, put her in the way of a job. Hackney Council, he had heard, were commissioning a study of immigrant housing. They needed interviewers. She could mention his name if she wanted. Anya applied, mentioned it, was interviewed, accepted, collected her briefcase full of questionnaires, and plunged into the darker ghettoes – both black and white – of London's East End. Here she found much to interest her and, every now and then despite her precautions, something to surprise. The job wasn't without its hazards: after one narrow squeak, she consented to accept advice about the places *not* to go after dark if she didn't want her skull smashed in. London was a lot rougher than she had grasped while viewing it from Princes' Gate and Mayfair. But that was all right: it was also more real. The boring old world was beginning to do its stuff, and *she* wasn't going to be the one to complain of over-excitement.

And imagine her surprise when one of the families for interview, listed simply as Mr and Mrs Lester, turned out to be Annabel and Sam. She had never thought of Annabel as having a surname, let alone an address. This was a new London she was discovering, but it was also the old London where she had roots, where she belonged. Her interview schedule rather went by the board that evening, while Annabel plied her with best Jamaican rum and caught up with all the news. Anya talked as avidly as Annabel listened. In a curious way, it reconnected her with Laczi, who was turning remote and strange to her inner view. It might have been Annabel's rum, but she went home warm – warmer than she'd felt since the winter began. More likely it was the enveloping physical presence she knew of old – 'the comfort of black', as someone had called it. She fought back of course. There was nothing she liked less than the emotional muddledom that treated individuals as representatives of something – class, race, predicament. But she fought as one who wished to be

199

vanquished, suspecting herself of patronage, but not caring. And she fell asleep with the sounds of Annabel's throaty voice – playful, quarrelsome, cajoling, accepting – still echoing in her mind like subdued laughter.

Laczi had to make do, down in Cornwall, with meagre dribbles of information. He was conscious of no right to claim more. Her departure had turned him into a permanent spectator – made him realize, rather, that he'd been one for a long time. Since she had not confessed to a pregnancy, her miscarriage had struck him like a meteor; and by the time he'd collected his scattered wits, she was gone. But now, in her scraps and jottings, he sensed an openness and briskness most unlike the sullen rancour of their last months; and though he was thoroughly excluded from it, he felt dispassionately pleased. Like a convalescent after a long illness, he took comfort from the existence of health, without quite believing yet in its reality for himself.

Early in the new year, he heard first of Jaswinder Gopal – one of the trophies, he deduced, of the new openness. The letter was both long and peremptory, telling him exactly what to think, but providing many materials with which to think otherwise. Anya clearly attached some importance to the meeting.

She had been doing the Saturday-morning shopping at the cluster of local shops. Jaswinder had just emerged from the dairy and her gaggle of clamorous duffel-coated kids were milling about for the distribution of ice-creams. Either it was turning-out time at The Crossed Staves (the communal swillery of the district) or else the winsome foursome of Anya's tale had run out of booze-money. Not drunk enough, he gathered, to resist being chucked out, they were quite drunk enough to resent it, and to feel that the world owed them a few reparations. In the circumstances, a clutch of immigrant kids would have been a gift. It was easy to imagine: isolated shoppers scattering into the gutters as the phalanx of black leather and dog-studs bears down on the Gopals, sending Jaswinder spinning breathless against the plate glass and knocking the cornets out of her grip. The largest lout places his boot on the fallen goodies, grinding them flat, and leers inanely. The smallest Gopal starts howling.

Anya had supplied the dialogue: 'Shaddup, yer snotty little coon! I already got me bovverboots all over shit wiv yer fuckin' ice-cream. So watch it! Don't push me!'

Guffaws and sniggers.

'Why don't youse all fuck off back to Coonland, coons?' Then, as

Baby Gopal continues to bawl, 'Belt up willya, yer bleedin' little runt!'

Jaswinder knows the game. They will provoke her into some flicker of resistance and then, by knocking down the child, they will guarantee her violence, to sanction theirs. So she keeps very still. The folk in the dairy have heads well down over the cash-register. Their plate glass isn't insured. The shoppers have thinned out, though there are a few faces in shop doorways – among them, Anya's turning purple, no doubt, with indignation.

The big lout leans over Jaswinder with a toothy grin, cunning in its stupidity: 'Wanna make sumfin' ov it, yer curry-shittin' cunt?'

Jaswinder, wary from long experience, knows better than to make anything. Not so our Anya, who elbows her way out of the greengrocer's entrance and swinging her shoulder-bag by its strap, fetches the youth an almighty clout on the back of the head. The bag is large, well-filled (as ever), and it has a solid brass buckle. Already off balance, he goes down like a felled ox, right at the feet of the startled Gopals, who scatter like pigeons. His skull hits the shop-front coping with a smart crack, where Anya, a little dismayed now (though she won't admit it), sees him crouched on all fours, blowing like a horse and shaking a stunned head – from which a bloody spittle swings – stupidly from side to side.

Anya has no plan, and she has exchanged one able-bodied enemy for three. The yobs are probably panicking too. This kick-back wasn't in the book of rules, and their bovverboss is unavailable to direct operations. But they daren't run out on him, so they come at Anya from three sides, heads ducked to avoid the bag she whirls round her head – like some crazed cowgirl lassoing steers.

'Stop the bastards!' she shrieks to the crowd which is now regrouping, though totally impassive. 'Don't stand there! Call the cops! Do something!'

A skinny youth has her in a rugby tackle and the other two close, to wrestle her to the ground. As the first fist comes crashing down on her kidneys and as boots are swung back for the kill, the sluggish public conscience (calculating itself to be by now in a moral majority) lumbers into action. A few hands drag them off, someone else hoists the injured bullyboy to his feet and shoves him on his way; a few platitudes of public order are ritually fired off, and the humiliated gang shambles off, jeering.

That's it. Crowd disperses. None of their business. None of hers come to that, the silly bitch! Teach her not to mix in it, next time. Each

201

to his own aggro. On with the shopping . . .

The epilogue Laczi could take pretty much as Anya gave it: 'Are you all right?' Jaswinder's small, clear tones. She has gathered her brood about her knees, but otherwise gives no sign of alarm. Voice perfectly steady.

'I think so,' says Anya, fingering what's going to be a fine blue bruise in the small of her back. 'Are you?'

'Oh, I am used to it.' Jaswinder dismisses the whole affair with a light movement of her hand which also serves to put a loose strand of hair back in place. 'You must forgive me,' she goes on, 'if I do not thank you. It was well meant, I am sure, but it will only make matters worse. I hope you can understand?'

'I didn't do it to be thanked,' says Anya, who hadn't, but is a little piqued, nevertheless, to be so decisively *un*thanked. 'I did it for the pure pleasure of battle. Scum like that needs sweeping into the gutter where it belongs.'

Jaswinder's smile, while not impolite, contains a shade of scepticism.

'I would be more careful next time,' she says. 'People will not always come to your help. And you cannot fight these thugs alone. There is always another gang around the corner.'

'Thanks for the advice,' says Anya, knowing it to be sound. 'I get these rushes of blood to the head. Do you mean,' she asks suddenly, realizing what has just been said, 'that they'll be back with reinforcements?' She's surprised how thoroughly it alarms her. The adrenalin has deserted her. The shabby ranks of shops, the bus-stop pole, the pavement with its grimy encrustation of bubblegum and lolly-sticks has turned suddenly alien, hostile.

'In daylight, probably,' Jaswinder is replying, 'they will not. But someone will be made to pay. Maybe you. Maybe me. Maybe someone else. But somebody. It is the way. You are new around here?'

'Yes.'

'It is not as bad as it looks. I find it best to ignore them . . .' (a tiny spherical gesture with her wrists, as if proffering a delicacy to a guest) '. . . for dignity.' The symmetry of the gesture is impaired as the eldest boy, who has been furtively picking his nose, has the finger firmly captured and imprisoned. He stares at Anya with round eyes.

'It's a bit hard on the kids, though,' Anya hints.

Jaswinder tucks a small, firm hand under Baby Gopal's chin.

'A few tears,' she says matter-of-factly. 'Last week it was the lion at the zoo that made him cry. What difference does it make? He has his fears. And he will grow out of them.'

'Certainly he has his fears.' Anya is intrigued by this novel philosophy, 'but he's lost his ice-cream. Let me get him another, at least.'

'It will be all right,' says Jaswinder, a trifle frostily, 'I have quite enough money, thank you.'

Things have come to a stand.

'Goodbye then.' Anya senses from what quarter the draught is blowing. 'See you around, I hope.'

'I also hope.' Jaswinder relents to the extent of a charming and quite unexpected smile, as she turns back into the dairy to get the replacement cornets.

It was the smile, Anya explained to Laczi, that really interested her most. It was what he, with his rotten English, would probably call 'a smile of equals'. And when you got one of those, it made you realize how rare they were.

Next time she saw Jaswinder, she made a point of speaking. And the next time . They exchanged names. They admired the material in each other's dresses. Mr Gopal turned out to be an importer of Indian fabrics. Anya confessed her former trade . . . Like the burst cornets on the pavement, the mistrust slowly melted, until there was only a faint stain left where it had been. And after a few weeks, with the traffic of time and feet, even that disappeared.

Anya invited Jaswinder home. But Jaswinder was having none of that: Anya must come to them. Like a city-state of ample amenity, the Gopals saw no call for missions abroad. What they did not already enjoy, they could always import. Anya was duly imported. Yet there was no insularity in the self-containedness, and no parsimony in her welcome. Whatever her notions of Indian family life had been (and I shall not betray her by setting them down in their native baldness), they had now to be abandoned. She sat among the gay clutter of ornaments, flowers, candles, lamps, and shrines, consuming delicacies that no curry-house had ever put her way, and enjoying a very free exchange of voluble opinion.

Conversation turned, unembarrassedly (for Anya was now an honorary Indian), on the racial troubles that had been much in the recent news. Grandpa Gopal was finding it surprising that anyone was surprised at these things: 'What do you expect?' he asked. 'If the English have a grudge against us, that is only natural. In India, in the old days, we did not love the English. There is nobody likes to be invaded.'

'Are you going to let them just walk over you, then?' Anya inquired. Passivity was one of the Indian traits she had come prepared to deplore.

Mr Gopal junior intervened promptly: 'Who is walking over us? We get on with our work. We make a living – a good living. Just because some foolish bully-fellow has too much to drink and opens his mouth too loud, am I to crawl into a hole and hide? It is nothing to do with me what he says. That same bully-fellow goes to the football games, so I hear. No Asians are there – apart from Ranjit, here, and he is not a real Asian . . .' He smiled slyly at a young man in denims. 'But what happens at the football all the same, you tell me? There are no Asians, so they beat up each *other*! It is not race, it is a social problem.'

'One or two "fellows" have died of your "social problem", squire,' said Ranjit laconically. His accent and intonation was pure London.

'Was I saying it wasn't serious?'

'They can die in India also,' put in Grandpa Gopal. 'In India they die by millions. So why make such a fuss about something over which we have no control?'

'That's old man's talk,' said Ranjit scornfully. 'How do you *know* we have no control? You can't control the monsoon maybe, but you can control a geezer with an iron bar. This immigrant mentality really gets on my wick! Just lie down and let it happen to you! God is over all! No wonder the racists are having a bleeding picnic!'

'It is a social problem,' reiterated Jaswinder's husband.

'It's all right for you,' snorted Ranjit, 'you've got your moneybelt to keep you warm. You should try living in Brick Lane on £30 a week.'

'That's exactly what I'm saying: poverty is a social problem – just the same for the English on £30 a week, as for the Indian.'

'But the English aren't *on* £30 a week, are they?' sneered Ranjit. 'Only the poor Bangladeshi. And why? Because they haven't got the brains to refuse. "Oh no, thanking you very much, sahib, I am so very happy to be cleaning lavatories at the Heathrow Airport! I think myself to be most lucky fellow." Peasants! Why do they think they were let in? To do the jobs no Englishman in his right mind'll *touch* any longer. And the silly bastards are grateful!' He turned to Anya for confirmation: 'Have you ever noticed,' he appealed, as if clinching the argument, 'how Asians always go for the ugliest white girls?'

The thought may have occurred to Anya, but she wasn't going to confess to it now. She wasn't sure, anyway, that it hadn't been as an 'ugly white girl' that she'd been consulted. But Ranjit reprieved her by plunging on: 'And talking about prejudice,' he said, 'for pure race prejudice, can anybody beat a Sikh? This same old man who comes here bleating to me about racialism (you know the one I mean, Jaswinder), will he let a son of his marry a girl from another caste? Will he hell! They may both come from the same culture, the same country, the same town, pray to the same god, work in the same bloody office, but, yah . . .' He became inarticulate with disgust.

'It may be,' said Jaswinder, pushing some food in his direction, 'that he is stuck in his ways, that he does not try hard enough to adapt.' Her voice, without being loud or contentious, flew through the air like a well-flighted arrow. 'But you, Ranjit, you try too hard. There is more than one way to lose your independence. Anyway, you are shocking Grandpa Gopal. If that is what you were wanting, you can stop now.'

Anya watched Ranjit, as he lowered his head over the plate, for some sign of resentment, but could make none out. He was simply enjoying his food. And Jaswinder, her rebuke delivered, was smiling again as if nothing had happened. A rebuke of equals – no hard feelings. She found it remarkable. Was there something in her own ethic of collision and abrasion that stood in need of correction? First Wavell, now this. Looking at Jaswinder's smooth brow and serene mouth, she felt the attraction of something more than 'charm' – though that was undeniable. Amanda Kovacs had been 'charming': this came from some deeper source and it left her feeling oddly chastened. Could it be that the white races, from long abuse of power, had become brutalized, and that civilization, all that while, had been passing into the keeping of those they oppressed? It was a thought with such surprising ramifications that she said little more for the rest of the evening, though she was extremely observant.

'I hope,' said Jaswinder, as she helped her into her fur coat, 'that you have enjoyed yourself?' The complacent smile that dimpled her cheek showed that the hope was benevolent rather than anxious.

'Yes,' said Anya. 'I did. Very much. Thank you.'

She went home to write a long letter to Laczi.

It was Laczi's own fault that he heard no more for over a month. He hadn't even the decency to reply. Composing letters in English was too wearisome, and he was in the middle of a bout of work which left him exhausted at the end of the day. A drink in the pub – where he was quietly mending the fences Anya had broken – was all he was good for in the evenings. He had become rather fatalistic about their curious long-distance marriage. What would be, would be. About her new multi-racial enthusiasms he was sceptical (having seen her take up people and causes before), but acquiescent. It was natural that she should seek new social outlets after the social starvation, largely self-imposed, that she'd suffered in Cornwall. Whether they would prove durable was another question.

Spring was advancing into summer when he received his next bulletin – a bulky package of many pages in her large, careless hand. There had been some talk of her coming down, and he presumed the length of this was offered by way of amends.

Dear Laczi,

You know what today is? May Day. MAY? Not even in the benighted bloody antipodes (where the seasons are all arse-over-tit anyway), not even *there* does it bucket down like this in *May*! I'm obscenely aggrieved. We had plans – Stace, Wavell and me (Wavell's her Spade boyfriend) – to celebrate the Big Red Festival of Spring by taking to the park. Watch the happy workers at play, sort of thing. Instead, I'll probably spend a grotty day in this gerbil-cupboard of a room (where, if I strained a little, I could touch *all four* walls at once!) staring at the waterfall on the windowpane. Very picturesque – like watching the street from inside one of those old-fashioned fish shops. For variety, of course, I can always study the dado-frieze peeling off the damp plaster, or admire my G-plan chairlet at its G-plan deskette. If I tuck the chairlet in *very* tight, there's a six-inch strip of lino for me to pace up and down on. ('G' stands for Gerbil – it's all gerbil-furniture in here. Gerbil pillows stuffed with chewed newsprint. Walls gerbilshit brown. Gerbilbars over the window. At night I run about squeaking. You must visit some time, see how you like hanging out *both* ends of my gerbil-divan.) Still . . . mustn't grumble. So they say. Though they never explain why not.

Anyway . . . I thought I'd while away the dripping day with a bit of reporting – to keep my hand in, and keep you up to date, you thankless old shit! Stand by to receive.

Yesterday I went on my first demo. Yes, you heard right. A demo. Little Annie has been personally Rocking against Racism. (Come to think of it, that may be why the skies have fallen today.) Don't panic,

I haven't actually *joined* anything, but I have to admit that I did lark about a bit on the fringes.

This is how it happened. On Saturday Bill and Bea turned up unexpectedly, with Annabel in tow. They'd made a special trip from Somerset to be in on the big anti-fascist shindig (you've read your papers, I hope). If you want my opinion, Bill has been suffering from CND cold turkey for years and had simply spotted a way of getting himself a canny fix. These solidarity-addicts are never cured. Anyway that, plus Stacy's multi-racist diatribes, and my neighbour Jaswinder's subtler persuasions, had so eroded my principles that I was anybody's for the price of a hand-held slogan. (You know how passive I am in the face of other people's convictions.) Well, at Trafalgar Square, someone shoved a lollipop-stick into my fist, and there I was – helplessly politicized. With 80,000 people roaring themselves hoarse, who was I to resist? 'We are bláck/We are whíte/We are dýn-a-míte!' Wow! 'Smásh the Násh — unal Frónt!' . . . and so on in thrilling kindergarten metre.

Crowds that big do funny things to my nerve-endings – skin starts prickling, genitals tingle, if I had hackles would they rise? I don't know, but there's some queer secretion from the Solidarity Glands that plays hell with my normal reactions – fear, contempt, loathing, you know.

Seriously though, it was hard to be serious about it – it was all such carnivally, festively fun. ('NF = No Fun' was one of the lapel-buttons on sale.) There were the usual po-faced solemnities of course: 'They shall not pass!' (Joint Examining Board against Nazis?) 'Never again! Stop the Nazi National Front!' (Auschwitz Veterans Wheelchair Brigade) 'One Race: Human Race.' The Bethnal Green Trades Union Council had the same banner that had been embroidered on crimson satin for the General Strike by loyal socialist needlewomen – 'Man to man the world o'er shall be as brothers,' and 'the world o'er' illustrated in bright picturegrams. Also the usual collection of riff-raff tagging along for the ride: 'Gay Rights for One-Legged Midgets', 'Brain Surgeons against Nazism', 'Binmen against Racists', ('Binmen against Brain Surgeons'?) 'Hackney Rape Crisis (affiliated with Manwar)', 'East End Federation of Anarchists' (*loved* that one – how did they ever manage to federate?), and one sad little placard: 'Christ is the answer' (but what was the question?) The amusing thing was that a lot of it was witty: 'Keep Britain clean [wire basket]: flush out the Nasties'; 'Famous Faeces' and a picture of Hitler as a pile of dogshit ('Do not permit your dog to foul the pavement'); 'Stamp out the Enochs: they are Overrunning our Cities, they are Breeding like Rabbits; they are Polluting our Rivers of Blood.' Well, if not witty, at least not mindless.

But the kids were having a ball. It was a kid's carnival – ageing hippies and moon-faced vicars completely outnumbered, faintly defensive actually: tending to mutter in corners about 'lack of historical perspective', and where was the 'ideological backbone' after all? But you don't need historical perspective to dance to a steel band (there were lorry loads of them) and your ideological backbone would probably snap if you tried. It was just Mardi Gras, complete with the giant *papier-mâché* heads of the NF bogeymen.

And the zaniest of punk fancy-dressing – outrageous, inventive, and very funny. There must have been dozens of Brides of Dracula, girl vampires with pancake make-up, blood-stained lips and demoniac eyes. And all those muscular male torsos, stripped to the tattooed waist, for them to sink their little fangs into! The black boys definitely cleaned up this section – *their* pimples didn't show and they strutted *much* more convincingly. And the hair!! What fun we were all deprived of, when they confined us to natural hair-colours. No Easter chick or Mohawk brave ever rose to *these* gaudy heights.

Of course (this was at the Trafalgar Square end) they kept distracting us with puerile attempts at marshalling, and even more puerile speechifying – everything that happened, from hard rock to hot dogs, happened 'regardless of race, creed or colour'. Or – in the case of the MP for somewhere, who wanted us to admire him for his political courage and his regional accent – '*ir*regardless of race, creed or colour'. 'This great occasion', we gathered, was somehow due to the wondrousness of his party's policy . . . The secretary of some tinpot union brings fraternal greetings to us, 'comrades, brothers and sisters', from the suffering workers of Piddlington-on-Pot. Ten seconds later he's tearing strips off us: apparently we haven't been properly supporting the Piddlington workers in their heroic struggle . . . A token black boy scrambles on to the hustings and gets entangled in his syntax and the microphone cord. He seems to be inciting a riot. ('Who *is* this schmuck!' grumbles Wavell disgustedly.) But the kid extricates himself with a bit of cheerleading: 'Black and White/Unite and Fight', and we yell back like maniacs, because today black is the only colour. Yes, my friend, I too yelled with the best of them. I don't like being unheard when there's a noise to be made. Besides I had to encourage Bill, who'd gone all shy on me.

Next, a tiny Indian lady with a shatteringly shrill voice. She's thanking us all for saving her and her family from deportation. (Don't thank us, lady, it was easy – we didn't even know we'd done it!) We're not really listening to all this – just waiting. Like you sit out an interminable grace (not that I ever have), knowing that it has to end, and then you can get your teeth into the meat.

There's a struggling mass of bare-chested yobs by the main procession banner – a huge blue-and-yellow affair. They've all *got* to be at the head of the march and they don't care whose jaw they break in the process. A young copper is handling them very well – banging a few heads together in a friendly way, and gradually getting them *behind* the banner, not in front. He carefully ignores the beer-cans and the bottles of suspect orange juice which the kids are hectically tossing down their throats. The fuzz behaved very well all day, incidentally – when they were in evidence at all, which wasn't often.

The only ugly incident I saw was a white Daddy with a black (adopted?) girl-child who was getting on Daddy's wick: 'Look!' he hisses in that special bourgeois hiss which loathes publicity but can't control its holy paternal fury, 'you've changed your mind four times! Do you want to go on the march or not? First you do, then you don't. Make up your mind! Anyway,' (he gets a pincer grip on the kid's neck – supposed to be chummily coercive, but you can hear the teeth grinding) 'we're here now, so we're going. OK?' The poor kid has no friends here, is part of no group, is merely a stand-in for his conscience, so what can *she* do? She's hating the whole affair.

The biggest cheer comes when we're finally released from the prosing arseholes on the platform. The pigeons on the National Gallery fly off in panic at that cheer. It's so big that the marshalling instructions get completely lost in it. The whole of Trafalgar Square gives a surge and a roar and we're on our way. (Well, after another half hour we are.) The chanters and shriekers take over.

Wavell says the march was routed through supposed NF strongholds. We never saw a sign of it. The faces on the pavement were anything from ecstatic to moronic, but the only noise of dissent came from a drunken old bum who could hardly stand up: he was bumping along the outside files and snarling something about Hitler having the right idea.

Oh, mustn't forget the ultimate politicized harridan (set it down for a warning!) marching under the banner of some splinter of a left-wing splinter-group, and trying to get a bit of noise out of the sheepish crowd of chaps mumbling-bumbling behind her. Modelling herself on Liberty in the French Revolution picture, I reckon, and with a voice-box of pure brass: 'SMASH THE NASH . . . What's *that*?' she bawls. 'Can't hear a bloody thing! Lost your voices or something? Let's hear it! SMASH THE NASH-UNAL FRONT . . . Christ Almighty, what's the matter with you? *I'm* making more noise than the rest of you put together. Let's be hearing you. SMASH THE NASH . . .' It's a lost cause – putting heart into this collection of puddings – but she doesn't care. It's the drama of it, the dominance, the great glare of publicity. Yes, *of course*, you dumbo! I was jealous. And, yes again, smart-arse! The harridan was a fine strapping wench with fire in her eye – a bit like your Ilona statue-girl. I detested her so much I actually tried to get in on her act (till Bill hauled me off): *Whaddawe want?* 'A few less slogans,' bellows me. *When d'we want it?* 'Yesterday?' I shriek. Got a few laughs, but no support. What is it that I haven't got, to make me into an Amazonian demagogue? I can yell. I can strut. I'm an exhibitionist. What's missing?

The best of the day, though, was the music (this was when we got to the park) – pumped out of a double tower-block of loudspeakers and amplifiers, and put through the head at such a volume that all thought died. Tens of thousands of kids thrashing and whirling and pogo-ing to it in ecstasy. I usually detest kids – all that fresh, blooming, untapped energy of youth, it's enough to make you throw up. I managed to hate the mc/presenter crud, who slouched on at the beginning, chewing gum. Fortyish, balding, with a ginger tonsure, red shirt, pot belly, and the face of a retired wrestler gone into the promotion-racket. A right bully-boy. He grabs the mike and roars into it: 'Are y'all right? Eh? I should bloody hope so. Got a little entertainment here t'day f'ya. All right? The sun is shining' (Cheers), 'the fuzz've gone home' (Louder cheers), 'and we're going to have fun' (Frenzied roars). 'What're we going to have? Fucking fun!' (Crowd goes wild) 'Got a few bands t'play f'ya. Be starting in a quarter hour or so. Little singer called Polly Ester . . .' (Mild cheers, nobody seems to have heard of the little singer) 'A coupla singing freaks called' (he suddenly screams) 'The Au Pairs !!!' (instantaneously the crowd screams back) 'And later on – presently on their way – stuck in the fucking traffic – expected any minute . . . (Bellows) THE CLASH!!!!' Not a line on his face suggests interest, feeling, enthusiasm – just contempt for the kids he's turning on and off like a switch.

'Right now' (recorded music fades in very loud – he signals angrily and it dies back) 'we're here to have fun.' (It never sounded less funlike.) 'Black and white – all having fun. Now there may be some yobbos who want aggravation.' (Roars and boos.) 'There may be some Nazi apes here who want trouble. There may be some who've heard there was a little aggravation at Lewisham and Brixton and Ilford, and they'd like some more. So whaddawe say to them? *We* don't want aggravation. If we get any aggravators, whaddawe we do? Eh? We sit on them. Got that? *Sit on their fucking heads!* There's enough of us here to sit on quite a few fucking heads, right?' (Roars of approval – not at all bloodthirsty. If his aim was incitement, it's fallen flat on its face.) 'Right! Stick around boys and girls. In another ten minutes – to kick us off . . .' (he wheels out the histrionic scream again) 'TOM ROBINSON' (deafening howls, whistles, screams and whoops from 80,000 throats – now he's talking!) Music fades up, but he's had an afterthought, snatches the mike and bellows out of the corner of his mouth, 'NAZIS OUT!' Replaces mike and slouches to the back of the stage where he spends most of the afternoon having grown-up talk with a collection of God-knows-what – bouncers? Touts? Pushers? Music moguls? – a seedy-looking bunch, anyway.

And over the front of the high paling-fence which protects the musicians from the fans – interesting, this – hang the groupie girls, blasé expressions, wan, washed-out faces, staring sightlessly into the masses of the unprivileged. Displaying themselves for Envy. Angel-faced kids with a touch of the sordid about them (on the junk, by the look of a few of them), all wearing that special expression of inane and cynical rapture you can see on 'Top of the Pops'.

Well, you can see I tried my best to hate it all, and they gave me all the help they could. We went as far away as possible, so that no animal magnetism could reach us from the stage. But once the music started up – the *live* music – and the bums of the black girls selling tea or squash or hotdogs began to wiggle happily in time with a beat that shook the ground even at a range of three hundred yards . . . well, there was nothing to do but join in. Couldn't help myself . . . All right, I'm sorry! I got into bad habits in the bad old Cape Town days. I still can't resist a good Afro beat, even if it's played by white slags and phoneys. It's all right, up here in the head: I *know* what meretricious assembly-line trash it is. About as individual as a fly-button. But it gets me somewhere below the organs of discrimination – and I'm a goner.

Upshot? I disgraced myself. Made a spectacle. Grabbed passing blacks, male and female. Grabbed whites too. Didn't care. Totally

211

indiscriminate. Had a ball. Had to be taken home forcibly by Bill and Bea. Left Stace and her bloke still pogo-ing like fiends. Want another show like it, next week. No, tomorrow! Believe in the brotherhood of man (one race: human race. Right on!) with all the fervour of a teenybopper. Love my black sisters all over from arse to tit. Feel like a new woman (wouldn't say No to a new *man* – preferably black). I am, in short, turned on by the Anti-Nazi League, all my sublime intelligence of the confirmed non-joiner swamped in the ecstatic muddledom of the political groupie. And I love it.

I remember trying to guess, in the course of that long happy afternoon, what would happen to any hapless NF skinhead who might have tried to stir up the fabled 'aggravation'. Answer? Nothing. He would have been absorbed, swallowed. There was nowhere for him to start, in all the squirming cavorting mass. If he had, nobody would have noticed him. Or if they had, they wouldn't have believed their ears – he'd have to be joking. He would have been neutered – no need for anyone to sit on his head.

The organizers had got it all wrong. They thought they were sponsoring a propaganda operation – leading us down the good old 'right path' with a few rock bands as bait. In fact, the propaganda was a wash-out and the only thing that mattered was that we were all there. The multi-racial society (shit! the cant has really got me!) simply existed. Black and white unite and *dance*! Forget the fight. It won't be necessary. It reminded me of what you said about Budapest, the day everybody sang, remember? What is it about music? It makes you feel that you must have spent most of your life in appalling solitude, and yet also that 'you'll never walk alone' again. Isn't that the favourite football song? Some connection?

Jee-sus! What a to-do about a bloody rock carnival! I think my brains are softening. But I did like the kids – I have to confess I liked 'em. They seemed to be going about the business of being kids in the right kind of reckless, arrogant, sexy way. What politics there were in it, all followed from that. I don't make a lot of sense – not even to myself. Can't handle this 'discovery' stuff. What am I doing, at my time of life, making discoveries? Don't I know it all already? *Disappointment*, chaps – that's what it's all about. Dance your little dance, but tomorrow comes Disappointment. The funny thing is how completely I forgot about Disappointment while I was dancing.

Anyway . . . I only mention these boring revels to explain why I didn't come down for the weekend – *supposing* that you looked up from your carving long enough to wonder. I suppose I'd have come

if I'd been hell-bent on seeing you, but I didn't. Or I wasn't. We seem to get on better at a distance. For the present. When it changes, I'll let you know. But write to me, you old bugger.
    Good luck,
      Anya
P.S. Stacy has just shown me the interview in *Sculpture International.* *And* the pics. Why don't you keep me informed, you miserable schmuck? Just because I fake indifference doesn't mean that you have to *believe* me! The editor seems to have done for your grammar 'the thing what I would have never achieved'. Could you ask him for lessons?

With 'The Prophet' duly installed in the Tate, Kovacs had become a name which the art journalists could no longer ignore. Soon after Anya had left for London, *Sculpture International* had despatched an expert to check out the new celebrity in his reported habitat. This art-watcher found the rare Hungarian bird not only at home, but positively singing on its perch. Perhaps Laczi was lonely. Perhaps he was flattered. Perhaps he was just very skilfully drawn out. But in any case, he told this stranger more about himself and his occupations than Anya had been able to extort from him in five months. She read it with avidity:

. . . Interviewer: Why granite? Is it not an exceptionally difficult stone to work?
Kovacs: All stone is difficult. The *kind* of difficulty is what makes each finished piece itself. But you are right: granite asks for much patience, and I can now spare the time. Also it asks for much muscle. I thought I would like to try it while I still have some.
You see it as a peculiar challenge?
Yes, I suppose so, I like a stone that fights back, shows some resistance. But there is also a something monumental that I am seeking these days. 'Monumental' is easily said, I know, but I mean figures that stand heavy on the earth – heavy knees, heavy feet, you see. Even the head is heavy – but not with thought, not a reflective weight. It is to be simply mass, not a concentration of the mind. The Egyptians used granite for this purpose, and they were right. With marble, say, or with alabaster, you do not *see* the mass. There is a certain deceiving of the eye that is occasioned by the finish – an illusion of lightness. With such stones one is betrayed into detail, into portrayal, into character. Perhaps I should not say 'betrayed',

for these things are not wrong if they are what the stone wants to do. But that is exactly why it does not suit me at present. I do not want character. I want mass.

You have worked extensively in bronze, in the past. Can you not achieve this 'mass' in bronze?

Bronze is for me a too 'invented' medium. (I speak only of today: tomorrow, who knows? I am fickle about mediums: for many years I would not carve stone.) The granite here in Cornwall, however, is not invented. It lies on the moors. It is given. I do not have to invent it.

You draw inspiration, then, from the natural rock-formations? From the tors?

Not at all. Not from the forms, at least. These are merely a stack of scones, or if you prefer, a stack of giant elephant-turds. No, no. There is for me no inspiration in the forms. Only in the fact that they lie there – so badly in need of transformation. So, I transform them. I thought once of making Roughtor, over there [the studio looks out towards Bodmin Moor], into a monster park of scuplture; but life is short, and even the thousands of years of stone-age men who lived up there left only a very little mark. And perhaps the National Trust would have a few words to say?

So you would not work like Henry Moore, say, when he evolves designs from flints or bones – from natural objects?

Does he truly do this? I know he *says* so, but I have some doubt. If he does, either he mistakes his interest (this is in humanity, not in flints or bones), or else he has forgotten in what century he lives. The eternally non-human – these stones and bones – that is what may come *after* us, if the world goes wrong. It is not for us, *now*, to give ourselves up to contemplating what will be left after we have blown ourselves in bits. History does not permit such detachment. What will be left is not sculpture, but detritus.

You find a 'false serenity' in Moore, then?

I do not complain of the 'repose' of a Moore figure. That is his very great virtue. It is his power. But only because it is eternally struggled for. You do not pick it up on the beach.

And there is also the question of scale. What am I to do with a flint as big as myself? Or a knuckle I can walk amongst? I do not know what to do with these things. There is only one scale: the human scale. The proper place for this flint is in a man's hand. And the bone should be put back in a man's leg so that he can walk with it. In themselves they are nothing.

When you talk of 'the human scale', of course, you are quoting Moore himself.

Exactly so. He should listen to himself more often. He says some excellent things.

You do not believe, then, in abstract form?

I do not know what it would be, when it is at home. These things are all objects. They exist. Where is the abstraction? The only question is whether they are worth the attention we are asked to give to them. I cannot give the same attention to a bone as I can to the man whose bone it is. It is the same with a stack of weathering rocks.

That sounds like the manifesto of an unashamed humanist.

Unashamed? I don't know. 'Humanist' is a word that has been dragged through the mud, and some dirt still clings. Affirmation, in our times, has always the taint of hypocrisy, so it seems to me. Anyway, I do not like to see '-ist' on the end of good healthy words. 'Human' is all right. We can agree on that. But a human*ist* is a man who makes a profession out of something that the rest of us have to *be*. Usually he expects to be paid for it, too.

You are not, then, a communist?

Please explain.

You believe in 'communes', but not in 'communists'? The same objection would apply?

That is difficult to say.

More difficult than to say whether you are a humanist?

Much more difficult.

Why is that?

Because a humanist offers to me nothing but his great big beautiful soul. This I do not need. I have one of my own. But the communist has a plan. He can do something. He will make change. In this I take some interest.

TWELVE

Scruples

The election campaign that ended four years of Labour misrule and initiated five of the other kind, was a grubby one. The lady who was to become Britain's first woman Prime Minister did not disdain, during the run-up to the General Election, to titillate white terrors by offering to salve them with fierce new immigration laws. The fact that these public-spirited plans were announced at Ilford (where the litanies of hate already adorned council-estate walls – *Versicle:* 'The Alien is in your midst' *Response*: 'The Alien will not be moved. He will bash your fucking brains out') . . . this was as fortuitous, no doubt, as the fact that there happened to be a bye-election going on at Ilford. Who would be so ungallant as to suggest that politicians study their audiences, or time their announcements? The Labour members, anyway – who were publicly shocked by the honourable lady's behaviour – had so much to do holding on to their own seats, that action unconnected with the ballot-box could hardly be expected of them. The verb 'to deplore' – never before so intransitive – was much in use, and the collective noun 'immigrants' took another semantic lurch towards excluding all white immigrants whatsoever, and *in*cluding many persons who had never 'immigrated' anywhere and were not likely to – unless 'assisted' by the fast-breeding tribe of the Enochs.

National Front candidates, meanwhile, held respectable election meetings around the country, in pursuance of their democratic rights. 'Inalienable' rights, you might call them. There were no Aliens in *their* midst, as they strove to put the Great back into Britain.

Perhaps nobody foresaw what it would all come to, though the head of the Special Patrol Unit must have had a shrewd suspicion as he stepped up recruitment and put his troops through some fairly stiff combat training. And at least one student of the newspapers, down in Cornwall, lay awake on more than one night, fretful with misgiving. His well-earned kip was by now thoroughly over. He had seen a little of Anya's new milieu, on a series of visits to London, and it left him extremely uneasy.

It mustn't be supposed, however, that on these visits he was simply visiting his wife. He had other problems. The granite was playing merry hell with his edge-tools, and he had not been able to persuade the local blacksmith to take a creative interest in the forging of points and chisels. For a while he tried running up his own; but it was a craft as subtle as sculpture. In the end there was no substitute for the old Whitechapel toolmaker, whom he had broken in over the years, and who needed no more than a hint to produce the exact and efficient implement. This was his excuse for coming to London every month or two – to spend a few restive nights in the bed Anya had grown used to having to herself, to meet some of her friends, to quarrel a bit, make up a bit, and then to depart, neither a wiser nor a sadder man – just a puzzled one. It wasn't yet time, he concluded – for either of them.

Then, over Christmas, Anya visited him. She'd decided she could risk it. The combined effect of the Cornish winter and the Christian festival would, she was sure, catapult her straight back to London, and all would be well. It didn't, and it wasn't.

Instead, she sank into a cosier, wintrier version of that first idyllic spring of their marriage. He worked. She read. And in the evenings they talked endlessly, chewing over the new matter of Anya's socio-political world, weighing and jettisoning, satirizing and collating with that tireless analytic verve they seemed to stimulate in each other. When every detail was rendered down to its finest constituent grains, they would go to bed . . . and begin again.

Cornwall itself let Anya down. The villagers were benign, all her old offences forgotten. They had forgiven her for Laczi's sake. And the winter gales, the icy horizontal rain simply put colour in her cheeks and a spring in her step. She walked the cliff-paths alone for days on end, remembering what it had been like to be really fit. Beginning, indeed, to feel it. Her solitude – until then a merely negative condition of deprivation – was becoming populous with perceptions and projects, which she hoarded up and carried home to try on Laczi, as he was trying out his sculptural projects on her. The old collaborative partnership was stronger than ever.

A month passed. Two. The clifftop heaths were starred with violets and primroses, and the gorse flowers were beginning to spread their tropic musk abroad on the milder air, before she was able – scarcely knowing why she did it – to tear herself away. And even so, before she left for the Smoke, she made Laczi promise to join her there in another month. Quite what he was supposed to do, cupboarded in her skimpy little flat, he could not make out and she could not explain.

Early in April he arrived. He had a very determined air. This time it was going to be settled, one way or another. He was not prepared to go on living as if under some kind of Separation Order. Their understanding had never been better. It was absurd to go on like this. If necessary, he would sell up in Cornwall and move several lorryloads of stone across the breadth of the country. But he was not going back to indeterminacy.

Anya was quite in accord about the indeterminacy, but over the property – though it was bought with her money and registered in her name – he could get no answers and roused very little interest. Some people, when they buy a house, embark on a proprietorial love affair. Every renovation, modification, even a coat of paint, deepens the sanctity of the bond. It is not any old place, it is 'my place'. Bill and Bea, like ivy on an old stone wall, had grown into Crabtree Cottage with that kind of affectionate closeness. But on the day Anya collected the deeds of *her* little grey home in the West, she began to lose interest. Sell it! keep it! . . . Did it matter? Yes, it would be useful to have the money. It would supplement the earnings from casual secretarial jobs, which she took up and then ditched every few months. Let him do what he wanted, and they'd split the proceeds. It wasn't important.

Well, it was important to him. Appalled at the prices, he began to look for a proper London studio. He was not prepared any longer to pursue long-term projects under the threat of eviction. He was 'established' enough to expect and receive something better.

But Anya – never *less* established – seemed to be enjoying the condition as if it had conferred new freedoms. In many ways, it had. Her old addiction to luxury – requiring as it did all the unwieldy impedimenta of repletion – had been a bondage. Now that she was mobile, and travelling light, she had no inclination to load herself down again. It might have been different if the child had come. Unthinkably different! But that option, now sealed off with a neat knot in her tubes, occasioned no regret. More than likely the impulse had been self-deceiving, and she could consider herself lucky to be saddled with no long-term consequences. No . . . things were best as they were – whimsically unsettled. Every attempt to lumber her with a future was met with jocose resistance. Anya faced her personal destiny with a cheerful flippancy that would not be inveigled into earnestness.

'You see,' she explained to Laczi, 'I belong to the replete generation. You chaps that come of ancient frugal stock wouldn't understand.'

'Frugal!' protested Laczi. 'You didn't know my father!'

'Well . . . maybe it's not congenital, but it *is* you. It's written all over your history. Now me – I hardly got around to knowing I *had* an appetite, before it was satisfied. Over-satisfied. That makes for dissatisfaction. You get a hankering to *experience* your hunger before some ample provider shoves a nipple down your throat. But the only way you're going to do that is by going native, or turning monk, or grabbing at some bogus poverty or other – which is completely phoney, because you only endure it for as long as you choose. It's not real hunger. You become a kind of poverty-gourmet, trying to get up an appetite after the years of stuffing yourselves senseless. Or your want to live in a hovel because your mansion bores you rigid.'

'It is the dilemma of capitalism. Pleasures held in private can only be competitive. And when they are competitive they cannot satisfy.'

'Capitalism, balls! The people I interviewed around Hackney weren't suffering from that dilemma. *Their* dilemma was whether to buy the kids shoes, or a decent supper. How would you fancy an English winter spent in sneakers and a cotton frock? Oh I know, *you* wouldn't notice!'

'But how have you escaped this "dilemma" what you speak of? Perhaps you sell your mansion and buy a hovel. But then you make a profit. And still you are playing at poverty.'

'I haven't escaped it at all, stupid! I've simply noticed it.'

'And now you have noticed, what next? Do you sell all and give to the poor?'

'Don't be fatuous!'

'What then?'

'You tell me. You're supposed to be the expert on structures.'

Laczi had gone uninterpretably gloomy: 'I think you time this. Just when I begin to enjoy my little bit of affluence you try to poison it for me. Is most unkind.'

'Well, you let me enjoy my little bit of frugality then, and don't come bothering me with your damned property deals. You talk like the Juhacz. Buy yourself your studio and belt up. I've got better things to occupy my mind.'

'Sure,' he said with a grin, 'I think that is just what I will do.'

'The replete generation,' she announced a few days later – the germ of thought had been proving prolific – 'has a fascination for disaster. Little miseries won't do – they might just be the side-effects of repletion, like bad digestion. It's got to be a big disaster. If there are no earthquakes, they have to invent them. And it can't just be personal disaster either – that's too narrow. You enjoy it, but it's too "subjective". You want something that's definitely "out there", whether you're looking at it or not. That's why public schools kids go on voluntary service to famine areas. People are actually dying. Makes 'em feel marvellous. They're not.'

'This also is why you go on marches?'

'I go on marches, chuck, because I like the company and I like the occasion. I told you that ages ago: it satisfies the exhibitionist in me.'

Laczi gave a small snort of derision.

'Well?' she challenged. 'You know better, I suppose. Come on. Out with it!'

He rumbled for a few seconds, deploring the need to nail down such palpable evasions, then spat it out: 'You *hate* them – these marches of yours. Do you think I am blind?'

'Oh yes?' She repelled the intrusion loftily.

'I watch you those mornings. You are at the mirror three – maybe four times before you leave. You worry how you look. This is how I know something is wrong.'

'Oh *that*!' Brightening, she hastened to the aid of his misconstruction. 'Of *course* I worry how I look! You take one pace to the left these days, and you're liable to get mistaken for the lunatic fringe. Can't be too careful. I am not fighting,' she declared doughtily, 'for the freedom to be hairy and unwashed. I stand for decency. And cleanliness.'

'So?' he nodded his enlightenment. 'At the mirror then, it is behind your ears you are looking?'

'Where else?'

'I see.'

Evidently he did, for she presently made a concession: 'It *is* just the tiniest bit embarrassing, though. You have a kind of a point.'

He waited.

'I don't seem to be able to keep up my end of the banner for very long. Weak wrists, I suppose.' She ran a hand nonchalantly through her hair, letting him examine the weak wrists for himself.

'Sure,' he soothed, 'I know. Is very worrying for you when you do not keep your end up.'

'I knew you'd understand,' Anya replied tartly. 'Of course,' she mused, 'there's the element of surprise too. You shouldn't overlook the Element of Surprise. Going on a demo is the sort of thing Anya doesn't do. So when I do it . . . it's a surprise.'

'I have felt this myself,' Laczi was bound to admit it: 'surprise'.

'Well there you are.'

He pondered for a moment.

'This is then a small blow for personal freedom what you are striking?'

'Not just *personal* freedom,' she corrected, smoothing her hair down primly. 'I'm an old-fashioned girl, underneath. Believe that certain things are right and certain things are wrong. I'm not altogether sure you'd understand . . . Principles, you see? I know it's old-fashioned, but I've always been like that.'

Laczi's furrowed brow showed what an effort he was making to understand.

'And the moralist in you?' he asked. 'She is also satisfied?'

'Who are you calling a "moralist"?'

He shrugged calmly, discounting her resentment: 'Sorry! I thought it was moral to want to be connected with the rest of the human race. I don't know what else would be moral.'

' "Connected with the human race"!' Anya allowed the phrase its full fatuity. 'I'm not *that* old-fashioned.'

'Only trouble is,' he pursued, quite undeterred, 'marches won't do it for you.'

Anya sighed for his obtuseness: 'I was afraid you wouldn't understand what I meant by "principle". You make it sound insufferably prissy.'

'And so it is. But it is an appetite like any other. And you have it. You need to be connected.'

'Bah! "Connected"! You talk like an electrician.'

'Just so. An electrician. You want to be "plugged in" and "turned on". Connected. Isn't that what you keep telling to me?'

'I don't know why I waste my –'

'And what is more,' he cut her off brusquely, 'you never will be.'

There was a pause. She looked miffed.

'How can you be so sure?'

He shrugged: 'The human race will not allow it.'

Anya looked grim: 'We'll see about that!' she said. 'Damn the human race! When I set my heart on something, I get it.'

He gave a small whistle of mock admiration: 'This is sure some "connection": what you have got there!'

He treated it lightly, but he was troubled – more *for* her, than *by* her. He knew what happened to people who grabbed humanity by the scruff of the neck and insisted on being connected: they got their shins broken when humanity kicked back. And for all her fancy footwork, this girl was grabbing. Yet he couldn't argue: he had lived by some such unrealizable ideal of brotherhood all his life. It was an appetite not to be denied, and he himself had been at pains to point out the havoc its denial had made in Anya's world. Now she was escaping the 'merely personal', just as he had so long exhorted her to do. Why was he uneasy?

It was, he decided, because of the company she was getting into. Not individually . . . Wavell, Jaswinder, Stacy, Annabel, they were all sound enough. Good folk. But the zealots of the Anti-Nazi League gave him a sick feeling in the pit of his stomach. These were the *Gauleiters* of unplanned expeditions, the Moseses who didn't bother to inquire into the availability of manna and quails. Nor was he entirely assured that their zeal was of a different kind from the zeal of the National Fronters. It was nasty to be thinking these things, but one had to be clear: there was a very similar conviction in both camps, that the opposition, by the mere fact of being opposed, had forfeited human status. The rhetoric which denounced, regularly assigned them to the bestial orders – they were apes, beetles, shit. And rhetoricians, eventually, must use their sticks to beat something more than the corporate drum. He berated himself for going wishy-washy in his old age, but the misgiving persisted. He had seen some sights in Budapest . . . Unlike some, he was not convinced that it couldn't happen here.

Usually, they did not drink in the Crossed Staves. It was a sordid tramshed of a place with an atmosphere of suppressed violence that soured one's beer and whetted one's acrimonies. The licensee – known to the initiate as 'Grievous Bodily', on account of a rumoured, if unlikely conviction – was ominously saturnine with the raw youths who milled round the football table, frostily acid with the middle-elderly ruins who were making their pints last half the night, and implausibly hilarious with some colourful ladies who congregated by the beer-pumps and cackled their evenings away in his company. He was also dully suspicious of strangers. But on a night of squelching diagonal rain, when they'd run it rather close to drink-up time, the Kovacses sidled in. For half an hour they reckoned they could put up with the gloomy place. It was better than getting soaked, and arriving too late, at its more genteel twin.

It was an appropriate setting, anyway, for the argument they were having . . .

'It's pure fatalism, what you're saying,' complained Anya, 'as if the intentions of the individuals, and their reasons for being somewhere, had nothing to do with it.'

'That is correct. They haven't.' He located his glass carefully in the centre of the beer mat.

'What? Is there some monstrous "force of evil" that takes over as soon as people get together to do something? I thought you were *against* superstition. When I think of the roasting you gave me for my black devil-man!'

'The psychology of the mass is not the sum of the individual psychologies. It is another thing altogether. Join the mass and you will find out.'

'What "mass"? There are a lot of Indian families that live in Hucklington – some of the Gopal clan among them. I go with my friends, I don't "join a mass"!'

'I did not mean "join" like that. You have only to be present.'

He lifted his beer, turned the mat over, centred the glass and lowered it. The design on the obverse was more satisfactorily symmetrical.

She watched these preparations with amusement: 'Are you going to drink that? or just play with it?'

It did not touch him.

'I will tell you something I saw,' he said. He had lowered his voice, so that she had to lean over to hear him properly. 'It was on the streets, during the troubles. There was a quiet bit in the fighting. There were perhaps a dozen standing about, perhaps more – leaning on their rifles, sitting on steps, chatting. Ordinary people. Good! There is a black car coming across the square, not fast, slowly. No passengers, a driver by himself. There were not many cars those days, but that was the only thing unusual. When it gets near us, suddenly some girl starts screaming, "Avo! Avo! Avo!" That is the name of the Secret Police, yes? Avo. We have all had our troubles from the Avo. We are very bitter with it. So some other one throws a cobblestone at the windscreen. The car stops with a squeal . . . Now everyone is screaming "Avo!" Probably me too. I can't remember.

'But I remember how they all went berserk. From the steering wheel they drag him. I did not see him well, because almost at once he goes down on the road. It is like a football scrum. There is no referee, but they are taking turns, thrashing around and screaming like pigs. Or maybe it is the one on the ground what makes the noise. I can't tell . . .

'I ask you, what were they doing?' He held out two shaking palms. 'They had guns. They could have shot him. But this is not enough. Everyone must have had their little bit of sweet revenge, with their boots and their rifle-butts and their fists and their fingernails – I think also with their teeth. I don't know how else he could have been so . . .'

Laczi paused, and swallowed on a very dry throat.

'It lasted . . . perhaps a minute? Then suddenly everyone has gone very quiet. They do not want to be here. They do not want to look at each other. And in especial they do not want to look at the mess on the cobbles, which is enough to make you throw up. I will not tell you how he looked, but he was very dead. I can see him now, because everybody else has melted away. Nobody left in the whole empty square.

'I was expecting an Avo uniform. Nothing. Civilian clothes, ripped and torn and bloody. How did they know he was Avo? *How did they know?* The girl who screamed out "Avo", she might have known. The others didn't. I didn't. Probably no one was sure.'

There was a pause, during which Anya noticed, for the first time, angry voices raised at the pool-table behind her. It affected her with a kind of subsidiary rage, a kind of dream-anger, though her conscious attention was focused on Laczi who seemed plunged irrevocably in thought. Heavy thuds were coming up from the floor and vibrating her calves.

He raised his eyes to her: 'So you see,' he said, 'you do not have to "join", you do not have to intend anything, you just . . .'

At last he realized what was happening, grabbed her wrist and pulled her violently towards him, out of her chair, as a cast-iron table behind her went over with a crash. Two figures were writhing on the floor among the broken glass, with a few others dodging about, searching for the spot to put the boot in. The furniture danced with the heavy impact of feet and bodies. There was a light of battle in Anya's eyes, too, and he could feel her straining and quivering away from him like a restive colt. She was crazy enough to mix in, this one, if he didn't hold her back. He hung on grimly.

But her help was not needed. Grievous Bodily and his barman were quite up to it. As suddenly as it had begun, the 'aggravation' ceased. It might have been some sort of cynical demonstration whose bluff had been called. The two sheepish combatants, with their ears pinned in an armlock, one under each arm, were being dragged squirming across the floor. The others were pitched out after them – with such violence, they could think themselves lucky not to get brained on the wall opposite. And one non-participant who looked sideways at the proceedings had his pint snatched and was packed unceremoniously after.

Laczi looked at Anya's wide strained eyes, heard her excited breathless laugh, and shook his head.

'Let us get out of this sty of pigs,' he said contemptuously. 'We never should have come.'

'You think I shouldn't go.' She delivered the pronouncement (it was not a question) into his ear where he lay turned away from her. The divan – a gift from Stacy – knocked together from planks, with a slab of foam on top, was only honorifically 'double'. And since Anya, in bed, generated heat like a furnace, he tended to lie on the cool outer perimeter, stretched out straight like a horizontal knobkerrie.

She blew into his ear: 'Hullo? Anybody there?'

He indicated that he was still alive by entwining his toes round her ankles.

'Jesus!' she exclaimed, with an intake of pained breath, 'can you *sleep* with feet as cold as that?'

'I wasn't planning to.'

'Well I certainly can't.'

She reached into the black depths and hauled the offending blocks of ice towards the surface, lodging them firmly between her thighs: 'There,' she said, repressing her shudders. 'Devotion can go no further.'

'Nice,' he said lazily.

'For you perhaps.'

'When I have thawed,' came his muffled voice,' I will reward you.'

'Gawd!' she said vulgarly. 'All my birthdays are coming at once.

Don't put yourself out, will you?'

'I would prefer,' he replied delicately, 'to put myself in.'

She dismissed it scornfully: 'You talk muck. And it's not even funny. You *know* you can't make jokes in English, so why try? You're much funnier when you don't try. Real barrel of laughs.' The feet were less icy now.

'Hey!' She shook his shoulder. 'I asked you a question.'

'You didn't,' he mumbled. 'You told me what I think.'

'Well, don't you? . . . think I shouldn't go?'

'What difference does it make? You take no notice.' Being ignored didn't seem to be distressing him much.

But she blossomed into indignation: 'Yes I do,' she retorted. 'I just don't let it show. And now when you've got me at a disadvantage . . .' she rubbed herself insinuatingly up the slope of his back, coming to rest cosily on his shoulder, 'you can do anything you like with me.'

She paused, pondered.

'Do you like me "sultry"? she inquired. 'I could work on it a bit. Give it some polish. Just say the word.'

The knobkerrie heaved, stirred, and took her in his arms. The only reason he had deferred it was that he knew how completely it would corrupt the independence of his upright soul. With an armful of Anya, he experienced pitying contempt for all lovers of thin bony women and a voluptuous sensation of his own riches. If only she didn't radiate heat like a grill!

'This is "sultry"?' he said, blowing out a gust of air. 'What then will be torrid? If I was of wax I would be by now a small puddle at the bottom of the bed.'

'The phrase is, "My bones melt with passion." '

'So they do.'

'Could've fooled me.' She paused to wriggle into a more comfortable clinch. 'Are you still fretting? About the demo?'

'Perhaps a little.'

'I understood your story, you know,' she remarked to the hairs that grew around his breastbone. 'It's a risk. But I'm not quite the madwoman you think. *You* stood back when the others ran amok, didn't you? I would have done the same.'

'I stood back, yes. But even now I do not remember why. No more than I understand why the others didn't. It was perhaps fear? Some chance of the situation? A freak of the genes? An accident of timing, I don't know. I didn't *decide*. That is where my worry lives.'

She pulled her head back far enough to get a look at his puzzled frown: 'Why don't you let your worry die? It's only a peaceful sit-down in the middle of the road – all impeccably Ghandian. They might arrest a few of us for obstruction, but that's the worst that could happen. Trust me. I know what I'm doing. Probably it's the first time I *have* known – in the cool, rational way of seeing something necessary to be done, and doing it. That's good isn't it? You shouldn't knock it. You're the *last* person to be preaching disengagement.'

'I wish however,' he murmured, 'that you had learned this good lesson at the house of some other teacher.'

She laughed softly: 'It's sweet of you to be so concerned, O Fount of Wisdom, but I promise not to hold Teacher responsible. So trust me, there's a good old fruit. Eh? Is that all right with you, old cock?'

The old cock appealed to with a soft and supple hand, seemed inclined to concede this, or any other, point. It was no time for wrangling. Though his head buzzed with misgivings, other parts throbbed with something more peremptory and he had no choice but to sign her release. She must do, they must both do what they must.

Anya did not *have* to go to the protest at Hucklington. (The National Front had organized an election rally in the town hall of that predominantly Asian suburb, and the local Indians had decided that it must be visibly opposed.) She could have prudently stayed at home. In the most crushingly obvious sense, it would have been 'better' if she had.

But the stories of people who are interested only in the obvious sense of the word 'better' . . . such stories are hardly worth telling.

She might have been mistaken but she felt she had to go. She had discovered a strange, new, frail quality called duty pushing its little pallid crest up through the accumulated twigs and leaf-mould of her thirty-three years. How could she grind it back into the earth? It was 'life' – as Caspar would say. You don't crush life.

THIRTEEN

The Demonstration

When Gordon Sagger's secondment to the Special Patrol Unit was confirmed, he went to inspect his new headquarters. He was pleased by the move. Apart from the fact that it was obviously 'up' and not 'sideways' (despite his remaining a nominal 'PC'), he had been getting rather frustrated lately by the routine beat and panda-car work. You had to sit like a tin duck in a shooting gallery while they let fly at you. And there was so very little you could do about it.

Only the other day he had been going with the super to inspect a squat, and this little black git had deliberately stepped in front of the super, blocking the way up the alley and refusing to move. Gordon had asked the kid nicely to step aside and the kid had replied, 'What the hell you going to do about it then? Gonna nick me then?' And you know what the super said? 'Never mind, son. We'll go round the other way.' And if they hadn't got their skates on, the kid would have been waiting for them there too. That was no way to police the streets! Every inch you gave they took a bloody mile. You'd see them standing on street corners, paring their nails with a Stanley knife and daring you to run them in. 'Hey man, ain't this an offensive weapon? How offensive is this weapon, man? Tell me, man.' And if you made a move – like the other day when they'd done a Rasta for openly smoking a reefer on the street – the whole damn betting-shop pours out and wades in. It's their Saturday-afternoon entertainment: clobber a copper. And with a weak boss like the super, and the whole damn tribe of community-relations milksops and bleeding-heart local councillors, and the bloody sociologists aiding and abetting, you might as well pack it in and go home to your fire. Let 'em get on with their dope-pushing and granny-bashing and pretend you don't notice. The top brass, with their softly-softly ethics, were living in the middle ages. At least, at the Special Patrol Unit, they knew what time of day it was.

He was shown round by a pleasant young chap with a northern accent. Called Wilson. Transferred from Huddersfield at his own request because he thought he'd like the work. He did. It was a smart outfit with a bit of pride about it, he said. Soft-spoken bloke, nothing noisy about him, but hard. You could tell that, even from the way he walked – something springy and alert and very tough in his bearing. Gordon was impressed by the facilities and especially, as it happened, by the size of the personal lockers assigned to each officer. They amounted almost to a small wardrobe apiece. Here, out of harm's way, was a home for his collection. On the day he took up duty, he brought the locked box with him. It fitted perfectly across the floor of the locker, taking up very little space. It might be a bit difficult getting at it, but he probably wouldn't need to, often. Too much else on hand, with the training programme they had lined up for him.

It mustn't be supposed that the rehousing of the artefacts was a symbolic act either for Gordon Sagger or for the Special Patrol Unit. For him it was simply a solution to a logistical problem. For the SPU, during the investigations that followed the Hucklington affair, it became an acute embarrassment, not at all symbolical. It was indeed very naïve of him not to see how odd his Nazi memorabilia would look when discovered in a police locker-room, but he was a naïve man. He wanted the world to be orderly. Everything in its place. He found it hard to conceive of a thing that did not *have* a place – the kind of man society needs, in short, for the proper enforcement of its own sense of order.

The training commenced. Some of it was familiar from cadet-school days – the usual commando stuff of unarmed combat, scuffling, tackling, overpowering and so on, though in this academy they took off the gloves and faced the real fight-situation. The unmentionable became mentionable: after all, sooner or later you might have to put the boot in an uncomfortable place, if riot control was what it was about. The thing was to know exactly how to do it with maximum effect.

But the best part of it was the way they were drilled as units, learning to act in a concerted way which made them twice as effective – real team-work. You might be outnumbered, you usually were, but with proper discipline, striking fast and together, you could put the fear of God into a sizeable crowd which couldn't begin to match you in organization.

They learned the use of riot-shields, not just to keep off the bricks, but to get right to the centre of a disturbance. You could lock them together, in 'the tortoise', to make a complete protective carapace, and then, moving steadily in an unbroken line, get safely within charging-distance; or into 'the wedge' to split a threatening mob down the middle. There were a few unofficial uses for the shields too, once you began the charge. It was as well to know about them, and provided you weren't too blatant, nobody could identify the face behind the visor: *they* didn't know what was happening, and *you* did. This was really modern policing, responding (at last!) to the modern conditions. It made the old-fashioned baton-charge look like a war of sling-shots – though they had some ingenious suggestions about baton-charge technique, too, when it came down to it.

Even the drivers were integrated into the operation. Instead of just being ferry-shuttles that shifted personnel from place to place, the carriers became part of the whole act. Drive at a crowd at exactly the correct speed and you could split it straight away into smaller, more manageable, and more demoralized groups. They watched films of the technique in operation, and it was amazing how fast you could go without actually knocking anybody down. 'This is one of my favourites,' said the instructor. 'Just watch this feller skip out of the way.' He directed them with his pointer. 'That's what the old adrenalin will do for a sluggish demonstrator. You can count on the adrenalin. It's on our side.' The instructors were very clued-up about the psychology of surprise and very expert at its application.

They even sprung surprises on the trainees, to see if they could keep their cool under pressure. A stranger would appear in the group one morning, and suddenly start behaving crazy. You suspected he was a plant but you couldn't be sure. If you went soft on him, all hell broke loose. Some of the unit would have been worded up to take his side. It really smartened up your reflexes, though a few noses tended to get bloodied in the process.

After two months of this, Gordon found he was really looking forward to getting out on the job. This time, they'd given him proper training, instead of throwing him in the deep end to sink or swim. He felt sharp, mettlesome and hard as nails, ready for anything. It made him realize how much, in the past, he had dreaded going out on the beat, though he had never let it show, not even to himself. This time it would be different, he told his wife, who had a tendency to worry. He'd be safer in the middle of a *riot*, with this outfit, than he'd been behind the desk in the station, before! He could see she didn't believe him, but at least she shut up. It was real man's work, this was. You couldn't expect a woman to understand.

But the best thing about his new set-up was the way his colleagues understood his point of view. They weren't all pulling in a dozen different directions, these men. They knew what policing was about: it was about getting a bit of order back into society, getting a grip on the unruly elements – fascists, trade-unionists, demonstrators and the like – who'd been allowed to get away with murder recently. It was all very well for the police chiefs clucking about like hens, trying to be politicians and TV personalities and social workers and community-relations officers all rolled into one; but meanwhile the commies ran riot on the street. He'd always said, Gordon had, if a law is being broken, someone has to be arrested for it; but up till now there'd always been ifs and buts, and maybes and perhapses. Now, when he said it, there was a solid consensus – a chorus of 'Yeah, yeah, that's just it. Right on!'

True, he got a bit of ribbing when he suggested (it was one of his hobby-horses) that it was all this slackening of divorce laws that had started the rot in society; but at least they gave him a hearing first. They were sensible blokes with a responsible view of society and they could grasp, once he explained it to them, how bad it was for kids to see their parents getting out of their duties, just because they felt like it. What would happen if villains who had been put away for a fifteen-year stretch were told it was up to *them* whether they served it or not? You couldn't run a society like that! It was like finding MPs on a picket-line: you got the idea you could get away with anything, when people who were supposed to be in authority turned out and joined the anarchists. Why should *you* keep up standards, if they wouldn't? It stood to reason: if you were a politician you had political duties to fulfil. If you were married you had marital duties. It made no odds what you happened to feel privately about it. There they were – Duties. The lads might titter a bit at his vehemence, but they knew what he was on about: 'Gordon, lad,' they'd say, 'we're relying on you to keep up standards, and do your marital duty.' It was good to be understood and respected.

And as for the anarchists . . . well, the SPU was there to make sure they toed the line, whether they wanted to or not. To teach them a bit of Respect – which was one thing they were never going to learn from pussyfooting old fogies like his last super. 'The trouble is,' Gordon said, 'there are too many extremists around. Left-wing, right-wing – I don't care what they call themselves – they're troublemakers the lot of them. Extremists! If it's extreme they want, we'll show them extreme, eh?' (When he got steamed up like this his eyes would dart about and his gingery moustache bristled. 'Basil Brush', his mates had nicknamed him, because of that foxy, gingery moustache – 'Give us a laugh, Basil!' they'd say.) The inspector in charge of their unit smiled at Gordon's enthusiasm, but he didn't argue. He knew what time of day it was.

It was very disappointing for Gordon, after all this, when the first mission turned out to be a routine cannabis snatch. The old boring dawn-raid stuff. What had all the training been for, if they were going to be wasted on this? It wasn't that there weren't any riots around. The extremists seemed to be squaring up to each other all round the country – Battersea, Islington, Leicester – there was something in the papers every second day. Why waste all this expertise on a clutch of run-down degenerates, half stoned out of their minds?

The Hucklington briefing cheered them all up.

This was something like! Two to three thousand men on the ground, and the SPU as the crack troops of the operation! The only fly in the ointment was that he'd been assigned to a carrier with a WPC at the wheel. A woman driver for this sort of an outing! Christ! What was the inspector thinking of? If the equal-opportunity bullshit started taking hold in the force, where would it end? He didn't try to give birth, did he? So why were they trying to police the streets? Just pray to God that the bloody woman's nerve didn't crack at the crucial moment!

'You may have quite a wait,' the chief super, told them. 'You'll be in position by ten and the election meeting isn't until 19.30. So I'd take a book.' Laughter. 'Or a pack of cards – *provided*,' he held up a solemn finger, 'it doesn't have the ace of spades in it. We don't want to be accused of incitement, do we?'

'On the other hand,' he went on, more soberly, 'there may be trouble long before that. The situation is volatile and our Asian friends are very steamed up. When they find they can't hold their demonstration, they may get *more* steamed up. The strategy is containment within cordons, on all four approach roads to the town hall. But they may not hold, and that's where we come in – to disperse the mob, if necessary. Yes?' He pointed to the questioner.

'Can we have maps, sir?' It was the WPC who was the driver of Gordon's carrier.

'I shouldn't worry. It's a simple cross-roads lay-out. You can't go wrong. Give yourself a short Cook's tour when you first arrive, if you're bothered; but don't be too conspicuous about it. Yes?'

'Truncheons, sir?' asked Gordon.

'*If* the order is given. You know the rules – only to be used when an arrest cannot otherwise be effected, and only on arms and legs, or, at a pinch, shoulders and back. But *not* skulls. Those are the rules. Never mind . . .' with a horizontal sweep of an ironic palm, he anticipated the objection, '. . . that we've got a riot on our hands: we stick by the rules or we'll have the media down on us like a ton of bricks. (Incidentally, confiscate any cameras you see – the mob tends to play up to cameras.) So . . . shoulders and back only. However . . .' He lowered his eyes to adjust a button on his tunic, 'it may happen that you aim for the shoulders, and the suspect moves. That can't be helped, not with a riot on your hands. All I ask is a bit of discretion.'

'Which truncheons, sir? short or long?'

'There is only one regulation police truncheon . . . as I'm sure you know.' He paused, pursed his lips. 'You are trained officers. You'll have to make your own assessment of the seriousness of the situation. I think I can leave it to your discretion. I shall be directing operations from the helicopter, so I expect we can keep it all pretty orderly. Whoever else loses his cool, it won't be the SPU. Of that I'm confident. All right?'

Apparently it was.

'Dismiss.'

It was about four on a damp Saturday afternoon when Anya, Jaswinder, Stacy and Wavell got off the train at Hucklington station. Most of their fellow-passengers had been shoppers or folk returning from work – Asians mainly. The place was milling with people, but they battled their way up the ramp, discovering, at the top, the cause of the congestion. A hundred yards or so up the Station Road there was a heavy cordon of police.

'Huh!' said Wavell. 'The pre-emptive strike. The town hall's up there.'

'What's the matter? – How do I get home? – What's going on?' came agitated voices on all sides.

'What shall we do?' Stacy asked Wavell who, from his superior height had a better view of the situation.

'If you can stay here,' he said coming down off the tips of his toes, 'I'll try getting round to the community centre. The guys there'll know what's going on. OK?' Wavell had friends in an unofficial centre which ran self-help groups and was home-base for a reggae band. He set off to the right, hoping to circumvent the cordon.

He had only been gone a minute, when the cordon began to move forward, compressing the citizenry. One or two placards could be seen, but the crowd seemed to be composed largely of ordinary residents cut off from their homes. An officer in a peaked cap and with a couple of shoulder stars was stomping around at the head of the advancing cordon, pushing people about at random:

'OK, you folks. Move along now. A bit of exercise does you good. Stops you getting constipated – after all those curries you people eat. Move along. Come on now, move it.'

The girls retreated down the station ramp as the crowd began to disperse to right and left along the streets that were not blocked.

'I hope,' Jaswinder remarked confidentially to Anya, 'that he knows more about policing than he does about curries and constipation. It is a most surprising theory.'

The officer had stopped in front of them. The two white women were rather noticeable in this particular throng.

'Didn't you hear me? I said move on.'

'We're waiting for a friend,' said Anya, without moving.

'I dare say.' He looked her up and down thoughtfully. 'You people always are. When you find your "friend", you just watch your step. I've got a good memory for faces.'

'We'll have to go the other way.' Wavell was back. He took no notice of the officer.

'Oho! so that's what you mean by a "friend" is it?'

Wavell took Stacy's arm and they set off to the left.

'Don't forget, I've got a good memory for faces.'

'Ignore him,' said Wavell quietly, walking them as fast as the crowds permitted.

For what was supposed to be an Asian ghetto, the streets through which they passed were surprisingly cheerful. Gaily painted Victorian and Edwardian houses with neat front gardens gleamed immaculately on either side. Anya nudged Stacy to note the house-names carved in the stone lintels – 'Ivanhoe', 'Robroy', 'Abbotsford', 'Kenilworth' – and under the lintels, in doorways that were mostly open, were brown faces, crimson caste-marks, nose-jewels, turbans, saris, sights which would probably have surprised Sir Walter, since they surprised Anya, who had come prepared. There was such an invincible air of placid prosperity and decorum here, that race-riots seemed an impossibility. Yet the faces were anxious, the shoulders of

234

children were clutched rather hard, and from somewhere over to their right, came sounds of chanting, an occasional wall of sirens, and the steady background roar that bespoke a large concourse of people.

The street took a right-angle turn towards the noise. At its farther end they could see shops, a supermarket, and what looked like a cleared space of roadway, littered with indistinguishable objects. They might just be walking into an ambush, but there were so many others, ahead and behind, that there seemed no cause for alarm. The police were not likely to launch a frontal assault on a crowd of peaceful pedestrians. A light but penetrating rain was falling. Anya opened her umbrella. Wavell touched her arm and waved a negative hand: 'Risky,' he said laconically. 'Offensive weapon. Draws attention.'

She bowed to experience, collapsed the umbrella and pulled up her headscarf.

At the T-junction with the main London road, the situation became clear. On their left was a line of police carrying the long transparent shields of reinforced plastic which covered them from nose to knee. They wore crash-helmets with perspex visors down and their air of corporate menace was enough to keep the crowd on the right at a wary distance – though an occasional youth would dart out and pitch a can or a stone or a bottle across no-man's-land. But they took good care not to advance far enough to be collared. The spent missiles littered the roadway.

They had no choice but to turn right and join the crowd. As they did so, Anya caught sight of a second cordon, three or four deep, on the farther side of the crowd. They were completely hemmed in between cordons and shop-fronts.

'This is a novel way of keeping the peace,' she remarked to Wavell as they picked their way through the debris.

'About as novel as war,' he remarked drily.

Even more novel was the behaviour of one huge shield-bearing warrior who, every time a kid scurried out to hurl something, broke ranks and came forward arms spread wide, bellowing, 'Come and take me! Come on, the lot of you. Come and take me and I'll have you, you black rubbish. Come on.' Goliath insulting the puny David could hardly have bettered the performance, and you could see that some of the young yahoos were sorely tempted. His fellow-officers seemed as little pleased by it as the crowd was by the yahoos. Both parties tried to pull the delinquents back into their ranks.

The party from Stoke Newington managed to wriggle their way into the packed mass. It was unthinkable to stand in front of it, and those who, by chance or design, found themselves there, looked distinctly edgy. Flank-rubbing is supposed to be a propensity of the lower animals; but after their scuttling transit across no-man's-land, Anya and her friends had a proper value for flanks. Received gratefully into the warm damp throng, solidarity became a sensation.

A helicopter flapped monotonously overhead, like a gigantic insect of uncertain intentions. Anya glanced up, taken short by an apprehensive pang which had constricted her chest. Something in memory stirred. Sharpeville, *that* was it! The day after the shootings . . . out on the playing-fields with the Herschel girls – all day long the choppers had circled the city, polluting the sky and menacing the populace. There was something obscene about being overlooked like this. What business had they supervising people from on high? Normal human beings walked about on their own two legs.

In this unnatural stasis they stood for perhaps an hour. The demonstration, plainly, was not going to take place.

The crowd, now that they were part of it, seemed predominantly sober and respectable: a fair sprinkling of puzzled bystanders, whose puzzlement, as the minutes passed into hours, was converting steadily to resentment. Indian women in sensible coats over vivid saris, their headscarves pulled up against the steady drizzle. A spatter of umbrellas and a surprising number of turbaned greybeards of dignifed mien. One of these managed to collar one of the stone-throwers and shouted angrily at him in Punjabi.

'What'd he say?' Anya asked Jaswinder.

'He told him to show some respect.'

'For what?'

Jaswinder smiled and shrugged in ironic deprecation: 'It's a good principle,' she said.

'Though of uncertain application.'

'What do they think they do?' appealed a blue-turbaned Indian in overalls who was standing beside them. The common plight made such interventions natural . . . 'I am returning from my workplace. I want only to go to my home. My wife she is ill. She is worry by this.'

'I suppose,' Stacy suggested dubiously, 'you might ask them to let you through.'

'I have ask,' he said agitatedly. 'Already I have ask. You look at those fellows. Can you talk as a man to such fellows?'

It seemed unanswerable, and the more so since the line of shields now began to advance slowly across the devastated zone.

'If they do not have a riot yet, they will have it soon.' The speaker was a handsome young Indian in a camel-hair coat under which a well-cut suit was visible. 'I have come here, you know,' he added confidentially, 'to help with legal advice, and I find that the police have sealed off the aid centre and nobody can either come or go. Even if it were not stupid in itself,' he adjusted the rimless spectacles on the bridge of his nose – 'which it is – it looks so very bad, doesn't it? As if the police are *afraid* that people may get legal advice. And now,' he gestured towards the advancing line of riot-shields, 'they are proposing to make us the meat in their sandwich. It is so very senseless!'

'I suppose it's what they mean by "crowd control", Anya shouted back. 'What's the legal advice about?' she appended, planting her feet firmly as the crowd began to heave and surge around her.

'Arrests. Bail. Injuries.'

'Are there many?'

The young lawyer nodded: 'Quite a few.' He had to raise his voice to be heard, as the crowd grew more noisily restive. 'They have, in their wisdom, arrested all the stewards of the demonstration. I think it was the red armbands. They did not like the colour. Anyway it made them very easy to pick out. So now we have no stewards. Tomorrow they will be complaining that the demonstration, which they have disrupted, was not properly organized.'

The man in the blue turban had rushed forward and was plainly trying to explain, again, his reason for being allowed through the cordon, while his interlocutor bumped him remorselessly back towards the crowd with his shield.

'Move it. Move it.'

'My wife she is ill.'

'Sorry, we don't understand English any more.'

'What do you mean? I speak English good. I tell you . . .'

'No savee. Go home.' (Bump.)

'But that is what I wish. I tell you . . .'

'Go home.' (Shove.) 'What're you people doing on the streets anyway? You've got it coming to you.'

At this moment a small flaming object flew over the front of the crowd and landed in the second row of the police cordon. There came a roar of pain from that direction and a flurry of conflicting shouts from the crowd: 'What is it? – Petrol bomb? – Firecracker! – Where? – The pigs are on fire – Hooray! Jolly good!' The small flaming object flew back, landing this time in the middle of the already compressed crowd. There was a panicked scattering and a couple of people went down. 'Gas! Gas! Gas!'

'They're using CS!' roared a bull-like voice. And as one man, the crowd gave tongue: 'OUT! OUT! OUT! OUT!'

Riot-shields notwithstanding, things looked nasty for the police. 'OUT!! OUT!! OUT!!'

The crowd's confidence grew as the noise increased. Someone in the line of locked shields lost his nerve and began to retreat. That was all it took: the crowd poured through the gap like a released tide. With miraculous suddenness the massed blue phalanx had broken into small beleaguered knots of helmets. You caught the flash of raised batons and cries of pain carried over the menacing roar. The crowd had had enough. They were turning into the mob they were not.

Something was approaching at what seemed like insensate speed. A blue police coach, driving straight at the struggling mass that blocked the roadway. Dozens of people leaped, or were hauled to safety. There was a scream of sirens, a roar of an engine at peak revs, and the line of blurred helmeted heads flashed past, miraculously failing to crush anybody on its way. They were bringing in reinforcements.

'Idiots! Bastards! Cretins! Somebody could've been killed!' screamed various enraged voices.

In the space cleared by this violent trajectory, a policeman could be seen lying in the road, his body sprawled in a curious zigzag line that seemed incompatible with normal bone-structure. Two of his mates slung his arms over their shoulders and dragged him back to where, to marshalling shouts, the line of shields was regrouping. A trail of blood ribboned out between his stuttering boots. The crowd went hushed. But it was just beginning.

Sirens again, coming from further away. The young lawyer craned his neck. 'Green transit vans,' he said. 'I would advise you to cover your heads. They are sending in the SPU.'

The crowd was better prepared for this swoop. As the two vans roared towards them, they pressed back on to the pavements. But there were too many people and not enough space. An ominous creaking came from the plate glass of the supermarket.

'The window!' screamed a woman's voice, 'the window's going!'

Then everything seemed to happen at once. There was a squeal of tyres, a crash of glass from the supermarket, the rear doors of the vans flew open and visored men from everywhere amongst the crowd, snatching people by their clothing, wrenching heads under their arms, twisting wrists, wielding truncheons. The door of one van caught Jaswinder on the shoulder, spun her about and flung her to the tarmac. Anya rushed to her aid. She was groaning, but conscious.

'Pigs! Nazi pigs!' Anya screamed, now totally out of control. She could see one great ginger-moustached pig climbing out of the van which had felled Jawinder. 'Look what you've done, you cretin!' She could see the little piggy eyes that were rolling about in his skull come to rest suddenly on her, the tight lips pulled back in a grin that stretched itself over the clenched lower jaw. Everything that was detestable to her in the human physiognomy was concentrated in that snarling red face of the bully-blusterer. She rose to her feet, planting her fists on her hips, inviting combat.

She would certainly have got it if the crowd around the prostrate Jaswinder had not been both large and ugly. But ginger-moustache was already behindhand. He couldn't tackle that lot. His mates were dragging their prizes to the van. He had to be quick. They exchanged a look of pure hate which made up in intensity for anything it lacked in duration, before he veered aside and, catching sight of a blue turban turning to flee, grabbed it violently by the collar. Its wearer made choking sounds:

'I am not struggling. I am not struggling,' howled the husband of the sick wife. 'There is no need . . .' He was being jostled and pitched so violently that he could hardly keep his feet. Just as they reached the van, ginger-moustache, who was using his captive as a battering-ram to part the crowd, saw the half-door close before him. It was too late to stop and the turbaned head hit it with a sickening clang and he sank to his knees. Ginger-moustache pounded on the half-closed door. If they left him now, he'd be lynched. But it opened and some hands hauled the shaking Indian aboard by the scruff of his neck. Ginger-moustache, last of the pack, climbed aboard. As the van squealed around in a tight U-turn, he saw the red-haired trollop shaking her fist in the air and yelling like a demon, while beside her stood – wouldn't you know it – a big buck nigger with a beard. These commie sluts were all the same! Do anything for a hot-meat injection from a Spade!

On the roof of the supermarket, an inspector from the local Hucklington station – who had by now recovered from the illusion that he was in charge of his own patch – saw a gang of youths leaping two-footed at the coping of a low brick wall. It would begin to break up in a minute and that would provide murderous weaponry. As the two green vans spun about, they were hit by a hail of cans from the supermarket window. Somewhere out of his line of vision a woman was emitting a continuous high-pitched scream.

He bawled into his radio: 'We've got a full-scale riot on our hands. Send everything you've got.' (But not, he muttered to himself, knowing the futility of the reservation, *not* the bloody SPU. Dear God, what do those blokes think they're doing?!)

In order to understand the events of that day it is necessary to know what the bloody SPU had been doing, before they were finally pitched into action. They had been sitting in a closed van for eight hours – nine, if you count the journey over. There is a limit to the number of happy hours that can be spent playing poker for matchsticks. Gordon, anyway, didn't play cards. His parents had been religious.

Because it was raining outside, they had to sit, at the ready, in their macs. The windows were forever steaming up and having to be wiped down, and a continuous rivulet of sweat trickled down the channel of your spine, drenching your underpants and fraying your temper. Through the reinforced mesh of the side windows you could distinguish nothing clearly. But there was no obscurity about the distempered roar of the crowd. Amplified by the tin diaphragm of the van, it was like the bellowing of some primeval monster of the swamp, out seeking its prey. The moments when sounds became distinct were a positive relief: at the chant of 'Nazis out!' some wit could retort, 'Commies in! Nazis in!' – which was amusing, though not perhaps very apt. But they had to identify the common threat somehow. It was the only conceivable topic of conversation, in this tiny authoritarian ghetto, for men who might at any moment be pitched out at the feet of a raging mob, to devour or be devoured. Who can be surprised that their identifications were purely hostile, or that they followed the lay-lines of their native prejudices? Even if the eradication of prejudice had figured more significantly than it had in their training, they were now in a situation where its resurgence was certain. Nothing nurtures prejudice so well as isolation, fear, and ignorance.

Their only information came via the crackling chatter of the VHF, or verbally from the radio-operator, who was trying to keep in touch by monitoring other channels beside their own. But for all his efforts, no clear picture emerged. The pieces were too fragmentary and the only certain thing was that some of our blokes were getting it in the neck. One PC stabbed near the station. Which station? Police? Or railway? No telling. Not one of ours, was it? Don't think so. Typical, eh? These bastards were always handy with a knife. Nobody said, Next time it may be me.

After midday there was a series of false alerts which finally buggered the card games and resulted in the spilling of a whole thermos of coffee on the floor. That was bloody marvellous! The way they were sweating, they needed all the liquid they could get. Did the chief really know what he was doing, anyway? His messages from the chopper (*when* you could hear them above the fizz of the engine and the whopping of the blades) were none too lucid: nothing but 'hold your position' for hour after bloody hour.

They heard the siren of the coach as it raced past. Things were obviously hotting up. Spencer, peering out the rear window, said he saw a petrol-bomb thrown at the coach, but when they wiped the glass there was nothing visible.

'An officer's been burned in the legs,' Sparks reported. ('Where? How? What with?') 'Shut up! I can't hear.' Pause. 'They dunno.'

At last, a firm order: 'Stand by to proceed down High Street. Riotous mob. Arrest all suspects – one per officer – and then withdraw. Helmets. Batons drawn.'

The longest five minutes of all followed.

'GO!'

The WPC threw the starter and whirred away. No contact. Jeee-zuss!

Gordon ground his teeth: 'Bloody woman-driver. She's flooded the fucker.'

But she hadn't.

This is it. The adrenalin which is their ally begins to pump into their veins. Only it doesn't feel like an ally.

Only now, as they peer forward through the windscreen, do they realize that they have no idea what they will encounter, or what they will have to do. They are trained officers. It is left to their discretion. The baying of the mob is all around them, any second now . . . The WPC brakes too hard, the men who are half out of their seats tumble over each other towards the front of the van, scramble up, and surge toward the rear doors. As Gordon throws the door open it hits something outside and flies back in his face delivering a stunning

241

blow to the side of his head. Someone is hammering on the roof, making a thunderous noise which feels as if it is inside his own brain.

'That bloody woman,' he curses, shoving the door open again, while the other five tumble past him. He jumps down and suddenly, nothing is as it should be. He can't see the rest of his unit. Where have they all gone to? He can see only an indistinct multitude of faces, and something lying on the road with an angry knot of foreign-looking people around it, brandishing fists and yelling. (Where can all these wogs have come from?) Every eye he meets is full of hate and contempt, as if he has no right to be there – whereas he is the only one – the only one – who has. The pain in the side of his head is intensified by the sick cramp in his gut. It would almost be a relief if he could shit himself. (Dear God, let me not shit myself!) A red-headed virago is shrieking abuse at him – at him! Gordon Sagger, trained officer of the Special Patrol Unit! He hardly knows how he manages to make his prescribed arrest and knows even less of the person he has arrested. All he wants is to get back into the safety of Carrier V13, where he can put his boots on the necks of the struggling scum they have laid out on the floor, and grin shakily at his comrades opposite.

'You Asiatic roobish!' says Wilson, the lad from Huddersfield, looking down at their cargo in contempt. 'What right 'ave you to be here? You're the cause 'v all this trooble.'

Inspector Murdoch turns sharply in his seat at the front of the van.

'Can it!' he snarls. 'We can do without the small talk.'

They exchange knowing glances. He has to say that. He doesn't mean it. It begins to feel a little bit more like normality.

Gordon's Indian is groaning. He settles his instep across the ridge of his neck.

'How's that feel, sonny?' he says, with a crooked smile for Wilson, 'more comfortable?'

They made two more runs. Gordon had hoped to nail the red-headed slag – he remembered now that she'd called him a 'pig' and a 'cretin', which would be quite good enough for a charge-sheet – but he didn't see her. Nevertherless it went more smoothly these two times. With each snatch they got swifter, fiercer, and were less at risk. It was really just a matter of getting the knack of it. His gut felt easier now. You couldn't expect everything to come together first off. But when it did, there was an exhilaration in the very danger – it certainly wouldn't have the same zest without it.

And then came another holding order. (Why, for Christ's sake?!) The noise of the mob was getting louder. What were they waiting for? The VFH was crackling away to itself. Sparks was having trouble hearing.

'Shut up, can't you?' he yelled, forgetting to shield the mike. '... Sorry sir. Where sir? Ferndale? Where is . . .? Yes sir, right away, sir.'

But where was Ferndale? There was a babel of advice.

'Simpson's been hurt,' cried Sparks, lifting one earphone, 'caught a brick in the head. Critical.'

That put the lid on it! A vindictive murmur ran round the van.

The insector gave an order. They backed up, roared off down a side street. A nameplate flashed by. This isn't Ferndale! – No, but we'll get to it from the other end. They didn't. They backed out of the cul-de-sac, engine screaming, reversed into the High Street and back the way they'd come. Everybody was being thrown violently about, which wasn't improving tempers.

'Bloody woman-driver,' muttered Gordon through clenched teeth. 'Bloody woman-driver!'

'Right!' yelled the inspector. 'Helmets, shields, truncheons. Drive the mob down Ferndale. The order is to disperse. They're right out of control.'

They skidded sideways into the neck of another side street. This one *was* Ferndale. The doors swung open.

'Hey, isn't this a dead end?' shouted Wilson, but didn't wait for an answer. The remains of a decimated crowd was streaming past him and he set out in pursuit.

Gordon, as junior door-holder, was last out. A few yards away a police uniform with something inside it lay in a pool of blood. The helmet had been removed and placed neatly beside what must be the head – though it was covered with a wad of stained tissues. Could that thing be Simpson? He looked away, down Ferndale, and saw to his dismay that the backs of the mob were retreating fast. That stupid bloody WPC had got them here too late. He tucked his chin-strap under, and sprinted off.

At about this time, a coachload of National Front supporters arrived at Hucklington Town Hall. All the other goings-on – the massive deployment of police, the rioting, the injuries – were merely incidental. This was the central event. Without it there would have been no police, no riot, no injuries. Democracy was proving itself to be shipshape and in good order. Despite the disruptive efforts of assorted subversives, the election meeting would take place. This was what firmness and determination guaranteed impartially to citizens – Democracy. As a senior man at the Met observed that evening in a radio interview: 'We fought two wars to preserve the right to free speech.' Nobody was so pedantic as to remind him against whom one of those wars had been fought.

The National Front coach-party – mostly under-age – paused on the steps to give a Nazi salute and have their pictures taken. Grinning from the tabloids next morning, they looked (apart from the flattened palm) like young football supporters cheering their team on and defying the opposition. Which was probably pretty much how they saw it. One inexperienced little Nazi, it was true, couldn't get the palm flat and had put his arm up at such a sharp angle that he appeared to be requesting permission to pee. With his slightly squinting eyes, set too close together, and his feeble flubber-mouthed imitation of ferocity, he didn't look much of a threat to democracy or anything else.

Photos over, they turned and filed into the hall, closely scrutinized by the Front stewards. No troublemakers were going to sully this respectable constitutional occasion.

An audience of fifty, finally, heard the speeches of the national leadership (and of the foredoomed candidate). It was not composed of Hucklington constituents. Even those who were old enough to vote did not come from the district. That was why the coach had been necessary. In addition to these bussed democrats, the stewards admitted fifteen journalists and five members of the public who had been allowed through the police cordon (several local councillors were turned away), before declaring the hall full and closing the doors.

There was no violence. Everything went off peacefully. The strategy of containment had worked perfectly. It was a pity there were so few to witness this triumph of crowd-control; but for a radius of two hundred yards around the town hall there was nobody, apart from two thousand policemen.

After the first wave of vans had retreated, Anya got Jaswinder to her feet. Her wrist was at a strange angle, her hand was turning blue and her teeth chattered uncontrollably. They had to get her out.

'Isn't that the road we came up?' Anya pointed to the farther side of the High Street.

'No,' said Wavell.

'But it goes towards the station. It's better than staying here, anyway.'

She hitched Jaswinder's sound arm round her shoulder, grasped her round the waist and set off. The crowd made way with expressions of concern and cries of 'Shame!' But they were halted by the next snatch raid, and again by the next. Jaswinder's face was grim with stoic endurance as her injured arm was bumped and jostled by people who apologized but could not help themselves.

Just as they reached the neck of the sidestreet (they saw the sign 'Ferndale Avenue') the police made their first concerted move of the afternoon (though the purpose of the concert was clear to no one in the crowd: omniscience resided on high). The cordon at the town hall end moved quickly forward, the phalanx of shields closed in from the opposite direction, and several hundred people were funnelled into the narrow opening where Anya had hoped to find shelter. And as if the panic caused by this was not enough, the demonic green vans came at them again.

The crowd stampeded. In the *mêlée* people were racing, stumbling, falling, yelling. The truncheons were out again (some witnesses were to claim that, this time, they were white and looked unnaturally long. A greengrocer, who was watching from the flat above his shop on the corner, told the inquest. 'The police came pouring out of the vans, laying about them like madmen. I thought, God help anyone who gets in their way.' God didn't.)

Anya caught sight of the young lawyer, just at the moment that a truncheon clacked into the back of his head. With a curiously graceful movement he skipped forward two steps and with even more amazing dexterity caught the glasses that had pitched off his nose neatly in one hand. Then he disappeared behind the blurred profiles of other fugitives, running with their necks craned forward, looking for all the world like scrawny chickens fleeing from the axe. How absurd it all was, she thought. How absurd! And how *wet*! And her umbrella was broken too.

Swept along on the fringe of the human tide, she tried to protect Jaswinder, but they had to move slowly. One more jolt and she would pass out altogether. She noticed Indian families standing in their doorways and in the tiny front gardens. They seemed to be offering help. Doors were being held open. Two pairs of hands reached for Jaswinder. Anya had time to scream, 'Mind her arm,' before she was struck a shattering blow by a riot shield which knocked her sideways against the brick fence. She tried to go back, to the house, to Jaswinder, but the copper charged her again with his shield. She saw the truncheon rising and took to her heels. Stacy and Wavell were nowhere to be seen. Though people were still running in all directions, the crowd seemed less dense.

She panted round the left-hand knee-bend at the foot of the street and saw another green van blocking the road. Were they planning an ambush and massacre, or what? Two policemen were running full tilt at her. No, it was not at her; they were chasing two Asian boys, who vaulted a fence and disappeared through an open door with the fuzz in hot pursuit. A few stragglers seemed to be slipping past the obstructing green van, though they ran a gauntlet of cuffs and menaces as they did so. (The inquest was told that this particular carrier had arrived there by mistake – they too had been hazy about the location of Ferndale Avenue and had, consequently, impeded the dispersal their colleagues were so energetically prosecuting.

Anya thought she could get her breath back and assess the situation. It seemed quieter now. Just as she had decided she might be able to slip back to the house that had taken Jaswinder in, another van, very late on the scene, skidded to a halt at the High Street corner. She stood very still, flattened against the wall, watching the troops run past her, and marvelling at the mauve-and-purple extravagance of the painted window-frames opposite. (Why was it, she wondered, that Asian colour-schemes ran to such inspired monstrosity?) Now she could make it . . .

'Where d'you think you're going?'

She thought it best to keep her eyes humbly lowered, lest the full blaze of her contempt should break forth.

'I've lost a friend.'

'Pfah!' The hatred in the voice made her look up and meet the gimlet eyes of ginger-moustache. 'Move, you commie slag!'

Anya fought for her calm: 'I'm going to her because she's injured – by your lot, as a matter of fact.' She was still blocked in. 'Out of my way, you stupid knucklehead!'

He banged her back against the wall with his shield.

Oddly she felt no fear, just a kind of unhoping, unimpassioned blankness. He leered at her, skin tight across the projecting jaw. His voice had gone voluptuously soft.

'You're not going anywhere, you slut. Shall I tell you where you're going?'

'Tell me.'

'Where's your nigger boyfriend? Perhaps he'd like to come too.'

'You do have a way with words, don't you? Why don't you come a bit closer, so I can read your number?' A flash of fear crossed the reddened features, which she saw. 'Where'd you keep it, Mr Plod? On your hat?'

She had got her arm clear of the shield and, gripping the broken umbrella, took a swift swipe at his helmet. It bumped forward (pulling his chin up sharply by the strap), bounced off the wall and bowled along the gutter. He sprang back, completely taken off guard, and put his hands to his head in comic alarm. This was no moment to be caught without a helmet. He remembered Simpson. God knew how many brick-throwing coons were lining the rooftops slavering for his scalp.

Anya hadn't seen anything so funny all day, and she burst out laughing in her usual unrestrained, whooping fashion. Fending him off like a fencer, with her umbrella, she bent to retrieve the helmet. It had all become a game. She had just located the number when the truncheon hit the back of her skull . . . Plock! like a well-struck cricket ball. She pitched forward on to her knees with the force of it, deducing rather than feeling that she was in pain, and heard a man's voice, somewhere, miles away, screaming, 'You commie slag, I'll get you!'

Now the pain was reaching her. . . What was it mother used to say? 'I have a splitting head . . .' Not that she ever had. Not like this . . . A splitting head! No, no, he must be stopped.

Wrenching herself about, she half-staggered, half-crawled towards her tormentor, plucking at the wrist which held the baton, with imploring hands.

'No, no, please! Please, no!'

With her head thrown back to appeal to him, something wet and warm began running down her back. A splitting head? Now she knew. All functions had ceased but those that belonged to her fear. Her fear, and her superstition – for, dazedly now, she remembered how she had stood by, once, while other people were clubbed – the sickening memory merged into the nightmare of sickeningly present pain. Could it be that all the violence of the earth was subterraneously connected? That there was always retribution? That the black man had come as he had always threatened, finally to exact his revenge.

Locked on to the wrists of her assailant, she hauled herself to her feet. It was as if she would fling herself about his neck like a mother on the neck of a long-lost son. She was whimpering in supplication, anguish, self-pity, her face smeared and blubbered in her terror, like a baby's.

'No, no! Please!'

If she had lain where she fell, stunned, he might have left her to bleed. But this horrible, blubbering, emotional intimacy filled him with loathing. Her terror touched a terror in him which he must not know. He shook off the frantic, scrabbling hands, tucked the baton's retaining loop snugly over his wrist, and swung high and hard . . .

'Easy on, it's a girl!' It was Wilson, returning from the chase. The Asian boys had got away. For a second, Sagger's arm hung in air, tormenting him with incompletion, then in a luxury of fulfilment it swung down, as he screamed in a voice that echoed off the surrounding walls, 'She's a nigger . . . loving . . . *cunt*!' All the riches of his satisfaction were expressed in the word. He had timed the impact to coincide exactly with it.

Wilson had him by the elbow. 'Hey, hey, hey!' he was saying confidentially, urgently, 'lay off! We don't want an incident, do we?'

He led him away, back to the carrier. The show was practically over.

Anya crawled to a metal pole she could just make out through the mists of blood and tears. A red-and-white No Entry sign stood on its top. She hauled herself nearly upright, then slid to her knees again. What on earth was she trying to achieve? She hung there, breathing shallowly.

Two officers came round the corner. One of them took her by the arm.

'Come along now, lady. Move on. We want you people off the streets. Move on.'

She got as far as the wall, where she leaned. The two officers seemed to have gone. She was grateful to them for being so gentle, so considerate. Her back slid down the wall, and she sat with a bump. Well, she'd come here to rest . . . to sit down . . . and they'd tried to stop her, but now – damn their eyes! – she was resting. That'd show 'em! But there was something she should . . . something she . . . Jaswinder. Jaswinder was hurt.

She tried to rise and lost consciousness.

As soon as the coast was clear, Mrs Bhatti and her son crept out and carried her indoors, out of the rain, into the warm. She tried to thank them, but her tongue would not come down from the roof of her mouth. The front parlour looked like the dressing-station in some barbarous war – there was a young boy with a head-wound and another man with a damaged hand, apart from Anya and Jaswinder. An ambulance had been called.

Jaswinder watched Anya in alarm. She was trembling from head to foot. In the open mouth her tongue had curled back, and her eyes too had rolled up into the top of her head. Mrs Bhatti mopped up the blood on her face with a white towel, but it still dripped steadily from somewhere in the thick hair. She was offered a drink of water, but the glass fell from her hand and bounced away across the carpet. If the ambulance didn't come soon . . .

It arrived at the same time as a desperate Stacy. Wavell had been arrested, but that seemed a mere pin-prick now. She stood stunned in the doorway: 'Oh, my God!' she groaned, 'what's the matter with you?'

There was a flicker at the corner of Anya's mouth. Some ghost of humour still haunted her reflexes. Was it the foolishness of a question to which the answer was so obvious? Or had she recalled the same question being asked on another occasion, in another world? There was no time for speculation. The stretchers were at the door. Anya pointed at Stacy with a feeble finger: let her come with me. They did. Stacy squeezed the limp hand for as long as they would let her. The head she dared not touch.

At the hospital, as they lifted the stretcher on to a trolley, Anya rolled over on one side and vomited a kind of bloody jelly. They undressed her, preparing for theatre as fast as they could; but she was thrashing about, making the job extremely difficult.

In the theatre-lift her respiration slowed, and by the time they had her to the operating-table, she was dead.

One might plausibly reconstruct Anya's thoughts, on her last journey – in so far as she was capable of having any through the blinding anguish that compressed her brain, as the blood from smashed arteries slowly filled the cranial cavity. Perhaps – though it seems unlikely – she reaffirmed the decision that had brought her to this extremity, bravely accepting the high cost of Duty. Perhaps she sent wordless messages to Laczi, forgiving him, for the last time, for being right. Perhaps she was conscious only of Stacy's fierce grip which distracted her from other anguishes. Perhaps, more horribly, she gave way to the hideous superstition that had always lain in wait for her acute receptivity . . .

But the thoughts of dying people are singularly futile – for nothing can come of them. It is for the living to go on thinking. It is the only relevant compassion.

It was past midnight before Stacy could find Laczi. He had been dining out with Borthwick, planning an exhibition of the Cornish granites – a collection of large figures, mainly female, which had been, in their way, the most sustained tribute he had been able to pay to Anya and to the revolution she had made in his life. It made no difference that some of them had been carved in estrangement: it was Anya that they honoured none the less.

Now they brought him to look at the ultimate monument, carved by human folly and fallibility – a stupefying tribute to the failure of humane imagination, from which he believed he would never recover. It was inevitable that he should feel the failure as his own. Many people had a part in it, and he could not be exempt.

He stood in the white and silent room, while Stacy, deprived of Anya's hand, gripped his instead. A great shuddering groan, which began in his bowels and threatened to crack his rib-cage in its passage, shook him where he stood. He tottered, but he stood firm. The wave passed.

It was succeeded by a bleak and terrible clearness.

'It's me.' His numb lips moved without sense or feeling. 'I have done this.'

'Don't say so,' Stacy murmured, knowing that he must.

His head swung from side to side in violent negation: 'I say it because it's true. It's me! I let her believe in causes, when I have known, *known*! how all such causes would end. How could I forget it?'

She was mute.

'Where is the cause that is worth this . . . this stupidity?' he demanded, expecting no reply. 'I should have never interfered. She knew best what was her own way.'

'She *took* her own way,' Stacy insisted, racked with pity for him.

It was not clear that he heard, for he stood immobile as the dead girl herself, at whom he stared fixedly as if intent on wringing her mortal secret from her. The electric wall-clock, the only living thing in the room, twitched its second-hand around the laborious minutes.

'No,' he said finally, 'this was not her way. It was her *fear*, but it was not her way. It is my fault.'

His stillness frightened her. It was not the living silence of a great anger. It was the quietude of despair. What words, what protest could make itself heard in this howling waste which was as silent as the tomb? White walls, white sheet, white cheeks. Only the rust-brown of her hair, from which a few clots of blood had not been properly washed, lent any colour to hope. He picked out the stuff, hardly knowing what he did, put the strand of hair back in place, and left the room.

Before he was allowed to leave SPU headquarters in the small hours of the morning, Sagger and the other officers who had been in Ferndale had faced some angry questioning. A heavyweight stranger with commander's pips on his shoulders was stamping about the place in a blue fury. Their truncheons had been impounded and they had all been placed on unofficial suspension, with orders to report again at ten.

Sagger thought he could trust Spencer and Wilson to keep their mouths shut. They'd all been laying about them pretty merrily and he sensed some wordless commiseration that *he* should have been the poor sod to have the bitch go and die on him. It could have happened to any of them. But everything was poisoned now. He hardly slept a wink, running up against the fact, from whatever angle he approached it, that his career was ruined. It might be worse than ruined: a manslaughter charge? Murder? They wouldn't do that to one of their own, surely? But they might – if they wanted a scapegoat badly enough. And you couldn't trust the bastards if it was a case of saving their own skins. Law of the jungle was all they knew.

Even his breakfast bacon and egg tasted like cardboard. There was a bilious slime on his tongue which he couldn't wash down with tea. Deidre Sagger watched her husband with concern. He'd always had his moods, but this was ominous. She reached out timidly and laid her hand across his wrist.

'What is it?'

He shook her off violently. The imploring touch had revived those clammy hands that had clutched at him, frantic with a kind of demented tenderness ('Please, please, no. No!'), that stumbling, shambling figure that had tried to throw itself into his arms . . . filthy slut to the last!

He staggered to his feet, making for the bathroom.

'What is it?' came the terrified voice.

Fucking women! Fucking women! Always pawing and plucking at you.

He leaned on stiff arms over the toilet-bowl, dry-retching till the tears stood in his eyes. Nothing would come. He hammered with his fist on the lid of the cistern:

'Bitch! Bitch! That bitch has ruined my life!'

His wife was pounding on the locked door.

The following morning a well-known liberal daily reported Anya's death – on an inner page. It was the only paper to do so. But on its front page it printed a picture. Against a background of misty streets and looming warehouses, it showed a tall policeman holding a girl of ten by the hand and wheeling her bike for her with his other. They were walking away from the camera, apparently in friendly conversation. The caption explained that the little girl had got accidentally caught up in an anti-Nazi march in Bradford, and the friendly copper was taking her home to her mother.

Good citizens could sleep quietly in their beds. Under flagrant provocation, there had been an aberration, but the police had now reverted to their normal role of holding little children by the hand. We mustn't get things out of proportion.

It is true. We mustn't. But what is proportion?

The corpse in the hospital mortuary could not tell.

Nor could the sculptor who stood for hours on end, motionless in the little box of a bedroom, staring into space. On an obscure impulse he had got all Anya's clothes from the closet and spread them on the bed – preferring, perhaps, the misery of recollection to the numbness of unbeing. It hadn't answered. There they lay in soft multicoloured profusion – for, despite her latterday frugality, Anya had never got around to pruning her wardrobe – but he could not see them. Nothing answered any more. Apart from the dripping rain, the whole world had turned to stone. And it was a stone upon which not even the most finely tempered steel could make the slightest impression.

252